A
Glimpse Into The Past

Andrea Best

i

A Glimpse Into The Past

First Edition.

Book typeset by Ruth – raawpro@gmail.com

Cover Design: Covers in Colour.com

Printed and bound in Great Britain by Amazon

ISBN: 9781739712426

DEDICATION

My sincere thanks to my sister, Carolyn Best-Campbell (aka. Shelly) and friend, Sonia Alridge-King, for being the beta readers of the rough draft.

You both loved the first novel, Second Glances, and gave such positive feedback that I knew I wanted you both to be the first readers of the sequel.

Thanks very much for your invaluable input, which was greatly appreciated.

ACKNOWLEDGEMENT

A big thanks also to the individuals of the writing group that I belong to. You know who you are …. Saleah Micci, Lilly Brown, Iyabo Oba & Jacqueline Codrington ….

We have supported each other's creativity over the years and continue to be that 'safe place' where we can be vulnerable with our 'babies' before they come to full term and are exposed to a wider audience.

Let's continue producing content that makes us proud and aligns with our Christian faith.

CONTENTS

CHAPTER ONE

It was a slow and laborious process. What seemed like an eternity, was only four months. However, Steve was making great progress. The physiotherapists at the rehabilitation centre where he was based were confident that he would be out of there shortly. Their update of his progress delighted Steve to no end. He was extremely lucky to have come away from the car accident with his life intact. Unfortunately, the driver of the car he had the altercation with wasn't so fortunate and, sadly, lost his life. Steve knew that luck had nothing to do with it, but rather his life was spared by the God he had put his trust in.

Steve's recollection of the night of the accident was still a little sketchy. The trauma to his head when it hit the steering wheel at such force, affected his ability to remember how the incident happened. But deep down he knew it probably had something to do with him being upset with Olivia and the Chris saga. That bit of the night he did remember. He just wanted to exit Olivia's house as fast as he could, but any memory after that was still a blur.

As a result of the accident, Steve experienced memory lapses and paralysis in the lower part of his legs. The doctors who were treating him when he was first admitted to the hospital reassured him that his condition was temporary and that with hard work he would get movement back in his legs. Now that Steve had been in the rehabilitation centre for three months, following his month's long stint in the hospital, for the first time he was starting to feel slight twinges of movement in his legs. This was the light at the end of a dark tunnel that Steve had been waiting for, and as a result, he continued to push himself extensively to get back to where he was prior to the crash.

Olivia was a frequent visitor to the centre. The staff loved her ability to change the atmosphere whenever she was there, bringing a fragrance of

1

something different than that of the other visitors. They soon realised that difference was due to her faith and the positivity she lived by.

Olivia wanted to reassure Steve that this accident made no difference to the plans they had initiated months earlier, but Steve's lack of enthusiasm and indifference towards her revealed a different story. In his mind, physically, he wasn't the same man that she had made those initial plans with, and he was not in the right frame of mind to see past his disability, however long that disability was to last.

"Here you are."

Olivia gave Steve a warm smile as his nurse positioned his wheelchair at the side of his bed and endeavoured to help him get into the bed. Olivia had arrived early and was told that Steve was still with the physiotherapists, but that she could sit by his bed and wait for him.

The ward was light, airy and spacious and smelt of antiseptic, which considering the number of visits she had made, Olivia found manageable. The decor of neutral grey & white colours was a dead giveaway that it was a male only ward which housed eight beds. Four on each side, with small lockers situated by the left side of each bed. The flowers that Olivia had brought Steve a couple of days prior were now starting to bud, which Olivia felt helped to brighten up Steve's area. She also arranged the numerous cards he had received in a precise way. Visible so that he could see them and know how much he was loved. Everyone was devastated when they had first heard about Steve's accident and as a result, a lot of prayer was said on his behalf for a speedy recovery.

"I thought that as it's a Friday, you would have been anxious to get home and start your weekend."

Steve's voice was sultry as he made himself comfortable, pulling the blanket over his feet, giving Olivia his full attention.

"You have practically visited every day this week. It's not like I'm going anywhere anytime soon, is it?"

Olivia could hear the slight irritation in Steve's voice, but she wasn't going to rise to the bait. She appreciated how frustrating it must be for him. One minute being a fit, strapping able-bodied man and in the next breath not being able to walk and function adequately. However, her visits were intended to be positive and bring him hope and she wasn't about to let the enemy get a foothold in their relationship and try to sabotage things.

"Don't be silly," she giggled.

"I enjoy visiting you. Plus, Jen is away for the weekend. She's gone to Cornwall to visit her parents for her cousin's wedding, so I've got nothing to rush back for."

Changing the subject quickly to defer from talking about weddings, Olivia cleverly said,

"So, how has your day been then?"

"Well, we've had a whale of a time in here today," Steve said sarcastically.

"We've raced each other up and down the wards in our wheelchairs and I came out the winner."

Olivia tapped him playfully on the shoulder.

"Well, I'm glad to hear that you've still got that competitive streak in you."

Steve half cracked a smile from the side of his mouth. Deep down, he admired Olivia's tenacity and the fact that she did not let things get her down. She would always look for something positive to say, regardless of how bad the situation looked and that's what he loved most about her. But how could he be the husband that he knew she deserved and had always longed for? It was a thought that kept him up at night and the fact that Olivia kept visiting religiously did not help the matter and his resolve. Prior to the accident, they were making good progress in the plans they were making for their future, but how long was he expected to be tied to the contraption of the wheelchair that he was confined too? That was a question that only lady luck could answer and one he had to be patient in as he watched how his recovery was going to pan out.

Steve had interacted well with his fellow patients and had especially been drawn to a young man who came to the rehabilitation centre shortly after he had arrived. Like Steve, he too was in a motor accident, but his was self-inflicted. He and a bunch of his friends were intoxicated and joyriding. Driving recklessly up and down the roads, they lost control of the car and swerved into a tree. The young man, whose name was Jack, was in the driving seat and bore the brunt of the impact. His friends were fortunate to get out with their lives intact and only sustained a few minor bruises. However, Jack was the one that ended up with life changing injuries. As a result of the accident, he lost a leg, which was amputated straightaway to save his life. After a period in hospital, like Steve, Jack was brought to the centre to work on his rehabilitation, enabling him to get to grips with learning to walk with a prosthetic leg.

At first when he had arrived at the centre, Steve noticed how quiet and withdrawn his demeanour was. He attempted to make conversation with him and to include him in the banter that the other patients were having, but Jack was having none of it. His guilt had taken a hold of him very strongly and he couldn't accept why he was the only one that came out of the accident with life changing injuries.

Also, there was the fact that none of his 'so-called' friends had even visited him once. In fact, they really weren't friends in the truest sense. They had used him for what they could get out of the situation. Jack, being the rich kid, meant they could get things on tap. Money, rides in swanky cars and exclusive entrance into the top night clubs where they lived, because of Jack's influence. His parents had always warned him that he was to watch the type of characters who tried to hang around him. But as an only child, developing relationships was very important to Jack.

Steve had learnt a bit of Jack's backstory and wanted to reach out to him. Not only because of the type of work he did in working with troubled young people, but also because Jack's story really resonated with him on a personal level. Steve knew what it felt like to be the rich kid on the block, as well as growing up as an only child. It was lonely and hard work trying to decipher who really wanted to genuinely be his friend or who had ulterior motives. Thankfully, he became a Christian in his teens and therefore relied on the Holy Spirit to help him choose his friends wisely.

On her visits, Olivia would always try and engage with the other patients, especially if she saw that they did not have many visitors. Whilst that was not the case for Jack, as his parents would often visit him, bringing with them a supply of goodies such as comics, chocolates, sweets and fizzy drinks, Olivia still felt especially drawn to him. There was something about his dark brown eyes that pierced through her soul as if to draw all the empathy out of her that she had reserved for loving individuals. Steve had already told her a bit of Jack's backstory, so she was already aware of the difficulties he had faced.

"Jack isn't looking so happy today; I wonder what's up with him?"

Olivia said in a whisper as she leant over and drew close to Steve's bed. Previously, whilst she was sitting and waiting for Steve to finish his physio, as her eyes spanned the room in her normal inquisitive manner, Olivia had noticed that Jack didn't seem himself. Not that he was a happy chap at the best of times, but on this occasion, he seemed to be even more sullen than usual.

In a whispered tone, Steve replied,

"Yeah, I guess he's missing his parents. They had a cruise booked that they could not get out of, so they are away for 14 days, and he hasn't really had many visitors in the last couple of days. I do feel it for him because he is a troubled soul and needs as much interaction with individuals as possible if he is going to beat this thing."

It was Steve's mission whilst he was in there to ensure that Jack was going to deal with whatever demons were troubling him. This was his expertise area and if it was the only reason that his accident was for, to reach that young man, he was determined that he was going to let God use him to be a role model to Jack if it was the last thing he did.

Steve shuffled nervously in his bed as he was about to make a statement that he knew Olivia would not like, but he felt it needed to be said.

"I was thinking that you don't really need to visit me tomorrow or Sunday. It's the weekend and I know how hard you work in the week and that you love to relax and unwind during this time."

Olivia's face appeared perplexed as she wondered what was behind Steve's sudden change of heart.

"Oh, I am fine you know. I just fit visiting you around the other things I have planned, so it's absolutely no problem at all."

Steve could see that Olivia wasn't going to back down and therefore he slightly raised his voice in an irritated tone.

"Look, my parents are in town and have said that they are coming to visit me this weekend, so you don't have to worry about me being left on my own. I'm a big boy and can handle it."

Olivia was still insistent and was not backing down but perked up at the thought of finally being able to meet Steve's parents.

"Oh, that's great, Steve. I haven't met your parents yet and it would be a good opportunity to meet them prior to the wedding, don't you think? You seldom talk about them, so I think it would be nice to make their acquaintance."

The conversation was like playing a game of competitive tennis, with each opponent determined to win the point.

"It's not that I don't want you to meet them, but I just feel this isn't the right setting. And I want it to be in a happy place when we all sit down to have tea, or whatever one does when introducing one's fiancé to their parents for the first time."

On second thought, having processed what Steve was saying, Olivia appreciated the challenging situation he found himself in and deduced that he was right. First impressions did count, and she did not want to meet his parents in an uncomfortable setting for their first encounter with one another.

Olivia composed herself and responded with a tinge of maturity.

"I guess you are right, Steve. It most probably is the best course of action so I will respect your wishes and allow you the time to spend with your parents without any undue pressure from me."

Deep down Olivia felt like she was being side stepped by Steve and wondered if he really wanted to introduce her to his parents. She couldn't put her finger on it, but Olivia felt that perhaps there was something that Steve was holding back from her and bearing in mind the secret that bulldozed its way into Michael and Carol's relationship the previous year, she did not want that to be their reality also. One of the care assistants disrupted Olivia's thoughts as she rearranged Steve's table to place his evening meal on it.

Being Friday, the evening meal was their standard fish & chips delight. The food at the rehabilitation centre was quite palatable, considering food at such establishments wasn't always the best. Steve was getting used to the style of dishes and the fact that you could predict with your eyes closed as to what dish would be served up on any given day. He longed for some sort of variety and was grateful for the odd occasions when Olivia sneaked in food to change the monotony. As Steve ate his meal, he and Olivia continued to converse in conversation up to the point when visiting hours was over and Olivia had to leave.

Even though his parents were due to visit over the weekend, Steve knew he needed a bit of time to mentally prepare himself for their visit. His relationship with them was hard work at the best of times, purely because of the standards and the way they lived their lives. Having been brought up in Catholicism, they weren't really practising Catholics. Steve found faith in his youth. He was invited to a Pentecostal church by a school friend and felt more comfortable with that style of worship. His parents had good morals, which is why he often described his upbringing to others that he grew up in a Christian household. But the reality is that they were not followers of Christ in the sense like he was and did not always understand the choices that he had made for his life, and he felt it a constant battle to fight to maintain his Christian standards.

It was a bright Saturday morning, and the sunlight flooded the ward, waking up the patients as they adopted their normal morning procedures. Some were physically able, albeit somewhat slowly, to take themselves to the bathroom to prepare for the day, whilst others needed assistance from the staff. Even though Steve had made significant progress since he first came to the rehabilitation centre, he still needed to be assisted, as he found it challenging to negotiate his wheelchair in and out of the bathroom. It frustrated him to no end that he still couldn't do, without assistance, what was once considered a basic task. That months earlier he would not have given a second thought to, due to him having been such an independent man for most of his adult life. He often fantasised about the day when he would finally get rid of his wretched wheelchair and could share with Olivia that he was back to normal. However, he knew that he still had some progress and hard work to undergo, if that day was ever going to manifest.

Steve had a session in the hydrotherapy rehabilitation pool prior to his parents visit, which was designed to relax and strengthen his legs, allowing him to relearn some of the skills that he had lost due to the accident. He particularly enjoyed these one-to-one sessions with his physiotherapist, Matt, who also was a Christian and communicated with him on a spiritual level. In a way that none of the other staff could. Matt would help him push through the pain by encouraging him with scriptures like 'He could do all things through Christ that strengthened him'. Another favourite was 'With God, all things are possible'. As Steve would mentally recite these scriptures, he knew it was a case of mind over matter. He was determined that he would not spend the rest of his days tied to a wheelchair, which gave him the tenacity to push pass the pain to gain his end goal.

After breakfast and following a short time in the afternoon interacting with the other men on the ward, Matt came to collect Steve for his session in the hydrotherapy rehabilitation pool. Matt had designed a simple programme for Steve, but one designed to work specifically on his problem areas. Steve needed to improve his balance and to strengthen the core muscles in his legs.

"You're doing great, Steve. Just continue to push pass any resistance you are feeling, as the muscles in your legs will loosen up as the water pushes pass them."

Matt gently guided Steve around the pool, ensuring that he did not fall and that he was steady on his feet.

"So, I hear your parents are due to visit you today. That should be interesting."

Matt playfully rolled his eyes. In their time together, Steve felt comfortable sharing with Matt some of his personal challenges. Being in the pool was quite therapeutic. It felt like being in a therapist's office and having a counselling session. Steve had shared his challenging relationship with his parents with Matt. Whilst they meant well, they really couldn't understand their son's deep faith in God, which meant that they didn't always see eye to eye on matters of integrity. Like telling a little 'white lie' here and there if the situation warranted it. Whilst they were not bad individuals in themselves, it was their view on certain matters, that did not always sit well with Steve's conscious and that was predominately their bone of contention.

"Don't remind me,"

Steve said nervously, trying not to let the thought that he would soon be in their company cause him to stumble and lose his poise. The pool was the place where he mentally went to offload any negative thoughts he was dealing with, allowing him the opportunity to relax and free his mind as he concentrated on his recovery.

"I think it gets challenging because they can't understand why I must go all out and openly declare my faith, when I could just be like them and be religious as and when it suits. But I can't live my life like that."

"I hear you," Matt said sympathetically.

"Individuals don't always understand that it isn't about adopting a religious persuasion at all but rather having a personal relationship with Jesus. As Christians, we believe in the abundant life that Jesus died to give us, which we so readily rely on in our day-to-day lives. And it's that hope that you must rely on to get you out of this place. Steve, you are doing so well. The progress you have made since you have been here has been exemplary. Olivia must be excited about the progress you are making."

As Matt mentioned Olivia's name, Steve took a slight stumble and Matt caught him.

"Steady on, mate. It looks like the mention of your girl makes you go weak at the knees, eh?"

Matt smiled as he teased Steve who was trying his best to stay steady on his feet.

And he had to make a bold confession to Matt. Again, like if he was on the couch having a counselling session.

"I haven't really told Liv about the movement and strength I have been feeling in my legs."

He bowed his head like a little boy who was being scolded for something he did that he knew he shouldn't have.

"Why not, Steve?"

"Errr… I just don't want her to get her hopes up as she'll start thinking we can go back to making plans for the wedding."

"And what's wrong with that?" Matt wanted to challenge Steve's thinking.

"I would have thought that was a good enough motivation for you to ensure that you get out of this place within the next couple of months."

"Yes, but what if I don't? What if this is as good as it gets?"

Matt was a good physiotherapist and positive in his manner.

"Look, mate, I have seen individuals come in this place with worse injuries than you and in no time, they end up walking out of this place on their own two feet. And that will be your testimony too. So enough of this negative self-talk, we have work to do."

Matt ensured that he walked with Steve another few laps of the pool before allowing him to retire for the evening to have a rest before his parents were due to visit.

CHAPTER TWO

Visiting time for the evening session had begun and Steve had his eyes intently on the door as he watched various individuals enter the ward and made their way straight to the person they had come to visit. He smiled on the inside as he observed how happy his fellow mates appeared and their demeanour changed instantly as they welcomed family and friends, which noticeably changed the atmosphere and created a buzz of excitement in the air. His heart sank, however, as he glanced over to Jack's corner, realising that he wouldn't have anyone visiting that evening. He held up a thumb to him in a gesture to communicate that everything was going to be okay. Jack coyly cracked a smile and returned a thumbs up to Steve and then went back to playing on his Gameboy. Jack's Gameboy was a welcome distraction, which was going to be his company until visiting time was over.

As Steve found himself caught up in the emotions of feeling sad for Jack, he heard a firm, yet polite voice wafting towards his bed.

"Hello Steven, how are you, son?"

A petite lady with silverish hair politely kissed him on his cheek, smoothed the fringe of his hair to the right-side of his face and sat down. Steve smiled at her as he embraced her affection.

"Hello, Mother. Thanks for coming. Hi Dad; you're looking well."

A tall, well-built man with dark hair and black rimmed glasses smiled at him as he extended his hand to Steve to shake it.

"Hello son. It's good to see you."

His father seemed a little agitated, awkwardly bumping his leg against the side of the table.

"It took longer than we had anticipated, due to the traffic. Plus, not being familiar with the area either. Oh well, we're here now."

Mr & Mrs Adams occupied the two spare empty seats that were allocated to Steve's area and made themselves comfortable.

"Now, I'm sure you would have wanted us to bring you a load of chocolate, sweets and biscuits. But we bought you some grapes, bananas and oranges instead, which are much healthier. And I am sure your doctors would agree are far better for your ongoing recovery."

Steve's mother was very health conscious. Even though she was in her late sixties, she looked after her body well, ensuring she attended Pilate classes and regularly went for walks to keep up her stamina.

"We are sorry we haven't visited you until now, Steven. As you know, we went on that month long cruise to the Caribbean. Which was fabulous, I must say. Then some other business had us occupied. We are sorry that this is the first opportunity we have had to come and see you. How have you been, son?"

Before Steve could answer, his mother continued with the agenda of points that she had mentally made a note of in her subconscious to bring to Steve's attention.

"You look well. Although your complexion could do with a little bit of perking up. Good job we brought you the fresh fruit."

Mrs Adams screeched out a laugh in a loud manner as she tapped Steve on his arm.

"I am getting there, Mother. They are looking after me well in this place and are pleased with my progress."

In a deep, husky voice his father looked him straight in the eye and said,

"You know that we can get you into a private facility that would probably speed up your progress. Just say the word and I will make a few calls and get you out of this place."

His eyes circled around the room in an up and down motion as he mentally took in his surroundings.

"No, Dad, I'm fine. They are looking after me satisfactorily."

Steve had to be strong and firm in his response as he knew how snobbish his parents were and only dealt with the finer things of life. If he were to let them, they would certainly make all the appropriate calls to get him out of the rehabilitation centre and choose a facility close to where they lived. But Steve was comfortable where he was and trusted the professionals who were assigned to work with him. He also did not want to move away from the friends he had worked so hard to establish over the years. And certainly, he did not want to be miles away from Olivia. Even though he was giving her a difficult time of late, she really was his rock and if truth be told, was the motivation for him working doubly hard to ensure that he recovered speedily.

"Thanks Dad, I know you guys mean well, but I have my friends who are nearby. And I'd like to keep the connection ongoing with them. Besides, you'd get me into a facility near to where you live, and I wouldn't know anyone in the area."

Steve hoped that he had done enough for his parents to realise that he was happy where he was. However, his mother had other ideas.

"Actually, Steven, I was meaning to share with you some good news."

A big smile came across her face, almost as if she was bursting with excitement to share a long-kept secret. She grabbed and held Steve's hand tightly.

"Charlotte Bramwell is back in the UK and only the other day was asking after your welfare."

Steve's face seemed puzzled. He couldn't work out how the correlation came about. One minute they were talking about finding a new facility for him and in the next breath, somehow, Charlotte's name got dropped into the conversation.

"That's nice, Mother, but how did we get from talking about my rehabilitation to Charlotte being back in town?"

"Well, you said you wouldn't know anyone in the area. But since Charlotte is back home now, she is someone that you could reconnect with. Perhaps picking up where you left off."

Suddenly, the penny dropped and from the conniving look on his mother's face, Steve saw where this conversation was going and it wasn't going to end well, for either of them.

Charlotte Bramwell was a family friend who both of their parents wanted them to be together, as in the grand scheme of things, they felt it was good on paper and made sound financial sense.

Charlotte's family had a successful, prestigious law firm with offices worldwide, and she had recently returned from the States after working in their New York office for several years. The name Charlotte Bramwell was like a blast from the past for Steve, not having heard it since his university days, and his mind wandered to the time when they first met.

They both studied law at Oxford University and instantly connected on a friendship level. Charlotte would have been every parent's dream for their son as she was astute and knew her mind. From the early days, it was evident that she would be successful in life and go all the way. Steve liked the fact that she challenged his thinking on various subjects and for him it was refreshing for a woman to be on that same intellectual level with him.

Over the years, their friendship developed deeper to the point that both sets of parents had a relationship with each other. And because of their similar backgrounds, there were shared events that the families attended. At the time, Steve knew that Charlotte would be his parents' first choice in a spouse for him. But he did not feel the romantic connection, even though he loved her as a close friend. Charlotte's personality was bold and vivacious, and on one occasion, she told Steve in no uncertain terms that she liked him and wanted to have a future with him. Whilst Steve appreciated her honesty, he had to let her down gently and vividly recalled that weighty conversation.

"Charlotte, I love the friendship that we have developed over the years, and I wouldn't want to spoil that. I think we both know that our parents want this more than we do, don't you think?" Charlotte smiled and dipped her head.

"I suppose you are right, but nevertheless, you are one good catch, Mr Steve Adams. There's a woman out there who is going to be lucky to have you." Steve blushed at Charlotte's compliment.

"And likewise, Miss Charlotte Bramwell. Your Prince Charming is out there too. You just need to wait for him. Don't ever allow yourself to settle for second best. You deserve all that God has predestined for you to have."

And it was on that mutual agreement that the subject on the matter was closed, never to be spoken of or brought up again. After university, they both went their separate ways and somehow lost contact with each other when Charlotte left for the States.

"Mother, I have already told you that I have met someone and have asked her to marry me, and I am pleased to say that she has accepted."

Steve knew that his choice of a spouse was never going to be accepted by his parents, as that was what it was like growing up for his whole life. From the time he was born, his life was mapped out for him, down to the preparatory boarding schools and university he would attend. He was even expected to follow in his father's footsteps and be an investment banker. However, that's where Steve drew the line. He had always had an empathy for helping others and wanted to be able to pour into individuals so that he could make a difference and change the course and trajectory of the lives of those who needed his help.

Steve's father piped in,

"Who is this young lady then? Do we know her family? What line of business are they in?"

Steve rolled his eyes and muttered to himself, '*Here we go*'.

"Dad, I haven't really met her parents yet, but from all accounts, they are good people. If you are asking me what the nature of their pedigree is, then I'm sorry as that's not a priority on my list of the qualities of what I want in a wife.

I'm marrying Olivia because I love her and not for what I can get from her or her family for that matter."

Steve was starting to feel slightly irritated with his parents as everything always had to revolve around a person's financial standing and that wasn't what he wanted to be known for.

"Steven, mind your tone with your father. I think Daddy is just trying to make sure that this young woman is not trying to marry you for the wrong reasons and because you are wealthy."

"Actually, Olivia doesn't really know about the money or my family background. We were getting around to that session in our pre-marital course, and then I had my accident and as a result ended up in this place."

Steve shrugged his shoulders whilst throwing his hands in the air.

"Well, what I am saying, son, is prenup all the way. We've worked too hard over the years for what we have built up. We can't afford anyone coming into the family jeopardising things if for some reason this marriage wasn't going to last. You make sure you get yourself protected."

Steve's dad was deadly serious and was all set to have his solicitors draw up the necessary paperwork at the appropriate time.

"Dad, lower your voice please. I don't want everyone overhearing my personal business. And, for the record, I have no intentions of asking Liv to sigh a prenup. If it means walking away from my trust fund, then she's worth it and I am willing to do so."

Steve could sense that his parents were not comfortable with his sense of direction and knew this would not be the last he would hear on the matter. They were like a dog with a bone when they had a matter that they wanted to go their way and could be relentless to secure the deal.

Steve cleverly deflected away from the subject by asking his parents where they were going on their next trip, and that got them talking about all things regarding their travels up until they were ready to leave. Steve felt mentally spent. Conversations with his parents were always challenging and he felt slightly guilty that he was pleased that they hadn't visited before and probably wouldn't get to visit for some time again.

"Well, thanks for coming all this way to visit me, that was very good of you."

Steve let out a large yawn as he stretched his hands in the air to release the built-up tension that he was feeling.

Mrs Adams started to clean and tidy up Steve's table, arranging his fruit neatly before she left.

"Steven, we can see that you are looking a bit tired now, so me and your father are going to leave you to rest now. We may not be able to visit again for a while, as it is quite a distance from where we live. Are you sure we can't get you into somewhere nearer to us?"

"No, Mother. As I previously said, I'm fine here and I believe I will be out in no time, so please don't worry about me. Don't forget also, that I'm only a phone call away, so you can always call anytime you like."

Mrs Adams perked up and felt reassured.

"Oh yes, that is true, I can speak with you on the telephone, can't I?" She let out another one of her loud screechy laughs.

"I feel much better now." Steve's mum tapped her husband gently on his shoulder.

"Come on, Daddy, let's get on the road as it's going to get very dark soon."

Mr Adams stood up and cracked his knuckles, making a loud sound.

"Son, you take care of yourself. I wish you the best and the next time we see you, we hope that it isn't in this place and that it will be in the comfort of your own home."

The bell to indicate that visiting time was over reverberated and Steve's parents, along with the other visitors, said their goodbyes and made their exit. The ward returned to a less quiet atmosphere with the buzz of the guests leaving with them.

Olivia approached the weekend with the realisation that this was the first weekend she did not have to divide her time between doing things around the house and then rushing off to visit Steve at the centre. She did not want to admit to herself that she wasn't Superwoman and therefore couldn't always be there mentally and physically for everyone else and their needs. It was time for her to think of number one for a change. Olivia allowed her mind to wander and think of something special that she enjoyed doing. It was a long while since she really pampered herself with a manicure or pedicure and decided to give the beauty shop, Nails by Design, which was located on the high street, a call to see if they could fit her in.

Olivia was in luck as they had had a cancellation that morning and was able to fit her in. Now that her nails were sorted, Olivia contemplated what else she could squeeze in before she visited Carol later in the afternoon. She had arranged the visit at short notice after Steve so abruptly dismissed her from visiting.

'I wonder what that really was all about. And how the visit with his parents went? I would have loved to have met them. It's almost as if he didn't want me to meet them. But I'm going to have to meet them eventually, and I would have thought that would have been the ideal opportunity. But I guess Steve is right, as the setting wasn't conducive for first introductions of their new daughter-in-law. Plus, I hope he has mentioned to them that I am black'.

Olivia started to get herself dressed for her appointment by taking out a pair of black skinny jeans, which complimented nicely with her Black Lives Matter T-shirt. 'I might as well make a statement whilst I am out and about'. She smiled to herself. Olivia wasn't really a radical activist regarding her black heritage, but she felt it was important to keep the matter alive and in the forefront of the mind of others that all lives were important and mattered, especially to God. She realised that her T-shirt would cause a few raised eyebrows from some, but that didn't seem to deter her from wearing it. She was a teacher and was used to dealing with conflicting opinions. Albeit the ones she dealt with on a day-to-day basis were mere five-year-olds and were easier to silence.

Olivia got to her 11.30 am appointment in good time. The shop was heaving with women of various ethnicities, young and old, which was often the case, and Olivia knew she was extremely fortunate to bag a last-minute cancellation. Olivia enjoyed being pampered for a change. The nail technician took great care with her hands, being gentle and professional, as she started off by soaking them in a pungent solution. After her hands were thoroughly massaged and her nails manicured, when asked what colour she wanted her nails painted in, Olivia felt that bold, feisty spirit rise on the inside again and settled for a vibrant bright burgundy colour with glitter running throughout. Olivia felt sure that Steve would have thought she had gone mad as she was usually more predictable with the French manicure look that she would normally have gone for. Olivia felt in a daring mood and her inner alter ego was emerging. Olivia also decided to push the boat out and went for a pedicure too, having the same colour varnish on her toenails. After feeling thrilled with her nails and feet, and tipping the nail technician generously, Olivia treated herself to a coffee in a local coffee shop, where she sat in a corner by the window and caught up with her text messages. She was surprised to see that there were several messages from Steve:

'Hey babes, just wanted to say hi and hope your weekend is going well. Missing you; can't wait to see you soon,'

and other messages along the same lines.

'Ahhh, that's sweet of him. He must have had a good conversation with his parents as he seems a lot more upbeat'.

What Olivia could not have foreseen is how challenging the conversation with Steve's parents turned out to be. Which only reinforced how important Olivia was to him and that he really did want to marry her as soon as he was fit to do so. Unknowingly, Steve's parents did Olivia a massive favour by making him see what the priorities in his life were and what he had that he didn't want to lose. After leaving the coffee shop, enroute to Carol's house, Olivia popped into her local supermarket and bought some flowers and a bottle of red wine.

CHAPTER THREE

Olivia wasn't too far from Carol's home and took her time to drive the few miles needed to get there. Olivia was looking forward to seeing Carol as whilst she spoke to her on the phone, they had not met up for a while and Carol had not been at church for some time either. Olivia had lots to discuss with Carol, and she also wanted to share with her some of the more intimate discussions that she had been having with Steve, if only to get a second opinion on the matter. Or, in her view, to get another woman's perspective on the situation. Olivia pulled up to the drive and manoeuvred herself next to the car that was already parked there. Olivia gathered her things, trying hard not to damage the flowers in the process, and got out of the car and walked to the door and rang the bell. Having waited for about five minutes, she pondered whether anyone was in. But the car was there, so Carol must be at home. Olivia rang the bell again.

A few moments later, Carol emerged at the door, panting and trying to catch her breath.

"Alright, alright, Miss Impatient. You need to allow me time to get to the door, you know,"

Carol said sarcastically, but in a humorous tone. Carol looked radiant and her bump was visible to see.

"Ohh myyy goodness, look at you."

Olivia practically dived towards her and gave her a big hug, even though Carol's bump got between them both.

"Yes, we are doing well," Carol said as she rubbed her stomach and beckoned Olivia to come into the house.

"And these are for you."

Olivia extended her hand to give Carol the flowers whilst smiling from ear to ear.

"Well, thank you my dear. And they are my favourite too. How very thoughtful of you."

"Anything for my favourite girl, you know that. Anyway, let's sit down. How are you? Well, I can see how well you look, but honestly, how has pregnancy been so far? And how far gone are you now?"

Carol smiled as she sat down and took the weight off her feet.

"Oh, gosh, so many questions. This is like the Spanish Inquisition."

Olivia had to laugh.

"I know it is, but this is new for us, Carol, as neither of us have done this before."

As Olivia said the words, it was almost as if she wished she could have taken them back, as she recalled that Carol had been pregnant a very long time ago. Olivia put her hand to her mouth and her face sank.

"Oh, I'm so sorry Carol. I didn't mean anything by that comment, and…"

Before Olivia could finish, Carol stopped her in her tracks.

"Liv don't worry. It was an innocent mistake, and I know exactly what you meant. And you are right, none of us have got to the point of being pregnant and carrying a child to full term. Well, in my case, it's not one, but two, because as you already know, we are expecting twins."

Carol sighed as the thought of having two screaming children running around the house at the same time filled her with a bit of trepidation to say the least. Olivia felt more at ease when she realised that Carol's past was exactly that and she wasn't going to let it spoil the beautiful experience of what she was now feeling.

Olivia started to laugh in a teasing way.

"Twins… that could only happen to you, Carol. I just can't wait to see how you are going to cope. Thankfully, you'll have Michael by your side. By the way, where is the man of the house? I bought this bottle of wine for him."

Olivia was looking around to see if there were any signs of him in the house.

"He's fine, thanks. He went into work this morning just to sort out a few things with Joan. There is a lot going on there, which I'm not at liberty to discuss at the moment, but just to say, there are going to be some very big changes happening there."

Carol raised her eyebrows and motioned as if she was zipping her mouth to indicate that, whatever the situation was, it was top secret and had a time and place as to when it could be discussed.

"So, in answer to your question, I'm five months along now and it's going well. Although I do get out of breath a bit when I have to do strenuous things. And my ankles get swollen from time to time, which is why I haven't been at church much, but I've just been watching it online."

"I'm sorry to hear that," Olivia said sympathetically.

"But I bet Michael is a Godsend, isn't he?"

Carol sighed and rolled her eyes.

"Oh pahleeze. That man has been driving me crazy. All he has been doing is fussing and annoying me. Bombarding me with facts about the do's and don'ts in pregnancy, just because he is the professional. Well, I know my body too, so that's something his textbook can't give him; the personal experience."

"Ah, leave him alone, Carol. He's an excited father to be and you know how special this is to him too, so let him have his time."

"I knowww. You should have seen his face when we were first told that we were pregnant. I thought he was going to faint."

They both laughed at the thought of Doctor Cool losing his cool. And Carol's thoughts went back briefly to that moment all those months ago.

Michael clasped onto Carol's hand as they waited nervously for the doctor to come back into the room with the results. Both had their own internal dialogue going on inside their heads for those brief moments. For Michael, it would be a dream come true, as he thought his chances had been taken from him due to the bombshell Carol had earlier delivered to him. And for Carol, she was filled with dread on the thought of being a mother. Especially when she didn't think she had one maternal bone in her body.

Also, she was a bit confused. How could she be pregnant when she was led to believe all these years that children would never factor into her life? And that was something she held to and ended up being comfortable with the prognosis of the medical profession at that time. How could they have got things drastically wrong? Michael was always saying to her that medical professionals were not God and therefore were prone to mistakes. If she was pregnant, then this one would have to go down in the history books as one of their all-time catastrophes.

The doctor came back into the room and Carol brought her thoughts to a head and smiled nervously with Michael. The news that they were about to receive had the ability to change the trajectory of their lives one way or the other. Michael had more to lose and squeezed Carol's hand tightly. The doctor sat down opposite them and looked intently in their faces with a big smile on her face.

"Well, Mr & Mrs Mills, it's good news. You're pregnant and are going to be parents sometime in the not-too-distant future. May I be the first to congratulate you both. You must be very pleased. Let me leave you both to have a moment to process the news."

A startled, but elated Michael was the first to respond.

"I think I'm going to faint. This is great news."

He turned towards Carol and gave her a big hug.

"We did it Caz. We blinking well did it. No matter what the enemy wanted to throw at us, God said, 'not on my watch' and turned the tables."

Carol, however, was less bursting at the seams regarding the news, but only because everything she once thought to be true now wasn't the case. Yet she did not want to rain on Michael's parade and spoil the moment he had been waiting his whole adult life to be... a father. And she smiled and went along with his euphoria.

"Well, I wasn't expecting that if I were to be completely honest. No pun intended. So, I'm going to be a mother. Well, I hope I do a good job as everyone knows I'm not very maternal."

Michael tried to reassure her.

"Caz, you're going to be great, and you've got all of us to help you. Me, Jenny and even Olivia. She's used to dealing with toddlers and I'm sure she'll have lots of advice to share with us."

Carol smiled. She appreciated what Michael was trying to do. He was trying to calm her fears, yet the internal anguish was almost deafening her as to her ability in being a good mother. After the shock of learning they were pregnant, the second shock came at the first scan when it was revealed by the sonographer that she could see two heartbeats and that indeed they were having twins. And it was at that point that Carol felt she was going to be the one to faint this time around. Michael felt as though God was rewarding them for all the drama that they had endured and was using this opportunity to give them a fresh start.

"Earth to Carol. Is there anyone there?"

Olivia was tapping Carol gently on the shoulder as she had gone off into a deep thought.

"Sorry hon. Talking about things took me back for a moment back to when me and Michael first got the news and then later were told we were having twins. I'm good with the information now, but back then, it was a little bit daunting to say the least."

Carol rubbed her stomach and stood up to stretch her body.

"Are you okay hon?"

"Yeahhh, I'm fine. Just changing positions as sometimes sitting still for too long can feel a bit uncomfortable. Excuse my manners, Liv. Would you like something to drink?"

"I wouldn't mind a coffee, if it isn't too much trouble. I don't even mind getting it myself."

Carol rolled her eyes.

"I'm not completely helpless yet, Liv. I think I can manage to get my best friend a cup of coffee. Now in a few months' time, that might be a different story."

They both had a giggle as the thought of Carol waddling along helplessly was something to behold.

"Anyway missy, enough about me, what's been going on in your world and how is that fiancé of yours doing with his recovery?"

Olivia sighed, wondering how much she should divulge to Carol or whether to keep her and Steve's issues private and just between the two of them. But Carol was her best friend after all and surely that's what best friends were for. To use as a sounding board when difficulties came to a head.

"Where do I start, Caz? It's been challenging to say the least. Not in a bad way. I would say more like I feel he's trying to push me away because at the present time he can't seem to handle his injuries. Because he doesn't see himself as a whole man. He keeps saying that he is not the man who I said yes to. And I know we haven't said those famous vows, but I still believe that for better or for worse, you stand by the person you are committed to. And I have no intentions of bailing out just because he can't walk at this moment in time."

Carol brought over a cup of coffee to Olivia and lent up against the wall.

"I hear what you are saying, Liv, but you must remember what guys are like. It's a pride thing. And I don't mean that he is full of pride or anything like that, because we know Steve's not like that. But he wants to be the provider, and right now, he can't see how that is going to happen. And that could be the cause of what is troubling him at present."

Olivia pondered.

"Ummm, I guess I didn't think of it like that or from his perspective. But how can I reassure him that I'm here for the long-haul?"

Carol hesitated before proceeding with caution.

"Well, you know I'm not the expert on all things smooth sailing in a relationship. And I guess I'm the last person you would want to take marital advice from, but I'd say just be patient with him. Everything at this moment in time seems to hinge on his recovery. I believe that as he continues to make progress, that will give him confidence, and he'll be back to the old Steve that you fell in love with. Although, if truth be told, the man was right under your nose for the longest time, so God only knows when you eventually fell in love with him."

Olivia chuckled, whilst surrendering her hands in the air.

"Okayyy, okayyy. Some of us take longer to state the obvious. I know. Anyway, nothing before its time, eh? And stop putting yourself down, Caz, you are certainly qualified to give marital advice. One mistake doesn't disqualify you from the game, so cut yourself some slack. You can give me advice anytime."

Olivia paused.

"Now whether I act on that advice is another story."

They laughed out loud. No matter what they were talking about, they always had the ability to make each other laugh hysterically.

"Changing the subject slightly, has anyone heard from Chris since he left abruptly?" Olivia said slyly.

Not that she was the slightest bit interested in what he was up to these days. But curiosity was getting the better of her, and she did not want to bump into him unexpectedly and then feel awkward in the process.

"Actually, I think he is back now. Apparently, the business he went back to sort out did not turn out as bad as was envisaged it would. But part of his story has to do with some of the changes that will be happening at the surgery. Which, remember, I am not at liberty to say at this moment in time."

Carol was sticking to her guns, especially as Michael shared the plans with her in private and she wanted to show him that she had changed and could be the type of wife he could entrust with work related matters.

"I must say, Caz, I'm really impressed. The old Caz would have been falling over backwards to share the latest gossip. You've really changed."

"I know I have, haven't I. Perhaps it's my hormones playing up." Carol winked at Olivia.

"No, seriously, Michael and I have had some hard discussions since finding out that I was pregnant and him moving back home. And we have been having counselling sessions with PT over the last few months. I am trying hard to win his trust again. I let him down very badly, Liv, and I never thought it would come to him moving out and us being apart for a considerable amount of time, which was horrible. But it seems these babies have been the catalyst to saving our marriage.

I feel like God has given me a second chance and I don't intend to blow it this time around. I feel blessed. I never thought I would say that about being pregnant, but I'm really looking forward to meeting these two little people who are growing on the inside of me."

"That's beautiful, Caz, and their auntie Olivia can't wait to meet them too."
Olivia looked over at Carol and noticed she looked a bit tired as if she needed to go and have a lie down.

"Caz, you're looking a bit tired. I don't want to outstay my welcome and it was just supposed to be a quick visit to see how you were doing."

"Yes, I am feeling a bit tired. I get exhausted so quickly and don't seem to have much energy for anything lately. Thankfully, I have good staff, and I can do some things remotely from home. Like the design side of various projects. Michael is very good too and comes home from a hard day's work and then starts the dinner. I feel a bit guilty, but if it was left down to me, he'd probably not get anything to eat until 10 PM that evening. It's not even funny," Carol said, putting her hand over her mouth so as not to laugh out loud.

"So, thanks for asking and yes, I will go and have a nap now. What will you do for the rest of the day then?"

"Well, I'm not going to see Steve tonight since he has banished me from visiting for the whole weekend, so I'll probably just go home, potter around the house and then get myself ready for church as I'm teaching tomorrow."

"Is Jen not around then?" Carol enquired.

"No, she's away for the weekend in Cornwall. Gone home for her cousin's wedding. So, she'll probably be back on Monday."

"Oh, well you enjoy yourself, whatever you do. I'm going to take a quick nap now before Michael gets back. I think I might even order us a takeaway, so that he doesn't need to feel the pressure of having to slave away in the kitchen. Plus, we occasionally have takeout on a weekend, so I believe he'll welcome the surprise."

Carol got up and walked with Olivia to the door and they embraced each other with a big hug.

"Thanks for your visit, hon. I really appreciate it, but don't leave it too long next time, okay?" Olivia smiled.

"Nope, I won't. You take care of yourself and get some rest."

Olivia walked to her car and, when she was securely belted in, waved goodbye to Carol and drove out of the drive and went straight home.

CHAPTER FOUR

It took Chris a couple of months to sort out his affairs in Melton Mowbray, but he and Ben were now back in Bricket Wood. He had been busily trying to secure a new live-in nanny since Mrs Jenkins was unable to return to her previous role. Whilst Chris and Ben were away, her husband had had a stroke, and Mrs Jenkins had become his full-time carer and contacted Chris whilst he was away as soon as it happened to explain that she could not carry on in the same capacity. She wanted to give him sufficient time to find a suitable replacement.

Whilst Chris appreciated all the work that Mrs Jenkins had done for them in the past, he knew he wasn't going to find anyone as hard-working and as dedicated as she was. However, he felt this time around that he needed to employ a live-in au-pair instead, so that there could be someone permanently on hand to assist him when he was tied up with surgery or hospital appointments. That way, Ben could be collected from school, and he would feel comfortable knowing that he did not have to run round frantically to try and pick him up.

Regarding the issue he had with Olivia some months prior, he was considering taking Ben out of Newmont Primary School altogether and looking for a new school for him. However, he had to admit that Olivia had done such a good job with his son when he first went to the school, and as Ben was settled and made friends for the first time, he had to put his own personal pride aside and think about Ben's needs for a change. He even thought about having a meeting with Mrs Barrett to see if Ben could go back to his original class with Ms Rogers, but as he had so much overshadowing his mind at present, he had to put that on the back burner until he had got things squared with his job.

Returning to Melton Mowbray was no mean feat. Chris had to deal with his demons. Firstly, he had to contact his in-laws and try to make amends for the way he abruptly left and ripped apart their hearts as their only grandchild had also left. It was bad enough coming to terms with losing a daughter, but to shortly lose contact with a grandchild too, who was their world, was inconceivable. And they let Chris know in no uncertain terms of their disappointment in him for the poor decisions he had made.

Whilst at first it took a while for Ben to remember his grandparents, he soon found a fondness towards them as they spoilt and smothered him with love and attention, something he wasn't used to. When Chris left to go back to Bricket Wood, he had to promise his in-laws that they could see Ben regularly and that he could visit them for a couple of weeks in the summer. That wasn't something Chris minded, as it would help him out in the summer break and he wouldn't need to find various activities, like summer camps, to keep Ben occupied for the 6-8 weeks that the school children would normally be out of school for.

However, his conversation with Tilly would not prove as smooth sailing. She was a tougher nut to crack and even then, he still left with some unresolved issues still hanging in the air. However, he could not get things sorted with his former practice, and clear his name, until he had spoken to Tilly first to try and reason with her to drop whatever enquiry she was trying to pursue to have him struck off the medical register.

She was living in the same house and area she was when Chris first met Jill as she and Tilly shared a house together, so she wasn't hard to find. When Tilly had descended on his doorstep and startled him with her presence prior to him returning to Melton Mowbray, she was disoriented and confused, and he couldn't get much sense out of her. She just wanted him to know that she had found him and would always find him, no matter how far he ventured. It was almost as if she delighted in being his stalker. At the time, with everything that was going on in Chris' life, he wasn't in the mood for Tilly's games and dismissed her and told her to go home. She screamed at him that she was in the position she was because of him and that he shouldn't have messed with her feelings if he had no intention of acting on them. Again, Chris was not about to start a full-blown argument on his doorstep and Tilly left, with the next time him seeing her was when he went to Melton Mowbray to speak with her.

Chris pulled up into the drive of the house where Tilly resided. Her metallic red Corsa was in the drive, so that gave him a strong indication that she was probably at home. Chris got out of his car and walked to the front door and rang the bell. After about five minutes, Tilly emerged and opened the door. For one split second, Chris felt as if he was seeing double and looking at Jill all over again and his memories with her started to flood back. The ladies were identical twins, so when you saw one, you saw the other. Tilly's appearance looked a bit dishevelled, as if she had just come back from the gym and seemed out of breath.

"Oh dear, look what the cat dragged in. Mum and Dad said you came around grovelling to them. I wondered how long it would take for you to make an appearance." Chris felt bewildered.

"Hi Tilly. Nice to see you too," he said sarcastically whilst rolling his eyes.

"So, are you going to let me in then or are we going to air our dirty laundry on the doorstep for all your neighbours to hear?"

"I don't care either way." Tilly walked off whilst leaving the door open.

"I've just come back from the gym so come in and make yourself comfortable. I believe you know where everything is. I'm going to take a shower and will be back down when I am refreshed."

Tilly darted upstairs of what appeared to be a massive house for one person. Chris was surprised that she did not sell the place when Jill left to marry him or perhaps get a flatmate. But then again, he wondered who really could live with Tilly because she wasn't the easiest of personalities to deal with.

He walked into the main lounge area and noticed that Tilly had made some considerable changes. He felt that the interior decorating she had done was nicely finished, with the pastel colours lending a warmth to the room that perhaps wasn't captured before. There were pictures of the sisters fixed to the wall and positioned on the mantelpiece which made Chris appreciate that losing Jill was just as hard for Tilly as it was for him.

Jill was in Tilly's life for a lot longer than she was in his life and therefore Tilly's memories would span several decades, consisting of fun, laughter and shared secrets, as well as good times and bad. He never really took the time to reach out to Tilly after Jill's death and offer his support. Perhaps that's what Tilly meant when she screamed at him that she was in this position because of him. Although, he couldn't quite work out what 'this position' signified. Chris sat quietly on the settee and reminisced over the various occasions he would pull up into the drive to come and visit Jill. And the smile that would be on Jill's face as she came running out the door for him to whisk her off to whatever date he had planned for them both.

Deep in thought, he hadn't heard Tilly come into the room. Her medium-built physique hugged neatly a white T-shirt and navy jeans with a towel around her neck, as her hair was still dripping.

"Okay Chris, so what's this all about, since you're the one who dismissed me when we last saw each other."

Tilly sat at the table opposite him and started to dry her hair whilst talking to him.

"If I remember rightly, your words were 'go home Tilly'. So, guess what Chris; I'm home."

She threw her hands in the air as she continued to provoke him. Chris hated the bantering he always felt he had to tolerate with Tilly. She could never give a straight answer or have a decent conversation.

When he first met her as a Rep at the surgery he worked at, she seemed pleasant enough. But there was something about her that he could not put his finger on. Yet when she introduced him to Jill, he realised that even though they were identical twins, their personalities were miles apart. And it was the warmness in Jill's demeanour that made him want to pursue and get to know more about her in depth. And it was as he and Jill got closer, he noticed a change in Tilly's behaviour towards him, and from then on, she never had a good word to say about him.

"Look Tilly, I didn't come here for an argument. You've said some very disparaging things about my character, and I am here to ask you to consider withdrawing those accusations. This is my career that's on the line here."

Chris sounded exhausted already and the conversation had only just begun. Tilly had him exactly where she wanted him, and he knew it. He could either start a slanging match with her and he would get nowhere. Or he could play the game and pamper to Tilly's every whim in the hope that she would see sense and drop the complaint. Tilly finished drying her hair and left it to nestle down the back of her neck.

"Do you want something to drink?"

Tilly asked Chris sheepishly as if to apologise for not offering him a drink in the first instance. Chris felt swayed by the question but wasn't going to let it distract him.

"No… No… I'm fine; thanks."

"Okay, Chris. For the record, I did not lodge a complaint about you. I just asked your surgery if they could investigate the drugs, you were handling around about the time that Jill died. Something just doesn't add up. Jill was doing fine and shouldn't have declined so rapidly over the two-week period from when she appeared fine until when she unexpectedly passed away. Everyone knew at the time that you liked experimenting with new drugs. I'm just wondering if you administered something to her that you shouldn't have, as you weren't her doctor, Chris. She had her own team that was managing her condition well."

Chris rose to his feet and his voice heightened.

"Tilly, if you are saying for one minute that I had something to do with Jill's death and deliberately did something to assist her dying quicker, then you are crazy. And way out of line to even suggest what you are purporting."

Tilly carried on in her matter-of-fact tone.

"I don't think it's crazy, Chris. You had access to the drugs, so you could easily have wanted to help Jill out of her pain. No one would have blamed you; it would have been perfectly understandable."

Chris fired back as quick as Tilly's darts were flying at him,

"And I daresay, you could have done the same. You're her twin. It must have been devastating to think that you were losing the one person that was always constantly there for you. And you also have the same access to a supply of drugs, perhaps even more so than me as you go around the country endorsing them. Who's to say that when I was at work and you were sitting with her that you didn't give her a little something to ease her pain? After all, she was your twin, and you would have done anything to relieve her of her discomfort."

"That's preposterous, Chris, and you know it." Now Tilly was the one raising her voice and getting agitated.

"No more preposterous than you thinking that I as her husband could do something like that. It doesn't sound nice when the boot is on the other foot now does it?"

"No, it doesn't," Tilly said as she felt made to eat humble pie over the whole matter.

Chris continued in a drained and exhausted tone,

"Why don't you say we call it a truce? You and I are never going to be friends and that's alright. We both loved and have lost her. And throwing around unwanted accusations isn't helping anyone. I could potentially go to jail over this, and what would happen to Ben in the process? And would Jill have been pleased to know that we were at each other's throats over this matter? I daresay, she wouldn't and would turn in her grave if she could even hear us now."

Chris' tone was more mellow, as he wanted to reason to the softer side of Tilly, which he knew had to be in there somewhere.

"Okayyyyy. I'll withdraw my enquiry,"

Tilly said reluctantly, knowing full well that she did not have any evidence to back up what she was purporting.

"But I want you to know that I'm only doing it for little Bengy and not for you."

"Tilly, whatever your reason is, I am very thankful and appreciate you withdrawing your complaint against me."

"It wasn't a complaint I told you, but rather an enquiry from a concerned family member."

"Okay, well whatever you want to call it... thank you. Can I leave it for you to contact them straightaway then, as I have a meeting with them in two days' time and would like to know I am going in there confident that it was just a big misunderstanding on your part?"

"Ummm, I guess so." Tilly shrugged.

Chris headed towards the front door.

"Well, thanks, Tilly, I better be off now. You take care of yourself." Tilly walked behind him and waved him off.

On the day in question, Chris had arrived 15 minutes early at the surgery for his appointment with Dr Nathan Kelly and the board. He wanted to be sure that there was nothing on his part that would hinder the board from giving him a favourable response. He sat nervously in the waiting room, and the receptionist assured him that she would let him know when they were ready for him. Chris prayed quietly that Tilly had kept her side of the bargain and had withdrawn her enquiry, which he felt was totally out of line on her part. Chris knew Tilly was capable of doing crazy things, but he did not believe she could stoop so low and deduced she obviously had her reasons for doing so. He hoped this would be the end of the matter and that he would not have to have any further dealings with Tilly. He knew she could be a loose cannon at times, and he did not have the energy to entertain her unpredictable ways.

The receptionist beckoned her voice to Chris.

"Dr Harris. They are ready for you now; please go in."

Chris was familiar with the layout, with it being his former surgery, and made his way down the slim corridor to the bottom, where the board room was situated on the right-hand side. The room was occupied with three other gentlemen, as well as Dr Kelly, sat around an oblong table, and one other female who had a notebook and sat away from the desk in a corner where she could still hear the conversation and make notes.

Chris recognised all the men, bar one, as his former colleagues and Dr Kelly signalled with his hand for Chris to take a seat in the one space that was reserved for him. The meeting lasted for an hour, and Chris was pleased to learn right at the start of the meeting that the enquiry that was made against him had subsequently been dropped. And even though there was nothing further to investigate going further, Dr Kelly expressed to Chris, in no uncertain terms, his disappointment in the abrupt way that he had left the surgery, reminding him that professionals don't act in such a way, but that they dealt with whatever issues had arisen in their lives in an orderly fashion.

Dr Kelly had appreciated that Chris would have been under an enormous amount of stress, having just lost his wife. But he still had a duty of care to his patients and should have asked for his compassionate leave to be extended if he felt that he had needed more time. Chris apologised profusely and agreed that he did not handle the matter as best as he should have. Dr Kelly summed up the meeting by saying that they would forward a reference to his new practice in order that he could practice legally as he was a good doctor and appreciated that everyone deserved a second chance.

Chris got up from the table extremely lighter than he had come in and thanked the board for their understanding in the matter. As he exited the room, Chris felt relieved that everything he came to Melton Mowbray to achieve was now ticked off his list. He had built the bridges that were broken with his in-laws and established a workable way forward for Ben being able to see his grandparents.

He had cleared the air with Tilly and got her to drop her enquiry. And finally, he was able to have a meeting with the board and get the necessary reference that he would have secured, had he dealt with his affairs a lot better than he originally did. All in all, it was a successful trip, and he was glad that he and Ben could go back to the place they had now called home with no skeletons in the cupboard to come back to bite them.

CHAPTER FIVE

C hris appreciated the fact that Mrs Jenkins had given him prior notice that she would not be returning as his housekeeper. It gave him the opportunity to start looking for an au-pair to live in. He had gone through a local agency that did the checks and references for him. Which meant that all Chris had to do was rely on his intuition when choosing the right person that he felt bonded well with himself, but, more importantly, with Ben.

Chris interviewed four individuals and felt comfortable with the second person he had interviewed. A 25-year-old young lady called Natalia, who was of Slovenian origin. Natalia's references were impeccable, and her last job was with an American military family, whose five-year term in the UK had come to an end. Natalia was an au-pair to their two children for the five years and had grown quite fond of the nine-year-old boy and seven-year-old girl that she looked after. Natalia had only been with the Harris family for a week and was finding her feet. She had made an instant connection with Ben and seemed to understand his quirkiness and unique character.

Chris had not gone back to the surgery yet and was due to go in the following day. He wondered what type of reception he would get from Michael and Joan, but at least the reference they so longed for would now be with them, so that was one thing that could be ticked off their list of requirements. Natalia had prepared breakfast earlier and was now upstairs in her room. Chris hadn't planned on going to church that morning as he wanted to spend a bit more time explaining Ben's routine and some other housekeeping matters with Natalia.

"Natalia. Could you come downstairs for a moment please?"

Chris shouted upstairs to Natalia for a quick chat, whilst Ben was occupied in his room playing a video game.

A medium built young lady strolled elegantly down the stairs. Natalia had a lovely olive skin complexion with blondish highlights running through her thick curly auburn hair.

"Yes, Dr Harris, you wanted to have a word with me?" Chris directed Natalia to the lounge area.

"Natalia, I keep telling you that you don't have to be that formal. I am perfectly fine with you calling me Chris. Anyway, you make me feel old when you keep referring to me as 'Dr Harris' in my own home." There was a slight humour to his voice.

"I'm sorry. It's just that you're my boss and I don't want to be disrespectful in any way." Natalia took a seat on the settee.

"Well, I respect that, Natalia, but I have given you permission to call me by my first name, so you aren't being disrespectful."
Natalia conceded, "Very well then."

"Right, I just wanted to go over once again the routine for Ben. The time you should leave to take him to school. The time to pick him up and the time to give him something to eat and to make sure he does any homework that he is given.

As I'm sure you've already observed, Ben can get a bit distracted. So, you're going to have to be quite firm with him, just so that you can establish quite early on that you're the adult and he needs to respect your authority. He's a good boy really, but I believe establishing boundaries at the first instance in any relationship is key."

"That's fine, Chris. I'm sure that Ben and I will get on like a house on fire. He already seems like such a lovely little boy and I'm going to enjoy getting to know him and trying to help him in any way I can."

Chris continued with his list of things for Natalia.

"Ohhh yeah. And Ben's teacher's name is Olivia. Sorry, I meant Miss Dupont,"

Chris quickly corrected himself. Now he felt like he was the one being disrespectful by referring to Ben's teacher by her first name in front of Natalia.

"When we first moved to the area, Ben struggled with interacting with individuals, and Miss Dupont was instrumental in working with Ben and really helping him to come out of his shell. She really is an excellent teacher, so I hope Ben is still in her class. Although, I'm not sure, with us being away for a few months, whether things have changed or not. But anyway, when you get to the school tomorrow, you'll be able to check if that is still the case. I noted from your references that you used to do the housework and laundry for the last family you were with. I'm assuming that this is something you'll be able to do for us too."

"Yes, of course, Chris. As an au-pair, that's all part and parcel of the role. Unless you want to relieve me from doing all my duties?"

Natalia teased as she attempted to help Chris understand the role more fully.

"In reality, some au-pairs only look after the host children and solely do their laundry etc. But I am happy to do any additional tasks since it is only you and Ben that I would be expected to support."

"I'm sorry Natalia. I've never employed an au-pair before so I'm totally clueless as to what I can or cannot ask you to do. We only had a housekeeper before and Mrs Jenkins did not live in, so I was clear on what her role was and what we needed her to do for us. She was an absolute Godsend. No disrespect to you or anything like that. She was just amazing and a great cook too." Natalia smiled.

"No offence taken, Chris. Good staff is not easy to come by, so when you lose them, I can appreciate how difficult that must be. But I can assure you that I too have worked up a good reputation for myself. And overtime, I will make for you some dishes from my home country in Slovenia, which you won't be able to resist."

"Oh, is that so?" Chris smiled.

"We shall have to wait and see then, won't we? Okay, thank you for your clarity. I will get the agency to adjust your contract to reflect these changes. Anyway, I think that's all I need to say for the moment. I have a few things to do, so I'll be in my office if you need me. I do my best thinking in there, so you'll get used to finding me in there if ever you can't find me in the house."

Chris was referring to his 'man-cave' which was situated at the bottom of the garden. It was his place of escape where he would often go to hide away and retreat to deal with his inner thoughts.

It was a brisk Monday morning. Michael and Joan were already in the surgery, having had an early meeting to attend. Janet was as efficient as ever and got in doubly earlier than the two doctors to ensure that everything was prepared for them in the boardroom, with the appropriate refreshments of fresh filtered coffee and croissants from a local bakery that they used for their various catering needs. As the meeting was rounding up, Joan took the opportunity to speak privately with Michael.

"I see Chris is due back today, isn't he?"

"Yep, I guess he is,"

Michael said in a matter-of-fact way. He really had lost his initial respect he had had for Chris, what with everything that had gone on, the incident with Olivia and the bigger issue with his position at the surgery. Was he now expected to just brush everything under the carpet and pretend as if nothing untoward had transpired? That wasn't really Michael's style. But he knew he had to put his professional hat on over his emotional hat. In the past few months, he had learnt a lot about forgiveness, having had to forgive Carol for her deception and what she had put him through. If he could forgive Carol, then he knew that God would expect him to forgive Chris too. And, with him being a born-again Christian, it was the right thing to do, regardless of the fact as to whether his flesh had an issue with it or not.

Joan continued in a whispered tone, as Janet was walking in and out of the room clearing away the crockery and leftover pastries,

"Do we tell him of the changes today, or should we leave it for the moment?"

Having had their long overdue inspection with the CQC, it wasn't the end results that they were hoping for. Unfortunately, there were quite a few issues that were flagged up, which meant that they would have to make some drastic changes all round for the good of the surgery going forward. Whilst the Chris saga wasn't the straw that broke the camel's back, it didn't bode well for the surgery that they were practising with a doctor that did not have the appropriate references and credentials in place at the time of his tenure.

Michael lent forward, whispering back,

"Let's ease him back in gently and slowly. The changes will affect him also and we'll need him to be on side if our plans are to succeed. I don't see any reason to just dump this in his lap right now. Let's give him a few days and then redress the matter."

Michael and Joan were obviously sitting on something that was significantly big and important, which would affect the lives of the staff, the surgery and its patients. The fact that they were even concealing the information from Janet, ensuring that nothing was left on their desks and password protected all folders on their computers containing the documents, meant that it was top secret and could not be divulged until the time was right to disclose the information to all related parties.

Janet was aware that something was brewing in the air but couldn't quite put her finger on it as to what the nature of it was. Ever since their failed CQC, she observed a lot of unscheduled meetings taking place with external individuals and noticed Michael and Joan whispering a lot and ensuring their doors were fully closed before engaging in conversation. That wasn't their usual style in the surgery, and even though Janet was the practice manager, overseeing the reception area, she did not feel any less important than the doctors. Janet felt slightly offended that whatever it was that Michael and Joan were concealing that they did not deem her worthy of being entrusted with the information.

Janet walked back into the boardroom as Michael and Joan were winding up and about to go back to their respective offices.

"Is there anything further you'd like me to do before I go back to my desk?"

Janet had 30 minutes to kill before the doors to the surgery would open. After that, she would be inundated interacting with the patients and not have a spare moment to sort patient records and update them on the system until the end of the day.

"No, Janet, I think we pretty much got everything covered. And thanks so much for getting the pastries for our meeting this morning. They went down a treat." He chuckled.

"By the way, you do remember that Chris is due back today, right?"

"Oh yes, I do. I'm looking forward to seeing him. He and his humour were sorely missed. And I know his patients will be glad he is back too."

"Well yes," Michael said hurriedly. Singing Chris' praises was the last thing he wanted to be engaged in.

Joan reiterated Michael's sentiments.

"Yes, Janet, you're a star. I don't know how we will cope without you."

Joan caught herself and attempted quickly to redeem herself and chuckled.

"Sorry, what I meant to say is that I don't know what we would do without your meticulous ways."

Michael rolled wide his eyes at Joan, mindful that Joan was just a little too loose with her words. Janet did not read anything into Joan's slip of the tongue and went back to her area, leaving Michael and Joan to go back to their respective offices.

Chris was grateful that he had found Natalia. She was an enormous answer to his prayers, which meant that Ben would get to school on time and going forward he could be in the surgery at a decent time too and plan his schedule accordingly. Chris was greeted with a friendly face when he arrived at the surgery.

"Welcome back, Dr Harris." Janet gave him a warm smile as he approached her desk.

"And I hope Ben is well too."

Chris appreciated the fact that he didn't sense any friction in Janet's voice or in her demeanour towards him and hoped that he would get the same response from Michael and Joan. Although considering how he had left the surgery, and the anger he had experienced from them, he knew he was clutching at straws.

"Ben is well, thanks. He enjoyed reconnecting with his grandparents and aunt, and I was glad to get some business done and dusted. I assume the others are already in?"

Chris enquired as he tried to gauge the atmosphere.

"Yes, there was an early meeting that they both attended. If truth be told, there have been several ad hoc meetings of late."

Janet knew she was talking out of turn, but Chris was a colleague and therefore shouldn't be left in the loop like she was.

"Oh really? What type of meeting would they be having on a Monday morning then?"

Chris said inquisitively. He wondered if perhaps he was still the hot topic of conversation, even after his references had been sent to the surgery prior to his return.

"Your guess is as good as mine, but I can tell you, something isn't sitting right with me at all."

Chris had never seen Janet like that before. Almost on edge. Janet was always very calm, cool and collected. But something had ruffled her feathers, which he felt in due time he would get to the bottom of. For the moment, Chris was only interested in getting that initial conversation over with his colleagues and for him to get back to the flow of things and doing what he loved best: helping his patients.

As he was engaging in small talk with Janet, Michael came walking towards them.

"Janet, do we have… Oh Chris, I didn't know whether you were here yet. Hi. Is everything okay?"

Michael tried to keep his tone upbeat as he did not want to make Chris feel any more awkward than he was already probably feeling.

Chris started to nod his head. "Yes, I believe everything is okay and hopefully you got the information that you were waiting for from my previous surgery?"

"Yep, we heard back from them. I believe Joan dealt with it and she was happy with the content. In fact, it was a glowing reference."

Michael had a look of approval on his face which put Chris at ease.

"And how is Ben?"

"Ben is fine, thanks. We have a new au pair, Natalia, as Mrs Jenkins' situation changed. Her husband had a stroke, and she has become his full-time carer."

"I'm sorry to hear that. I know how much you relied on Mrs Jenkins to help you out in the past. I hope it works out with the au-pair. Look, I'm going to head off now. Welcome back." Michael started to walk back to his office.

"Janet, if you can get me those x-ray results I asked for, that would be great as I need it for my first patient."

"Yes, Dr Mills, I'll get that for you straightaway."

Chris threw his coat over his arm and headed towards his office. He just wanted to get back to life as he knew it. Too much time had passed. He had made some silly mistakes. No, in fact, they were huge mistakes and, whilst he was away, he had had time to reflect on his inexcusable behaviour. He owed Michael and Joan an apology for him not being upfront with them regarding his position when he first joined the surgery. And he also owed Olivia an apology which he was dreading the most.

He had put Olivia's newfound relationship with Steve in jeopardy when he had made disparaging comments to him with regards to her character. If he could have erased that chapter from his life, he would have done so in a heartbeat. He wondered whether Olivia would even talk to him again. But as she was his son's teacher, it was obvious that their paths would cross again in the future.

As Chris reminisced over that dreaded night, the look of horror on Olivia's face would forever be etched in his mind. He recalled being in a low place with his emotions at that time. However, that was no excuse for him forcing himself onto Olivia in such an unsavoury way and causing her to feel threatened in her own home. As he sat at his desk feeling remorseful with himself, his intercom went off. It was Janet letting him know that his first patient was on their way down to his office.

It was a busy morning at the surgery, yet none of the doctors had the opportunity to interact with one another as they tackled their own workload. Chris had pre-empted that his first day back was going to be a busy one and brought from home a ham & salad sandwich, together with a packet of cheese and onion crisps. He had got himself a bottle of water from the fridge in the kitchen and went back to his room. As he ate his sandwiches and caught up with the emails in his in-box, there was a knock on his door.

"Come in," he said as he took a gulp of water. A head emerged around the door.

"Hi Chris. Welcome back."

It was lunchtime and Joan had taken the opportunity to pop over to see Chris, if only to be polite.

"Oh, hi Joan. Sorry, it's been a frantic morning, and I have been glued to my seat so to speak."

He attempted a feeble joke in the hope it might ease any uncomfortableness between them. The last conversation they had engaged in was when Joan was angry and annoyed with him and she did not mince her words. Joan sat down opposite Chris, and he attempted to move his lunch to one side so as not to seem rude whilst talking with Joan.

"I'm not sure if Michael said anything to you, but we eventually got the references back from your former surgery, so thanks for getting things sorted. I'm sure having to up and leave everything wasn't the best timing, but it was imperative that we had things in order prior to our CQC inspection, but sadly the reference didn't arrive in time."

Chris was apologetic for any problems that he may have caused.

"I know, and again, my sincere apologies. What kind of report did we get then?"

Chris was genuinely concerned to hear how well they had done.

"Well, we didn't quite get the results that we had hoped for, and we have a lot of work to do to remedy the situation. But that's something we can discuss at a later stage, once you have your feet firmly on the ground again."

Joan was quick to shut down the conversation, which she did not want to tackle on her own without Michael's input.

"Right. I'm going back to the grindstone as I need to have a quick bite to eat too before my next patient. Take care." Joan hurriedly walked out of Chris' office and went back to hers.

As the day ended, Chris was relieved that he got through it with no major drama. Several patients expressed how much they had missed him and were glad to see him back. Chris was looking forward to going home and seeing Ben. He was also curious to see how Natalia had done on her first day and if she had met Olivia, and if so, what the dynamics of the conversation were like.

After everyone had left for the day, Janet gave the office a once over, ensuring everything was left in an orderly fashion for the cleaners before locking up the surgery for the evening.

CHAPTER SIX

Two weeks later...

Steve had made significant progress and had worked hard to get to where he was now. With a positive mindset and the assistance of Matt consistently putting in the extra work, Steve was now in a place where his legs had gained strength. He still had to use his crutches when his legs got tired, but the centre was confident that Steve could go home, organising him with home care to assist him further for a couple more weeks, assigning Matt to help him with his physio until he was fully recovered. Steve finally found the courage to confide in Olivia that he had been gaining strength in his legs, which delighted her to no end and excited her that they could finally start to get their plans back on track. Olivia had agreed to pick him up later that afternoon, taking him back to her house for a few days to allow him the ability to get used to fending for himself again.

In the two weeks that had passed, Steve had spent a lot of time with Jack, trying to convince him that his life mattered. Jack really wasn't in a good place, and it was affecting his progress. His parents were in the process of having him transferred to another rehabilitation centre, where he could get more individual one on one care, but Jack showed little interest in what they were planning to do.

Steve didn't want to leave the centre without him at least getting Jack to a better place.

"Buddy, you know I'm leaving today, don't you?" Steve gingerly walked over to Jack's bedside, aided by his crutches.

Jack took the headphones out of his ears to acknowledge Steve's presence.

"Hey. You leaving too Steve? Everyone leaves this place except for me, and I'm just stuck in this dump."

Jack was having a pity party. Whilst in the centre, he was forced to observe individuals come and go home whilst they made significant progress. And yet his progress was slow and prolonged.

"Look, here's my card. I have already told you that I'm not about to desert you, just because I won't be around. I want you to call me whenever you feel you need to talk, and I'll be there for you. Remember the chats we have had, when I told you that God loves you."

Jack wasn't in the mood for being cheered up with the 'God talk'.

"Well, if God loves me, why has He allowed this to happen to me, eh? Or you for that matter? What kind of God shows His love in such a sick way?"

"Jack, I understand your hurts, and it is hard to process everything that you have gone through. But I promise you. It does get better. Look at me. I thought I'd never get back on my two feet when I first came to this centre. And now I'm literally walking out of this place. That's down to the mercies of God over my life. I don't want you to give up on life because you have so much to live for and a heck of a lot to do with your life."

Steve had years of experience dealing with young people who were down on their luck and instead chose to give up on believing that they could make anything of their lives. He did not want to see another statistic in Jack and was determined to ensure that he would be a mentor to him, even after he had left the centre. As Steve had Jack's attention, he continued with his pep talk.

"When I get out of here, I will continue to make sure you are okay. I don't want you to think that I'm just waffling to make you feel good, as I'm giving you, my word."

Jack could see the sincerity in Steve's eyes and believed him, even though he always had friends who only had their own interests at heart when dealing with him.

"Well, my parents are arranging for me to be transferred to another centre, so we'll see how that goes. Anyway, I appreciate you taking the time to talk to me whilst we have been in here. It helped pass the time."

"Oh, thanks, mate. Is that all I was good for? To pass time by for you?"

Steve said sarcastically, managing to get a smile out of Jack in the process. Steve went back to his bed and attempted to pack the rest of his things before Olivia was due to pick him up.

The news that Michael & Carol were pregnant and expecting twins came as a huge shock yet was a pleasant and welcomed surprise. However, they still had a way to go in working on the trust in their relationship. PT had suggested that they have counselling to help them communicate their feelings and how they were going to progress forward without letting what had happened affect their future. They had been meeting with him and his wife, Linda, every two weeks for some months and he had given them homework to do at home prior to their next scheduled session.

At the beginning of the counselling sessions, it was quite a slow progress with Michael trying to understand what would possess Carol to do what she did. Carol did not have anything concrete that she could put her finger on, apart from the fact that she didn't want to lose the best relationship she had ever had, and it was her way of ensuring that Michael did not slip through her fingers. Michael still struggled that their whole courtship was based on a lie, and this was the main bone of contention where he was concerned.

They both arrived for their 12.30 PM appointment promptly, which was held in PT's office on the church premises. Throughout the pregnancy, Michael had been proactive and hands-on, trying his best to navigate around Carol's mood swings, putting it down to her being ratty at times due to her emotions. Michael held the door open for Carol as they entered PT's office. It was always such a welcoming environment, with the fresh smell of lavender that enveloped the airy, spacious office. The office was where PT prepared some of his best sermons. And if the walls could talk, they would divulge many a story of various couples whose relationships were salvaged, purely because they took the time to invest in their relationship and get counselling.

Counselling could be viewed by some as a taboo subject, with couples not wanting to admit that their relationships were less than perfect and that they needed a third party to help them navigate whatever difficulties they were experiencing. However, for those who were brave enough and could put aside their pride for the sake of their marriage, they were the fortunate ones and left PT's office with their marriages intact.

Counselling was PT's speciality. He and his wife, Linda, were the perfect partnership. Having been married for 25 years, they helped couples go back to the beginning of their relationships to try and recreate what drew them to each other in the first place and to work from there. PT and Linda were sitting on one side of the beautifully crafted solid oak wood desk, whilst Michael and Carol sat opposite them. Following the formalities, PT was keen to see how they had got on with the last homework that he and Linda had set them.

"So how did you get on with that last activity we gave you?"

PT's voice was deep, yet direct, but had a kindness and warmth to his tone. Linda sat quietly until it was her time to interject and make any relevant contributions to the conversation. The task in question that was set for Michael and Carol was to go on a date to one of the places that they had gone to whilst they were courting. They were asked to try and recreate the ambience and conversations that they could recall and then make notes of how it made them feel.

Michael was first to respond. "Yeah, I guess it was alright."

It appeared obvious that there was more Michael wanted to divulge, but PT and Linda were going to have to prise it out of him if they wanted to learn more about the activity.

"Michael, I note you used the word 'alright'; is that all it was to you?"

Linda intimated, as she wanted to let Michael know that his answer wasn't really cutting it, and he would have to do better.

Before Michael could answer Linda's question and get his next words out, Carol quickly jumped in to give her interpretation of the situation.

"We went to a Thai restaurant that he took me to on our very first date, but instead of recreating the atmosphere, we just argued the whole time, so I don't really think we achieved what you wanted."

Linda continued in her pleasant and sweet voice.

"Carol, you aren't doing this exercise for us so that you can come back and report that you ticked off what we have asked you to do. This exercise is for your benefit to remind you both that at some point in your relationship, you got on and enjoyed each other's company. And, if truth be told, I believe that you still do. Unfortunately, somewhere along the way, your marriage collided with a roadblock and that's why we are here to help you get back to where you were and to go forward stronger and better."

PT wanted to get to the bottom of the nature of the argument and sought to explore that further.

"Michael, what was the argument about?"

Michael, embarrassingly, dropped his head. After a few minutes of silence, he composed himself.

"It was down to me really. I feel bad, as Carol is trying hard, but the problem lies with me. I find that I am dissecting everything. Every conversation. Every thought. To me, everything was based on a lie and that's what I am finding hard to get pass. How do I differentiate between what was real and what was fabricated?"

PT rubbed his chin with his right hand.

"I understand there is still deep hurt within you, Michael, but I thought in our previous sessions you had agreed that at some point you must forgive Carol and let it go. Because if you don't. You might as well call quits on your marriage right now because you won't be able to fully move forward. Is that what you want?"

PT gave Michael a few moments to ponder over his words. Following which, Michael shook his head.

"No, it isn't."

PT directed the same question to Carol.

"How about you, Carol? Is that what you want?"

Carol articulated what she had consistently voiced, that she wanted to save her marriage and would do whatever it took to do so also.

"So, this is easy," PT said confidently.

"You are both on the same page and therefore have the recipe to effectively save your marriage, providing you put the work in. Now, Michael, what is it going to take for you to move forward once and for all, and completely forgive Carol? What do you want from her for you to do so?"

Michael felt a sense of relief that he was asked the question and decided he had nothing to lose in being totally honest with his response.

"I need for Carol to be truly repentant. Because at times I get the impression that she isn't genuinely sorry about her deception, but only sorry that she got rumbled. Had I not had a deep desire to be a father and have children of my own, would this deception ever have been exposed?"

Michael threw his arms in the air and gave Carol a look that penetrated deep into her soul.

Linda could see that Michael was about to lose it and go deeper into his rabbit hole and she wanted to run after him before he got stuck and refused to come out.

"Carol, can you understand where Michael is coming from? What can you say or do that is going to reassure Michael that you are deeply sorry for causing pain to him and your marriage?"

Carol shook her head whilst tears rolled down her cheeks. She took hold of Michael's hands and delicately squeezed them.

"Michael, I am deeply sorry for the way I deceived you. You're a good man and did not deserve being put in such a position. I knowingly made the decision to keep certain things regarding my past from you, and if I could go and turn back the clock, I would."

Carol let go of Michael's hands briefly to retrieve a tissue from her bag to dab her swollen eyes and continued with what she knew Michael desperately needed to hear.

"Back then, following our initial first meeting, we were getting on well. Yet I could see that June Black had her sights on you in our home group at church and I let my jealous thoughts get the better of me. I realise that I like to have my own way on my terms, and sometimes I am not always appreciative of the feelings of others. That is something I have been trying to work on, but from the bottom of my heart, I am asking you to forgive me as I am truly sorry and repentant for all I have put you through."

Michael looked directly into Carol's eyes and for the first time he sincerely felt Carol's heart and knew she had finally bore her soul and was truly sorry for all that she had done, contributing to the breakdown in communication within their relationship. His countenance radiated as he gazed deeply into her eyes and affectionately rubbed her hands.

PT was keen to interject at this juncture.

"This is very good, folks. I believe we have made real progress. And I can see from the tears in both of your eyes that you have truly come to a mutual place of respect and forgiveness. Can we now safely say that you will both draw a line under this matter?"

They both looked at each other and nodded. PT carried on.

"Michael, this means that you can't ever throw this subject in Carol's face again, even if in an argument it comes to the surface of your mind. When God forgave mankind for their sins, the Bible tells us that He remembers them no more and He expects us also to adopt the same attitude."

"I understand, PT, and I don't intend to. For the first time, I felt the sincerity in Carol's apology, and I now know that she is deeply sorry and repentant. That's all I ever wanted to hear and perceive. I am now willing to definitively put this matter to bed. I want to thank you and Linda for helping us to get here."

Carol also agreed with Michael.

"I too would like to reiterate what my husband has said. We are truly grateful. There was a point I wondered if we would ever get to this juncture, so I'm glad you encouraged us to seek counselling."

"Well, I can certainly sense a change in the air. And from the look on the two of your faces, I see that you can feel it too," Linda said with a glee in her voice.

"Yes, Linda, you're quite right. I think these two will leave here a lot lighter and be pleased with themselves that they have made significant progress."

PT wanted to get Michael and Carol back on track with their overall plan.

"Right, now the homework for this week will be the exact same task that you failed to successfully complete the last time. So, I want you to go back to a place you once visited, whether a place you first got together or one when you were courting, and recreate that magic. So, let's see you both back here in two weeks' time to see how you got on."

Michael and Carol felt like they were the last two students in the class that didn't quite get the required pass and therefore had to re-take the test to get PT and Linda's mark of approval.

As Linda had reiterated earlier, the tasks set were purely for their benefit and if they both committed to putting in the work, they were guaranteed to get the best results.

Michael and Carol thanked PT and Linda again and both gave them an affectionate hug as they left the office. Having got to their car, they both exhaled and breathed a sigh of relief.

"Well, that was heavy duty, wasn't it?" Michael said as he revved up the car.

Carol was pulling the seatbelt over her bump to try and get herself comfortable.

"Yep. It sure was. To be honest, I really didn't think we would ever get to where we are now, but we did it."

Chapter Six

Carol was pleased that she finally let her guard down and was completely vulnerable by showing Michael the softer side of her personality that she often tried to conceal because she did not want to feel weak or beholden to any one person. Because of what she went through when she was younger and having been abandoned by the father of her unborn child, she had promised herself that no one else was going to hurt her like that. Especially not another man. She was forced to grow up fast and as a result developed a backbone spirit that would ensure she was not walked over by anyone again.

It was that backbone that got her to the place she was as a top designer and then build up her own business from scratch. Meeting Michael caused her to let her guard down slightly, but even then, she wasn't about to let him see the 'real' Carol and sought to stay in control to protect her heart. It was now time for change and Carol was grateful to God for a second chance, which she was not going to mess up this time around.

CHAPTER SEVEN

Same Day…

Olivia was frantically rushing around, trying to get things in order before Steve's arrival. She worked out that she had about 45 minutes before she would have to leave to pick him up and bring him back to her home for a few days. Jen was also at home, having had the weekend off from work.

"You certainly are rushing around like a headless chicken, aren't you?"

Jen observed how stressed-out Olivia was making herself and wanted her to slow down and chill out. As a paramedic, Jen knew first-hand the affect stress could have on the body, the result being that Olivia would not be well enough to help anyone, let alone Steve in his time of need.

Olivia stopped her rushing around to address Jen's comments.

"Tell me about it, but I just want everything to be perfect. He's been in that rehabilitation centre for quite a while now and I just want his environment to be a pleasant and positive one when he comes out. Plus, one that doesn't feel clinical or smells of antiseptic,"

she smirked.

Changing the subject, Olivia wanted to double-check that Jen was onboard with Steve coming to stay.

"Jen, you're okay about Steve staying here for a couple of days, aren't you?"

Olivia had run the idea by Jen previously, but now the time had come, she just wanted to be double sure that there would be no awkwardness with her.

Jen felt taken back by Olivia's comment but understood where she was coming from.

"Of course, I don't. It will be good for him in the first few days of his transition period. He's lucky to have someone as caring as you to look after him."

"Well, he's my beau and I need to start practicing the whole 'for better or worse' vernacular prior to the real thing if you know what I mean."

They both chuckled. Jen wanted to explore that topic further, since after all, she was considered the lodger and would need to know what that meant for her in the long-term. Would Olivia be selling up and going to live with Steve after they were married? Or would they both sell their houses and buy a new one together? It wasn't something they had had the opportunity to talk about yet, since Steve's accident seemed to shut down the conversation on the matter.

"So, how are things between you and Steve with regards to your wedding plans?"

They were both in the lounge area and Jen had made herself comfortable with her feet up on the settee, enjoying a cup of coffee.

Olivia's countenance changed slightly, which gave Jen cause for concern, wondering if she had gone too far in her line of questioning and whether she was now prying into something that was considered a private matter between Olivia and Steve.

"Gosh, that has certainly been a sore topic of conversation between the two of us lately." Olivia sat down also to slow down from the tidying up that she was doing in the lounge.

"Why? What do you mean?"

Jen could see that Olivia seemed as if she was carrying the weight of the world on her shoulders. And whilst she would normally pour her heart out to Carol, Carol had her own issues to deal with regarding her pregnancy and trying to get her own marriage back on track. Olivia felt comfortable talking to Jen and exposing her vulnerability.

"I have been trying to keep things alive in the planning of our wedding, if only to keep Steve's mind occupied to give him hope for the future. However, he has the opposite perspective to me and doesn't see how he can be planning a future with me in his current state. He feels he is not the same guy who proposed to me, and thinks he is trying to save me from any future heartache, especially if he doesn't fully recover."

Jen could see that it was really affecting Olivia, even if to the world she was trying to put on a brave front. She had lived with her for close to two years now and they both learnt to appreciate each other's persona and quirky ways.

"So do you think he is suffering from some sort of depression, as well as his physical limitations?"

"I never looked at it that way before. Perhaps." Jen continued,

"Do you think he would be open to seeing a therapist? Because I know of some good ones from the hospital that I could put you in contact with."

"Whilst that might not be a bad idea, it's something I would need to discuss with him first. But at present, I don't want to heap too many things on his plate. I think if we concentrate on the physical side first, anything affecting his mental health we can deal with after."

"Well, let me know when you'd like the information, and I'll set the wheels in motion for you. And remember, seeing a therapist isn't a bad thing. It has such a negative connotation when it shouldn't. As it's no different than going to a doctor when you are ill. Or seeing a dentist if you have a toothache or even visiting the optician if you have difficulty with your eyes. I'd have no problem in seeing a therapist if I needed one."

"Thanks Jen. I appreciate your advice. I believe he has been confiding in his physiotherapist, Matt, and he seems to have had a positive effect on him. I believe he has been instrumental in Steve's extraordinary turn of events, in terms of his progress. He's a real great guy… handsome too."

Olivia winked at Jen with an expressive look. At a poignant moment in their conversation, Olivia's mobile rang, and she could see that it was Steve's name that illuminated. Olivia put her finger in the air to indicate that she had a call.

"Sorry, Jen, Steve is calling. I just need to take this call." Olivia excused herself and went out to the hall.

"Hi hon, is everything okay? I should be leaving shortly."

Steve had called to let Olivia know that Matt needed to go to the hospital which was en route to Olivia's house and didn't mind escorting Steve to her place.

"Oh okay, well, tell Matt that would be great if he's sure it is no trouble."

Steve assured Olivia that Matt practically insisted, so there was no issue there.

Olivia walked back into the room, feeling slightly relieved that she didn't have to rush and could finish getting the place ready for Steve's arrival. Her tone and persona were a lot more upbeat also.

"Thankfully, Steve said that Matt was driving through the area and didn't mind giving him a lift here, so that's me off the hook." Olivia threw her hands in the air and chuckled.

"That's great. Do you want me to make myself scarce to give you both some time to settle him in?"

"No, not at all. You're going to be in the house whilst he is staying for the few days anyway, so let's just try and act as naturally as possible."

"Okay, cool. I'm happy with that. Well, at least let me help to ease the load off you and prepare lunch or dinner, whichever one is needed."

Jen hoisted herself from off the settee and started to make her way to the kitchen.

Olivia responded favourably.

"You are a lifesaver. That would be great. I owe you one, girl."

"No, no. Don't you worry. I'm very happy to help. You finish up here, and I'll look in the freezer and see what I can rustle up."

Jen excused herself and headed for the kitchen. She was thinking of doing a lasagne, but having checked the freezer, they were out of mince. As the fridge was full of a variety of vegetables and Jen was a resourceful cook and could work with anything, she decided to make a vegetable version instead, accompanied with garlic bread and a green salad.

Olivia went into the spare room where Steve was going to be staying, which conveniently was on the ground floor and had an en-suite, to finish off the little touches to the room. Like putting a set of fresh towels at the bottom of the bed and placing bottles of water on the side cabinet for his comfort. Lastly, she sprayed the room with air freshener, which encapsulated the room with a fresh vibrant fragrance that would linger nicely until Steve got there.

It wasn't long until the doorbell rang, and Olivia excitedly shouted, "They're here, I'll get it."

She ran to the door with a huge grin on her face, opening the door to her guests.

"Hi there. Welcome guys, please come in."

Even though Steve had graduated to crutches whilst he was at the centre, Matt brought him to Olivia's house in a wheelchair, which was easy for him to help Steve with and manoeuvre him around quicker.

"Here, let me open the door wider for you. Is that okay, Matt?"

"Yes, that's great. Thanks, Olivia. Why don't you go in first and then let us follow you? I think that would be easier."

The front door was a generous wide size and Matt comfortably pushed Steve through to the hall and then went back to his car to get Steve's bag and his crutches.

"Right, that's everything now. So where do you want us?"

Matt directed his gaze to Olivia, waiting to be directed as to where he was to wheel Steve to.

"Yes, Matt. Please take Steve to the lounge area for the moment and I will take his bags to the guest room and then bring the crutches into the lounge."

Matt took Steve to the lounge and helped him out of the wheelchair onto the settee.

"How does that feel? Are you okay?"

"Yep, that feels fine."

"You shouldn't need the wheelchair, so I am going to take it back with me. Plus, you should be getting used to not having to rely on it."

Steve nodded in agreement and made himself comfortable in a room he had frequented often, and fond memories of spending time with Olivia and the many chats they had had flooded his thoughts. In that moment, he realised that he had been hard on Olivia lately and none of what had happened to him was her fault. Yet he was unfairly punishing her because he was hurting as he couldn't get a handle on the way his life was spiralling out of control, even though he had made significant progress and his healing was manifesting.

Olivia came back into the room and interrupted his ruminating.

"Can I get either of you a drink?" Matt responded first.

"I don't mind having a quick coffee before I leave, if that's no trouble."

"Of course, it isn't. How do you like your coffee?"

"Black, no sugar and not too strong would be great."

"How about you, Steve, can I get you anything?"

Steve was still in his reflective mode but asked for a glass of water. Olivia went to the kitchen to get the drinks, where Jen was still cooking up a storm.

"Ummm, something smells nice."

"Thanks. Just a little something I am rustling up with the leftovers. We need to do some shopping," Jen said in a headmistress-like toned voice.

"Yep, I know. I was meant to go last night but had a lot on my mind and got slightly distracted."

"No, I wasn't having a go at you. I should have picked up a few things myself. I'll go and do the shopping later, so don't worry about that."

"See, you definitely are my guardian angel today and again, I'm in your debt."

They both smiled. Olivia almost forgot what she had gone into the kitchen to do.

"Let me get the drinks for the guys before they wonder whether I have nipped out to Starbucks instead to get them." Jen giggled.

"Jen, you should come in and say hello. I'd really like you to meet Matt."

"I don't like the way your voice is sounding, Olivia. You better not be up to anything."

"Me?" Olivia said suspiciously. Olivia made Matt's coffee and poured out a glass of water for Steve.

"I'll see you in the lounge then."

"Okay, I'll show my face quickly, finish off cooking and then run to the supermarket."

Olivia went back into the lounge and gave Matt his cup of coffee and Steve the water he had requested.

"Is Jen home?" Steve enquired.

"Yes, she is. She was just preparing some lunch for us. I have asked her to quickly pop her head in to say hello, as she is going to the supermarket later.

Matt, can we tempt you to stay for some lunch with us?" Matt put the cup on the saucer he had in his hand.

"That's very kind of you Olivia, but I really need to get to the hospital soon for a private session with another patient, so I'll have to take a rain check on your kind invitation. Perhaps another time."

As Matt was finishing his conversation, Jen came into the room.

"Well, hello, Mr Adams," Jen said as she walked over to Steve and gave him a hug.

"You're looking well. I'm so glad to see that you are making a speedy recovery."

"Thanks, Jen. It has been a long laborious process, but with the help of this good man, he has got me back on my feet. You haven't met Matt, have you? Let me introduce you to each other."

Olivia interjected almost immediately, "You beat me to it, Steve, as I was getting around to introducing them."

Matt rose to his feet as Jen directed her gaze towards him and instantly there was a spark in their eyes towards each other. Jen recognised him as the hunky physiotherapist who occasionally did sessions at the hospital and who was the hot topic of conversation amongst the women paramedics. She wasn't aware of his name but glimpsed him from time to time and had to agree with the hysteria amongst the women that he indeed was extremely good looking.

Matt was the first to break their gaze. "Hi Jen, it's nice to meet you. Don't you work at Sunningdale Hospital?"

Jen was stunned by Matt's statement. *How on earth does he know that? He doesn't know me.*

"Err, yes. I'm a paramedic. I work mostly in the A&E, but I don't believe we have met... Have we?"

Jen felt slightly paranoid as to whether they had met, as she could not remember. Although, she was pretty sure she'd remember meeting a handsome face like that.

"No, we haven't but I've noticed seeing you there whenever I have had a client to see."

'So, he's noticed me, eh? Eat your heart out, female paramedics. Anyway, sort your thoughts out, Jen. You aren't looking for a relationship at this moment in time. You're taking a break from men to get yourself sorted out first before you go back down that rabbit hole. Don't forget. Your last attempt at romance wasn't a positive one and look at the trouble it got you into. Now get yourself out of here quickly before you fall under the spell of those big brown eyes.' Jen was keen to get going.

"Well, it was nice meeting you. I'll be certain to say hello the next time I see you at the hospital then."

"Yes, that would be great as I don't know that many people there. I've only just started operating out of that base."

"Please excuse me as I need to go and do some food shopping."

Jen started to make her way to the door to exit the room. Matt did not want the conversation to end there and offered to give Jen a lift to the shops, but she reluctantly declined, as she needed to take her own car to bring the shopping back in. It would have been nice for her and Matt to have a bit longer to chat and get to know each other better, but realistically it would not have been very practical. Jen left the room to get her bags.

"Well, I better make tracks myself." Matt rose to his feet.

"Thanks for the coffee, Olivia, it really hit the spot."

"Steve, take care of yourself and remember the exercises I have taught you. Do them as often as you can, as they will help increase your progress."

"Thanks Matt, I believe I have the hang of them now, so I will practice them profusely. You know what, I have a few more things I want to discuss with you. Olivia, I wonder if it would be okay if Matt could come over for lunch tomorrow, if he is free."

"Yes, that would be fine. I had invited Michael and Carol for lunch too as they are really looking forward to seeing you. I was going to tell you later, as I didn't want to bombard you with so many things when you first walked through the door. I thought we could go to church together and then all have lunch after."

Steve didn't feel ready to see a whole lot of people because mentally he didn't want others to treat him differently and start to feel sorry for him. Therefore, he made an excuse to Olivia that he was still a bit tired from all the travelling and transition from the centre to normal living again and wasn't quite ready yet. Olivia understood and did not want to push Steve into doing anything he wasn't comfortable with. Matt agreed that he was available to come for lunch and appreciated the gesture. He made his exit and left.

Jen left shortly thereafter to go and do the shopping, leaving Olivia and Steve to enjoy the food that she had prepared for them.

Olivia and Steve had a pleasant time just the two of them and enjoyed the vegetable lasagne, garlic bread and green salad that Jen had prepared for them. Afterwards, Steve was feeling slightly tired, and Olivia showed him to his room where he took a nap for a few hours.

CHAPTER EIGHT

Next Day… Sunday

Olivia and Jen were super early for church, which meant that they could pick the best seats at the front. New Dawn was a popular church, and the services were usually packed to the rafters with individuals having to go into an overflow room to watch the service on a big screen if the main auditorium was full. Worshipping from the overflow room didn't quite have the same impact as being upfront with the worship team and musicians and experiencing the worship first-hand. It almost felt like a detention room where you got sent to for being late to church. Olivia recalls being in the overflow room once when she first attended the church, and that memory was enough for her to ensure that she was never late again.

Once the church was filled and everyone had settled and quieted themselves, the worship team led an inspirational time of worship, which was heartfelt and anointed. As the first song played, Olivia connected with the song in an emotional way as it spoke directly to her heart and touched on some of the things that she was going through personally. The song reminded her that she was to cast all her cares upon the LORD, because He cared for her. Jen noticed that Olivia was crying and bent down to retrieve a tissue from her bag, which she gave to Olivia. Olivia appreciated Jen's sensitivity as she placed an arm around her to comfort her. The word PT shared also resonated with her in a powerful way. It was almost as if it was her day to be totally immersed in the presence of God as He showed Himself intimately to her as the Father who could deal with anything that was troubling her that she was not able to deal with in the natural.

As the service ended, Olivia pulled her emotions together.

"Gosh, I really don't know what came over me today. It was like every song, scripture and even the sermon, was tailor made for me."

"Yes, it was a great service, but I think that you've been through quite a lot recently, so you were bound to have a moment at some point when you needed to exhale. And what better place to do it than in the presence of God?"

Olivia nodded in agreement and whilst she continued to dab her eyes, she could hear her name being called.

It was Carol and Michael, who were waving at her and walking towards her. Carol looked radiant in her polyester turquoise maternity dress, which swayed from side to side as she waddled over to Olivia and gave her a hug.

"Hey hon. You guys must have got here early that you had the coveted front seats," Carol said sarcastically.

"Hi Jen, how are you?"

"I'm fine, Carol. You're looking glowing. How long have you got to go?"

Carol rubbed her stomach and said, "I think about four months. Is that right, hon?" Carol turned to Michael who was closely behind her.

"I always forget, so I leave it to the doctor to work it all out," Carol teased.

Michael joined the conversation.

"Hi ladies, it's good to see you both. Take no notice of Carol as she knows exactly how long she has left, because she often complains that she can't wait for the babies to pop out now. Let's just say, we're shy of 3 ½ months away to meet our little ones."

"That's not too long now then. Do you know what you're having?" Jen asked with an air of curiosity.

Carol was quick to answer that question. "Yes, we do, but we aren't telling."

She quickly grabbed hold of Michael's arm for reinforcement. And he complied to support Carol.

"That's right. Our lips are sealed. We want to keep that element as something special for ourselves that will be a surprise to everyone else when they are eventually here."

"What! Not even Olivia knows?" Jen teased.

"Not even my best friend," Carol declared.

"We made this decision together, and that's something I must honour. I'm learning." Carol rolled her eyes in submission, as she knew she had to continue to work hard to prove to Michael that she had changed to keep her marriage intact.

"And she's doing very well too, because I've tried to tease it out of her a number of times, I can tell you," Olivia chuckled.

"So, are you guys coming over straightaway for lunch or are you going home first?"

Carol responded quickly.

"If you don't mind, I just need to go home to put my feet up for an hour or so and will come to you for about 3 PM. Is that okay?" Olivia nodded.

"Sure, it is, as I need to finish preparing the food anyway. We're having a roast, and I left the bird in the oven cooking, so hopefully it will be finished by the time we get home. All I have left to do are the accompaniments, so that's plenty of time."

"Okay, Liv and Jen, we will see you later."

Michael had his hands on Carol's shoulders and started to direct her gently towards the back of the church where the car park was. Olivia and Jen also started to walk towards the car park.

"Well, I can make myself scarce whilst you all have lunch together."

Jen was under the impression that Olivia & Steve and Michael & Carol would be having lunch together. And as she would be the odd one out, she didn't want to feel like a spare wheel as such. Olivia's expression caught Jen by surprise.

"Are you joking me? You're having lunch with us too." Jen's head timidly dropped.

"I would feel slightly awkward having lunch with two couples and feeling like I was the odd one out."

"You're not going to be the odd one out as Matt is coming for lunch too." Jen's eyes widened.

"Matt is coming?" Olivia smiled and reassured her.

"Yes, Matt is coming. After you left yesterday, Steve asked if he could have lunch with us today and I said that it was fine. You're not going anywhere, missy; you're going to entertain the hunky therapist." Olivia giggled as she grabbed Jen's arm and pulled her to the car.

"Okay then. Guess I don't have a choice, do I? Seems you have it all planned out, don't you?"

"I do indeed. Now come on. We've got work to do before our guests arrive."

Steve had the morning to himself to reflect on where he was in his life. He felt guilty that Olivia had gone to all the trouble to make him feel comfortable and welcomed him to stay at her home, and he couldn't even return the sentiment and go to church with her. He felt a stirring in his heart from the Holy Spirit and knew that he needed to start making changes to his attitude if he did not want to lose Olivia. It was only months back when he was in the friend zone and Olivia did not have a clue that he was holding a torch for her.

He recalled how he longed for her to feel the same way about him that he had felt about her. But Olivia did not see him in that way. When Olivia started to embark on the relationship with Chris, it broke his heart to the core. He couldn't understand it. Olivia did not know who this person was, and yet she was quick to dive in and start a relationship with him. And look how that turned out. Yet Steve was under her nose all the time, but she did not give him the time of day in a romantic sense. Thankfully, Steve did not give up and tried a different approach when he arranged the trip to Rotterdam. And it was there that he laid his cards on the table and told Olivia how he really felt about her. To his amazement, she responded favourably, and the rest is history.

'Steve, are you going to throw away the best thing that has happened to you in a long time because of your ego and pride?'

The internal thoughts were eating away at Steve, and he determined within himself that he was going to apologise to Olivia when she came home and ask for her forgiveness. He also resolved that he was going to talk to her about finalising their marriage plans so that they could be married within the next few months. He did not see any reason why they needed to wait any longer if they loved each other. He also decided that it was about time Olivia met his parents. Even though he wasn't looking forward to the prospect, remembering how his parents reacted disapprovingly in the rehabilitation centre, he knew he could not put it off any longer.

Olivia and Jen returned home in a jovial mood. Olivia took the opportunity all the way home to tease Jen about the prospect of Matt being their guest and that she was to ensure that he got special treatment. Jen did her best to try and ignore Olivia's matchmaking efforts yet meeting him again made her feel weak at the knees and warm and fuzzy on the inside. Matt was extremely handsome, and she did not know how she was going to get through lunch having to sit at the table with him in a room filled with loved up couples, but she was going to try and get through it with her poker face intact. Steve was still in his room when he heard the playful interaction, although he couldn't quite make out what they were saying, since they were whispering and laughing under their breath.

He got his crutches and made his way out to see what was going on.

"Hey, you're back. How was church?"

"Hi, Steve, it was good, but I'll let Olivia fill you in with the details. I'm just going upstairs to refresh myself."

If Jen was going to see Matt again, she was going to make sure that she put her best foot forward and have a refreshed face too. Olivia laughed as Jen ran up the stairs because, as a woman, she knew exactly what that meant.

"Hi Steve. Church was a blessing, as you know it would be. I was a complete mess though." Steve seemed concerned.

"Oh dear, what happened?" Olivia thought she'd better clarify what she meant.

"Well, a complete mess in a good way and not a bad one. I was just very emotional and moved by everything. From the worship to the testimonies, scriptures shared, and even PT's word touched me to my core. I felt the presence of God in a strong way this morning and some things that I had been holding onto inside of me just lifted. I feel much lighter and positive about life."

"That's great, hon. I wish I had come with you now. But I also had a good opportunity to reflect on some things in my life. Do you have a couple of minutes to have a chat?"

Steve felt the time was right for him to lay his cards on the table and tell Olivia what he had also concluded in his mind that morning.

"Well, I was just about to run upstairs to put my things down and then come back down to finish off the lunch. If you don't mind sitting in the kitchen with me, then we can talk whilst I work."

What Steve had to talk to Olivia about needed her full and undivided attention and he did not want her to be distracted by peeling potatoes, sorting out vegetables and all the rest of things she would have been involved in to finish things off for the lunch.

"No. You're good. We can talk later when everyone has gone home. If that's okay?"

"Actually, that might be better you know. Why don't you go into the lounge and see what's on TV. Or I have some good DVDs that you might like. Amongst all my romcoms, there are a few crime suspense ones. If nothing appeals to you, then just turn on Netflix. There's an endless range of movies on there; I'm sure you'll find something that you like."

Olivia ran upstairs to put her things away and ran back down, went straight to the kitchen, pulled her sleeves up and got to work. The chicken that she had left cooking in the oven had browned nicely and putting the meat thermometer into it confirmed that it was cooked through. The potatoes were already peeled and prepared, and she put them in the oven with the Yorkshire puddings. The vegetables were also prepared by Jen earlier that morning and all Olivia had to do was turn on the fire underneath the pot and they took care of themselves.

Jen had come back down the stairs all dolled up and went into the dining room to set the table. She selected the crockery that only came out for special occasions, made of bone china with a gold rimmed edge. The flute glasses also had a gold rimmed edge which she positioned on the right-hand side of the place mats. As she was meticulously making sure that everything was neatly in its place, she could hear Steve laughing from the other side of the room. He had found a comedy to watch and seemed to be enjoying himself.

Just then, the doorbell rang. Jen shouted out to Olivia that she would get the door. When she opened the door, Matt was on the other side holding a big bunch of flowers and a bottle of red wine in front of him.

"Hi Jen. I'm not too early, am I?"

"No not at all."

Jen gave him a big smile, and he followed her through to the hall. He extended the bright bouquet right in front of her.

"These are for the ladies of the house, and I thought this bottle of wine might accompany whatever we are having for lunch."

"Thanks very much. They look lovely." Jen took the flowers and wine from Matt and asked for his jacket, which she threw over her arm whilst struggling to balance everything and trying hard not to admire his muscly biceps.

"Are you sure you're okay there? I seemed to have dumped all my stuff onto you." Matt sighed as he realised what he had done.

"No, I'm okay. I'm used to balancing things. I'm a paramedic, remember, so I've had a lot of practice." They both laughed.

Jen informed Matt that Steve was in the lounge watching TV and that he could go in and join him. Matt found Steve exactly where he had left him the previous evening and hoped that he had at least moved from the spot and did some of his exercises. But as he wasn't officially on duty, he thought he'd give himself and Steve a well-deserved break.

Chapter Eight

Jen went to find Olivia in the kitchen to show her the impressive bunch of flowers and bottle of wine that Matt had brought, which looked like it must have set him back a few pounds. Olivia confirmed that they were lovely, and Jen found a suitable vase to put them in. "So how are we doing? What's left to do?" Jen enquired.

"I've pretty much got things organised and everything is nearly finished. Just need to wait for the last two guests and then we can eat. So how did Matt look?"

Jen laughed to herself. Even though Olivia wouldn't have admitted it, she was a lot like Carol in many ways when it came to trying to pair individuals up. And whilst she appreciated what she was doing and that it was coming from a good place, she still questioned within herself if she was ready to dive into another relationship.

In the back of her mind was her parents' marriage and the foundation that it was built upon. Her mother did not really hold out for what she wanted and settled for someone who was not her first love. Whilst in turn she learnt to love Jen's father, she spent many years being miserable and pining for another man. Jen grew up not seeing a pattern of someone who waited on God for their future spouse, regardless how long that wait was. Jen did not want to repeat history by doing the same thing her mother did. She had always promised herself that she would marry for true love and under no circumstances would she take second best. Being a content and fulfilled single was better than settling for a loveless marriage. Could Matt be that true love she had always dreamed about? Or would this be just another failed attempt of trying to find the one?

Olivia's voiced pulled Jen back into the land of the living.

"Why don't you put those flowers in the lounge? They would look nice in there."
"Errr… yes, I will."

"You okay, Jen? You looked a bit lost in thought there."

"No, I'm fine. I was just thinking about my mum. I must give her a ring sometime just to touch base with her." Jen tried quickly to deflect from what she was really thinking about.

"That's nice. Your mum is very sweet. Whenever she calls here for you, sometimes we have a quick chat, and she always has positive things to say about you. As her only child, she is very proud of you. You are blessed to have such caring parents."

"Yes, I am, Olivia. But so do you, you know." Olivia chuckled.

"Yeah, I know. Anyway, let's go and see what the boys are doing."

Michael and Carol arrived promptly at 3 PM and everyone sat around the table for lunch. Olivia and Jen brought all the food out and arranged it in the middle of the table and everyone helped themselves and ate till their hearts content. Carol complimented the chefs and commented that as she was now eating for three that it was only right that she had a second helping. She had the other guests in stitches of laughter. Carol could always be relied on to bring the humour and Olivia noticed that lately she was in a much better place and seemed a lot more chill and happier too. She was pleased to see that the interaction between her and Michael almost resembled how it was when they were first married, and her heart was full to know that her friends were making progress and on the right track. Now all she needed to do was get her own relationship back on track and wondered if what Steve wanted to talk to her about had anything to do with that. She hoped it would, because it was time that they both started talking about their future and where exactly it was going. Olivia was a strong character and braced herself for the inevitable. If Steve wanted to call things off and end their relationship, it would break her heart, but she would have to respect his wishes. She had never begged a man to stay with her ever. And if his heart wasn't in it anymore, she had no intentions in starting so now. Whatever Steve wanted to talk about, she would hear him out.

CHAPTER NINE

After dinner, the guys huddled in the lounge to talk man-to-man whilst the ladies retreated to the kitchen to do what ladies do best: scrutinise each other's relationships and try to put the world to right. Carol was the first to break the ice.

"So, who's this Matt guy then?" Olivia responded with a glee in her voice.

"He's Steve's physiotherapist."

"And is that all he is?" Carol said blatantly, glaring at Jen.

"What? You girls are too much. You'll frighten him off the way you two are carrying on," Jen screeched.

"Okay, you all know that I've turned over a new leaf, and I've given up the meddling business. But the chemistry between the two of you at the dinner table was sizzling. I thought at one point I was going to need a fire extinguisher to hose you both down."

They all laughed hysterically. However, Jen was quick to defend herself.

"I must admit he is a very good conversationalist, and I was fascinated with some of the places he has visited and the things he has done. What's wrong with that?"

"Oh, nothing," Olivia said.

"But were the two of you actually aware that there were four other people at the table too?"

"I wasn't aware that we were monopolising the conversation," Jen said light-heartedly.

"Don't mind us old fuddy-duddies, it's nice to see young love in full bloom before our very eyes," Olivia said, winking at Carol.

"Who said anything about love? We are just two individuals who were having a conversation. How does that equate to love in your minds?"

Carol and Olivia both gazed at each other with 'the look'.

"We've seen enough individuals who first meet each other and have a spark like yours to know how it ends missy. So, you mark our words. This is the making of something special and will go very far," Olivia acclaimed.

"Well, I'm not reading anything into it right now. After what happened with Chris, I think I need a break from men for now."

"Oh pahleeze," Olivia said.

"There's absolutely no comparison. For one, you can see that Matt is a pure gentleman and isn't a narcissist like Chris Harris. Chris played a good game, but his true colours were soon exposed because you can only lie for so long before it catches up with you."

Carol was enjoying a big bowl of Neapolitan ice-cream whilst sitting comfortably taking it all in, trying hard not to revert to her old ways, but it was too tempting not to.

"So has anyone seen Chris lately?" Carol thought she'd put the question out there, since his name had surfaced, to see what the consensus was with regards to him.

Olivia dived in. "I haven't seen him in person, but I do know that he has a new au-pair, because I've seen her drop and collect Ben from school. She's a young girl. Quite pretty. Poor thing though, having to live under the same roof as that monster. I just hope he doesn't pounce on her as we know, from personal experience, that he has form."

"Well, I haven't seen him and nor do I want to. I don't want to be reminded of a lapse of judgement I had when I allowed him briefly into my life. Especially when I knew it wasn't really going anywhere but just tried to pretend, I couldn't see what I blatantly knew was obvious. It was apparent that we weren't compatible with one another. He was at least 10 years older than me but was just trying to turn me, bit by bit, into his late wife."

Jen shivered on the inside as she contemplated what a lucky escape she had had.

"Well, all I know is that he is back at work and keeping a low profile, according to Michael. So perhaps he came back to turn over a new leaf. Only time will tell, eh?"

"Indeed," Olivia said whilst taking the opportunity to clear away the lunch things with Jen.

Michael wanted to maximise the opportunity to get acquainted with Matt whilst the men were on their own.

"When did you get assigned to Sunningdale, Matt?"

"I've only been going there for the last three months, but I will be doing some regular work in the future, so will be there more often. Do you work out of there too then?"

"Yes, I have clinics that I attend to from time to time. It's a good hospital and the Board of Directors run a tight ship. So, how's this old man doing then?" Michael said as he playfully slapped Steve on his back.

"Well, at first he was a tough nut to crack, but I soon whipped him into shape,"
Matt said jokingly.

"No, in all seriousness, Steve has worked extremely hard and has made significant progress in comparison to where he was when I first met him. I always find that clients who have a purpose and drive to want to get well, do just that. And they walk out of that place, even if initially it is on crutches. Within a few weeks, Steve will lose his crutches altogether and hopefully should be back to normal. Well, normal..ish."

"That's great," Michael said.

"As I can't wait to destroy him on the squash court. We can get quite competitive and like to play badminton and squash to let off steam from time-to-time." Steve laughed out loud.

"You wish, mate. I've been strategizing in my mind how I'm going to crucify you when we are next on the squash court, so you just hold that thought." Steve wasn't about to lose face to Michael's threats.

"Matt, do you play the game?" Michael curiously asked.

"As it happens, I do. But I can tell you, you wouldn't be able to catch me. I'm just putting it out there."

"This one is very sure of himself. Steve, where did you get him from?" Michael chuckled.

"You know these young men. They think they can wipe the floor with us. But they don't know that our secret weapon is our experience," Steve bragged.

"Well, Matt, if one day you're looking to let off some steam, give me a call and we'll see what you've got." Michael leant over to Matt and handed him a business card with his details.

"Cool, that would be great." Secretly, it was a challenge that Matt would relish and look forward to.

"How's work, Michael?"

Having been in the centre for a few months, Steve had lost contact with his friends so wasn't up to date, back then, with all that had been going on. Neither was he in a good place to connect with his friends. Olivia had tried to keep him current with things, but he would often adopt a deaf ear policy, blocking out what she was trying to communicate to him. His philosophy was, if he wasn't in a good place, then he didn't want to hear about the successes of anyone else either.

Michael sighed and scratched his head.

"There's a lot going on at the present time with a few changes that we are about to implement. But it's all a bit confidential at present, so I really can't divulge much."

Michael was careful not to say more that he was permitted to share. And with Matt also being in their presence, he really did not want to say anything that could get back to another practitioner. He could not vouch for Matt, having only just met him, even though his initial gut reaction was that Matt was a decent guy. However, he made that mistake once before by trusting someone at face value and it turned out to be a nightmare on preposterous levels.

Steve read between the lines and understood what Michael's comments would have meant and decided to take the emphasis off Michael and instead switched gears in a totally different direction.

"Hey Matt, what do you think about Jen? Pretty girl, huh?" Steve wasted no time and was as direct as an archer's arrow hitting the bullseye.

Michael laughed. "Don't hold back, mate. Ask what you really want to know."

"What!" Steve threw his hands up in the air, looking all sheepish but trying hard not to let his sniggering be seen.

"I'm just asking because they looked very cosy in their conversation earlier. They seemed to be getting on like a house on fire, considering it was their second date."

Steve couldn't keep it in any longer and let out a thunderous roar of laughter. Michael came to Matt's defence.

"Matt, this is something that you will learn quickly about this group. They just love to get into people's business, even without you asking."

Matt blushed slightly, as if he had been caught out.

Yes, he thought Jen was an attractive young lady and he was perfectly aware that they were both flirting openly with each other in full view of the others' presence, but he really wasn't fazed by that. He enjoyed talking with Jen and found that they had a lot in common. Matt had not dated anyone in a long time, since his work and the hours he clocked up prevented him from having any room for a social calendar.

Apart from going to the gym a couple of times a week, he really was a home body. Yet from his first interaction with Jen, even though it was brief, he felt something in his heart that he hadn't experienced in a long while. He had allowed his imagination to run ahead of him and concluded that if for some inexplicable reason they ended up together, at least they would have something in common and could appreciate each other's world.

Matt pulled his thoughts together and mentally brought himself back into the conversation, undetected by the others that he had left briefly.

"In answer to your question, Steve. Yes, Jen is beautiful and having had the opportunity to speak with her more deeply today, it's good to know that there is a depth to her and more importantly, that she has a faith. It would be nice to explore things a bit further, but I don't know. She might even already have a boyfriend."

Both Steve and Michael looked at each other and rolled their eyes. Steve was happy that he could give Matt the information that he was probably fighting internally with.

"Well, I can tell you that she hasn't, mate. And she's a nice girl too and deserves some happiness." Michael glared at Steve as if to say, *'zip it and quit while your ahead'*.

"What do you mean by 'she deserves some happiness'?" That last statement caught Matt's attention.

Steve had to think quick on his feet as he did not want to say anything out of turn that would cause Matt not to want to pursue Jen.

"Mate, I just meant, I've known her for a couple of years now and if anyone deserves to be happy, then it's Jen. She has such a sweet spirit and deserves to meet someone who would recognise her worth and treat her like the princess she is." Matt smiled and let out a huge sigh of relief.

Michael wanted to affirm Steve's glowing report of Jen.

"Carol and I only know Jen through Olivia as she took the place of my wife who used to be Olivia's housemate. But I would have to agree with Steve. Jen is a very humble and kind human being."

Matt got the reassurance that he had prayed for and decided that when the time was right, he would pursue matters further.

"And now that you know she hasn't got a boyfriend, you better move pretty quickly before someone snaps her up from right under your nose," Steve exclaimed.

'Do they read minds also, God?' Matt felt naked as these two men were challenging him in ways he was clueless about.

"Anyway, we can talk about it another time as I can hear cackling which means the ladies are on their way back to join us."

Olivia, Carol and Jen returned to the lounge as the men were just finishing up their conversation.

"I notice the conversation has gone a bit quiet since we have come back into the room, ladies. It makes you wonder what they were talking about huh!" Olivia said teasingly.
"Wouldn't you like to know," Steve said as Olivia nestled and cosied up next to him.

"Now that we're altogether I think we should do something fun that involves us all" Olivia said.

"So how does a game of monopoly sound?"

"Only if I can be the banker," Carol shouted as she waved her hands in the air like an excited child in a frenzy who had just heard the chimes of the ice-cream van in the street.

"Please don't let my wife anywhere near the money," Michael teased as the others laughed.

"Yeah, I'm game Olivia," Matt said.

"Count me in too," added Jen.

"That settles it then. Monopoly it is."

Olivia retrieved the monopoly box from a side cabinet, and everyone sat around the table poised for a game of wit and strategy.

Two hours later, as the game was nearing an end, the competitive claws were striving for the finish line. Michael had accumulated most of the properties on the board, with Matt closely behind him in his portfolio of properties. Carol decided to stay in jail, as she was low on money, and Michael was being unkind to her by not allowing her to pass by his properties without paying the rent due if she landed on any of them.

The others were just trying to get around the board and accumulate money to acquire the expensive properties that were left, like Mayfair and Park Lane.

Carol's yawn and sigh was an indication that she was getting tired, which Michael picked up on.

"Okay Caz. We can see that you are waning so let's call it a day. I've probably won anyway with the most cash and properties to my credit," Michael said with a smug grin on his face.

Steve threw his money down in a sigh of surrender.

"I don't know how you always win at this game. You're obviously in the wrong job. You were born to be in real estate, mate."

"What can I say. I'm just gifted." Michael laughed smugly.

"It's been a very nice day with you all, but I am feeling tired now."

Carol rose to her feet and rubbed her stomach. Michael pulled the chair out to help Carol with her bag.

Matt also took the opportunity to excuse himself.

"I too should be making a move. Ladies, you put on a great spread today and the lunch was delicious."

Matt didn't think it would be right to approach Jen in front of everyone and decided to leave it for another time when they had the opportunity to be on their own. Perhaps he might catch up with her at the hospital or be able to prise her number out of Steve.

"You are more than welcome. We have loved having your company, even if you bought up all the properties that I was going for." Matt smiled.

"Steve, you take care of yourself and follow the plan I have set out for you, and I'll see you later in the week. Michael and Carol, it was nice making your acquaintance. And Michael, I look forward to that game of squash whenever you're ready."

As Matt was saying his goodbyes, Jen walked with him, escorting him to the front door. "Thanks for a lovely day, Jen," Matt said as he gave her a hug. Jen was taken aback as she didn't think he would be so forthcoming.

"Oh, you are welcome. Hopefully we'll cross paths again at the hospital."

"Yes, I hope so."

Matt realised that he had blown it again. He was alone with Jen, away from the earshot of the others, but failed to ask Jen if she'd like to go for a coffee or to the cinema some time. Now, he really would have to rely on randomly bumping into her at the hospital and who knows when that would be.

Jen waved Matt off. As she was about to shut the door, Michael and Carol emerged and headed towards her, with Olivia close behind and Steve behind her on his crutches.

"Great seeing you guys again. Take care of yourselves."

Jen embraced Michael and Carol and made her way back into the house and retreated to her room to allow the others some privacy for the rest of the evening. Olivia and Steve said their goodbyes to Michael and Carol, waved them off until their car left the drive and returned to the lounge.

"That was a good time with everyone, wasn't it?"

Olivia was pleased with the way the day had gone. She loved to entertain and especially enjoyed spending time with people that were dear to her. Steve, however, was glad that they were finally on their own as he had a lot on his mind that he needed to offload, but before he could respond to Olivia's question, she enthusiastically continued reminiscing on how the day had panned out.

"And did you see the body language between Jen and Matt? There's definitely something percolating there, so watch this space. Did he even mention anything to you guys?"

Olivia was curious and hoped that they had.

"Yes, Michael and I noticed the interaction between them too and we really grilled him about it when you ladies were in kitchen, and I can confirm that he really likes her."

"Yes. I knew it." Olivia punched her fist in the air as if her favourite football team had scored a home goal.

"You all looked a bit guilty when we came back into the room. Caz and I did tell her that the body language between them was clear to see, but after what happened with her and Chris, it is understandable that she wants to be cautious and tread carefully."

Steve didn't want to spend the rest of the evening discussing other people's relationships when he needed to sort out his own and was keen to veer the conversation towards them as a couple. When Steve found a pause in the conversation, he switched gears.

"Olivia, do you remember earlier I told you that I had something I wanted to discuss with you?"

"Yes, I do recall that." Olivia's stomach sank.

'Is this the conversation when he tells me it's been nice whilst it lasted, but now it's over?' It's almost as if Olivia was bracing herself for the worse.

"Firstly, I want to start with a massive apology to you with regards to my behaviour since the accident."

Olivia's stomach stopped churning. Her eyes widened and Steve had her full attention.

"I have been angry and feeling sorry for myself. All you were trying to do is make me feel better and keep my spirits up. However, all I did was throw a spanner in the works and behave badly. I am very sorry for that, because you didn't deserve any of that. If anything, you have been the one positive influence in my life which has kept me going."

Olivia slid her hand over Steve's to reassure him that she accepted his apology.

"Whilst you were at church this morning, I had a long hard look at my life and what I wanted and it's to be with you. I think we should resume the planning of our wedding and get married as soon as we can. And it's about time that you met my parents too, so I'd like to arrange a suitable time and make that happen."

That was a lot of information dropped on Olivia's lap in one go, which was a stark contrast to the conversation she thought Steve wanted to have with her. And whilst she was pleasantly surprised and happy, it was just a lot to process.

"I agree, we have a lot to sort out and I'm excited that things are back on track. I also look forward to finally meeting your parents as it would be nice to see if there is a resemblance and which one you take after. I also appreciate you being vulnerable by apologising. That took a lot of courage and humility. You will get through this, Steve. Your healing is manifesting daily, and God has a purpose for your life. For both of our lives. Just promise me that if you are ever feeling low again that you will talk to me. Don't bottle it in because that doesn't help you or me."

Steve nodded and promised Olivia that he would handle his disappointments better and not internalise things and retreat to his man cave.

"Look, it's been a long day and I'm sure you also are tired, so why don't you go and get some rest? I'll finish tidying up here and then I have some work to attend to before school tomorrow."

Steve agreed with Olivia that he could do with a rest and felt lighter now that he had offloaded his heart to her.

CHAPTER TEN

Monday...

There had been several top-secret meetings conducted at Bricket Wood Surgery in the past couple of months, right under the nose of all the staff, who were not privy or aware of what the meetings entailed. Janet, however, made a mental note of how often the meetings were taking place, especially as she was redundant in having anything to do with the set-up of them, which was unusual for their small practice. As the Operations Manager, Janet was always privy to what was going on, even before the other staff were told. But for some reason, these meetings were different, and the shoe was now on the other foot, in that she was the one being excluded which made her realise how the other staff must have felt being left out of important matters in the past. Janet had her suspicions, however, and speculated whether Michael and Joan, as Senior Doctors of the practice, were going to ask Chris to leave the practice.

Following the recent CQC inspection, she had perused the report, which highlighted the difficulties that Chris' non-regulatory position had caused the surgery and wondered if it was the reason Bricket Wood Surgery had failed to get a satisfactory result from their last inspection. Also, the fact that Chris had not been invited to any of the meetings, even after he had returned to the surgery, Janet put two and two together and deduced that this had to be the reason for the inconspicuous discussions. Perhaps they were interviewing for his replacement, which would make sense as to why they did not want to involve her on such a delicate and sensitive matter.

Prior to leaving the office the previous week, Michael had asked Janet to set up a meeting with Joan, Chris and himself for the following Monday at 4 PM in the Board Room. As Janet contemplated Chris' fate, she felt sad as she had warmed to Chris and got on well with him in a working capacity. She had found him pleasant and approachable but agreed with the report that it was unprofessional of him to have taken up another position at a new surgery without the proper references and credentials rightfully being in place.

The surgery had a busy schedule for a Monday morning, with all three doctors having appointments back-to-back. Janet was dealing with patients in reception adequately, as well as answering external and internal calls as they filtered through. There were two other part-time staff that Janet managed who were perfectly capable of answering the calls and dealing with the menial tasks. But Janet found it hard letting go of the jobs she used to carry out before being promoted to Operations Manager, to the frustration of the two ladies, Rose and Kate, who were employed on a job share basis. Whilst Janet was a lovely lady, and no-one could say a bad word about her, she was old school and set in her ways, which at times left the other ladies twiddling their thumbs with Janet doing their work as well as her own. Janet lived for the praise, accolade and the way the doctors relied on and made her feel valuable, which is why her confidence was dented somewhat not knowing what those private meetings were all about.

Rose observed that Janet was free from dealing with patients and approached her with a query that Chris had raised. He had carved out some time in his schedule to go back to looking at their immunisation programme but could not find the files that he had originally created on his computer. After an extensive search, neither could Rose.

"Janet, do you have a moment?" Janet gave Rose her full attention, relishing the thought of being needed and able to be of assistance to her.

"Yes, I do. The mayhem has died down now. One minute it's quiet and then the next there's a mad rush. But then again, it is a Monday morning and is to be expected. What can I do for you Rose?"

"Well, it's a bit of a mystery really. Dr Harris can't seem to locate some folders on his computer with regards to the immunisation programme. I've checked for him, but I can't find them either. I know they were on his computer, as I've assisted him with accessing the folders before. He also wanted to check if anyone was using his computer whilst he was away. I know I didn't and I'm not sure if Kate would have either, as she doesn't usually get involved on the computer side of things, not being that techy."

Janet smiled. "Don't you worry, Rose; I'll deal with this matter and go in and have a word with Dr Harris. Can you oversee things in my absence whilst I pop in and have a word with him?"

"Yeah, sure I can. Thanks a lot, as he wasn't very happy when I left him. He seemed agitated to say the least."

Janet beamed as if the power laid with her to solve the matter in hand and save the day. Janet made her way down the corridor to Chris' office and knocked the door. When Janet heard the words giving her permission to enter, she made her way into Chris' office.

"Ahhh, Janet. Thank goodness you're here. Now can you please tell me what is going on? Where are all my files regarding the immunisation programme?"

Chris had spent the best part of 30 minutes trying to establish where the files he had created relating to the programme and some other projects he had been working on had gone. Janet took a seat next to Chris so that she could easily show him the area where some of the folders he had created were moved to.

"I'm sorry, Dr Harris, that you have wasted precious time trying to sort out admin matters. This is something we should have informed you of when you got back. There is nothing to worry about as the files and folders have been moved to a new drive which had been specifically created following the CQC inspection."

Janet leant over and manoeuvred the mouse to the dedicated area where some of the folders had been moved to.

"And what was the need for changing the system? I thought the previous system worked perfectly well prior to the rehaul."

Chris seemed more infuriated that neither Michael nor Joan had had the decency to give him the heads up that something quite important that he had been working on was not even discussed with him, especially as both had ample opportunity to do so.

"Here you go, Dr Harris, the files you are looking for are now in the one-drive under 'Senior Doctors', and within that folder, you can then find the specific files in the folder marked 'immunisation programme'.""

"Well, that seems fairly easy to find when you know how," Chris said sarcastically.

Janet tried to access the folder denoted 'Senior Doctors', but it was password protected, and she could not get into it without the necessary password. Janet recalled that this was something she had encountered prior when she tried getting into some other folders on the system and found she could not do so.

"Dr Harris, it appears that the folder is password protected and unfortunately, I don't have the password." Chris' expression changed and he became infuriated, raising his voice.

"What do you mean password protected? And who has the password? Oh, let me hazard a guess. Michael and Joan perhaps," Chris said in a tongue and cheek manner.

Janet moved away from his computer and desk.

"Yes, I guess that is most likely the case. Do you want me to go and check with Joan if she is available and can give you the password?"

"No, that's quite alright, Janet. I've wasted enough time. I can come back to this another time, I guess. I have a meeting with them both later this afternoon, so I will bring the matter up then. Thank you for your help. It looks like both of us are being phased out of the inner circle, eh?" Chris said flippantly.

"Yes, perhaps so. Anyway, I better get back and relieve Rose who I left on reception to come and assist you."

As Janet left Chris' office, she could not get the phrase that he had voiced aloud out of her mind *'being phased out'*. Surely, there wasn't something more sinister going on than what she had suspected. Janet hurriedly made her way back to the reception area and thanked Rose for keeping an eye on things in her absence.

Chapter Ten

The busy Monday pandemonium at Bricket Wood Surgery had subsided as most appointments had been carried out by the three doctors, apart from the appointments scheduled to be seen by the nurse. Janet had already prepared the board room in readiness for the meeting that Michael had asked her to schedule in the three of their diaries for 4 PM. Since his conversation with Janet earlier in the morning, Chris had not ventured out of his office. Therefore, he did not have any interactions with Michael or Joan all day, which gave him time to mentally calm down and gather his thoughts as to how he was going to broach the subject, if it was not on the agenda.

Chris' Outlook reminder alerted him that he had 15 minutes to the start of the meeting. He took out his mobile phone to send a message to Natalia to remind her that he would be home later than his usual time and for her and Ben to go ahead and eat dinner without him. It was moments like this that he was glad he had the extra help in place, which gave him that added peace of mind. And now that his in-laws were back in Ben's life, they were keen to make up for lost time and had already contacted Chris a few times to see if they could have Ben over for a weekend.

`Chris reflected on what life would have been like if Jill was still alive. She had always wanted to be a mother. It was her heartfelt desire, and high on her list of things she wanted to achieve, and in the short time that she got to be a mother, Chris felt she was a natural. The high pitch screech Jill made when she first found out that she was pregnant reverberated in Chris' thoughts as he pondered, taking a glimpse into the past.

"Chris, get in here quick."

Jill heard the front door close and yelled at Chris in an excited tone to quickly come upstairs into their bedroom. Chris ran up the stairs, wondering what the commotion was that greeted him as he came home from a long day at the surgery.

"What's all the fuss about? From downstairs, your screech sounded like the house was on fire." Jill laughed and tapped him playfully on the shoulder.

"Now sit down and close your eyes. I'm just going to get something from the bathroom." Jill went to the bathroom for a short moment. Chris was intrigued and shouted after her.

"What are you up to?" All sorts of scenarios were going through his mind and the obvious one excited him to no end.

"Chris, I know you. Stop cheating and keep your eyes closed."

"Okay, okay," Chris said as he covered his eyes and waited for Jill to resurface. After hearing rustling going on in the bathroom, Jill came out of the bathroom with her hands behind her back.

"Okay, you can open your eyes now."

Chris opened his eyes, expecting to see Jill in a sexy negligee. Instead, she was standing in front of him, fully clothed, but with the biggest smile on her face and her hands extended towards his face.

"I've done at least three of them and they all say the same thing."

Jill placed in Chris' hand one of the pregnancy tests that she had taken earlier that day.

"They all say the same; we're pregnant, baby."

That was the furthest thing from Chris' mind, but nevertheless he was ecstatic by the news and couldn't contain himself. He picked Jill up in his arms and squeezed her tightly. They had been trying to get pregnant for a while, but with no success. Chris had suggested that they try a round of IVF if they did not get pregnant within the next six months.

"This is great news, babe. Sometimes when you take your mind off the pressure of trying for a baby and just relax, then nature takes its natural course," Chris said, sounding like the doctor he was.

"Wowww. We're going to be parents." Jill's thoughts immediately turned to her twin sister.

"I can't wait to tell Tilly. She's going to be beside herself. Especially finding out that she's finally going to be an aunt. Of course, you know she'll spoil the child rotten, don't you?" They both smiled and nodded their heads in agreement.

"More importantly, you're going to make a great mum," Chris remarked as he slid his hand gently over Jill's stomach.

"This will be the first of our growing brood. You mark my words."

"Steady on, doctor. Let's get through this pregnancy first and then we'll see what the future holds, eh?"

The phone rang, interrupting Chris' thoughts down memory lane. It was Janet letting him know that it was ten minutes past four and the other doctors were in the board room waiting for him. He hurried to the board room and made his apologies to Michael and Joan as he entered the room.

"Please accept my apologies. I even set myself a reminder so that I wouldn't be late but then got caught up in some last-minute things."

Chris was never going to admit to them that his delay wasn't work related at all, but rather, he was caught up in reminiscing over his late wife's memory. Those were his private thoughts and memories that he reserved for moments when he wanted to escape and be reminded of the good times and how life was when Jill was by his side, and everything made perfect sense.

"Not to worry, you're here now. We should get down to business now since we all have homes to go to and I'm sure none of us want to be here any longer than is necessary."

Michael was firm in his delivery and was keen to get down to the real core of why the meeting was called. Joan kept quiet and allowed Michael to take the lead on matters. They both had already agreed beforehand the tone of the meeting and where Joan would be expected to interject, so that the two of them were singing from the same hymn sheet so to speak.

Chris made himself comfortable and waited for whoever was going to speak to start proceedings, since clearly, he could read the body language in the room to recognise that he was walking into a loaded situation.

"Right Chris. We, I mean Joan and myself, called this meeting with you, as we wanted to update you on a few matters that have recently arisen, which is going to have a significant impact on the surgery and its long-term future."

Chris continued to listen intently, noticing that Joan was looking slightly nervous, the dead giveaway being the way her cheeks appeared flush and bright red. Also, Michael struggled to give him direct eye contact. When Michael spoke, he would either look at Joan or instead fiddle with the papers in front of him, which Chris found distracting. Whatever was at the heart of the meeting, he wished that they would just hurry up and get on with it, as he would rather be at home with his son than where he currently was.

"Since you've been back, I'm not sure if you've had a chance to go over the CQC report?" Michael directed his gaze towards Chris since his question was intended directly at him.

"No, I haven't yet. No one brought it to my attention so I assumed the report went smoothly and there was nothing of importance to flag up, since if there was, you would have spoken to me beforehand or when I first got back from my time away." Again, Michael shifted apprehensively in his chair.

"Ahhh. Well, we did not want to bombard and overwhelm you with matters when you first got back and thought we'd give you an opportunity to settle back into the swing of things."

"Okayyy. But as I said, if there was anything urgent, I am sure you both would have thought it appropriate to speak with me straightaway, regardless of whether I had just come back to work. So how did the inspection fair then?"

Michael looked at Joan, permitting his eyes to do the non-verbal communication. Since the CQC was really Joan's baby, he felt it only right that she should share the details of the inspection and answer any questions that Chris might have as a result.

"Let's just say, we did not get the results we were hoping for. We knew that there were matters that might be flagged up, but we weren't prepared for the rating we got."

Joan cleared her throat as she continued, but the daggering looks that she was getting from Chris' direction wasn't helping in her execution of trying to get to the crux of the matter.

"Look Chris, there is no easy way of saying this, but we didn't do well. We were given a rating of 39-62% 'requires improvement'. Which means that our service is not performing as well as it should, with recommendations of how our service needs to improve. We have been scheduled for another inspection in six months' time."

Chris processed inwardly what he had just heard before attempting to speak.

"And did my non-compliance status tip things over the edge then?"

Chris was aware that his actions might have been the difference of them failing or succeeding and a tinge of regret for his actions pierced his heart. Michael felt he needed to interject at this juncture.

"To be honest, Chris, whilst that really did not help matters, it wasn't the main factor. The truth is, as a practice, we've dropped the ball massively on a few issues and therefore, we all have to take responsibility for the results. I had my own personal issues going on and my head wasn't always in the right place. Joan would admit that she also had her own private matters to contend with, as did you. So, no, there is not one person that we could lay the blame on. Therefore, I don't want you to think that you are solely to blame as that would not be fair. I certainly wouldn't have felt comfortable attributing all the blame at your feet."

Chris felt relieved that for once, he wasn't going to take a blow for the team.

"So, is there anything we can do within the next six months to improve upon?"

Chris appreciated that there was a problem and was keen to move forward with working on a solution to turn the situation around.

Like a tag team, Joan jumped back into the driving seat.

"We've had a long conversation about the matter, and we believe there is only one practical solution that would make sense and perhaps is best for the surgery and our patients…"

As Joan was about to land the plane, Michael jumped into the pilot's seat and swiftly took control of the steering wheel.

"…So, we are going to close the surgery and consider a merger with a larger establishment."

The confidential secret that Michael and Joan were careful to ensure wasn't leaked until the negotiations were underway was finally out.

Chris lent onto the table with his elbows, and a confused expression on his face.

"Close the surgery? Where on earth did that come from? Why would we do that? Are things that bad that we can't try to see how we can improve upon things so that we can meet the CQC's requirements?"

Chris was especially interested to understand how Michael and Joan thought that closing the surgery was the best decision for the good of the surgery. Michael went onto give Chris some historic information that he would not have been privy to with regards to the lease of the building. The lease was due to be extended shortly. However, the landlord was new and the lease they currently were on was at a much lower rate, which had to be honoured whilst their existing contract was in place. The new landlord was not prepared to lease the building to them at the rate they were paying and wanted almost three times the amount instead, to bring things in line with current market rates. As a small surgery, they could not sustain such an increase and still be expected to maintain staff salaries and all the other costs required to run a growing practice. Michael also shared how they had approached a larger surgery to ascertain considering a merger and that talks were still being negotiated regarding the finalisation of the contract.

"Well, it certainly looks as though you've both made up your minds about this. But did you not feel that my opinion mattered too, prior to making you final decision?"

"Yes, I understand how this might look, Chris. And you are right. If you were a partner, we couldn't have done anything without your input, but as it stands, you aren't a partner. You sealed your fate when you failed to properly allow matters to follow the correct procedures and therefore your partnership was not procured."

Michael's crass summation of Chris' shortcomings was a low blow, even if it was the truth.

"We apologise, Chris, but we had to act quick on this and with you being away, we just made the decision to crack on with things."

Joan did not want Chris to conclude that things were done quickly behind his back whilst he was away and therefore could not have a say in the matter. An opportunity was presented to them at the right time, and it just seemed a no brainer to strike whilst the iron was hot.

"We aren't quite there yet with the negotiations. There is still a lot of toing and froing to be discussed, so would value your input when we next meet with their board members."

Joan had thrown Chris a lifeline and it was now up to him to decide if he wanted to come on board.

"Yes, that would be good, especially as my future would be at stake too. I am presuming under this new merger that there will be a surplus of doctors and staff and therefore not everyone's services at Bricket Wood Surgery would be required."

"Yes, you presume right. But as I have said, this is what we are trying to negotiate, and you don't have to worry as your job is safe," Joan said, smiling as she tried to reassure Chris.

"Well, we can have another meeting soon and pick up on that further as I'm sure we'd all like to wrap this meeting up. I know for one that I have a hormonal wife waiting for me to get home to make her dinner," Michael joked to end what was potentially a heavy meeting on a lighter note.

Chris raised his hand. "Umm, there's just one quick matter I wanted to raise."

"Sure," Michael said.

"It was the fact that I can't get access to some of the files that I had been working on. Janet tried to help me earlier today, and whilst we did locate them on the new drive that has been set up, we couldn't get into them as they are password protected. What's that all about?" Joan was quick to relieve Chris' concerns.

"Sorry Chris, that was my fault. I should have sat down with you and had a conversation as to why we had to change the system. But let's have a quick chat tomorrow morning and I'll go through everything with you. There is a perfectly plausible reason why we had to implement the changes."

Michael rose to his feet.

"Well, if that's everything now, let's touch base again at a convenient time and continue our discussions. And Chris, please keep what we have spoken about in this meeting to yourself as we haven't divulged news about the potential merger to anyone in the practice. Not even Janet. And we'd like to keep it that way until we have sealed the deal."

Chris responded quickly, "Don't worry, she won't hear anything from me. But I wouldn't like to be either of you when she does eventually find out." Chris tried hard not to sound so smug.

"You leave Janet to us. At the proper time, Janet will be notified of the necessary information she needs to be aware of," Michael reassured.

The three doctors agreed that they would continue to keep their covert operation under wraps until negotiations were agreed upon and finalised. The time was 5.30 PM, and the surgery was duly closed. Michael did a quick check of the building, engaged the alarm system, and locked up as they all left together.

CHAPTER ELEVEN

Two weeks later…

Steve had been pushing himself to get back to his old form. He had a lot to prove and organise with regards to his impending wedding. Having previously put his cards on the table with Olivia and promising her the world, he now had to deliver on making that happen. One of the first things he knew he had to make right, which was long overdue, was introducing Olivia and his parents to each other. Steve waited until his parents had got back from their latest travels and agreed to meet them later that day at a restaurant close to where they lived. Olivia was excited that she was finally going to meet Steve's parents and had restless nights wondering what they were like or if they would warm to each other. Steve wasn't back to driving yet, and Olivia had agreed that she would drive them both to the restaurant.

Ahead of the lunch date, Steve had booked a session with Matt and was keen to show him the progress he had made. Within the last few weeks, since Matt had taken back the wheelchair, he had made huge strides and had got a lot stronger. On cue, at 10 AM his doorbell chimed, and Steve strolled leisurely to the door to let him in.

"Hey there Matt., Good to see you. You're like clockwork. I can set my clock by you." Matt laughed at Steve's comment.

"Well look at you. No crutches. I see someone has been putting in the work."

Matt followed Steve through to the living area, where a dedicated area on one side of the room was set aside so that they could work on the routine that Matt had designed for Steve's progress.

"I have been meaning to ask you. Are you still in contact with Jack? He isn't at the rehabilitation centre anymore and I wasn't assigned to his aftercare."

"Yes, we have spoken on Facetime a couple of times now. His progress isn't as progressive as it should be though, but I just think that's down to his perspective on life. I really want to visit him in person but for obvious reasons, haven't been able to at the present time. I'm due to give him another call, so I will tell him that you enquired about him. It's a shame that you weren't assigned to be his physiotherapist because he could use someone like you, who has a positive outlook on life from a spiritual perspective."

"Well, if he isn't happy with the physiotherapist he has, he can always ask to be reassigned to someone else."

"Ohhh, can you do that? Would you be willing to take him on if I was able to persuade him to do that?"

"Yes, of course I would. From what I remember of Jack, he seemed a good kid and just needs a break."

Steve felt ecstatic and hopeful as he knew what it felt like when he hit rock bottom but felt fortunate with the individuals he had in his life to support and encourage him. Jack did not have that. He was an only child. After the accident, not one of his so-called friends stayed in touch and he only had his parents as his core support. Steve felt confident that if Matt started working with Jack, not only would he benefit from the physical side of things, but his mental and spiritual health would be significantly impacted as well.

"That would be great, Matt, as he could do with someone like you championing in his corner."

"Well as I said, he has got to want it and if he does, then I'm happy to work with him. Now let's go through your routine and see if you're as good as you look."

Steve smiled and the competitive nature rose up in him. He was always one for a challenge. If someone put down the gauntlet, Steve was ready to take them on. That was why he and Michael were so competitive with each other.

"You've done well, Steve. The muscles in your legs have really strengthened as you are doing these exercises with ease and with no signs of pain. I see I'm going to have to up the ante to get you over the final hurdle."

Matt ended the session by setting Steve a new routine, confident that he only needed a couple more sessions until he was fully back to form.

"I know you have the lunch with Olivia and your parents to go to shortly, so let's call it a day. You've done extremely well. I'm very pleased with how you've thrown yourself into everything I have set for you. Also, your positive mental attitude has been key to the speed of your recovery. You'll confidently be walking down that aisle sooner than you think."

Steve appreciated all that Matt had done for him. There was a time a few months back that he thought he would never ever get back on his feet or even get married to the woman of his dreams. Yet he was now on the verge of having all his desires become a reality.

As Matt was packing his things away, he was a little curious as to how Steve was feeling with regards to his parents and Olivia finally meeting one another.

"Steve, I know when we have spoken in the past, you were concerned about introducing Olivia to your parents. Do those concerns still exist?"

Steve thought long and hard, whilst fiddling with his chin, before answering Matt's question.

"Look mate, it's still something that concerns me, but Liv is the woman I plan to spend the rest of my life with, and they are going to have to get used to that. I know my mother would have preferred that I chose a wife from her social standing, but a person can't help who they fall in love with, can they?"

Steve flung his hands in the air as a gesture that the matter was what it was.

"Well, if we are talking about my love life, what about yours? Have you even asked that sweet girl out yet? Or are you still stalling?" Steve's voice heightened in a sarcastic tone.

Matt realised he had been rumbled as by now they should have at least had a date.

"Wow, you got me there. Guilty as charged." Matt put his hand to his chest as if a dart had penetrated his heart.

"I've been swamped with work, so the problem lies solely with me and not Jen."

Steve could see what was happening and felt it was his duty to rescue this lovesick workaholic novice.

"Matt, she isn't going to fall into your lap like some little lamb you know. As the man, you need to put in the work. She's too sophisticated to chase you. And why should she? The man should be the pursuer. I fear that if you don't get your act together, you might just find that someone else snaps her up from right under your nose. Do you want that?"

Steve knew first-hand what it was like to hold a torch for someone for a long-time and miss opportunities because of not acting quick enough.

"No, I don't. I really like her and found her easy to talk to. Plus, we have heaps in common with each other."

"Do you still have her number that I gave you well over two weeks ago?" Matt looked sheepishly at Steve and nodded his head.

"Then go for it mate and ask her out. What have you got to lose?" Matt continued packing up.

"No, you are right. I've left it long enough. Now is the time. I'll call her after my shift later today."

"Now that's the spirit," Steve said as he slapped Matt on his back. The small pep talk with Steve was the kick up the butt that Matt felt he needed to have the confidence to ask Jen out on a date.

"Well, I guess I'll be seeing you in a week's time but well-done, Steve. You've made great progress in these last few weeks. You must feel proud of how far you've come. Throughout my career, I've worked with individuals whose injuries were less serious than yours and some of them haven't even made half as much progress as you have."

Chapter Eleven

Steve felt fortunate and knew that the part he played was small in comparison to what God had done for him in miraculously healing his body. As well as giving him Matt to help him on his journey to recovery.

"I honestly didn't think I would see this day, but I am grateful to God and to you for making it happen."

"You don't need to thank me, mate, I'm just doing my job, and my only reward is seeing my clients succeed."

Steve walked Matt to the door and waved him off as he mentally prepared himself for the next part of his day.

Olivia was looking forward to finally meeting Steve's parents and wanted to make a good first impression. As she opened the wardrobe, she scanned the fully crammed rails. The amount of clothes she had made her choice that much harder. Should she go smart casual or just go for it and dress to impress, she pondered. That was the dilemma. From the way Steve had described his parents in the past, it sounded like they appreciated the finer things of life.

'I know, I'm going to go for a smart jacket and tailored trousers. Surely, they won't turn their noses up at that.'

Olivia chose a white blouse, black tailored trousers and a red blazer, with silver buttons. Now she just had to decide what to do with her mane. Olivia wasn't familiar with whether Steve's parents had had many dealings with people of colour and didn't want to startle them with a wild and outlandish hairstyle. She brushed her hair back and tied it with a scrunchie and put it in a bun. Olivia took a step back as she looked at her reflection in the mirror.

'Who is that woman? I don't recognise her, but I can't afford to get this first impression wrong, as you don't get a second chance to make one.'

Olivia was happy that she looked the part and would not let Steve down.

'Right, now where are my keys?'

Olivia found her keys on the side dresser, grabbed them and her bag and darted down the stairs. As she got to the bottom, Jen was coming out of the kitchen carrying a drink and sandwich that she had just prepared for herself.

"Someone looks and smells good," Jen teased.

Olivia seemed flustered. "How do I look? I haven't overdone it have I?"

Olivia looked at herself again in the mirror in the hall, checking that her lipstick hadn't smudged on her teeth.

"Oh, girl stop it. You look great. You always do. You have a figure to die for. That red blazer really suits your bronze complexion too." Olivia smiled.

"Ahh thanks hon. I'm glad I've passed your approval. Now I just need to pass my future in-laws' scrutiny as to whether I'm good enough to marry their one and only son."

"They will love you. Now get out of here before you're late and really give the wrong impression." They both chuckled.

"Anyway, how come you aren't working today?" Olivia asked.

"I changed shifts with a colleague who wants to attend a family wedding next weekend, which would have been my weekend off. I'm looking forward to chilling out today. I'm going to wash my hair later and then perhaps go and see a movie. They've got one of those Marvel movies on and I like the action and getting lost in their make-believe world."

"Going alone or on a date?" Olivia felt sure she knew what the answer was going to be but was hopeful that Matt would have got his act together by now.

Jen gave a long sigh. "Alone I'm afraid. I guess Matt wasn't as keen as he made out as I haven't heard from him."

Olivia started walking towards the door, realising that she was on the verge of running late and Steve was a stickler for time.

"Listen girl, don't give up hope. I get the impression that he's shy, but will come good, so just trust God on this one. Girl, I'm out of here. Byeeeee."

Chapter Eleven

Olivia left Jen loitering in the hall whilst she flew out the door in a dash to pick up Steve.

Olivia got to Steve's house with minutes to spare. She was glad that she wasn't late as the two of them rocking up to the restaurant in an argumentative mood wouldn't bode well for the image she was trying hard to portray. Olivia blew the horn, and Steve came out walking gingerly to the car and got in.

"Wowww, look at you then. No crutches. Are you sure you don't want to bring them just in case you get tired?"

"Olivia. I'm fine." Steve rolled his eyes.

'Why can't she see how far I have come and just congratulate me?'

Olivia's comment annoyed him, but he wasn't going to create a scene and allow the moment to spoil his happy place. Olivia pulled off en route to the restaurant.

"You look nice," Steve said as he complimented Olivia on her outfit.

"A tad overdressed I would say, but at least Mother will be impressed so you'll pass."

Steve was teasing Olivia as he knew how important this introduction was to her. Even though he had reassured her time and time again that she should just be herself, he understood what this lunch meant and how important it was to her.

They were first to arrive at the restaurant, with the reservation made under the name of Mr & Mrs Adams Snr. The waiter showed them to their table. As Olivia made herself comfortable, she couldn't help noticing how ornate the surroundings were with high crystal chandeliers glistening and brightening up the area. Their table was in a prominent location of the restaurant, which suggested that Mr & Mrs Adams dined there regularly and were highly respected by the management of the establishment.

"Wowww. This place is posh," Olivia whispered as she gently nudged Steve with her elbow.

"I'm so glad I made the effort to dress more conservatively. Unlike you I might add,"

Olivia tutted as she looked Steve up and down, making the point that he really didn't make much of an effort with his outfit choice, a long sleeved dark blue polo shirt and beige slacks.

"As I told you before, Liv, I don't make any special effort for my parents to try and impress them. They ought to accept me for who I am and not something that they think I should be."

Steve did not anticipate that it was going to be a straightforward lunch as he could never predict what would come out of his parents' mouth, especially his mother's.

"Oh look, here they come now." Steve could see his mother's high-top hat, with its distinct coloured feather, before he saw her as the waiter escorted her and his father to the table.

"Mother." Steve stood to his feet and greeted his mother with a kiss on her cheek. Mrs Adams smiled as she enjoyed her son's gesture.

"Hi, Dad." Steve shook his dad's hand as he walked over to the other side of the table.

"Mother and Father, I'd like to introduce you to Olivia. Olivia, these are my parents."

Olivia smiled. "I'm very pleased to finally meet you both."

Mrs Adams was the first to speak, responding to Olivia's comment.

"Indeed. He's been hiding you away and I can see why. You're a pretty thing, aren't you?"

Olivia didn't really know what Steve's mother meant by her comment but did not take it to heart. This was her first time meeting the woman, so she wanted to give her the benefit of doubt before making up her mind about her future mother-in-law.

Mr Adams had greeted her in a fatherly way and Olivia found herself warming to him more and surmised quite early that she would probably get along with him a lot better than his wife.

Having given the waiter their choice of food from the menu, Mr Adams suggested a Merlot red wine to accompany their meal, which he felt everyone would enjoy. Talk soon turned to the elephant in the room, their impending marriage.

"Olivia. Steven tells us you're a teacher. Do you find fulfilment in your job?" Mrs Adams was gentle in her delivery, yet inquisitive all the same.

It excited Olivia that Steve's mother would ask about something so dear to her and the passion in her response was evident as her countenance brightened.

"Yes, I do. My kids are a delight to teach. I always find that we can learn a lot from them too and have their childlike spirit."

"That's a lot different to the work Steven is involved in. Do you think you are going to continue teaching once you are both married?"

Mrs Adams wanted to gauge what the plan was once they were married, since Steve was keeping things close to his chest.

Steve felt this was his opportunity to jump in and try and steer the conversation. He knew what his mother was like and once she started down a particular rabbit hole, she wasn't coming out without the trophy prize.

"Mother. Of course, Olivia is going to continue teaching after we are married. There isn't any reason why she wouldn't."

"Oh, well, I just thought with you both being slightly older, you might want to try for a family straightaway. You're not going to deprive me of grandchildren, I hope. We hardly see you at the best of time, so goodness knows when we would ever see our grandchildren."

Before anything more could be said about any impending grandchildren, the food arrived. Mr Adams did the honour by tasting the wine first that the waiter had poured in a red wine glass for him to sample.

"Ahh yes. That's good. Thank you."

The waiter poured the Merlot in the glasses of everyone around the table and told them to enjoy their meal. The conversation was quiet as dinner was consumed, but once everyone was finished, Mrs Adams picked up from when she left off.

"So, are your people happy about your impending marriage to our son?"
Steve rolled his eyes.

'And there it is. I was waiting to see how long it would take her to put her foot in her mouth. To be honest, she took longer than I had envisaged.'

Steve's hand slipped over Olivia's to reassure her that he had her back and that she wasn't to react to the ignorant choice of words that his mother had used. Before Olivia could respond, Steve took the lead to protect his fiancée's honour.

"Olivia's parents are the nicest people you would ever meet. They are very humble and down-to-earth individuals. And very accepting of all individuals, without judgement."

Steve recalled briefly the first time he met Olivia's parents. He did not know how they would receive him, with him being from a totally different culture. However, they made him feel at ease very quickly which gave him a sense of their approval. He had wished Olivia's response with his parents could have been as positive as his was with hers.

There was further grilling by Steve's parents over a variety of subjects as they tried to ascertain how Olivia would fit into their family and the value she would bring. Steve was quick to wrap things up and was the first to make a move in suggesting the lunch came to an end.

"Well, it was nice meeting up with you both, but Olivia and I have a lot of things to finalise."

Steve's mother appeared disappointed as there were still so many other questions that she needed answering. And the expression on her face did not hide her disappointment. Plus, they hadn't even had dessert yet.

"Olivia, it would be nice if you and I met up for tea some time, so that we can get to know each other a little bit better, without the men. They just get in the way, don't they?"

Mrs Adams was trying to end on a lighter note as she could tell from the look on Steve's face that he wasn't too impressed with the way they had come across. It wasn't so much Steve's father, as he was quite harmless and only went along with his wife to save the peace. However, his mother was the real culprit and didn't always discern when she was being offensive and insensitive.

Olivia was trying to stay positive as it was important to her that they approved of her.

"Yes, I would like that. Just get my number from Steve and give me a call."

Mrs Adams was happy that Olivia was open to them meeting up on their own and embraced them both as they prepared to leave. Mr Adams also rose to his feet and gave Olivia a kiss on her cheek and tapped Steve on his back. As Olivia left the restaurant with Steve, she felt it went better than she had been fretting about and was looking forward to meeting up on a one-to-one basis with her future mother-in-law.

Jen spent the afternoon washing her hair and leisurely pottering around the house. She had checked online to see what timeslots the movie was scheduled to show and had decided to go to the 5 PM showing. As she was relaxing on the settee reading her Bible, her mobile phone rang. She didn't recognise the number but decided to answer it anyway.

"Hello."

"Hi, is that Jen?"

She recognised the voice to be that of Matt and was pleasantly surprised that he had finally called.

"Yes, it is, stranger. I was beginning to think that you didn't have my number."

Jen wasn't going to make it easy on Matt and thought she'd have some fun listening to him try to squirm his way out of why he left it so long to contact her.

"Ahh, sorry about that." Jen could hear the embarrassment in Matt's voice.

"I have been meaning to call. And then just got a bit distracted with work. I hope you can forgive me, as I have really wanted to touch base with you. We have a lot in common, and I'd like to explore that further, if you are also open to that?"

Matt waited patiently to hear Jen's response. He hoped his inability to strike whilst the iron was hot had not caused him to miss out and that Jen was still as keen as he was to see where their friendship could go.

"Yes, I forgive you. You sound like a wounded puppy. How could I not accept your apology?" Jen chuckled so that Matt could gauge that she wasn't annoyed in anyway.

"Ohh, that's great I appreciate that. Thank you," he said, somewhat relieved.

"So, I wondered if you were free this evening? Would you like to do something?"

"Well, actually, I was going to the cinema later."

"Ohh, okay. On your own or with someone else?" Matt was secretly praying that he wasn't too late.

Jen paused for a while, still having fun punishing him for not calling sooner. But then responded putting him out of his misery.

"No, I'm going on my own."

"Phewwww. That's a relief. That would have been awkward. What were you going to see then?"

"I was going to see the latest Marvel movie that is out."

Before Jen had a chance to finish her sentence, Matt responded with excitement in his voice.

"Gosh, I love the Marvel franchise. I've watched most of their movies. I'd love to join you, if that would be, okay?" Jen's facial expression heightened, not that Matt could detect it.

"Yes, I'd love the company. I was thinking of going to the 5 PM show, if that would work for you?" Matt hesitated.

"What time was the next show due to start as I am still working and have one more client to go and see?"

"I think the next show starts at 6.30 PM."

"Can we go for that time instead?" Jen was happy with the later time as she really didn't have much going on.

"Yep, 6.30 PM is fine. Shall we meet each other there then?"

Jen didn't really know what the protocol was or what Matt was thinking and didn't want to make any assumptions.

"Is it okay if I come and pick you up, as I'd rather like us to go together rather than us having to wait outside the cinema for each other?"

Matt was old school and had been taught that a man should offer to pick a woman up if he was taking her out.

"Err, yeah, that will be fine."

"Okay, that's great. I'll be there at 6 PM, so I'll see you later then."

"Yep, see you at 6 PM."

As Jen put the phone down, she pondered how quickly things had changed. One minute she was making plans to go to the cinema on her own. And the next minute, she was going to the cinema on a date with someone of the opposite sex.

LORD, you sure do have a sense of humour, don't you? Perhaps Olivia was right. I should just leave everything in your hands and not try to micro-manage my own destiny. Father,

I am glad Matt called and I'm going to let you order my steps on this one. I'm not going to jump into things so quickly like I did with Chris. And I'm going to look out for any red signs that you show me and act on them sooner rather than later.'

CHAPTER TWELVE

True to his word, Matt had arrived at Jen's place on time to pick her up for them to head to the cinema. Matt did the gentlemanly thing of opening the car door for Jen, which immediately ticked off one of the points on her list of 'must haves' that she had mentally erected in her mind i.e., a man who is old-school and knows how to treat a lady.

The Marvel movie they went to see, 'Spiderman; Homecoming', had them intrigued and mesmerised all at the same time, especially the stunts and imagery of Spiderman flying from one place to the next. At the end of the movie, neither of them was ready to go home, as they still had lots to talk about whilst leaving the cinema. It was Matt's suggestion that they look for somewhere to eat to extend the evening. He allowed Jen to pick the restaurant, which was a Chinese restaurant. And he happily went along with her choice, which in his opinion was a good call.

Once settled at their table, they ordered a platter with various dishes so that they could enjoy a selection of food that they both liked.

"So how long have you been a paramedic and what's the best thing you enjoy about your job?"

"Ooooh, that's a good question." Jen finished what she was eating and cleared her throat.

"Well, I've been a paramedic for about three years. And the best thing I enjoy about my job is the fact that no two days are alike. I love the variety of people I meet on a day-to-day basis. But more importantly, I feel blessed to be able to support individuals and help them to their path of healing and recovery."

Matt excitedly agreed. "I feel the same way too. My greatest reward is seeing my patients recover and regain the life they once had before their injuries. There's nothing quite like it."

"So, what would you say are your hobbies, or the things you like doing?"

Jen hurled the candid question right back at him as the conversation continued to flow effortlessly between them.

"Well, I'm quite sporty and athletic, and do enjoy some healthy competition from time to time. In fact, the guys have been spurring me on to play squash with them when Steve is back to his full strength. But I wonder if they both know what they are letting themselves in for, as I don't suffer fools gladly," Matt said with a cheeky smirk on his face.

Jen thought to herself, 'He may be shy in some respects, but I like this side of him that I haven't seen before. It makes him an interesting character to unpack.'

Matt continued. "I told Michael that we could probably get in a few games, in the meantime. My problem is that I don't always know how to prioritise my schedule and make time for a social life. It's something that I am working on however."

He looked directly into Jen's eyes as if to say he hoped that she would be the person to help him get the balance right. Jen thought she could read the same thought in his mind by the way he was glaring at her and embarrassingly looked away from his gaze. She didn't want to give the wrong impression of her being too eager or desperate to change him. She liked that edge to him and did not want to ever change a person to suit her. She appreciated that as a wife, the biblical approach was for her to be a helpmeet to her husband. However, she was getting way ahead of herself in her imagination as this was only their first real date. There was still a long way to go. She had rushed things with Chris. Or more like she had allowed herself to be swept along a path that she wasn't totally comfortable with and should have spoken up earlier, when it was clear that he was not the one.

"I also like to paint."

"Oh yeah. What kind of things do you paint?" Jen was intrigued as the layers to his personality were slowly peeling away.

"Landscapes mainly. If I ever get to go hiking or spend times outdoors, I like to take my canvas and paints with me and paint what I see."

Jen was seriously impressed. "Wowww. I think that's amazing. Have you sold any of your pieces? Or aren't they that good," she said teasing him.

"I'll have you know, young lady, that I have actually. A local gallery took some of my pieces to put on display. I didn't get enough to make me want to pack up my job and change my profession, but I was chuffed all the same that someone believed in me. And equally individuals paid for something I did for fun."

"Well, it sounds like you are better than you are letting on. I'd like to see your work some time."

Jen quickly tried to justify herself. "Not that I'm trying to get myself an invitation to your house or anything like that..."

Matt smiled as he tried to help her out of the hole, she was digging herself deeper into.

"Don't worry, Jen, I know what you meant. And, at some point, I'd love to show you, my work. I would especially be interested in your honest opinion."

Jen felt humbled. "My goodness, you don't need my approval. You've had a gallery purchase your work. In my book, that speaks volumes."

"Well thank you for that; I appreciate your kind words."

They had spent over two hours just talking and getting to know each other better. It was clear that they both enjoyed each other's company and wanted to spend more time together.

"Well, Lady Jen. I better take you home or your housemate is going to want to know where you are."

"Oh, you mean Olivia. I guess she and Steve may be doing something fun of their own or making plans for their big day."

Jen's mind drifted to imagining seeing Olivia in her wedding dress, the bridesmaids all dolled up and of course, Steve waiting at the end of the aisle, for her, suited and booted, looking dashingly handsome.

It was her greatest desire to get married herself, but only to the right person and for that she knew she had to wait patiently on God if she wanted His best. Whether that would be Matt or not, time would tell. But over the last few months, Jen had grown and significantly changed her perspective in terms of accepting who she was and what she deserved. Her self-esteem was devalued in her relationship with Chris and to move forward, there had to be inner healing and forgiveness on her part.

If she hadn't chosen to forgive Chris and herself, any future relationships going forward would suffer and be impacted negatively as a result. And Jen could not credit arriving at this resolution on her own. Rather, it was a truth she had learnt from Olivia who helped and counselled her when she needed a shoulder to cry on. She also found that reading the Word and listening to worship music was extremely valuable for her emotional and spiritual wellness.

Matt dropped Jen back to where he had collected her from earlier that evening. He jumped out of the car and ran around to her side to open the door. As they walked towards the front door, they both felt a bit nervous as they didn't know what each other was thinking in terms of what was expected. Matt quickly took the initiative and gave Jen an affectionate hug, which made her feel at ease and respected.

"Now don't leave it so long as you did last time, eh?" Jen said teasing him as she unlocked the door.

"No. Definitely not. I now need to ensure that I make time for my social calendar to be active. So, watch this space."

They both laughed in unison. Matt watched Jen close the door and he walked back to his car feeling satisfied with himself that the evening was a great success.

One week later…

Chris was disappointed with himself. As usual, he hadn't got his act together with his time management between his work and home life balance, the result of which meant that it had an impact on others and the plans that they had made. He was supposed to have taken Ben for the weekend to stay with his grandparents on the Friday evening after he had got back from work, but the clinic that he was working in at Sunningdale started late, which meant that subsequently he would finish late. Thankfully Natalia had packed Ben's bag, and he was excited and ready to go, but Chris was too tired when he eventually got home and told Ben that he would have to take him the following day instead.

The first thing Chris did was make the embarrassing call to his in-laws to let them know that he would be arriving the next day. They were extremely disappointed with him for not managing his time appropriately, therefore, reneging on his promise, as they had planned a full itinerary for the entire weekend to spoil their one and only grandson. But there was nothing they could do about it now and set out to rearrange a few of the activities until Ben arrived.

Natalia had the weekend off and had made plans to stay with friends. She didn't think it appropriate to stay in the house alone with Chris if Ben wasn't round to look after. Not that Natalia felt apprehensive of Chris, nor had he given her cause to doubt his integrity. It was just the way she was brought up and the boundaries she had put in place for her life as an au pair, which had always worked out well in her past roles.

Chris set off early on Saturday morning to try and make up for lost time and to stay in the good books of his in-laws, who clearly weren't impressed with him, following his conversation with them the night before.

The journey began smoothly, with Ben in the back, as usual, being kept occupied by his tablet. It wasn't an area he would have remembered, having left so young. This would now be a fresh start for him to create new memories with the family that he was reconnecting with. However, as Chris drove and got nearer, for him it was bittersweet memories of what was and what could have been. Things that he once had and those precious and dear things to him that he had now lost.

It was never his intention to keep Ben away from his family, but the constant accusations that were directed at him following Jill's death was just too much for him to bear. Especially since he was trying to hold things together for himself and his young son. Chris had felt that his in-laws should have been more supportive towards him. However, in those early days, after Jill's passing, they were clearly influenced and goaded on by Tilly who was relentless to apportion blame directly at Chris' door. And that's where all the trouble and ugliness with Tilly first began.

She had lost her twin, and she needed answers, and Chris was an easy target in her mind. Reminiscing over that time, and with hindsight, Chris realised how badly he had handled the situation by running away. He should have been more assertive, stuck around and challenged the accusations that were being hurled at him, but he was in a vulnerable place and wasn't thinking straight.

"Are we there yet?"

Ben's restless voice echoed from the back. He yawned loudly and stretched his hands in the air. Chris checked his rear view mirror and could see that Ben had probably had enough of staring at a glaring screen.

"Yep, buddy, we just have another 30 minutes and then we'll be there. So, sit tight and be a good boy for daddy. You've been great so far; I'm so proud of you. Did Natalia pack any snacks for you? Check your bag and have a look. There might be a packet of crisps in there or maybe a banana. I'm sure she would have put something in there for you."

Ben put his tablet to the side and had a rummage through his rucksack.

"Oh yeah, there's a snack box at the bottom of my bag."

"Okay buddy, well, open it up and see what goodies you can find."

Chris was relieved that Natalia had gone ahead and prepared something for the journey. He thought she would have as she was very efficient and always seemed to be one step ahead of him in knowing what was needed before being asked. That was exactly what he needed. Having lost Mrs Jenkins, who was familiar with his needs and quirky ways, he wondered if she could ever be replaced. And yet here was someone a lot younger but had an old head on her shoulders that made her perfect for their household. For the short time Natalia had been with them, she slid into her role seamlessly and without any issues, which was made easy with her being allowed to get on with the job.

Chris arrived at his in-laws in good time, giving them plenty of time to spend the rest of the weekend with their grandson. He drove up the drive which led into the green and spacious grounds, surrounded by large and perfectly manicured trees, with horses roaming the fields in the distance. After a few yards drive, they arrived at the stately home, the decor of which was something like out of a period drama and was breathtakingly stunning. Chris remembered how intimidated he had felt when he first visited the home and wondered what type of dynasty Jill had belonged to. Jill reassured him that he had nothing to be intimidated by as her family were down to earth and not pretentious in the slightest.

The house was a family inheritance that was handed down from generation to generation. She had jokingly teased Chris that one day the house would be theirs which is why they needed to have lots of children to fill it. Somehow, Chris had hoped that she was joking as it wasn't somewhere that he would want to live, let alone bring up a family in.

Mrs Hunter had been looking out through the window and waiting for their arrival. The sound of the engine pulling up the driveway prompted her to run out in excitement, with her husband close behind her.

"He's here. He's here."

Mrs Hunter ran straight to the back of the car door, waving at Ben before the car had made a complete stop. Ben smiled as he stared into the heart-warming face of someone, he had previously learnt was his grandmother and was excited that he now had grandparents just like the friends in his class had. As the car finally came to a stop, Mrs Hunter opened the car door.

"Hello Ben. How was your journey?"

Before he could answer, Mrs Hunter helped Ben out of the car and gave him a big hug and proceeded to walk him to the front door. She almost forgot to acknowledge Chris until she heard her husband greet him and then she remembered her manners and greeted him also. Her husband just rolled his eyes and muttered something under his breath as he took Ben's things from the back of the seat.

"Does he have any more luggage, Chris?" Chris got out of the car and walked around to the boot.

"Yes, he has a small bag also. Let me get that for you." Chris handed Mr Hunter Ben's bag.

"Would you like to come in for something to drink before you drive back?"

Chris shook his hand. "No, I'm alright. I best be heading back as I'm sure you both have got lots to keep Ben occupied for the rest of the weekend. I'll just quickly say goodbye to him and Mrs Hunter."

Chris followed Mr Hunter into the house, and immediately the smell of the house transported him back into the past. Mrs Hunter was a keen baker and there always appeared to be the smell of freshly baked bread lingering whenever he frequented the house. He recalled seeing Jill in the kitchen pinching away at the bread before Mrs Hunter had time to store it away and that memory brought a slight smile to his face.

"Sorry, Chris. I whisked young Ben away rather quickly. Will you stay for some tea before you drive back? I've made some fresh bread and have just taken out of the oven a fresh batch of scones that I made for Ben."

Chris smiled. Mrs Hunter was a feeder and if given half the chance, individuals wouldn't leave the house with their clothes still fitting.

"As I was telling Mr Hunter, I am fine and better head back as I have a lot of things to catch up with at home for work. So, what time should I come back for Ben? Say 5 PM?"

Mrs Hunter put her hand around Ben's shoulders.

"Now don't you worry about driving all that way tomorrow to come and pick Ben up, as we will bring him home. Won't we, Frank?"

She gave Mr Hunter a deep glare so that there was no way he would dare disagree with her.

"Of course, dear; it would be our pleasure."

"That settles it then," she said with a contented smile to her demeanour.

Chris had already robbed her of precious time with her grandson, and she was keen to spend as much time as she could with him until he had to go back home.

Chris bent down on Ben's level and gave him a big hug.

"Now you be good for grandma and grandpa, okay?"

Ben nodded in agreement. He did not seem agitated or scared as Chris thought he might have been. It's almost as if in his subconscious he had a memory of being at the house and interacting with them before, albeit vaguely.

"Will Tilly be visiting this weekend?"

Chris was concerned about Ben spending time with Tilly, even if she was his aunt and his mother's identical twin sister. There was still something that he did not trust about her and didn't know what her mental health was like or if she still had an issue with him. Whatever state she was in now, the less she saw of Ben the better was his motto. The response Mrs Hunter gave to his inquisitive question filled Chris with a sense of relief. Tilly was away for the weekend at a medical convention for work and they weren't expecting to see her until the Monday, by which time, Ben would have been back at home away from any influences she might have tried to project onto him.

"Okay, well, I think that's everything. You have my number. Please don't hesitate to call me if there's anything you need to know, no matter how late it is. I don't mind being disturbed and will take your call."

"I think we will be just fine, Chris. We have raised children before you know and had two to contend with at the same time, remember. So, I think we more than qualify in looking after our grandson."

Mrs Hunter's tone was warm-hearted which immediately put Chris at ease as he had never really left Ben on his own with strangers. But Ben wasn't with strangers. He was in good hands and was in for a treat, which involved being lavished with lots of love.

Chris said his goodbyes and made his exit for home.

CHAPTER THIRTEEN

Carol sat nervously in the waiting room until her and Michael's names were called. In the past week, she had been experiencing some uncomfortable pains in her abdomen. At first, she did not want to tell Michael, as she knew how paranoid he had become since finding out that they were pregnant. She only had to sniffle, and he was at her beck and call, self-diagnosing what she should do and letting her know the various medication she could not take that would be harmful to the babies. In all honesty, he was driving her around the bend. But at the same time Carol knew she had to give him some leeway and appreciate that she was married to a doctor, after all, and it was his natural default to care for individuals. Michael was a bit concerned with the pain that Carol described she was having when she eventually came clean and told him as the pain was excruciating, which is when he immediately booked an appointment with their obstetrician. Carol couldn't help but think the worse. When she was pregnant the first time, her pregnancy did not get this far, as it was still in the early days, so the pain she was experiencing was new to her.

'LORD, I'm not going to lose my babies, am I? Is this my punishment for what I did all those years ago and the deceit I showed to Michael? With the babies gone, would Michael even want to stay with me?'

Carol couldn't stop the thoughts from spiralling out of control, as deep down she wondered if Michael was genuinely back with her because of his love for her or was it just because of his future heirs. She looked over at Michael who was sitting there cool as a cucumber, reading some important documents that he had brought with him. After the appointment, he was due back at the surgery, and he, along with Joan and Chris were meeting with the rest of the practice staff to let them know the fate of the surgery's shelf life.

All the T's had been crossed and the I's dotted on the contract for the merger and they felt satisfied with the deal they had struck with the other surgery. There were going to be some redundancies, but they had worked out satisfactory packages for those who would be losing their jobs because of the merger. Michael appreciated that once they had spoken to the staff that they were going to be shocked and surprised, since the partners chose not to divulge any of the details until everything was finalised. The rationale behind their decision was that if the merger did not materialise, they would have unsettled the staff needlessly and, therefore, chose to wait until the ink was dried and the contract concrete and watertight.

"Mr & Mrs Mills."

The receptionist smiled as she directed Michael and Carol down the corridor to the last room on the right. Michael's hand was slid across Carol's back gently aiding her as she uncomfortably waddled slowly to the room. It seemed the further along her bump was growing that Carol was experiencing all sorts of unpleasant feelings. She privately confessed to Olivia, on more than one occasion, that she couldn't wait for it all to be over, as it wasn't the most pleasant thing she had experienced and didn't know if she would want to go through it again either. They arrived at the door and Michael opened it for Carol. They were greeted by Dr Wendy Thompkins, who had been looking after them since they first started having antenatal appointments. Carol made herself comfortable and described the pain she was having. A sharp stabbing pain.

Having made a note of the symptoms, Dr Thompkins got Carol to position herself on the bed whilst she gently probed her stomach, as Michael looked on intently. Her hands were gentle as she manoeuvred them around to the sides of Carol's stomach and then all around it.

"Let me know if anywhere is hurting as I probe." Carol's face was contorted as her stomach was being pressed left, right and centre.

"It hurts more towards the bottom of my stomach."

"I'm just going to check that everything is okay with your babies."

Dr Thompkins made Carol feel comfortable and then put some gel on her stomach and glided the ultrasound probe over her stomach.

Michael's face lit up. "There they are. God's little gifts to us. How are they looking, Doctor?"

Dr Thompkins' attention was fixated to the monitor, so she didn't really hear what Michael had said, and he repeated himself.

"Is everything okay?"

"…errr, yes. No, my apologies. I was just measuring the babies and notably one is a lot smaller than the other, but that's nothing to be too concerned with at this stage."

Dr Thompkins did not want to alarm the couple and once Carol had got herself cleaned up, Dr Thompkins had a conversation with them regarding what the issues to Carol's pain could be.

Dr Thompkins reiterated the risks of women over 35 getting pregnant. Such pregnancies had an increased risk of certain complications like preeclampsia, chromosomal abnormalities, as well as a few other risks.

"Carol, I'm concerned that your blood pressure may be too high at this stage of your pregnancy, therefore, I think it best we keep you in hospital just for a couple of weeks to monitor things. We can get some blood tests done and make sure you are taking sufficient vitamin D and the other essential vitamins your body needs, especially as you are carrying two babies. Are you going to be okay with that?"

Dr Thompkins could see from the look on Carol's face that it wasn't what she had anticipated.

And before Carol could even respond, Michael stepped in and took the reins of the situation.

"That's fine, Dr Thompkins. I think that is probably the best decision. I keep telling her to stop doing strenuous things at home, but she doesn't listen."

"I am in the room, you know,"

Carol said in a tone of disbelief that Michael just happened to plan her whole life out without taking her feelings into consideration. Although, it wasn't something Carol would have refused, if the doctor thought that it was the best course of action for her and the safety of their babies.

"Yes, Dr Thompkins, I am happy to do all that is needed to ensure that me and our babies are safe and healthy. And if it means staying in hospital to do that, then so be it. Plus, it will give me a chance to get away from 'you-know-who.'"

Her eyes flickered as she looked at Michael and then towards Dr Thompkins, who gave a cheeky grin in agreement.

"Great. Give me a couple of days to get you booked in and a bed sorted. That will give you time to get your head around the idea and get a small bag ready for your stay."

Dr Thompkins said her goodbyes and Carol and Michael left her office. As Carol was waddling back down the corridor, she was mumbling to herself, but loud enough for Michael to hear.

"I better start handing things over to my assistant as I wind down."

"Yes, I think that would be wise. You've trained Chad well and I am sure he's going to relish the opportunity to show you what he can do in your absence."

"Guess so."

"Anyway, let me drive you back home and I'll get back to work unless you wanted me to drop you off somewhere first."

"Nope. I'm fine. Take me home, Parker."

"Yes, m'lady."

They both smiled as they left the hospital hand-in-hand and feeling optimistic about their future.

Chapter Thirteen

Michael got back to the surgery and was not looking forward to the meeting that was scheduled for the end of the day. All the staff were told was that there was an important staff meeting at the end of surgery hours and that everyone was required to attend, even those who had a job-share or worked part-time. Janet pretty much had things wrapped up in her mind that the meeting was to let the staff know that Chris had been sacked. The fact that the surgery had failed their CQC inspection, someone's head had to roll for it and as Chris withheld vital information regarding his professional credentials, that was sure to be a reason worthy of asking him to leave.

Ever since the other staff were aware of the meeting, they tried to tease out of Janet was it was about. However, Janet acted like she couldn't divulge such information to them. Even though she herself was not privy to the details, she liked feeling important in the eyes of others and if they all felt that as management she would know, when she didn't have a clue, then so be it was her motto.

As a busy Monday in the bustling surgery was drawing to a close, the staff started to down tools and put away their things to get ready to head to the boardroom for the meeting, which was scheduled for 5 PM. Chris took the opportunity to call Natalia to remind her that he had a meeting after work, but that it wasn't expected to run too late. He wanted to check with her if he should stop by the chippy to bring in some fish and chips. However, Natalia had declined his offer, since it would have been too late for Ben to eat with his bedtime being so close to when Chris was due to return home.

Natalia reassured Chris that she had made Ben's favourite meal for him, one of her specialities that she had introduced to the family. Kranjska klobasa, a Slovenian sausage, which she was serving with French fries. Ben loved sausages and chips, but Natalia's version was slightly more flavoursome than the sausages his dad used to make for him. Natalia would tone down the spices somewhat so that Ben's delicate palette could handle it. She made a spicier version for herself and Chris, accompanied with sauerkraut and fresh focaccia. It was a dish that Natalia perfected well, as it was handed down to her by her mother, with some secret elements that only the family was aware of, which made it unique to them. Chris had to admit that the different Slovenia dishes that Natalia was introducing them to had him excited and titillated as the flavours were stimulating his tastebuds. It also took him out of his comfort zone. Mrs Jenkins' cooking was very good, but it was safe food, and he always knew what to expect. However,

Natalia's cooking was enabling him to broaden his horizon and appreciate food from another culture.

"Okay, Natalia, that's great. I'll see you later. Tell Ben I won't be too late and will be home in time to read him a story and put him to bed."

Just as he was finishing off his call, Joan popped her head around the door of his office.

"Are you ready for this?"

"As ready as I'll ever be. But I'm an innocent bystander remember. I'm leaving this one to you and Michael."

Joan smiled as they both made their way to the board room in anticipation of what was about to emerge.

Everyone was starting to settle in the board room except for Michael, who was just finishing off a call. There was an array of pastries, teas, coffees and bottles of water at the back of the room and the staff availed themselves of the goodies as they found a seat.

Michael eventually entered the room and apologised to everyone for the delay.

"Thank you all for your time in staying behind, as I'm sure you are wondering what the meeting is all about and why it was necessary for us to gather in this fashion."

His voice remained steady and professional as he started to break down the crux of the meeting.

"Well, as you all have probably heard, unfortunately we failed our recent CQC inspection. However, we were given a time frame to remedy some of the areas that we failed in, with the opportunity to have another inspection."

There was a sense of relief in the room as individuals were hopeful that with everyone pulling together and working hard, they would get a better review next time around. Michael's expression of optimism wouldn't last long with the next few sentences that he was about to deliver, and the staff also were unaware what was about to hit them.

"However, that being said, we, the partners, have decided to go down another route. We have made the very difficult decision to close Bricket Wood Surgery and merge with another practice."

Michael's words felt like a round of bullets that he had just delivered and there was a sound of gasps that reverberated around the room. There was a mixture of emotions as individuals were stunned, shocked and truly blindsided. Michael had a difficult job to do and could not allow the reactions of the staff to deter him from concluding what he had started.

"You will all be familiar with Belmont Medical Centre, which isn't too far from our vicinity. Belmont is the practice we will be merging with. There were a lot of factors that we took into consideration before making this decision and therefore, it wasn't taken lightly."

Chris' main concern was how Janet would take the news, and his eyes locked directly with hers. In her eyes he saw hurt, disappointment and a genuine sadness and she looked away from him and hung her head down, as she wiped away the tears that had started to stream down her face. One of the staff put up his hand to ask a question. Michael acknowledged his hand.

"Yes, John."

John spoke candidly as if he had read the minds and was speaking for all the other staff.

"So, I guess what we all want to know is will there be any job losses, since Belmont is a much larger and established practice?"

"That's a very good question, John. However, one that we won't be able to answer at this meeting. Over the next few days, we will be having individual meetings with each one of you, at which point we will have a frank discussion and share the outcomes we have arrived at."

Another person put up their hand. Michael also acknowledged the hand.

"Yes, Kate."

Kate did not mince her words since she shared her job with Rose and concluded that at least one of them was surplus to requirement.

"So, you want us all to do our work as normal with this uncertain cloud hanging over our heads? This isn't fair."

Michael sensed that Kate was understandably upset, however Joan speedily came to his rescue.

"Kate, we appreciate that this is all new for you and everyone else to process. And we understand that you all want answers now. However, it would not be professional of us to discuss the outcome of everyone's fate at this meeting. And we hope that you all will just bear with us as we deal with the matter as swiftly and efficiently as possible. I promise you that any questions you have will be answered and addressed openly."

After answering more questions from frustrated staff members, Michael took the brave decision to swiftly wrap things up.

"Well, if there aren't any more questions, let's call it a day, shall we? Is there anything you'd like to add, Chris or Joan?"

Chris waved his hand to indicate that he had nothing further to add, as did Joan by the facial expressions she communicated to Michael.

Janet would normally have been busy clearing up behind everyone, but she was the first one to leave the room, followed by the disgruntled others.

One individual mumbled under his breath, but loud enough to be heard.

"Well, I didn't see that coming. That was the last news I was expecting to hear. And I wonder how long they were sitting on this information, eh?"

When everyone had left the room, only Michael, Joan and Chris were left.

"That went down like a lead balloon," Chris whined.

"Well to be honest it was never going to be the easiest of conversations, was it?" Joan replied.

"I must admit, I thought there was going to be a bigger uproar than there was," Michael said in a rather matter of fact tone.

Chris couldn't believe his insensitivity and was not going to allow him to dismiss what was rather an emotional and scary meeting for a lot of them.

"Michael, how can you say that? Did you even look at their faces? Janet was absolutely crushed. I don't know if she'll even come back from this. The poor woman was mortified about being blindsided the way she was."

"We all knew that this was never going to be an easy meeting and that some understandably would be shocked. In the days to come, we will just have to deal with whatever the aftermath will be. Now I have a pregnant wife to go home to. Some of us have our own issues to deal with too you know. Carol will be going into hospital for a couple of weeks, so we need to prepare for that."

"Michael, I'm sorry to hear that. Is there anything we can do?" Joan said with a tinge of empathy in her tone.

"Yes, I'm sorry too. I hope she is going to be okay," Chris added.

"I hope so too."

Michael collated his things together and made his excuses, with Joan and Chris following close behind him.

CHAPTER FOURTEEN

True to her word, Mrs Adams had contacted Olivia to arrange for them to meet up. Even though Olivia was slightly nervous that Steve would not be there to hold her hand, she knew that she needed to forge her own relationship with her future mother-in-law and wanted desperately for them to get on.

Olivia had a great relationship with her own mother; therefore, she did not yearn that maternal bond with Mrs Adams. However, for the sake of Steve, she wanted to put her best foot forward.

Mrs Adams had booked afternoon tea for them at a prestigious hotel and was eager to know more about the woman her son had chosen to be his wife. Olivia was not her first choice of a wife for her son. Her and Mr Adams had hoped that Charlotte would be their daughter-in-law as it just made better sense. Charlotte's family was from a similar background to them and Charlotte had done very well for herself too.

Over the years, Mrs Adams had made several attempts to push Steve and Charlotte together, but Steve just saw her as a friend and therefore did not want to give Charlotte false hope, only to break her heart later down the road. Plus, Charlotte did not share his Christian faith and that was number one on his list of priorities; his wife had to share the same beliefs as he did.

Mrs Adams arrived at the hotel first and was shown to her table. As she waited for Olivia to arrive, she opened her bag and took out a compact mirror to check her reflection that everything looked satisfactory and to her high standards. She was an attractive woman for her age and took pride in her appearance and the way she looked. When Steve was growing up, he always felt proud when his mother waited for him at the school gates as she always looked trendier than the other mothers. But in the next breath would feel slightly embarrassed as she smothered him with kisses and affection. However, over the years, their relationship changed as Steve disliked the way his mother tried to control his life. She was overly protective and often would not respect that as an adult, he had the right to live his life the way he wanted to. And it was her meddling in his life that pushed Steve to distance himself from his parents to his mother's dismay.

Olivia arrived at the hotel in good time, 15 minutes earlier than the expected time, and was surprised that Mrs Adams was already there sitting at the table waiting for her.

'Ohhh nooo. I really made the extra effort to get here before her, but she just had to make me look bad, didn't she?'

Olivia smiled awkwardly as she was escorted to the table.

"Mrs Adams. Hello. You're here already," Olivia said as she nervously took her seat.

Shortly after their pleasantries, a waitress brought to the table two cake tiers, with a selection of freshly prepared finger sandwiches, warm scones with clotted cream and preserves, and a variety of mini home-made cakes and pastries. Another waitress brought to the table a selection of teas served in dainty bone china floral-print teapots with bone china cups and saucers to match. Mrs Adams was very particular in the teas she chose, which was Assam, a strong full-bodied tea from India, with a distinctive malty flavour, and Darjeeling, an aromatic and astringent tea, also from India, with a hint of almonds and wildflowers.

"I do hope you like my selection of teas, Olivia, as they are my favourite."

Olivia took a sip of both teas, but they weren't to her taste. Was she going to just accept what Mrs Adams had projected onto her, without even asking what type of tea she would have liked? Or was she going to make the bold decision to assert her own voice and not be controlled by her future mother-in-law just because she wanted to be liked?

Olivia decided that she was going to be herself and let her character shine.

"Actually, I find them slightly rich. I prefer lighter teas, so I am going to ask for a pot of lemon and ginger tea, with some honey."

Mrs Adams seemed surprised at Olivia's choice as she did not think much of it. Also, the fact that Olivia would refuse her choice and choose her own, she slightly admired as she was used to individuals just going along with the decisions she made.

"Well, that's not a problem, Olivia, we can order you a pot of whatever you like." Mrs Adams signalled the waitress to bring them over another pot of herbal tea for Olivia.

"So, Olivia, I know you are a schoolteacher. Tell me a bit more about yourself. I'd like to know who it is my son is smitten with."

Again, Olivia could feel that she was about to be interrogated and grilled, but she had already prayed beforehand and was ready for whatever Mrs Adams was prepared to hurl her way. Olivia took her time and shared with Mrs Adams about her passions, her hobbies and those things that were dear to her heart.

Mrs Adams gave the impression that she was listening and interested, but her body language was giving off a different emotion. Mrs Adams then started asking Olivia some intrusive questions about her financial situation and that of her parents. Olivia felt uncomfortable with the line of questioning but did not want to come across rude in anyway and answered the questions as best she could without divulging away too much of her personal information.

"I'm financially proficient; thank you. And my parents are comfortable also. Growing up, I never wanted for anything, and they did their best to teach me the value of money."

"That's good, dear," Mrs Adams said in a condescending tone.

"I'm glad you know how to take care of yourself."

Mrs Adams reached down in her bag and pulled out an A4 white embossed envelope and slid it along the table to Olivia. Her manner was cool, calm and collected.

"This is for you, Olivia, but you don't need to look at it now. Take it with you and have a look at it in the comfort of your own home."

Olivia seemed startled. It was almost as if the envelope magically appeared from nowhere, as Mrs Adams had it skilfully camouflaged underneath the table.

'Where did she whip this up from then? No wonder she was keen to get to the hotel first. I wonder what's in it.'

Olivia smiled politely as she accepted the envelope.

"Thank you, Mrs Adams. I will do just that."

Olivia was glad that she managed to get through afternoon tea reasonably unscathed. Mrs Adams had a smirk on her face like the cat that got the cream. Olivia wondered to herself what she was feeling so smug about but didn't feel it was worth trying to find out, as to be honest, she was quite exhausted.

"Well, Olivia, it was lovely getting to know you a bit better."

"And likewise; it was nice getting to know you too."

Olivia offered to contribute to the bill, but Mrs Adams confirmed that she had already paid online for the afternoon tea. Both ladies rose to their feet and awkwardly pecked each other on the cheek. Olivia felt it was the Christian thing to do by offering Mrs Adams a lift home if she needed one.

"Can I offer you a lift anywhere?"

"Oh, thank you, dear, but I have booked a driver to pick me up, but that was very kind of you to offer."

"Well, that's good. And again, thank you for afternoon tea. It was kind of you to pay. Perhaps next time I can pick up the cheque."

"Yes, that would be nice. Thank you, dear."

Olivia followed Mrs Adams out of the restaurant and waved her goodbye as she got into a silver jaguar car and smiled at Olivia as she peered over her glasses. Olivia walked to her car, which was parked a short distance away from the hotel, holding her mysterious envelope, and was eager to get home to find out what it contained.

As Olivia sat in her car, she stared anxiously at the envelope. It was almost as if it was goading her to open it. Olivia was bursting with curiosity to find out what was in the envelope. However, she talked herself out of it. Whatever was in the envelope had the power to make her happy or sad and Olivia was not ready to deal with her emotions, or the aftermath of what would follow as a result, just yet.

Olivia had asked for special leave, citing it was for a personal family matter, and had taken the day off to spend time with her future mother-in-law. Mrs Adams' gave Olivia a small window of opportunity for them to meet up, since she was going to be out of the country again on one of her trips. Since Olivia wanted to appear compliant to her urgent request, she agreed to the mid-week meeting.

With the rest of day to herself, Olivia made use of the time by catching up on some errands that she wouldn't ordinarily get the opportunity to do with her busy school schedule. Carol had also recently contacted her to say that she was having a stint in hospital, therefore, Olivia had agreed to go and see her following the afternoon tea with Mrs Adams. Plus, Carol had insisted that Olivia visit her straight after the meeting because she wanted to get all the juicy details first-hand.

After running various errands, Olivia arrived at Carol's house and an excited, heavily pregnant Carol greeted her with delight and couldn't wait to get her in the door. Once they had settled comfortably in the lounge area, Carol was beside herself to hear all about Olivia's meeting with Steve's mother.

"Girl, so tell me all about your meeting with Steve's mother. How was it?"

Olivia paused and then sighed, releasing the tension that had built up in her body.

"Interesting to say the least."

Carol's eyes opened wide.

"You're starting to worry me girl. Why? What happened?"

Olivia shared in detail the meeting she had earlier that day with Mrs Adams. She shared honestly with Carol some of the concerns she found that made her feel uncomfortable and wondered if Mrs Adams even approved of her being good enough to be her son's wife.

Olivia continued.

"Anyway, towards the end of the meeting, she pulls out this envelope. I swear it came from nowhere. And then she says, 'read it at home, dear'."

"Oh my gosh, so what was in it?" Carol was literally on the end of her seat in anticipation of what was in the envelope.

"I don't know. I haven't opened it yet."

"Are you crazy? I would have opened that envelope when I got back to my car." Carol laughed.

"Well, I'm not like you, am I! Remember, I'm the disciplined one out of the two of us."

"Okay, touché. I just don't know how you can sit on something like that without being curious as to what's in it. So, when do you plan to open it?"

Olivia tutted as she knew where Carol's line of questioning was hinting at.

"Honestly. You're incorrigible. If it's that important to you, Miss nosey, I'll open it now, but it's probably something and nothing. Perhaps it's the secret recipe to Steve's favourite meal and she wants to make sure I cook it just like she would."

They both chuckled as Olivia reached in her bag to retrieve the envelope. Olivia opened the envelope and as she slid the document out, she was stunned and just sat there staring at the wording at the top of the document in bold black letters.

"Liv, what does it say? Your face looks blank."

After a few more stares at the document, Olivia quietly mouthed the words as she trembled.

'Pre-Nuptial Agreement'.

"It says what, Liv?" Carol said in dismay with her hand on her heart.

"It's a pre-nuptial agreement, Caz, and the names of the parties in question are Steve's and mine. But I don't understand it. Why would Mrs Adams present this to me and not Steve?"

"What does it specifically say then?"

Olivia started mumbling through the contract so that Carol could hear the content of it.

"Erm, there's a clause that says, 'in advance of their marriage, the parties wish to provide for their rights and obligations in and to each other's assets and property including that which each of the parties currently and separately own, that which both will acquire together during the marriage, the event that the marriage is terminated'.

Etc, etc, etc. And there are other bits of legal jargon listed about who will be entitled to what, if the marriage is terminated etc. I really don't get this as Steve, and I have never discussed anything like this before."

Olivia was numb and couldn't quite process what she was clearly reading in black and white.

For once, Carol was gobsmacked and didn't quite know how to respond to a revelation like that.

"But Liv, do you think Steve even knows about this? Or could this just be the doings of his meddling mother to throw a spanner in the works before you both have had a chance to walk down the aisle?"

"Caz, I don't really know, but the document has both of our names on there and it details some personal information that she could only have known if Steve had given her the information. Or given whoever wrote up this stupid document. Would she go that far as to do something like that though behind her son's back? I don't know her that well to make that kind of assumption."

"So, what are you going to do, Liv? Are you going to talk to Steve about what his mother has given you or are you going to confront her first?"

"That's a good question, Caz, but I think I owe it to myself to first hear what she has to say before confronting Steve as to what the heck is going on and what this all means. I mean, it makes me sound like I'm some kind of gold digger... after the family heirlooms. Goodness me, what do they take me for, eh?"

Olivia was disappointed with the way she was being perceived by Steve's family.

"Call her now Liv and put the phone on loudspeaker. That way, I can be a witness to anything that she says. And if later, she states she didn't say the things she indeed said, then I'll be on her like a ton of bricks, I can tell you."

"Alright, alright; calm down, Mrs Marple. But to be honest, that isn't such a bad idea. Plus, I know she is expecting me to call as I recall the smirk on her face when she slid the envelope to me and told me to read it in the comfort of my own home. I suspect that's because she didn't want me to create a scene had I opened it there and then at the hotel. I'm starting to think that woman is shrewder than any of us can imagine. Right, I'm going to call her, and I need you to remain totally quiet Caz, as I don't need you trying to throw in your two cents amidst the conversation. Now do you think you can do that?"

Olivia said, looking wide-eyed at Carol, knowing how hard it was going to be for her to stay neutral and objective. Carol nodded her head and motioned with her hand that she was locking her mouth with an invisible key and throwing it away. Olivia smiled as she nodded her head at Carol's theatrical performance. Olivia reached for the phone in her bag and rang Mrs Adams' number.

After a few rings, Mrs Adams answered the phone, almost as if she was sitting by it waiting for Olivia to call. There followed a conversation between the two of them with regards to the content of the envelope that Mrs Adams had given to Olivia when they met up earlier that day. Olivia was keen to know why Mrs Adams was the one who presented her with the pre-nuptial agreement and not Steve and whether Steve was aware that she was going to be giving it to her when they met up.

Carol was sitting very quietly but bursting with rage as she listened to the conniving tone that Mrs Adams was using to get her points across. Mrs Adams confirmed that she and her husband did discuss with Steve about drawing up the agreement, but what she failed to tell Olivia is what Steve had originally said to them both. Steve was adamant that he was not going to be asking Olivia to sign one and that he was perfectly willing to walk away from his trust fund if that was what was required of him with regards to marrying Olivia as opposed to their choice.

Mrs Adams cleverly worded things as if Steve had asked them to go ahead and draw up the agreement and that he would discuss it with Olivia at a later stage.

"I'm sorry, Olivia. I was not aware that Steven hadn't yet spoken to you, so I can appreciate how this must have come as a shock to you. I think you and your future husband have some things to sort out in your relationship and will leave that to you both to handle. Steven can touch base with us when we get back from Mauritius. We're away for a couple of weeks. You take care of yourself, Olivia."

Before Olivia could say another word, she heard the abrupt tone ending the call and Mrs Adams was gone.

"Unbelievable," Carol screamed out.

"That woman is very difficult to have a conversation with, and she can be very manipulative too. I heard that tone she was using, and it certainly was her in the driving seat, with you in the back seat tagging along for the ride. But it does sound like Steve knew about it, which still surprises me. Especially with everything he witnessed between me and Michael transpiring before his very eyes, I would have thought that he did not want any secrets between the two of you that could potentially come back to bite you."

"Yeah, I agree, but I can't talk to him just yet. I need some time to process all of this. I think I'm going to talk to my parents before talking to him. I just need my mum right now," Olivia said in a sombre tone.

After such a heart wrenching time of emotions, Carol shared with Olivia details of the last visit she and Michael had with their obstetrician and why she needed to go into hospital for bed rest, as well as to have other tests. Olivia showed great empathy, and they ended their time together by praying for one another.

Olivia prayed that God would help Carol through the rest of her pregnancy and that her babies would be safe in her womb. Likewise, Carol prayed that God would intervene and put an end to the confusion that Olivia found herself entangled in. She also prayed that the truth would prevail and that whoever was not telling the truth would be exposed for all to see.

Their friendship could always stand the test of time, and they always had each other's back, no matter what the other one was going through. Olivia stood by Carol when her and Michael went through their rough patch, and she knew that Carol would stand with her as she navigated the obstacle course that she had to endure to marry her prince. He was the one that God did not allow to die as a result of the car accident he was involved in.

Olivia believed that God saved Steve for a reason, and she wasn't going to allow the enemy to ruin her happy moment, no matter what form he tried to adopt to do so. God was in control and Olivia just had to turn everything over to Him and watch Him put the puzzle together, since he had the original template.

However, for the moment, she needed time to deal with her thoughts and emotions as the revelation contained in her 'mystery envelope' really rocked her confidence.

CHAPTER FIFTEEN

With Carol confined to a hospital bed, Michael threw himself into work to take his mind from off things. Even though neither of them did not want to admit it to each other, they were worried about the pregnancy. Carol only had two months to go, and it was likely that the twins could come early if she carried on having stomach pains. As a doctor, Michael was fully aware of the complications that could happen at this stage of a pregnancy. Whilst most pregnancies led to a healthy baby, Carol was already pre-warned, in the early stages of her pregnancy, that she was at a higher risk of suffering from complications because of her age. However, it was a risk she was prepared to take for the sake of her marriage, as it was her pregnancy that saved her doomed relationship with Michael.

Morale had been low at the surgery ever since the announcement was made that the surgery was merging with a larger practice. Today was the first day of the scheduled round of interviews that needed to be carried out to inform the staff of their fate. It wasn't something Michael or Joan was looking forward to, but as senior partners, the lot fell on them to schedule the interviews in between appointments over the space of a week. Janet was the first interview that was scheduled, and Michael had a few moments to gather his thoughts together prior to meeting Janet and Joan in the board room.

He reflected upon the time he interviewed Janet when she first got the job and how conscientious she appeared, which put her head and shoulders above the other candidates. And over the years, Janet proved her weight in gold, showing great dedication and loyalty to everything, she did, as she was promoted to more senior roles throughout the years.

Michael knew that Janet's interview was probably going to be one of the hardest, which is probably why he and Joan wanted to tackle the most emotional one first. Thereafter, they would then be able to gauge how the other interviews would pan out.

Michael got to the boardroom, where Joan was already waiting for him. Once he settled and organised the papers in front of him, he let out a deep sigh. Joan looked at him with concern and responded,

"It's going to be a hard one, but we've got this."

She put her hand over his to reassure him that it might not be as bad as they were envisaging.

"Yes, it is going to be hard since Janet has been a key member of staff keeping this place ticking over. I know she will have been disappointed when she found out of our decision with all the rest of the staff, but we had no choice. We had to keep things close to our chest for fear of the information getting out and something potentially sabotaging the merger. I hope she will understand our reasoning."

"I hope so too. Anyway, lets rap this conversation up as I can hear footsteps coming."

Janet knocked on the door before going in and taking her seat. Her demeanour was quiet, and she didn't seem to be the bright and cheery individual that they had grown to love.

Michael started the conversation off, trying to be as professional and respectable as possible.

"Janet, thank you for your time today and for giving us the opportunity to have a chat with you regarding the future."

Janet finally looked up as her head was lowered from the moment she walked into the room. Her eyes looked sunken, and she couldn't hide her emotions and what she really thought about the whole situation. Janet felt blindsided and that was the last thing she would have imagined could have happened to the surgery.

Joan followed on from Michael's introduction.

"Firstly, Janet, we'd like to apologise that you heard about the merger with the other staff. As Operations Manager, you ordinarily would have been privy to such information, but the negotiations were extremely sensitive and the less people that knew about it, the better. We did not want to put you in a position where you would have had to keep sensitive information that would have had a significant impact on your colleagues. The fact that you too were oblivious to what was going on meant that your colleagues couldn't accuse you of not sharing the information with them. I hope you understand that."

Between Michael and Joan, they gave Janet a bit more information as to why a merge with another practice was the best option. They felt that they owed her that respect.

Following their explanation, Janet's manner changed somewhat, and she appeared more optimistic.

"Well, yes, I can appreciate everything you have shared. It was just a real shock I guess, which is why I took the news quite hard. I have loved working here and the thought of that being taken away from me was a bitter pill to swallow."

"And we have loved every moment with you too Janet, which made the decision even harder not to factor you into the discussions,"

Michael said as he tried to reassure Janet that it was never personal towards her. Michael continued.

"Janet, as you know, a merger like this comes with its challenges in terms of staffing issues. We have been in long discussions to keep your Operations Manager role. However, Belmont Medical Centre already has two Operations Managers. They will be making one of those positions redundant but plan to keep employed the more senior manager who has been with them for several years. This means that we can't take you to Belmont in your current role."

Joan took over the conversation.

"So, what does this mean for you, Janet, I hear you say?"

"Precisely, that was my next question," Janet said inquisitively.

"Ahh, yes, I am coming to that," Joan reassured.

"There is good news and not so good news. First, I'll start with the good news. There is definitely a job for you at Belmont, so we don't envisage you losing your job. However, the not so good news is that it is just a receptionist role, which would mean a demotion as such. If that is not something you'd like to do, having done such a junior role many years ago, then we would be prepared to offer you early retirement. If you chose the retirement route, we guarantee you that the package would be very lucrative, as that is something we would ensure that you got the highest tier."

Janet sat back in her chair, deep in thought.

"There seems a lot for me to consider and think about so I would need some time to make my decision."

"We totally respect that, Janet. You take whatever time you need. What we will share with you though, which we haven't told anyone else yet, is that we are looking to finalise the merger within six weeks," Michael disclosed.

"Ohhh, I didn't think it was going to be that soon."

Janet was shocked that a merger could be done that quickly. But once things had been approved by the Local Medical Committee (LMC), it was then just a matter of preliminaries to be ironed out, like the TUPE of the staff and merging of the bank accounts, amongst other things.

"Okay, Janet, I think that about wraps things up, but we would just like to take this opportunity to thank you for all your years of service. You've been faithful and loyal, and we have appreciated having you not only as a valuable staff member, but also a trusted friend."

Michael's voice trembled slightly as he appreciated Janet by reassuring her of her worth. Janet walked out of the boardroom a lot lighter than when she first walked in, armed with more understanding of the situation to fully appreciate the reasoning behind their decision to merge with another practice.

Michael and Joan briefly summed up the meeting by making notes for their records. They both agreed that they were pleasantly surprised as they were bracing themselves for Janet to react more negatively. However, after treating her respectfully and laying all their cards on the table, Janet could see and appreciate why the merger had to go through. She had promised that she would let them know by the end of the week what her decision was, and they hoped that she would consider staying on and going with them to Belmont Medical Centre.

Following their first date to the cinema, Matt and Jen had a few more dates since then and had discovered that they were compatible and had a lot in common. Matt finally found the courage on one of their dates to ask Jen if she would be his girlfriend, which Jen accepted favourably. She had been giving the situation some serious consideration prior to Matt's proposition. She told herself that she needed to tread carefully after the Chris debacle and had no intentions of dating another individual if it was not potentially going to lead to marriage.

Jen had played out the scenario in her head several times and Matt was exactly the type of man she had prayed and asked God for. She even told her parents about him and her mother encouraged her that if it felt right, to go for it. As life was too short. Unlike with her brief relationship with Chris, Jen did not feel that she was compromising or just going along with the flow when she was in Matt's company. So, saying yes to being his girlfriend was a no brainer.

They had decided to meet up for lunch as they were both based at the same hospital and making the most of every opportunity was one of the advantages they relished. Matt arrived at the hospital canteen first and secured a table, nestled in the corner by the window. He would be able to see Jen as she arrived and wave to her to indicate where he was. Jen arrived about 10 minutes later, slightly flustered and apologetic.

"Hey Matt, I'm really sorry I'm late." Jen sat down, offloading the duffle bag from her shoulders and putting it on the chair.

"My last call dragged on, and I almost thought I wasn't going to make it. However, my colleague told me that he would finish up and for me to take my lunch break. Oops sorry…"

Jen leant over the table and gave Matt a kiss. They were being more affectionate with each other, but it wasn't too overtly and in your face. Just enough for what Jen could handle, and Matt was respective of that.

"Don't worry. I finished with my client early so I've just been sitting here watching the world go by and catching up with my messages. Let me get you something to eat and drink. What would you like?"

"Errm, can you get me an egg mayo & cress baguette and a bottle of orange Lucozade?"

"No probs. I'll be back in a mo…"

Jen was in a good place and could not believe how quick things could turnaround. After Chris, she had decided that she was going to give men a break, especially if she could not find the type of man that she wanted. And yet God had other plans and instilled in her that if she waited on Him, He would bring her His best.

Matt was kind, funny and very caring. He complemented her well and Jen loved the way Matt made her feel. He was respectful of her and because they shared the same faith, they were aware of the boundary lines. Matt came back to the table with their lunch, choosing a ham salad sandwich and fresh orange juice for himself. They talked about their day and about the recent Bible study that they had attended at New Dawn young people's fellowship group. They were studying the book of Jonah, learning what it meant to be obedient to God and what the consequences were if a person went down the disobedient route.

"Did you finish the assignment by reading the entire book of Jonah?" Jen asked.

"Yep, all four chapters, which I found quite interesting. I can't wait to delve into it further with the group tonight. How about you? Did you find time to read all the chapters?"

Jen looked down sheepishly and took a bite of her baguette.

"Actually, I've only read two chapters. But I'm leaving work at 4 PM so I'm going to rush home and try and finish off the other chapters."

Matt smiled at her.

"Miss Busy Bee always has a busy schedule. You need to slow down and prioritise your schedule."

"Tell me about it! Anyway, are you picking me up tonight?"

"Of course. You know, I'm always happy to assist. Hey, changing the subject. Can I ask you something? And if I'm being too intrusive, then let me know."

"Yeah, what is it?"

"Is everything okay with Olivia?" Jen tried to rack her brain to see if she noticed anything out of the ordinary.

"Well, she has been a little quiet, but I put that down to her having a lot on at school, plus she is planning a wedding. Why do you ask?"

"It's just the impression that I got from Steve recently. He hasn't been able to speak to her for a few days now and every time he calls her, it's almost as if she is fobbing him off. He even asked me if you had noticed anything strange regarding her behaviour and I told him that I would ask you."

"Well, if anything is on her mind, she hasn't shared it with me. Olivia is quite a private person and doesn't readily share information that she keeps close to her heart. If anyone would know if anything was going on, it would be Carol. Perhaps Steve could tap Michael's brain to see if Carol divulges anything."

"That's true, perhaps I will do that as he seems quite low, and he is in a good place at the moment in terms of his recovery. I don't want anything to jeopardise that."

"I'm sure it's nothing. As I said, Olivia probably has a ton of books to mark and is concentrating on that, unbeknownst perhaps that she is shutting Steve out."

"Thanks for your perspective on the matter as I didn't want to pry by making you divulge something that you weren't at liberty to share. Anyway, sweetheart, I've got another client in about 20 minutes, and I need to drive to their house, so I'm afraid I'm going to have to cut our time short."

"Not to worry, I've enjoyed our brief time together and look forward to seeing you tonight, so have a great rest of the day."

Matt cleared the table and emptied the rubbish in the bin. He kissed Jen on her forehead and they both walked out the restaurant to their appropriate appointments.

Jen had finished her afternoon roster and arrived home. Olivia was already home and was in the kitchen, making dinner. Jen followed the aroma to the kitchen.

"Hmm, that smells like salmon."

"Hey Jen, your nose is on point." Olivia smiled as she continued hovering over the cooker.

"Just going to do some stir-fry noodles and vegetables with it. You fancy some?"

"Okay, that would be great as Matt, and I have a Bible study tonight and he'll be picking me up later."

"Wowww. Things between the two of you are getting serious. You seem to be seeing each other quite a lot now."

"Well, I guess I should let you know that we are now more than friends. We are dating."

Olivia dropped what she was doing and put her hands on her hips with a smirk on her face.

"Didn't Carol and I tell you that we called it long time ago? We told you that we had a radar for these kinds of things."

Jen laughed as she remembered that day when Olivia and Carol were trying to force her and Matt together when they hardly knew each other.

"Ahhh. Young love. I'm very happy for you, Jen. You deserve to have a good man and by all accounts I would say that Matt is a great guy, so you hold onto him."

"Thanks, Olivia. So, what about you? How are the wedding plans going?"

Jen did not want to come outright and question Olivia as to where things were with her and Steve and decided to tease it out of her instead.

"Umm, most things have been sorted. I've just had a few things on my mind which I need to sort out, but I'll get there."

Olivia's demeanour changed somewhat from the cheerful person she was when Jen first walked into the kitchen.

"Anything I can help with?" Jen said with genuine concern in her voice.

"I'm good, Jen. Thanks for your concern, but this is something that only God can intervene and fix, so I'm going to leave it at His door and wait for His resolution."

"Sounds serious, Olivia. Has it anything to do with Steve? I only ask, as today Matt asked me if you were going through anything. He said he got the impression from Steve recently that perhaps you were avoiding him."

Olivia rolled her eyes and sighed.

"Ohhh boy. Yes, it does have to do with Steve, but I haven't really discussed it with him yet. I will do, but I need to properly process it in my mind first. Just pray for us, Jen, as that's all I can say at this moment in time."

"I hear you and yes, I will pray for you both. If anyone can put things back together between the two of you, God can."

"Thanks hon; I appreciate that."

Jen ran upstairs to take a shower and spent the rest of the time in her room, catching up on her reading for the night's Bible study. After she caught up on the last two chapters, she went downstairs and ate some of the food that Olivia had prepared. Shortly thereafter, Matt arrived to pick her up and she left.

CHAPTER SIXTEEN

Michael found himself at a loose end. Carol had been in hospital for a week now and the doctors and her team were pleased with the progress she had been making since being admitted. Her blood pressure had stabilised and the twin that was the smallest had increased in size, albeit still not as big as its sibling. Michael had been working late at the surgery dealing with finalising all the finer points of the closure of the surgery and the impending merger with Belmont, which meant that he wasn't eating properly and instead living off takeaways. For a change of scenery, Michael had arranged to meet up with Steve for dinner to catch up with him and to see what was going on in his life. They had agreed to meet up after work at a local Italian restaurant, which was a favourite of theirs and one they use to frequent often when Michael was a bachelor, and his time was his own to navigate it how he desired.

Michael was early and had arrived at the restaurant first. He was shown to a table in the main part of the restaurant, with it having two separate dining areas. As he sat there waiting for Steve to arrive, his mind drifted back to when he and Steve used to eat there in their younger days. In those days they did not have a care in the world. None of them was in a serious relationship and instead enjoyed cultivating friendships with the females in their church. They were both quite similar in their views in that they did not want to string women along if they could not see a long-term future with them. Michael always knew that he wanted children to factor into his future so that was the number one quality he was looking for. Steve was more laid back and wanted to feel that real deep connection with someone and was not going to settle until he felt that gut reaction in his stomach that told him the specific person he was potentially pursuing was God's best for him.

Steve arrived at the restaurant at the agreed time. As he was putting his coat and scarf on the coat rack in the reception vicinity, he could see Michael waving and beckoning him over to where he was situated. The restaurant was heaving with hungry customers and Steve found himself navigating his way through the tables, which were snugly positioned, until he eventually got to where Michael was sitting.

"Hey buddy; it's been a while that we've been out like this." Michael got up and man-hugged Steve.

"Yep, it has, but I was glad when you called as I could do with a good catch up and some decent food too."

They both made themselves comfortable, ordered some food, and shortly after the waiter brought their drinks to the table as they waited for their starters to follow.

"How is Carol?"

Steve was aware that Carol was in hospital, as Olivia had told him in a previous conversation.

"She's doing great. It was the best decision for her to be admitted, not only for the sake of the babies, but also for Carol's well-being."

Michael appeared chilled as he spoke passionately about Carol. Steve noted a glint in Michael's eye and knew his friend was in a good place once again.

"Hey man. It's great to see you and Carol doing so well. You've had a bad patch but somehow have managed to get back on track."

"I know. Can you believe it? God is good. That's all I can say. I'm glad that we both put our pride aside and agreed to do counselling with PT." Steve found himself immersed into the conversation by listening carefully to what Michael was sharing, dissecting his every word.

"So, do you feel that was the catalyst and the turning point to restoring your marriage?"

Michael looked intently at Steve and confidently said, "Absolutely and I would recommend anyone having problems in their relationship to give it a go. God can do the impossible. I'm a living testimony of that."

In mid-flow at the core of their conversation, they were interrupted by the waiter bringing their entrees to the table, a selection of the restaurant's appetizers: carbonara arancini, bruschetta with pickled okra and potato focaccia rolls.

"Wowww, this looks good. I didn't realise how many things we had ordered. Hope we'll have room for the mains when it comes."

Michael was salivating. The thought of eating something that was freshly cooked tantalised his taste buds, in comparison to the TV dinners he had recently been consuming.

Steve had a heavy burden on his heart that he needed to offload and was keen to pick up the conversation from where they left off before being interrupted. He allowed himself to do something that was often hard for men and that was to be vulnerable. Michael was his best friend, so he felt that he was in a safe space to talk directly.

"So going back to our conversation, I think something is going on with Liv and I, but I'm not quite sure what it is."

"What do you mean?" Michael asked sounding concern.

"So, I feel that Liv may be avoiding me and not taking my calls. I've not had a good conversation with her since she told me briefly about Carol, and we usually speak every day."

Michael put his cutlery down and looked straight into Steve's face.

"Mate, are you seriously telling me that you don't know why?"

There was a look on Michael's face that Steve could not decipher. It was as if Michael knew something that he didn't.

"No, I don't, and why are you staring at me like that."

Steve felt nervy but braced himself for what potentially was hiding behind that blank stare, which was piercing, causing his heart to beat fast in anticipation.

"Steve, you know I respect you. And you're my best friend, but I think what you did to Olivia, I've got to admit, man, wasn't your finest hour."

Now it was Steve's turn to put down his cutlery and respond with a blank stare, as his mind galloped into overdrive. The tone in his voice rose to a higher decibel.

"Michael, what are you talking about? I honestly don't know where this is going. Did Liv share with you something that I am supposed to have done to her?"

Michael felt he needed to enlighten Steve, since he was oblivious to what was going on. "Steve, it was the prenup you had your mother give to her. She confided in Carol, who shared it with me as she was quite upset with the way Olivia was feeling."

Steve almost choked on the food that he had previously put in his mouth.

"What! My mother did what?"

"Well, whether you know about it or not, when your mother met up with Olivia, at the end of their lunch, she conveniently handed her a prenup and told her to read it when she got home. Your mother gave Olivia the impression that you were in full knowledge about what she was doing. When Carol first told me about it, I did say to her that it didn't sound like your normal form, but Carol said Olivia was convinced that some of the personal information in the document must have been sourced from you."

Steve couldn't believe what he was hearing.

"Michael, you should know me by now. I would never be that callous or insensitive, especially to Liv.

My parents did suggest I get Liv to sign a prenup, but I was adamant that I wouldn't do that. And I told them in no uncertain terms that I was prepared to walk away from my trust fund, if that was what was required.

I cannot believe this. No wonder I couldn't get hold of my mother either, prior to her leaving for her trip. It's obvious that she too was trying to avoid me. I'm so livid, my hand is literally shaking."

Steve was visibly shaken, and his head was spinning with various scenarios.

"I wonder if my father was in on this also or if this was just my mother's doing? Or more like her meddling. I can totally understand why Liv would be upset and blindsided by this, as we've never discussed anything like this with each other."

Steve put his hands over his face and kept shaking his head from side to side. The blood rushed from his face revealing a slightly pale and somewhat discoloured complexion.

Michael wanted to probe further regarding what exactly Steve had shared with Olivia about his family and his inheritance.

"So, can I ask you a question, Steve? Have you told Olivia about your family's wealth?"

Steve took his hands from his face, so that Michael could see his facial expression. He looked dishevelled, as he shook his head from side to side.

"Nope. I didn't get the opportunity to discuss that part of my life, as my accident occurred right in the middle of our premarital sessions."

"And you haven't found the time to tell her yet?" Michael's demeanour was startling.

"Have you learnt nothing from what I went through with Carol, Steve? The number one rule when it comes to the opposite sex is that you leave nothing out. You share everything. No matter how hard it is. And then you allow the other person to make up their mind with the information they are given to process.

I know I'm not supposed to bring it up again, as I've totally forgiven her now, but it was Carol holding back significant information that led to the devastating issues we had. And you know how toxic and quickly our relationship went downhill, because you were there to pick up the pieces when I fell apart."

"I hear you, Michael, and it was always my intention to talk with Liv about my background. I know it's not an excuse, but following the accident, I went through a low point and at the beginning couldn't really talk to Liv like I should have. I was feeling frustrated and discouraged with my injuries and almost pushed her away. I wish I had told her now as she's only going to think that I didn't trust her enough to handle my personal story."

"Well, if I were you, I wouldn't waste any more time. You better get around there and visit her quickly, so that you can get this misunderstanding sorted out."

Michael continued to share some of the insightful tips that he had learnt in his counselling sessions with PT. He advised Steve to be repentant, to come clean, and to put his hands up and admit his shortcomings to Olivia, which wasn't intentional on his part. Michael knew exactly what Steve was going through, albeit it was not as intense as what he had encountered.

Steve appreciated all that Michael had to share, but his mind was playing the video tape over and over again of the deception his mother had exhibited and the audacity she had in drawing him into her lie under false pretences.

Steve's appetite had vanished, and he asked Michael if he didn't mind them wrapping up the evening as his concentration was all over the place and he couldn't guarantee that he would be good company any longer.

His intention was to act promptly on Michael's advice by going over to Olivia's house to have the conversation that he should have had with her long ago. He did not think it prudent to call her, since she wasn't answering his calls anyway. This was a conversation to have face to face and not over the telephone, where sentiments could be lost in translation. And he had already been guilty of that. Also, facial impressions could not easily be perceived through the airwaves, and he really needed Olivia to see how truly sorry he was for what his mother had put her through. He would also need to divulge with her things he should have shared with her at the beginning of their courtship.

Michael appreciated that Steve was fairly shook up with the information he had shared with him and quickly prayed with him quietly at the table before Steve departed. He told him not to worry about the bill, and to just go, as he would settle things. Steve's departure was swift like he had a bee in his bonnet.

Steve got to his car and just sat there for a while before driving off.

'Why would my mother do something like this? And who did she use to draw up this false document?'

Then almost as if a bolt of lightning dropped from the sky, the name 'Charlotte Bramwell' came into his spirit.

'Surely not. Charlotte would never do something like that behind my back.'

However, Steve couldn't shake from his mind that perhaps Charlotte was somehow involved, and he felt in his spirit that he should give her a call, if only to satisfy his curiosity. Steve took his phone out and called Charlotte. As he sat in his car, he opened the window slightly, as the inside had started to steam up with the condensation that was building up. He was also feeling quite warm and loosened the top button of his shirt.

"Hello, stranger." Charlotte was pleasantly surprised when she saw Steve's name illuminate on her phone.

"And what do I owe the pleasure of this call?"

Steve did not seem his usual confident self and Charlotte suspected something might be wrong since he wasn't saying much.

"Steve, you're starting to scare me. Is it your parents? Are they okay? Something hasn't happened to them, has it?"

Charlotte was jumping ahead of herself and suspecting the worse. She was aware that Steve's parents had gone away since Mrs Adams had mentioned it to her when they last met and wondered if Steve's call was to tell her that something bad had happened to them. Steve eventually put Charlotte's mind at rest.

"Charlotte. Nothing has happened to my parents. As far as I know, they are safely enjoying themselves halfway across the world."

"Then what is it, Steve, because your voice sounds like you have something on your mind?"

Steve cleared his throat and spoke directly.

"Charlotte, I'm just going to come out straight and ask. Did my mother ask you to prepare a prenup for my fiancée, Olivia behind my back?"

He paused and waited for Charlotte to rebuke him and declare that there was no way she could have done anything like that. However, to his dismay he was about to be shocked to his core.

"Yes. I did." Charlotte paused before continuing.

"Your mother had approached me with regards to drawing the document up. At first, I was taken back as I had informed her that I should be having this conversation with you. However, she informed me you had asked that I should start the ball rolling, as you were busy working on your recovery and the planning of your wedding."

Charlotte couldn't see Steve's expression, but his eyes were rolling, and his breathing was heavy and laboured.

"And you didn't think to contact me to check my side of things?"

"It did cross my mind, but your mother was so persuasive. You know what she's like. I wasn't to know that she was being disingenuous. I prepared the document and told her that it couldn't be finalised until you had approved it. She was to pass the document onto you for you to approve that everything was in order and that you were comfortable with the wording."

There was another pause on the line.

"So, am I right in thinking that the document isn't even legal for that matter?"

"Yep, that's about the size of it. In my position as a lawyer, even though I drew up the document without your input, that was just as a favour because of the relationship I have with you and your family. However, the ratifying of it, must come from you, and your mother was supposed to give you the document to look over, approve it and then send back to me."

Steve let out a nervous laugh.

"Ha! Ha! Like that was ever going to happen. Well, my dear mother betrayed me by giving the document directly to Olivia. And now she is mad with me as she thinks I had something to do with it. She probably thought I was a big coward using my mother like that, and now everything is one big mess."

"Oh Steve, I am so sorry. I had no idea that your mother would do something like that. I can imagine how Olivia must be feeling and I'm sorry that I had any part in causing such pain to you both.

I regret now that I did not stick to my professional guns and put my foot down when your mother first approached me. Therefore, I am partly to blame also."

Charlotte seemed genuinely remorseful for Steve's predicament.

"Look, Charlotte, don't blame yourself. As you said, we both know what my mother is like. She's been trying to get us together for years and I think my engagement to another woman has really thrown her."

"It has, hasn't it?"

Charlotte recalled in her mind when she and Steve were both students and when he first introduced her to his parents. They were besides themselves. Well Mrs Adams was, especially when they knew that she was a Bramwell.

The Bramwell dynasty were a well-respected brand, and Mrs Adams was keen to meet her parents, which is how they all became such good friends over the years. Charlotte could look back now and laugh at the countless times Mrs Adams tried her best to get the two of them together, but Steve always knew the kind of woman he wanted, as young as he was, and over time, Charlotte learnt that it wasn't her.

Steve saw her as one of his best and dearest friends and in time, Charlotte reciprocated those feelings and saw him as that too.

"Listen Steve, please don't worry as I will destroy the document. I know you are probably going to have to work harder than that to gain Olivia's trust again, but you always know the right thing to say, and I know everything is going to be just fine."

Steve mellowed slightly now that things were out in the open and Charlotte had fully explained the situation and how events unfolded.

"I like your optimism, Charlotte, but I don't think it's going to be that simple. She hasn't been talking to me for the best part of a week, and it was only tonight when I had dinner with Michael that I found out the real reason why. Anyway, this is my mess to sort out, but thanks for being honest with me and letting me have your perspective of the situation. Well, I better go now as I have somewhere to be. Wish me luck, eh? I shouldn't really say that, as I don't really believe in luck, but I know you do and that is something you would have said."

After such an intense conversation, there was a glimmer of hope in Steve's tone, and he started to mentally prepare himself for the next conversation he was on his way to have. Steve and Charlotte said goodbye, and ended their discussion on common ground.

The drive to Olivia's house was a strenuous one. A myriad of scenarios of how the conversation might pan out was galloping through Steve's thoughts. They had never had a heated argument before and had always got on by respecting each other's opinions. He was truly embarrassed and sorry for what his mother had done to Olivia, and it was his intention to go in there, put his cards on the table and be totally honest with her about everything.

Steve walked up the path to Olivia's house. Every step felt pronounced like he was delicately walking on eggshells. After ringing the doorbell, Jen answered attired in her PJs and comfy oversized fluffy slippers. Her appearance startled Steve, as he had been expecting Olivia to answer the door, which dented his confidence somewhat as he was all prepared with his rehearsed opening speech to spurt out on the doorstep. Jen seemed just as surprised, as a previous conversation with Olivia earlier in the week gave her the impression that she was not ready to talk to Steve until she had sorted out her feelings. Even though Olivia did not divulge what was bothering her, Jen suspected that it must be something serious for Olivia to not want to talk to him until she cleared her head.

"Hi Steve. I didn't know you were coming around. Olivia didn't say."

"Hi Jen. How are you doing?"

"I'm doing good. Had a busy day so I'm just vegging out in front of the TV watching a mindless reality show. Ssshhh. Don't disclose my secret to anyone," Jen teased.

Steve didn't forget the question that Jen had asked him and responded after the introductions were out of the way.

"No, Jen. Olivia doesn't know I was visiting. I was in the neighbourhood and just wanted to pop in and have a quick chat. Is she in?"

"Yes, she is."

Jen almost forgot she had kept Steve standing on the doorstep.

"My goodness. Excuse my manners, Steve. Please, come in."

The house felt warm and cosy like it always did when Steve had visited on previous occasions. Olivia had great taste, and the décor reflected her personality and flare.

After Carol got married and left the house that the two shared, Olivia wanted to redecorate the entire house. It was her therapeutic way of dealing with the gaping hole in her heart that not having Carol around would leave.

Jen shouted up the stairs, "Olivia. You have a visitor."

Steve stayed in the hall and waited for Olivia to come down the stairs.

Olivia came out of her room and shouted down to Jen,

"A visitor? Who on earth is it?"

As Olivia ran down the stairs, her facial expression changed when she clasped eyes on Steve.

"Oh. Steve. Hi."

Olivia seemed puzzled and surprised that he was just standing there and hadn't called to say that he was coming around.

"I wasn't expecting you."

"Yeah, I'm sorry. I was in the area and as we hadn't talked much throughout the week, there were some things that I wanted to discuss with you that I felt needed to be done in person."

Jen came out of the lounge.

"Olivia, I can go to my room, so please, the two of you use the lounge."

Jen was sensitive in reading the situation and acted quickly, since she was aware that Olivia was not in the habit of entertaining Steve in her bedroom and he had never really had the need to venture upstairs, since there was a downstairs toilet that he could make use of.

"Thanks Jen. I appreciate that."

Steve followed Olivia into the lounge and tried to make himself comfortable, whilst Olivia went straight over to the television and turned it off. The anxious feeling that Steve had on the drive down resurfaced, and his heart was palpitating fast.

Olivia sat opposite and waited for Steve to say what was on his mind.

"Firstly, I wanted to say that I have only just heard about my mother's actions, which is downright despicable. I had no idea that she was going to do something like that, nor did I give her permission to do so. And I apologise that you were put through such an ordeal."

"So, I'm curious. How did you find out?"

Olivia was inquisitive as to whether Mrs Adams had gloated to him that she had done the deed and was she now the brunt of their private joke.

"I've just had dinner with Michael. I casually told him that I hadn't spoken to you much this week and thought I might have offended you in some way, as you seem to have been avoiding my calls or putting off talking to me. He started to make accusations at the way I had treated you and what I did in allowing my mother to present a prenup to you in the first place. Which was the first I had heard about the situation. Why didn't you tell me about it when it happened, Liv?"

Olivia rolled her eyes in disbelief that Steve would be questioning her over why she found it hard to approach him about the situation, especially as she thought he was privy to it and was in cahoots with his mother.

"I guess what I'm struggling to understand is why your mother felt the need to present me with a prenup. It made me look like some kind of gold digger, but what does it all mean?"

The time had finally come for Steve to come clean about his background.

"I think I need to explain something to you, which I haven't had an opportunity to discuss with you yet."

Steve shifted nervously in his seat and painstakingly took the time to explain to Olivia about his background and the privilege that he grew up in. The preparatory school he went to. The family trips when he was young that took him all over the world and finally the trust fund he was bequeathed and the percentage he inherited within the family business. The estate he grew up on and the servants they had. He left nothing out.

"I know I should have told you all this before, but my accident happened which scuffled our premarital sessions and I did not get the opportunity to share that side of my life with you."

"Ahhh. Now things make sense,"

Olivia said, nodding her head as if the penny had finally dropped. Her eyes glared as she continued to process all that Steve had divulged. There it was. His mother was disappointed that her son wasn't marrying someone of their calibre and therefore, she was labelled as the one who was marrying her son to get a hold of their hard-earned cash. The fact that Steve was only now divulging significant information about his background worried Olivia as to what else he might be keeping back from her.

"Again, I can only apologise for the way you felt blindsided by what happened, which could have been avoided. I will be speaking with my mother when she gets back."

Steve was trying to communicate to Olivia how genuinely repentant he was. However, that was only the start of things slowly spiralling.

"Steve, the fact that you kept something as important as this back from me only makes me wonder what else you are not telling me. Perhaps we should meet up with PT, because right now, I'm not feeling great."

Steve sat apprehensively wondering what else he could to do to remedy things. The expression on Olivia's face wasn't one he had seen before, and he could see how hurt she was, her heart rocked to the core.

"I've made plans to visit my parents this weekend, as I need to be with my family at this moment, so we will have to continue this conversation when I get back. Perhaps the space between us will give you the opportunity to decide what else I need to know about you and your dynasty family," Olivia said flippantly.

"Yeah, I fully appreciate your decision, and I promise you that there aren't any more skeletons in the cupboard."

"We'll see."

Olivia rose to her feet, which was her way of communicating that the conversation was ended and it was time for Steve to leave. Steve rose to his feet and reassured Olivia that he was going to prove to her that she could trust him.

Steve left Olivia's house with a heavy heart. He didn't know if Olivia would come back from her parents with a changed posture or not. He could only pray that they would be able to salvage and repair their relationship for the better.

CHAPTER SEVENTEEN

Bricket Wood continued with the closing stages of the surgery with the impending merger of all their systems and records being transferred over. Chris discovered, albeit last minute, that he was nominated, out of the three doctors, to go away on a course for two days. There were specific qualifications essential for the doctors at Bricket Wood to have in place as part of the merger and Michael and Joan were preoccupied dealing with key matters that required urgent attention before their closure.

Since Chris wasn't given much notice that he was expected to attend the course, he was left with no other alternative than to contact his in-laws to see if they could look after Ben whilst he was away. With Natalia being new to the role, he did not feel it appropriate to leave her to look after Ben for two days. Thankfully, it turned out that he didn't have anything to be nervous about by calling his in-laws, as Mrs Hunter was only too pleased for the opportunity to have Ben stay over.

Albeit she failed to inform Chris, an important piece of information. On one of the days in question, she and Mr Hunter were going to be away for part of the day. Mrs Hunter did not think it would cause too much of a problem as she would ask Tilly to come over and look after Ben until they got back. Tilly had been at the house a few times when Ben had visited for weekends and she had taken him out on a few occasions, so Ben had got used to spending time with Tilly.

Ben had never mentioned to Chris that he had spent days out with Tilly, since he would not have been aware that his dad wouldn't have approved. At a young age, he was innocent and oblivious to any family drama that ensued. And, like any inquisitive kid, he enjoyed the outings he had with his aunt Tilly, as she allowed him to eat loads of junk food, like chocolate and ice-cream, unlike his grandmother, who was very careful that he ate balanced meals when he stayed at their house. Tilly had convinced Ben that it was their little secret and that she wouldn't tell if he didn't. Ben found it funny and enjoyed keeping the secret, which is why he probably didn't think to tell Chris about his expeditions with Tilly either, it all being part of the little game they played. And neither did Mr & Mrs Hunter feel uncomfortable with their daughter taking out her only nephew. In fact, they felt it was therapeutic for Tilly in helping her to bond with her late twin's son, which was like having a piece of Jill still around.

Chris made the trip to his in-laws the day before his conference. The drive was getting familiar to Ben and at certain landmarks, like the Drive Thru McDonalds they had stopped at before to get him a Happy Meal, prompted Ben that he didn't have far to go.

"You're awfully quiet back there, buddy. Are you okay?"

When Chris did not get a response to his question, he checked his rear-view mirror and Ben's head was flopped to one side. He was fast asleep that his tablet had fallen out of his hands onto the seat beside him. Chris felt a tinge of guilt as it was way pass Ben's bedtime and he should really have been tucked up safely in bed. Instead, he was being traipsed around the country being passed from pillar to post and once again not being his father's priority. Chris immediately recalled a promise he had made to Jill that when they had a family he would slow down and give more time for his family.

Jill was always trying to get Chris to put his priorities in order, but there were many evenings in their marriage where she had to eat dinner alone, as Chris couldn't quite pull himself away from work. Or in the early days, working on groundbreaking research work which he hoped would give him recognition and put him on the map.

Even after Ben was born, he tried extremely hard to fulfil his promise, but as soon as his paternity leave had ended, he reverted to his old ways and missed those crucial early bonding years with his son.

'You're struggling to cope, aren't you, Chris? I know I'm not around and you are left to parent alone and I'm sorry I left you so early.'

Jill's voice startled Chris.

He blinked his eyes a few times as he thought he was hearing voices. He took a quick glimpse to his side and there was Jill, right next to him in the passenger seat. Chris' voice was shaky.

"Is that really you, Jill?"

He carried on driving, trying to keep his gaze straight and his hands steady on the steering wheel. Chris wondered if he was having an out of body experience, or whether Jill's spirit was present.

'Yes, it's me. I'm in a central part of your memory that never goes away. But don't be alarmed. I'm just here to help you remember the things that you had promised to do. You agreed that you would slow down and always put your family first. Are you truly doing that, Chris? Look at poor Ben shattered back there, when he should be tucked up comfortably in his bed.'

Chris decided that since Jill was present in the car, and he didn't even know how that was at all possible, then he was going to engage in conversation with her.

'I'm sorry, Jill. It has been hard, and I have been trying to juggle being a good father, as well as a provider.'

Chris was nearing his in-laws' property. Still dazed whether the pizza he ate before he left was influencing his mental agility, Chris turned to ask Jill another question. He really wanted to pick her brain as to what other things she thought he needed to work on. However, the space was empty. His glimpse of Jill had evaporated, and, in its place, he was just left with the sound of Ben snoozing heavily in the back seat.

'Did I just imagine that whole conversation? It felt so real.'

Chris felt embarrassed that his overactive imagination had got the better of him. He was tired and had a lot on his mind, so the thought of an ongoing conversation with his deceased wife was comforting. Perhaps the fact that he was driving to Jill's parents' house brought to the surface memories of when he and Jill used to drive to the house on numerous occasions.

Whatever it was, he needed to get himself off the road and have a black coffee to keep him alert for the drive back. Chris pulled into the grounds and within minutes was parking up at the house. Mr Hunter met him at the car and assisted him by carrying Ben into the house, whilst Chris got his bags and his tablet. After he entered the house, Mrs Hunter asked him if he wanted something to drink, whilst Mr Hunter took Ben straight to his room.

The Hunters had decorated one of the rooms in their eight-bedroom mansion especially for Ben which was the smallest of their huge sized rooms, complete with an en-suite. It was decked out with a variety of toys for him to enjoy whenever he visited his grandparents, and he was spoilt for choice, having the best of both worlds.

Chris had an early start the following morning, so he didn't want to stay too late and wanted to get a good head start for the journey. However, he responded favourably to Mrs Hunter's offer of a drink.

"Thanks Felicity, a black coffee would be great. My mind seems to be playing tricks on me, so it would be good to have a clear mindset for the drive back home. Now are you sure I am not inconveniencing you and Frank?"

Chris was mindful that he did not give them much notice but was grateful that he had made his peace with them and that Ben had his grandparents back in his life.

Again, Mrs Hunter kept her schedule concealed and did not tell Chris about their plans to be away for some of the time Ben would be with them.

"Oh, don't be silly. This is our grandson you are talking about, and any opportunity we get to spend with him, we are going to grab with both hands." She smiled at Chris.

"Now let me get you that coffee so that you can be on your way."

Mrs Hunter came back with a mug of coffee for Chris. She was mindful that he wouldn't have wanted it in one for her porcelain cup & saucer set that she would normally serve drinks in and that he would probably gulp it down as quick as he could anyway, as he seemed fidgety as if he wanted to depart hastily. Chris took the mug from Mrs Hunter and immediately started to drink, despite it being quite hot.

"So, my course is for two days, Thursday and Friday, so I can come and pick up Ben on Saturday, if that's okay?"

Chapter Seventeen

Mrs Hunter seemed puzzled as she thought that they would have Ben for longer.

"Why don't you let Ben stay until Sunday and we can spend a bit more time with him?"

She put forward a convincing proposal to Chris in that it would give him a bit more time so that he didn't have to rush straight after the conference.

But Chris was mindful of the superficial conversation he had had with Jill in the car on the journey down and wanted to spend quality time with Ben.

"Actually, I wanted to spend Sunday with Ben before he goes back to school, which would be the only time we have been able to spend with each other this weekend. Perhaps another time."

Chris had almost finished his coffee, but his tongue was tingling from the heat. He wondered if he had scalded it and if he did, it would have been his own fault for not taking his time and always being in a rush. He swung back his head and put the last drop to his mouth.

"Right, that's me finished. Let me just quickly go and check on Ben and then I'll be off."

He was familiar with the house and went straight to the bedroom that was reserved for Ben.

He quietly opened the door and found that Mr Hunter had already undressed Ben, put him in his pyjamas and tucked him up in bed. He left the lamp at the side of the bed on until they were ready to retire for the night, when they would turn it off. As Chris observed Ben, he looked so comfortable and peaceful and he wanted to do right by him in ensuring that he would make a better effort to ensure that Ben was his priority, even if that meant saying no to work commitments that always vied for his attention. Chris closed the door behind him and walked down the stairs. He thanked his in-laws for helping him out and reminded them that he would be back on Saturday afternoon to pick Ben up. They waved him off and Chris started the journey back home.

Chris woke up half-tired after the drive back home from his in-laws the previous night, but there was nothing he could do about it, since he had to get ready to drive another two hours distance to his course. In all the mayhem in learning he was nominated for the course and trying to sort out childcare for Ben, it didn't even dawn on Chris that he hadn't called the school to try and explain why Ben wouldn't be in attendance for the next two days. The thought of having to justify to Olivia why Ben could not attend school just because he had a work commitment terrified him.

His mind became scrambled imagining all the thoughts that would go through her head of him not being a fit father and jeopardising his son's growth for selfish gain. But nevertheless, whatever he was dreading, the call still had to be made. Chris called the school and got through to the receptionist. He explained that Ben had come down with something and that he was keeping him off school for a couple of days so that he did not pass it on to any of the other children and would hopefully be back on Monday. As he put the phone down, his conscious got the better of him, which he justified away by asserting it was just a 'white lie' and that he had no other alternative. Olivia and the other staff would be none the wiser and, therefore, no harm was done. Chris gathered his things, got into his car and made his way to the course.

"Come on, sleepy head, it's time for you to rise."

Mrs Hunter walked over to the window in Ben's room and opened the curtains, revealing that a bright and sunny day was imminent. She smiled as she watched Ben fidget with the duvet covers that he was so comfortably nestled under.

"Is it time for school already?" he said, tossing and turning refusing to surface.

"No, Ben. Don't you remember that your father brought you down to stay with us last night? You're at your grandma and grandpa's for a couple of days and we have lots of exciting thing to do with you. Now come on, let me help you up and we will go to the bathroom. Grandpa is downstairs making your breakfast. Would you like rice krispies or a boiled egg with soldiers?"

"I'll have a boiled egg with soldiers, please,"

Ben said in a groggy manner as he literally fell out of bed. Mrs Hunter had grown accustomed to the types of food that Ben enjoyed, and it was always her aim to spoil him when he came to visit. Mrs Hunter helped Ben up and putting her hands on his shoulders, guided him in the direction of the bathroom. She shouted down to Mr Hunter to put on a couple of eggs for Ben so that his breakfast would be ready after he had washed and got dressed for the day.

The plan was that they would have a full two days with Ben, but on the Saturday morning they had a breakfast at their local rotary club, which was booked months in advance, and wasn't something the Hunters could get out of since they were the ones hosting the event. Mrs Hunter did not want to miss the opportunity of spending time with Ben all for the sake of half a day, which is why she agreed that Ben could stay with them whilst Chris was away.

After Ben was washed and dressed, he came alive and was his usual bouncy self. Armed with his iPad underneath his arm, he accompanied his grandma downstairs to the dining room and sat on one of the chairs at their large dining table. Mr Hunter could see how Ben was struggling to reach the table and smiled.

"Here Ben, let me get you a cushion so that you can be the right height at the table." Whilst Mr Hunter went to get him a cushion, Ben turned on his iPad and started to play a game. The noise of the game he was playing reverberated loudly in such a large space. Mrs Hunter came in with two boiled eggs and a plate of toast cut in strips for Ben to dunk and placed them on the table in front of Ben.

"Oh no, no, little man. There will be no playing on that device whilst we are having breakfast."

She was firm with her delivery, but not in a way to frighten Ben that he felt scared of her. It was something she was trying to get Ben out of the habit in doing, since she had to ask him the same thing on previous occasions. Ben tried to be cheeky, but it wasn't going to work with a feisty grandma like Mrs Hunter.

"But my dad always lets me use my device at home when we are having breakfast."

Ben seemed reluctant to give in, but Mrs Hunter wasn't taking no for an answer.

"Ben, I suspect your father usually has a hundred and one things to do in the morning and isn't always able to watch what you are doing. Anyway, it's a good discipline to just sit, talk and enjoy breakfast, without all that distraction."

"Okayyyyy, Grandma,"

Ben said as he half-heartedly put down the tablet and instead turned his attention to the strips of toast which he started to dunk in his soft-boiled eggs. Mr Hunter slid the cushion under Ben to give him some height at the table to enjoy his breakfast.

After breakfast, the Hunters had a whole day planned for Ben which was sure to keep him occupied with not a moment for him to complain that he was bored. They started off doing a children's puzzle together. After clearing the breakfast dishes from off the table, they scattered the pieces out on the table and got to work. Ben was excited, especially as he had sharper eyes and could find the pieces a lot quicker and keenly slotted the pieces in the correct places, although he wasn't aware that his grandparents were allowing him to think that he was a lot cleverer than them. The picture on the front of the box detailed a scene from space with colourful stars and planets, something that Ben was fascinated by.

Whenever Olivia taught on the subject at school, he always sat up keenly and absorbed everything she had to share. At one point, Chris was convinced that Ben wanted to be an astronaut when he grew up, but he soon fizzled out of that phase when another subject that he liked came up.

"Ben, you're very good at this, aren't you?"

Mr Hunter was impressed by the way that Ben could look at the box only once and yet seemed to work out quickly where all the pieces slotted together. Ben looked up into his grandpa's wrinkly face, smiled and then went back to the job in hand. Mrs Hunter excused herself from helping with the puzzle to prepare Ben's bag. After they finished the puzzle, they had planned to take Ben to the park, followed by a spot of lunch.

When the puzzle was finally completed, Ben had a big smile on his face.

"We did it, Grandpa, we put all the pieces in the right place," Ben said as he stretched his arms in the air proud of their accomplishment.

His grandpa had to agree.

"Yes, Ben, we did a great job together, even if your grandma didn't stay with us to finish off the job. When she comes back in, we can show her what we have done together. Anyway, I believe we are going out soon, so why don't you go and see where she is?"

Ben raced from the dining room to see where his grandma had gone. Mrs Hunter had got Ben's bag ready and had his coat in her hand.

"Ahhh, there you are, young man, here let's put your coat on." Mrs Hunter helped Ben to put his coat on.

"Where are we going, Grandma?"

Fresh off the back of his victory in getting the puzzle completed in quick succession, Ben was ready for his next adventure. He loved visiting his grandparents as he never knew what was coming next. There was always a surprise awaiting him.

"We're off to the park, Ben. I think you need to burn off some of that energy that you have accumulated, and they have a few animals there that you might enjoy seeing."

"Wowww. Yippee. I love animals."

Ben couldn't contain his excitement and ran downstairs to let his grandpa know where they were going next.

They arrived at the park, and for the next couple of hours Ben enjoyed roaming around the park, making up his own games as his grandparents watched from a parked bench where they had made themselves comfortable. When he had exhausted himself doing that, they took him to see the animals where he was able to help with the feeding of some of them.

After a spot of lunch at a fast-food outlet, which wouldn't have been Mrs Hunter's first choice and she would rather it was somewhere more wholesome, nevertheless she went along with the choice, purely because Ben had chosen it, after which they made their way home.

Over the next day and a half, the Hunters enjoyed having their grandson stay with them and continued to spoil him rotten, which Ben had no objections to. At home, it was just him, his dad and Natalia and there weren't always the one-to-one intimate connections, which he longed for and was why he often resorted to playing on his tablet and shutting everything and everyone out of his small world. When he was at his grandparents, they really took the time to treat him like he was the most important person in the world, and when Tilly came to visit, she equally treated him like he was her very own.

CHAPTER EIGHTEEN

It was Saturday morning, and the Hunters were getting ready to leave for their breakfast. Tilly was due to come over to stay with Ben and they were awaiting her arrival. Ben had already been washed and fed, so Tilly didn't have to concern herself with doing that, which Mrs Hunter made sure of. All Tilly was required to do was stay in the house with Ben until they got back in the afternoon.

The Hunters were patrons of a charity that supported sponsoring a Children's Charity in Africa and the breakfast was to thank and appreciate the sponsors who had faithfully supported the charity over the years, which was something they hosted on an annual basis. Ben had already been prepped that he was going to spend the morning with his aunt Tilly, which did not seem to faze him in the slightest. He liked spending time with Tilly, and he knew she would have something exciting for them both to do.

Just when Mrs Hunter was fussing around wondering where Tilly was, as she did not want to arrive at her function late, the front door opened, and Tilly walked in. Being the home Tilly grew up in, she still had a key to the front door, which was something she wasn't giving back in a hurry, even though she had a place of her own.

"Hey, it's me. Anyone around?"

Tilly put her things down in the hallway and carried on walking the length of the hall looking for her parents.

"Ahhh Tilly, you're here," Mrs Hunter said, all flustered.

"I thought you were going to make us late. We were looking for you at least half an hour ago."

"Sorry, Mother, I was just tying up some loose ends for work."

"I thought you said you were free this morning?" Mrs Hunter's facial expressions and rolled eyes revealed that she was a bit concerned.

"Well, technically I am, but I need to quickly pass round by a client who called me this morning urgently needing a replenish of supplies and then I will be as free as a bird."

"Ohhh, Tilly, you promised that you'd be available to stay with Ben."

"Mother, you panic too much. I'll take Ben with me. We'll be in and out of there in no time and then I'll head straight back home. Now stop worrying and go to your function with Dad. Ben and I will be fine."

"Well, you better be. I need you to be here when we get back. And none of your shenanigans either, as I know how sporadic you can be at times."

Mrs Hunter seemed agitated and started to gather her things, meticulously checking if she had everything she needed.

"Honestly, Mother, sometimes you forget that I'm a grown woman, and yet you treat me like if I'm still 12 years old. I said I have this delivery to do, and I'll be gone about 40 mins. An hour tops. And then I'll head straight back."

Tilly managed to calm Mrs Hunter's fears somewhat and after rehearsing all the things she needed Tilly to do that morning, with regards to preparing Ben's lunch, she and her husband left for their appointment.

Tilly found Ben in the lounge in front of the TV watching the Disney channel and called out to him. When Ben saw her, he had a big smile on his face and ran towards Tilly and gave her a big hug.

"Hey Ben, that's a great hug from my favourite nephew. Thank you. So, I'll be looking after you for a few hours whilst Grandpa and Grandma are at their function."

Ben did not seem surprised at all and responded in his usual cool manner.

"Yes, I know, Aunt Tilly, Grandma told me that you'd be coming to look after me. That's alright and thank you."

Tilly smiled at him as she smoothed flat a hair on top of his head that had got out of place.

"You're alright about it, are you? Well, I am glad you approve."

She started tickling him until he was limbless and couldn't control himself.

"Benjy, I just need to get some work stuff out of the way and then we can have lots of fun. Would that be okay with you?"

"Okayyyyy."

"Well go and get your coat and we'll be off."

Ben ran upstairs to his bedroom and armed with his coat in one hand and his iPad in the other, he ran back downstairs ready for his trip.

"Here, Ben, let me help you with your coat."

As Tilly helped Ben put his coat on, her phone rang. She paused assisting Ben and reached in her bag to answer the phone.

"Tilly Hunter; how can I help you? Oh, hi George. Yes, I do have your order with me, and I am on my way right now. I'm literally going out of the door as we speak, so see you soon."

Tilly was running late and became flustered in trying to get Ben ready and get on her way. She placed her phone on the side table, quickly zipped up Ben's coat and they both hurriedly ran out of the door.

After a 20-minute drive, they had arrived at Tilly's first drop off. Tilly wasn't quite honest with her mother and had quite a few deliveries to make that morning. Her mother's concerns were legitimate, since Tilly was not always the most reliable person, which was a stark contrast from her twin sister, Jill. Whenever Jill gave her word to someone or to something, it was her bond and she seldom changed her mind, unless it was particularly urgent that she had no choice but to cancel her original plans.

Even though they were identical twins, there were considerable differences within their characters and the way they did things that distinguished them from each other. Neither could they get away with some of the tricks twins normally play on individuals in trying to convince others that they were the other twin, since Tilly's erratic behaviour often exposed her identity.

Tilly pulled up at her first appointment. Helping Ben out of the car, she retrieved a few boxes from the boot of the car which contained pharmaceutical samples and made her delivery. It was quick enough. Just meeting the client, them checking that everything they needed was there, signing off a form and Tilly was finished.

She continued the format for another four more deliveries with Ben as her sidekick. Tilly was happy for her clients to assume that Ben was her son and did not correct them otherwise, especially in a weird sort of way she saw him as the son she never had, which is why she fondly referred to him as Benjy, as it was her special name for him that no one else called him.

After her last delivery, Tilly noted that the time was flying by and that she wouldn't have much time to get Ben home for his lunch, and instead decided to take him out to eat, with the plan being to head back home straight after. Having found a suitable venue, Tilly purchased their food and located a free table in a corner by the window, since the place had started to get busy with the lunchtime crowd.

Ben enjoyed his burger and chips, which was obvious from the way he was guzzling his food down, whilst Tilly took her time with minute bites of her tuna salad. Tilly made light conversation with Ben.

"So, Bengy, what has Grandpa and Grandma been doing with you, eh?"

Ben chewed quickly so as not to talk with food in his mouth, which was one of the disciplines he learnt from his Grandma. After a gulp, he responded,

"Well, we've been to the park, which had animals there, which was very cool and lots of other stuff."

Ben took another bite of his burger whilst smiling at Tilly. When he finished that bite, he continued.

"Oh yeah. Me and Grandpa did a puzzle together too."

"That's nice, Bengy. What was the picture"

Ben started to get excited as he tried to explain the description of the puzzle.

"It was all about space. I really like things like that. I want to be an astronaut when I grow up."

"Do you really, Bengy? You'd make a great astronaut. I believe there is a place close by where you can view space through large telescopes and see the stars and planets, as I've driven past it before."

Ben's eyes lit up, and he started to get excited.

"Can we go there, Aunt Tilly? Please can we go there?"

"Well, I'd have to check to see if we can get tickets as I'm not sure if you can just turn up without booking. Plus, it's on the way home, so we shouldn't be that late I wouldn't think."

Tilly rummaged through her bag for her phone but couldn't find it. Then she searched both pockets and it wasn't there either. She wondered if she had left it in the car and tried to mentally retrace her steps as to when she last had it and then the ball dropped. Tilly last used her phone when she was talking to George and put it down briefly to help Ben with his coat. She had left her phone at her parents' house.

"Oh, drat Benjy, I think I left my phone at Grandpa and Grandma's house so I can't phone them to check up, I'm afraid."

"Does that mean that we won't be able to see the stars and planets today then?"

Ben expressed his disappointment as he was really looking forward to going to the place, especially as Tilly really hyped it up and excited his curiosity.

"No, don't worry, Benjy, we will just have to drive by there and see what they say."

"Yipppeee," said an enthusiastic Ben as he quickly finished up his meal.

Tilly checked her watch and even though it was well past the time she should have been back by, she convinced her conscious that she was sure her parents would understand. Especially as she was taking Ben somewhere that was educational and was a nice thing to do for him. If she had her phone on her, then she would have called them, and they would probably have agreed anyway.

With those thoughts spiralling in her mind, Tilly set off on the road to locate the planetarium. After a short distance, Tilly spotted the place and pulled into the car park. As they looked for a parking space, the building was spacious with pictures depicting planets and solar systems. Ben was beside himself and could not contain the excitement that was welling up on the inside.

"Wowww, Aunt Tilly, this is cool. I've never been to anything like this before. I can't wait to tell my friends all about it when I go back to school."

Ben's approval was the green light that Tilly needed to justify her actions. Once inside, they were able to purchase tickets. And with their map in tow, they proceeded to make their way around the various interactive galleries. Ben particularly enjoyed the one where there was a life-size aircraft, where he jumped into the seat, took the controls and imagined what life would be like as an astronaut.

Tilly enjoyed seeing the way his little face lit up every time they encountered another gallery, and for her, that was more important than having to just watch over him in a boring house with nothing fun to do. Whilst Tilly wasn't the maternal type, it was always Jill's dream to be a mother out of the two of them. However, her recent feelings towards Ben was that he could have been the son she never had. And if things had gone right for her years prior when she first met Chris, perhaps Ben would have been her very own son, and this would have been a normal day for her, spending it with her son.

As hard as Tilly tried, she spiralled into a daydream of life as Chris' wife and the life they could have had. The reality of the fact that Chris chose her twin over her did not register with her at that moment and the more she got caught up in her fantasy world of make believe, the more the time was running away.

The Hunters returned home to what appeared to be an eerily quiet sound. Whereas there would have been the normal noises of the TV or a radio playing, or laughter and chatter, there was nothing. It was dead silent. Mrs Hunter took off her coat and hung it up on the coat rack and proceeded to walk through to the lounge.

"Tilly. Ben. Where are you both?" Mr Hunter was close behind her.

"I can't hear anything," he said in a puzzled tone.

"Perhaps they are upstairs,"

Mrs Hunter concluded and ran up the stairs, checking room to room for signs of life. She ran back downstairs flustered.

"They aren't upstairs either. Where can they be as it's well past 3 PM and they should have been back hours ago? We should have known that we couldn't trust Tilly to follow simple instructions. What on earth does she think she is playing at?"

Mrs Hunter sat on the couch and tried to work out where they could be until this late hour.

"Now, now, Felicity. There's no need you getting worked up over something that might have a plausible explanation. Anything could have happened. Tilly could have broken down somewhere in the car, waiting for help. Or there could be several other reasons why her and Ben aren't back yet. Let's just be rational and give her a call and then we can see where she is."

"An accident. Ohhh dear. I hope our Ben is okay."

"No, dear. I didn't say an accident."

Mr Hunter rolled his eyes as he rang Tilly's mobile. After a few minutes, a noticeable sound of a phone ringing was coming from the direction of the hallway. And it was Tilly's ringtone. Mrs Hunter jumped up and started walking towards the hall.

"That sounds distinctively like Tilly's ringtone."

Tilly's phone was on the side table, deafening them both with the ringtone of 'I'm every woman' by Whitney Houston chiming out.

"That's Tilly's phone. That's Tilly's phone," Mrs Hunter said hysterically, flapping around.

"How are we going to communicate with her now and what if she isn't back by the time Chris gets here? He didn't say what time he was due to arrive, but I know it probably won't be too long now as he'd want to get back home swiftly with Ben at a decent hour. What are we going to do if we can't get hold of Tilly?"

Mrs Hunter was besides herself with worry. She didn't want to have to admit to Chris that they weren't actually free for all the time they were supposed to look after Ben and wondered if this little incident would dampen any future opportunities of them being able to look after Ben.

"Calm down, Felicity. I'm sure it won't come to that. Tilly is a responsible adult and I'm confident that she will be back well before Chris gets here. I still think something has happened and Tilly will be doing her best to ensure that she deals with the situation and gets herself and Ben back home safely."

Mr Hunter was the softer parent and ever so the optimist. When the girls were growing up, he was always the one to go to if there was a problem that they wanted to squirm their way out of, as he wouldn't ask many questions and took everything, they said at face value.

Mrs Hunter on the other hand could always see through the girls' antics, therefore they never attempted to try and pull the wool over her eyes.

"You've always had a soft spot for the girls, Frank, ever since they were little. They could never do any wrong in your eyes, but I don't know about this one, Frank. I believe Tilly is being her usual stubborn self, doing things on her terms and will only come home when she is good and ready. We just need to pray that they both get back before Chris gets here or else there will be all hell to pay."

There was nothing more the Hunters could do. The situation was taken out of their hands. They just had to sit tight and hope the matter would be resolved satisfactorily.

It was an intense two days of trying to cram in information regarding various medical procedures and formats and Chris thought his brain was about to explode with overload. When the last class had finished, Chris eased his tie and felt a release as if he had a chokehold around his neck and was glad, he could relax and breathe again. He was now compliant and had the necessary qualifications that the new surgery required. And he felt pleased with himself that he had more credentials on his CV so that if at any time in the future he were to leave the surgery, he could apply for better jobs which required the qualifications he had just acquired.

It was something he was giving some serious thought to. Over the months, Chris had been observing what a positive effect his in-laws were having on Ben, and although he did not like to admit it, he needed a lot more input than having a nanny around to look after his son. Ben needed the stability and his wider family around him. And Chris knew that he could rely on his in-laws to take care of Ben if ever he needed to call on them, especially at short notice. If they moved back to the area where he used to live, then they would have the best of both worlds.

The training was now over, and it was time to leave. The thought of driving back home to put his bags down and then drive the distance to his in-laws did not fill Chris with much hope or enthusiasm. Especially since he knew what would most likely happen. He would get home, feel shattered and then make the decision to collect Ben the following day. That was his norm. However, the elusive conversation in his head with Jill a few days ago kept reverberating in his thoughts. He had to make Ben his priority. Therefore, Chris decided he was going to drive straight to his in-laws to get Ben. Even though he would get there much earlier than they were probably expecting him to arrive, Chris deduced that at best it would give him the opportunity to have a 30-minute rest before they both were ready to leave.

It was final and sorted in his mind. It was the plan he would adopt, and Chris got into his car to make a start on the long journey ahead.

CHAPTER NINETEEN

The drive down was smooth and leisurely, as opposed to Chris' normal form where he would drive at speed with the aim to get to his in-laws in the quickest time possible. Chris even afforded himself the opportunity to have a 15-minute stop-off toilet/coffee break before finally completing his journey and arriving at his destination. As he pulled in, the Hunters' distinctive metallic grey Jaguar was visible, which indicated that they were at home. Feeling satisfied with himself that he was going to see Ben shortly, Chris made his way to the front door.

The sound of the bell reverberated in the house, which made Mrs Hunter run for cover, since she knew what that meant. Tilly had her own key and wouldn't have needed to ring the bell. They weren't expecting anyone else, therefore the only plausible explanation to conclude was that Chris was on the other side of the door.

"Frank. I think Chris is at the door. I can't face him right now as I don't know what I'm going to say, so you answer the door and let him in."

The look on Mrs Hunter's face told Mr Hunter that he better heed her advice, since she was adamant that she needed time to compose herself.

"Okay dear, I'll talk to him first, but following that, you must come and join us. We need to do this together," Mr Hunter said in a hushed tone and through gritted teeth.

Mr Hunter walked to the door and opened it to see Chris beaming and full of life.

Chapter Nineteen

"Ahhh, Chris. Hello. This is a surprise. Well, when I say surprise, I mean that we were expecting you sometime later."

Chris wiped his feet on the mat as he entered the house.

"I know, Frank, that was the plan. However, the course finished early, and I just thought it made sense to drive straight here. How have you been?"

"Oh, I've not been too bad. The weather has been holding out and that's always a good sign."

Chris followed Mr Hunter into the lounge where the radio was playing loudly in the background.

"So where is Ben and Mrs Hunter?"

Chris found he had to talk loudly to be heard over the classical music that was playing in the background that was responsible for creating what felt like a relaxed and homely atmosphere, when in reality the tense atmosphere was anything but that.

"Sorry, Chris, I can't hear you over this damn radio, let me turn it down. Felicity just ran upstairs to do something and will be down in a few minutes."

Mr Hunter conveniently did not answer the part of the question enquiring where Ben was and wasn't about to start tackling that subject until Mrs Hunter was back downstairs to absorb some of the fallout. Mr Hunter went into the hallway and carried on with his charade. He shouted up the stairs,

"Felicity. Would you come downstairs, dear? Chris is here."

Chris scanned the room and was immediately drawn to the tell-tale signs that a little person was staying in the house. The Hunter's usual immaculate room had Lego pieces scattered in one corner and in other pockets of the room, some of Ben's things were left lying around.

Chris smiled to himself as even at his own home, he couldn't get Ben to be a neat freak and put his things away, so why would he be any different at his grandparents. Chris could hear whispering outside the lounge. The Hunters preferring to talk with each other in the hallway, as opposed to coming back into the lounge to converse with Chris.

After a couple of minutes, Mrs Hunter burst into the room, unaware that she was hyper and acting strangely.

"Chris. It's good to see you. I guess you must want a drink after your long journey. What can I get you? A cup of coffee or tea perhaps?"

Mrs Hunter's frantic mannerisms baffled Chris. However, he thought nothing untoward of it and just went along with the flow.

"Hi Felicity. A cup of coffee would be great; thank you. Is Ben still upstairs? Does he know I am here?"

Chris inquired, looking to see where Ben was as he didn't appear to be behind Mrs Hunter when she came into the room.

"Let me just get your coffee and I'll be back in to finish off our conversation."

Mr Hunter was already outside and followed Mrs Hunter into the kitchen.

"Felicity, we're not going to be able to keep up this charade for much longer. Sooner or later, Chris is going to have to know that Ben isn't here, so we might as well pull off the band-aid now and face the consequences."

"I know, Frank, but I'm terrified that he is going to lose it. Especially when he learns that Ben is with Tilly and that they have been gone since this morning."

Mrs Hunter proceeded to make Chris a filtered coffee, and they both walked back into the lounge, united with the devastating news they were about to disclose.

Chris sipped his coffee slowly, and following what appeared to be mindless small talk and pleasantries about the weather, he reiterated his earlier question as to the whereabouts of Ben.

"So, does Ben know I'm here then? I can't stay too long as we need to make a move shortly, especially if we're going to beat the traffic."

Mrs Hunter twitched nervously in her seat and realised that it was time for the truth to come out, no matter what the aftermath. Mrs Hunter took a deep breath and proceeded.

"Chris, I'm afraid, we have something to tell you. Unfortunately, Ben isn't here."

"Not here! What do you mean he's not here? So where is he then?"

Mr Hunter weighed into the conversation in support of his wife.

"Errr. That's the problem. We don't exactly know where, Chris. We had a breakfast meeting this morning that we couldn't rearrange, since we were the hosts. We asked Tilly to come over and stay with Ben for a few hours whilst we were out. However, she said she had an urgent delivery to make, and we were led to believe it was a quick job and that she would be back straight after. However, when we arrived home after our event, she wasn't here."

Chris' patience started to wear thin, and he couldn't hide the frustration in his tone, as events continued to unravel.

"It's well after 5 PM now. Are you telling me that Tilly is out there with my son, since this morning, and neither of you know where she is? Why haven't you called her yet? Let's call her now."

"That was the first thing we did, Chris, when we saw that she wasn't here, but sadly we heard her phone ringing in the hallway. She must have mistakably left it on the side," Mrs Hunter concluded.

"This is so typical of Tilly. I bet she thinks this is some sort of game to get back at me. Why would you let her look after Ben when you know our history? I left Ben in your care, not Tilly's. I didn't want to leave him with Natalia as we've not got to that stage yet in terms of levels of responsibility. Yet you assured me that you were available to look after Ben. Had I known that you weren't able to commit to the entire duration, I would have cancelled my plans and not gone on the course. Anyway, Ben hardly knows her and what if he's confused about where he is now?"

Mr Hunter tried to appease Chris' fears.

"You have nothing to be concerned about, Chris, as Ben will be safe with Tilly. He's been out with her several times before and just loves her company."

However, following his statement, and from the look Mrs Hunter gave him, he wished he hadn't opened his mouth, as he ended up adding more flames to the fire.

"Why am I only finding about this now? I don't believe Tilly is emotionally stable and certainly not someone I want around my son. Your memories are very vivid. You will recall that Tilly was the one who accused me of assisting my wife in her death to ease the excruciating pain that she was experiencing up to when she died. It took time to clear my name so excuse me if I'm a little paranoid that she is out God knows where with my son. Where do you think she could be until this hour? Do we need to call the police?"

"No, please don't, Chris," Mrs Hunter pleaded anxiously.

"Tilly has turned her life around and is sorry for what she put you through. She wouldn't hurt Ben. He's her nephew and she really cares for him. If you could just see them together, you would know that. Whilst we don't know where she is or why she has stayed out for so long, I believe there is a good explanation and that they have innocently lost track of time. Please, Chris. Don't call the police. Let's give them another hour or so and assess the position then."

"Okay, but no more than that. After the hour, I'll have to consider taking matters into my own hands."

In the time that ensued, the three sat in total silence, not knowing what each other was thinking, yet imagining that the same thoughts were prevalent in their minds. Where on earth was Tilly!

Chris sat quietly but annoyed as he recalled the last encounter he had because of Tilly. He was in front of a hearing trying to convince them that Jill died from her illness and that it wasn't because of anything he had done to ease her pain. Tilly's previous concerns left his employers with no alternative but to follow through with the complaint. The bitterness in Tilly's eyes towards him continued to haunt Chris for weeks after the hearing, even though he was eventually cleared since there was no substantial evidence against him.

Mrs Hunter wanted to occupy herself by making everyone something to eat or drink but dared not move and disrupt the silence. All she could think about was how this had now jeopardised any future chances they would have to look after Ben and because of that, she was furious with Tilly. What didn't Tilly understand about the instruction to stay put and look after Ben until they got back?

Tilly was always a law unto herself but this time she had gone too far, and even though Mrs Hunter was adamant not to involve the police, she couldn't wait to deal with Tilly herself and let her know in no uncertain terms how selfish and thoughtless she had been. Mr Hunter broke the deadlock by getting up to stretch his arms and legs and then left the room to use the toilet.

Tilly and Ben were still at the planetarium, having had a busy day, oblivious to the mayhem that was ensuing back at home. There was a lot of information to absorb and interactive galleries to explore that it was only after Ben wanted to go into a gallery that they had been in twice before that Tilly got a wake-up call and realised that they had literally spent the whole day there. She checked her watch to see what the time was and could not believe that it was nearly 6 PM.

'Ohhh no. Where did the time go? Mother is going to be mad at me.'

Tilly's intention was to see Ben content and to spoil and have him think that she was the coolest aunt ever. However, she now realised that perhaps she had overstepped the mark by going to the planetarium when really, she should had taken Ben back home as her parents had requested her to.

"Sorry, Ben. We've been in there a couple of times already. We're going to have to head home now. Grandpa and Grandma are probably frantic wondering where we are, especially since I left my phone at their home, so they can't get hold of us either."

"Ohhh. I've really enjoyed myself today. I hope we can come back. Thank you, Aunt Tilly; I really love you."

Tilly felt her heart melt as Ben threw his arms around her neck and squeezed her tightly. She had never known love like that since losing Jill. The relationship she had with Jill was like none other she had experienced. As twins, they had a special unique bond with each other and Jill dying left a gaping hole in Tilly's world. Having Ben back in her life helped in some way to fill her love tank again, but she didn't quite know how to manage the dynamics of the relationship in a healthy and responsible way. Tilly attempted to pull herself together emotionally, careful not to let Ben see the tears in her eyes. She grabbed Ben by the hand, walked him to the car and drove him home.

The stipulated hour Chris had set was almost up and Mr Hunter was nervously hovering near the window for the slightest flicker of headlights or the sound of a car. No-one knew if Chris would follow through on his threat to involve the police and Mrs Hunter hoped her prayers would be answered. Shortly thereafter, there was a sound of a car pulling up the drive.

"It's them," Mr Hunter shouted. "It's them."

All three of them ran to the door and awaited the individuals to emerge from the car.

Tilly observed that there was a welcome party waiting for them and knew that she would have to face the music for her actions.

"Hey Bengy, we're back. Wake up, sleepy head."

As usual, Ben would fall asleep as soon as he got into the back of a car. Chris ran immediately to the car and opened the back door.

"What on earth do you think you were playing at, Tilly? How could you be so irresponsible?"

Before Tilly got the chance to apologise, Chris had Ben in his arms and carried him into the house. Tilly made her way into the house with her head down.

"Tilly, do you know what you have put us through and the embarrassment you have caused us? You were supposed to have been back in the house this morning. What happened?"

Tilly knew that her mother was disappointed with her and no matter what she said, it would still fall on deaf ears. All eyes were on Tilly waiting for an explanation.

"I'm extremely sorry that a decision I made backfired. What I thought was something nice for Ben has impacted on you all and caused you worry and concern."

"You know what, Tilly? Your apologies are lame, and I don't want to hear any more. Because of your recklessness, I'll now be on the road later than I had planned and Ben is going to be all over the place regarding his sleep pattern. Felicity, could you get Ben's things please as we are leaving now?"

"Yes, of course Chris, I'll go and get them."

Mrs Hunter went up the stairs and came back down with Ben's things. As they walked out of the house, Mr Hunter helped Chris with Ben's bag, whilst Chris carried him to the car and belted him in. After waving Chris and Ben off, the Hunters came back into the house to finish off their frank discussion with Tilly. The conversation was heated in parts, with the Hunters expressing their deep disappointment with Tilly in no uncertain terms. Also, questioning the reasoning behind what she did and the impact it could have on any future opportunity they would have to look after Ben. Especially as Tilly would have known that Chris was due to collect Ben that day and he wasn't privy to the fact that Ben had spent time with her on previous occasions. During the argument, Mrs Hunter even accused Tilly of deliberately staying out to somehow get back at Chris. However, Tilly adamantly refuted that notion and stated that it was a genuine oversight.

Even though Tilly was sorry for the mayhem she seemingly caused in that everyone was unduly worried and concerned as to where she and Ben were, she was not sorry that she got to spend quality time with Ben. It gave her the opportunity to feel what being a mother could really be like and to her surprise she enjoyed it. She would have been the first to admit that there wasn't a maternal bone in her body, yet Ben brought the softer, more caring side out of her. It also made her feel close to Jill and she believed that had Jill been there, she would have understood and would never had thought that she could in anyway do any harm to Ben. Chris seemed extremely angry with Tilly, and she knew it would take time for him to trust her or her parents again. And for the sake of them, she had to try to make amends, since the last time Chris made the decision to keep Ben away from them was also because of her actions.

'Tilly, when are you going to learn to stop sabotaging the lives of others because of your reckless actions?'

Tilly was only too aware that this wasn't the right time to try and smooth things out with her parents and made the decision to leave. Mrs Hunter had already gone upstairs as she really couldn't bear to be in the same room as Tilly and it was just her father left with her to do what he always did in trying to comfort her.

"Honestly Tilly, what are we going to do with you?"

Mr Hunter pulled her into his embrace and Tilly rested her head on his shoulder.

"I really don't know, Dad. I make these decisions, which at the time sound right in my head, but it always has a negative impact on others. Mother isn't going to forgive me anytime soon, is she?"

Tilly relaxed comfortably on her father's shoulder, knowing that he would always be there to support her, no matter what craziness she was dealing with.

"Give her some time, Tilly. Her only priority is maintaining a relationship with her grandson, and if that is compromised, she will be impossible to live with. Somehow, Tilly, we've got to fix this... and fast."

"I know, Dad. I don't know how, but I promise you, I'll think of something, you mark my words. Well, I better go now and again, I'm truly sorry for everything."

Mr Hunter kissed Tilly on her forehead and walked with her to the door.

"Oh, don't forget this." He ran back to retrieve Tilly's phone from the side table and gave it to her.

"Oh yes, the dreaded phone that could have saved me a lot of trouble today, eh?" Tilly said as she raised her eyebrows.

Mr Hunter just gave her a fatherly smile.

"Get home safe, Tilly, and we'll talk soon."

CHAPTER TWENTY

Steve had not spoken to his parents since the revelation of what they had done and instead was busy concentrating on trying to repair his relationship with Olivia and her trust in him. They had had a few more sessions with PT and had finally completed their pre-marital counselling sessions, which had previously been put on hold following Steve's accident. In the sessions, there was a lot of information that was brought to the surface concerning trust issues, which was extremely important to Olivia and was one of her deal-breakers.

In the sessions, PT counselled them both on how important it was for them to put everything on the table now and not leave any surprises that could come back to haunt them after they were married. Olivia satisfied herself that Steve had now told her everything about his life that there was to know. And even though the incident about his background had caused a major scare, the love they had for each other was much stronger than anything anyone could do to come between them.

The wedding was back on track with only a month left to go. Olivia had practically spearheaded the whole event by herself, since Steve knew his strengths and it was not in wedding planning. He just nodded when Olivia showed him samples and provided the funds when things needed paying for. What they both agreed on though was that it would be a quiet affair. Only their nearest and dearest would be on the guest list, comprising of their parents. Carol & Michael, Jen & Matt. PT and his wife and a few close friends from New Dawn Church.

Regarding Steve's parents attending the wedding, they were aware that the relationship needed to be repaired first and as much as Olivia wanted to avoid having another confrontation with his mother, she knew it was something that

Steve needed to sort out. Her conscious wouldn't allow her to start off married life on such a sour note.

For weeks, she kept on pleading with Steve to do something about it and he had been dragging his heels and stalling the inevitable, but he had finally plucked up the courage to do so. He knew what the Bible endorsed about forgiveness, and it was something that he just needed to do for the sake of all parties concerned. Therefore, he called his mother and made the conversation brief. He asked if they both could meet him at a certain restaurant, which happened to be the same one where Mrs Adams had met Olivia a couple of months earlier. Mrs Adams was elated that Steve had finally got in touch and would have agreed to have met him anywhere for the sake of being able to see his face and talk with him again.

The day had arrived. Steve planned it meticulously so that his parents would arrive at the restaurant earlier than him, as he had a surprise for them that they would not be expecting. He arrived at Olivia's house to pick her up. He blew his horn and Olivia came running out, dressed in a navy-blue dress with a navy and white sailor styled jacket to match.

"Hey, you," Olivia said as she got into the car.

"Hi hon. You look very nice."

"Why, thank you. Thought I'd make the effort." Olivia made herself comfortable as she buckled herself in.

"Steve, are you sure this is a good idea? I thought you'd want to see your parents on your own when you were attempting to reconcile with them."

"Don't try backing out of this now. You're the one that has been nagging me to get my relationship back on track with them and I am not doing that without you by my side. And anyway, they need to apologise for what they put you through and for nearly wrecking our relationship."

"It might all end in tears you know, that's all I am saying. I mean, your mother will be beside herself when she sees me rocking up alongside her precious son. And did you really have to choose the same restaurant we met up at previously?"

Chapter Twenty

Olivia rolled her eyes as if to intimate that Steve was playing with fire. Whilst she wanted Steve's relationship with his parents to be restored, she did not want it to be at the expense of her being responsible for yet another fallout between them all.

"Yes, I did have to choose the same restaurant as I am re-enacting the scene of the crime."

He smiled as if he was Columbo, plotting out one of his famous scenes in catching his prey.

"You are so silly," Olivia said as she tapped him on his shoulder, and they had a slight giggle about the situation.

On cue and at the time Steve had told them, Mr & Mrs Adams arrived at the restaurant and were shown to a table reserved in Steve's name. Mrs Adams made herself comfortable as she pulled the black & white polka dot silk scarf from around her neck and placed it beside her, whilst Mr Adams poured himself a glass of the complimentary water that was already on the table.

"Do you want some water, dear?"

"Ahh yes please." Mr Adams also poured a glass for his wife.

"I can't wait to see Steve. It's been too long," Mrs Adams said with a big smile on her face.

"And whose fault is that then?" Mr Adams quickly chimed in with a sarcastic tone.

"Our son would not have distanced himself from us if you hadn't attempted to sabotage his life. I mean, what on earth were you thinking of getting a dummy prenup drawn up and dragging poor Charlotte into the mix too? Did you really think it was going to end well?"

Mrs Adams appeared repentant, as she hated it when her husband reprimanded her like that. She knew only too well that the reason Steve had cut contact with them was because of her actions. He had not even spoken to her since she met up with Olivia and she suspected that he was angry with her since he had never gone this long without speaking with them. "I know. I can see now that I was wrong, and I am deeply sorry for what I did, but I was…"

"It's no good saying sorry to me, it's that poor girl that you should be apologising too. And when Steve gets here, you're going to tell him that you want to do that and will apologise to his young lady in person. You'll have to set up another meeting with her and this time not on your own. Steve should be there also. I am surprised at you though, because you really do have a short memory."

"What do you mean by that comment?"

Mr Adams didn't like to drag up the past but felt it was necessary to do so on this occasion, to bring across a point and give his wife a wake-up call because of her actions.

"Well, you forget that we were in a similar situation, weren't we? Remember when we first started seeing each other? My parents didn't like you, nor did they want me to marry you either. But I still chose you. I went against their wishes and still married you anyway and it's a decision I'd do all over again."

Mrs Adams put her hand over her husband's and tears started to well up in her eyes. He was right. Their situation was not so dissimilar to her son's at all. What was she thinking? As Mrs Adams contemplated the memory her husband had brought up, her mind drifted back to those earlier years.

They had met in college, and she recalled Mr Adams being the most handsome boy that she had ever seen. Her girlfriends would often tease her that he fancied her every time they passed the field where the boys played cricket, and she had to admit that she did catch his eye a few times. They eventually connected and started going out with each other. It was evident to see that he came from good stock and that one day he would make something good out of his life because of his privileged head start in life. Yet she wasn't so much drawn to his wealth. Instead, it was his kindness and good nature that won her over.

Eventually the time came for him to introduce her to his parents and Mrs Adams recalled how nervous she felt in meeting them. And whilst they greeted her cordially to her face, she somehow felt that she was not the person that they would want for their son and felt a bit of a resistance from them as time went by. Just like what she was attempting to do with her own son. They tried to get their son to rethink his actions, but she was so proud of the way he stood his ground and knew what he wanted. And they eventually got married, without their blessing. However, over the years that ensued, Mr & Mrs Adams Senior finally mellowed when they realised that she was in the relationship for the right reasons and have spent the years ever since trying to make amends.

Steve and Olivia found an appropriate place to park and made their way to the restaurant hand-in-hand.

"Are you ready for this?" he said as he squeezed Olivia's hand tight.

"Of course, I am. I'm a born fighter you know."

There was a slight hint of nervousness in her tone, but Olivia did not want Steve to sense that she was absolutely terrified of how things might evolve.

"Good girl. We're a united front and nothing can stop us. Just you remember that. And with God on our side, we can conqueror anything."

On that strength, they arrived at the restaurant and were shown to the table reserved in his name. Mrs Adams spotted Steve as he walked towards the table and started waving her hand to beckon him over. Olivia was close behind him, but Mrs Adams' view was blocked from seeing anyone else behind him.

As Steve approached the table, Olivia's presence was now obvious and there was a nervous smile on Mrs Adams' face.

"Mother. Father," Steve said, greeting his parents as he showed Olivia to an empty seat that was next to Mr Adams, but directly opposite his wife. Mr Adams rose to his feet and embraced Olivia.

"Hello, young lady. It's nice to see you again." His embrace was warm and cuddly like being wrapped in a duvet on a chilly day.

"Likewise, Mr Adams. Great tie by the way," Olivia said as she smiled and sat down.

"Hello Mrs Adams. You look nice."

Olivia had been rehearsing her opening speech to her future mother-in-law all the way from the car, since they had not spoken following that dreaded one-to-one encounter by themselves.

"Thank you, Olivia. Likewise, you look equally lovely."

Olivia could not work out what kind of game Mrs Adams would be playing today, but she came armed and was ready to bat away any negativity that would come her way. Steve made himself comfortable and reached for Olivia's hand to give it another squeeze to reassure her that he had her back. After a few minutes of awkwardness, Mr Adams broke the silence.

"Anyway, before we start to dine, I believe my wife has something to say."

He was not going to allow her to sit through their luncheon without addressing first things first. Mrs Adams didn't realise she would be apologising so soon and was a little taken aback by her husband's directness. Nevertheless, she knew that she was in the wrong and had to put matters right.

With Olivia sitting directly opposite her, there was nowhere for her to focus her gaze except straight into Olivia's eyes. All other eyes were fixated on her, waiting to hear what words she would utter.

"Ahhh yes. I do have something to say." She cleared her throat a few times.

"Olivia, I owe you a sincere apology. What I did was wrong and out of line and I only hope you can forgive me for trying to sabotage your and Steven's relationship in anyway."

Olivia was shocked as she didn't expect an apology and thought that Mrs Adams would spend the whole lunch trying to deflect her actions. And yet there she was looking like a puppy, all droopy eyed and helpless. Olivia sensed a deep regret in her voice, and her body language supported the heartfelt words she had uttered. Olivia knew there and then that she had to accept her apology and move on.

"Thank you, Mrs Adams. I appreciate and accept your apology. I know deep down that you were looking out for the welfare of your son, and I get that."

At that juncture, Steve piped in.

"Yes, but it still wasn't a nice thing to do, but I'm glad, Mother, that you have finally seen the error of your ways. I love Olivia and she is the person I have chosen to spend the rest of my life with. And I hope that both you and father can accept that."

Mrs Adams put her hand on Steve's giving him her approval.

"And we do, son. We do indeed," she said, and Mr Adams also nodded in solidarity with his wife's sentiments.

The rest of the lunch went off smoothly with Mr & Mrs Adams showing interest in the wedding plans and asking if there was anything they could help with. Which was met with a bit of resistance born from the fact that as soon as Steve was old enough to make his own money, he had always been independent, even though he had a trust fund to fall back on if he ever needed to. Steve politely declined at first. However, so as not to offend his parents from wanting to contribute, he accepted their offer to pay for the honeymoon, which Olivia gladly accepted too.

After what turned out to be a pleasant lunch, all parties left, promising to stay in touch with each other with regards to the rest of the wedding plans. Having left the restaurant on a high, they all got into their respective cars and headed for home. As Steve and Olivia got into their car and settled in, the atmosphere appeared a lot lighter.

"Well, I've got to admit, that went a lot smoother than I was expecting," Olivia said, slightly surprised.

"Yeahhh, I would agree." Steve's tone implied the fact that there was more to the story than met the eye.

"I suspect my father had a word with her about the whole fiasco, because whenever she is that sheepish, it's because he has given her a good talking to. She doesn't like when he reprimands her by showing her the error of her ways and would do anything not to be thought of badly by him. Anyway, whatever it was that he said, I'm just glad that the air has been cleared. You got your apology and now we can move on from this."

"Me too. I really did not want to start off married life at odds with your parents. That was the one thing that was weighing on my mind, so I'm glad things will be more amicable going forward. Although, I hope your mother isn't going to keep bothering me too much with her ideas for our wedding. We promised that we were going to keep it simple, and I hope it will stay that way."

"Don't worry, you'll find things will be very much on our terms now as she'll not want to rock the boat again and will stay compliant with whatever we decide in order to stay in our good books."

They both looked at each other with a sense of relief that they could move forward on a more positive note.

Carol's stint in the hospital was successful, and the rest was certainly welcomed, but there were always things she found to occupy herself with around the house, since Michael wasn't the tidiest of persons to live with. Carol took her time as she attempted to put things back into their designated places. She was the clean freak of the two and had always been like that, even when she lived with Olivia.

Michael was more laid back and felt there wasn't any need to fuss since it was only the two of them living in the house and no-one would see the mess unless they had visitors.

Carol's obstetrician had warned her to take things easy as the babies could come early if she continued to run on all cylinders and not slow down. However, Carol believed she was superwoman and always did things on her own terms.

As she was bending down to pick up some things off the floor, she heard the front door open, indicating that Michael was home from work.

"Hey, Caz, I'm home. Where are you?" he said as he walked towards the lounge area.

"I'm in here," Carol said in a slightly strained tone.

Michael came into the room and saw Carol in an awkward position.

"Caz, what on earth are you doing?"

He rushed over to help her straighten up and assisted her to sit on an upright chair at the table.

"Caz, you're supposed to be taking things easy. Do you want to end up in hospital again? And you certainly shouldn't be bending over and doing strenuous things either."

Carol responded back quickly with her usual wit,

"Well, if you left the place tidy and didn't leave your things lying around, I wouldn't have to, now would I?"

"That's not the point. I told you that I will tidy up and put my things away when I'm good and ready. I've just had a lot on lately, what with settling into the new surgery and everything. The days just seem to be rolling into each other."

Michael felt exhausted not only with work life, but also with home life too. The onus was on him to get everything right, but he was starting to crack behind the scenes, unbeknown to everyone else.

"Oh dear. Sounds like someone had a busy day," Carol said as she rubbed her stomach.

"How are things going in your new environment? It must be challenging at times not being the one in charge and having to answer to someone else instead."

"That's the least of my worries. We all seem to be getting along well. I just need to find my feet. There's a lot going on there with the two surgeries merging and it's not long until the babies are here. I just want to make sure that we are ready for their arrival."

Anxiety had taken a grip of Michael's emotions, and he was trying hard to conceal his true feelings from Carol.

"Ahhh bless you, but these two will come when they're ready and I daresay, they won't announce their arrival to anyone either."

Carol tried to be light-hearted about the matter as she sensed Michael was worrying unnecessarily which was his normal manner.

Even though Michael did not have the day-to-day responsibility of overseeing what was going on at the surgery, he still felt invested in the lives of his former staff. He was delighted that Janet had decided to take early retirement and that he was able to negotiate a good settlement package for her. In his mind, she deserved it, and he would have fought to the hills to ensure that she walked out of the NHS with nothing less than what was due to her. Janet was in the process of working out her notice period and was due to leave at the end of the month. Michael had noticed a spring in her step as she went about doing her work, almost as if a weight had been lifted off her shoulders, which told him that it was the right decision for her.

Chris, on the other hand, had seemed a bit distracted in his work of late, and Michael had suspected there was trouble at home. He appeared very protected over Ben and the time he needed to spend with him and declined any extra hours at the hospital, when normally he would have jumped at the opportunity to have them. Chris had explained earlier to Michael that Ben would not be spending as much time with his in-laws as he had done in the past which confused Michael, since he thought they had re-established their connection and were all getting along amicably. However, Michael suspected that there was probably more to the story than Chris was divulging, but didn't want to press him for further details, since he was a private soul at the best of times and didn't always like to bear his all and let third parties in.

When it came to Joan, she was settling into her new environment suitably. She wasn't aware initially that one of the locums that worked at the new surgery was an old love interest, being someone, she had worked with whilst she was doing her training and had dated when they were in their early twenties. Somehow after their training, they had lost contact and went their separate ways.

Joan had got married but later divorced. However, the doctor in question did not marry and, therefore, was still an eligible bachelor. At least that was one staff member that Michael did not have to worry about, knowing that Joan could hold her own and would look after herself and emotions just well. The crux of the matter was that Michael knew, he had to stop trying to play God. He couldn't oversee and be involved in everyone's lives; only God had the ability to do that, and at that successfully.

No, Michael's job was to be present at work. Do what he had to do with the minimalist amount of stress and then return home to his wife and, in a few weeks, his new babies.

CHAPTER TWENTY-ONE

The months had flown by since Matt and Jen had started seeing each other. They were investing and spending more time with each other and their feelings for one another were deepening. Even though they were both still young, they had mature heads on their young shoulders and had already discussed things that would have ordinarily taken other couples' years to tackle. It was clear that their relationship wasn't just about being boyfriend and girlfriend and had more depth and a seriousness to it. Matt had felt early on that Jen was the person he wanted to marry but wanted to tread carefully to see how Jen felt about him before making any grandiose gestures. Matt had even taken the initiative to discuss the matter with PT regarding his feelings for Jen, who advised him to take his time, follow his heart and allow God to guide him with the rest. He had also already spoken candidly to his parents about Jen and the next stage was for him to introduce her to them. He had briefly mentioned it to Jen in passing whether she would like to accompany him the next time he visited his parents for the weekend, which she agreed to. In her mind, she wondered if things were moving too quickly, but Matt was such a respectful young man that she knew he was always one step ahead of her in perceiving how things were going to pan out for the future.

The weekend in question had arrived. Jen had packed a small holdall and wasn't sure what kind of clothes she'd need but chucked in an assortment of casual and smart casual just to be on the safe side. Matt had spoken so often about his parents and his twin sister that Jen felt she already knew them. Unlike Steve, Matt had told Jen upfront that whilst his parents weren't stinking rich, they were comfortable and with the way they carried themselves, they were often thought of as a well-to-do family. Matt's father was also a doctor, and his mother was a physiotherapist like he was, which inspired him to follow in her footsteps by becoming one too. His sister, who he was quite close to, was a veterinarian and loved all things animals, having a few of them herself that lived with her at her flat. Jen was not surprised to hear that Matt's parents did not live too far from Cornwall where her parents lived, since they kept coming across these coincidental similarities in their lives. She hoped they would have time to swing round by her parents' too and waited to see how the weekend would unfold.

Matt picked up Jen, whose excitement of their first road trip together she could not contain.

"Well, I'm ready," she said as she fastened herself in.

"So, let's get this car on the road."

Matt smiled as he pulled out of her drive. He loved Jen's sense of adventure and the way she just enjoyed life and saw the positiveness in everything.

"You do know that we'll be quite close to my parents. I have told them we are coming their way this weekend. Do you think we'll have a chance to pop in and say hello?"

Jen cheekily dropped the question in, hoping that she wasn't being disrespectful of the plans Matt would have meticulously put together.

"Of course not. I'd love to meet your parents. Perhaps we can see them on Sunday, if that is alright with them."

"Oh, that would be great, Matt, as they have heard so much about you and are just dying to meet you."

Jen realised the words that had come out of her mouth, but it was too late to backtrack and take them back, but Matt quickly picked up on what she had said.

"So, they've heard a lot about me, eh?" he said, smiling.

Jen tried to lower herself in the seat, putting her head down to hide herself, but there was nowhere to hide.

She tapped his knee playfully.

"You know what I mean, Matt. Stop teasing me," she said sheepishly.

"I just love to tease you. It's those dimples of yours that I like to see come out as they make you more adorable."

For the next few hours, they enjoyed playful banter with each other, listening to music from the various CDs Matt had in his car, and stopping off briefly for a leisure break to use the facilities and top-up on petrol.

The weekend they spent in Falmouth meeting Matt's parents and sister went off smoothly. They loved Jen as much as she loved them, especially his sister. Jen felt that she had gained a new sister and knew that they would be friends for life. Matt showed Jen around the area of Falmouth where he grew up and, on Saturday evening, he and his family took Jen to one of their favourite Turkish restaurants, where they all got to know each other in more depth.

On Sunday morning, Matt took Jen to the church he grew up in and called home, which was as vibrant as New Dawn and made her feel right at home in the style of how they did things.

After Sunday lunch, it was time to say goodbye to his family and en-route home, they got the opportunity to stop off and meet Jen's parents. Again, the reception towards Matt was very friendly and cordial. Jen's parents saw immediately what their daughter had seen in Matt and were grateful to God that she had finally found someone who they knew in no uncertain terms would end up being her husband. Before they left, Jen's mum cordoned her off to a quiet area and whispered in her ear,

"This one's a keeper, Jen. You've done well. You've done well." She hugged her tightly and Jen and Matt left to head back home.

On the drive home, Jen was beaming from ear to ear as things could not have gone more perfectly, and for the first time, she could see a future with Matt in it.

After they got back to Bricket Wood, Matt helped Jen with her bags and walked her to the door.

"Well, I guess that's the end of our road trip. I think it was a fruitful weekend getting to meet both sets of parents at the same time. It couldn't have worked out better."

Jen agreed.

"Absolutely, I concur. Your parents and sister are the best, and my parents really liked you too. You obviously made a good impression on them," Jen said, smiling from ear to ear that she finally had the opportunity to introduce them to someone decent who could potentially be 'the one'.

Matt quickly returned the compliment.

"As were your parents. Your mother is very sweet and caring. Now I see where you get those wonderful qualities from."

Jen blushed as Matt was flattering her and did not know where to put her face. He always said the nicest of things and she wasn't used to a man treating her with such respect and bringing out the best in her.

"I better get in and get my stuff in the washing machine and then get ready for work tomorrow. I have an early shift."

Jen took her bag from Matt. They exchanged a warm and lingering hug, which felt like it went on for ever, as neither of them wanted to let the other one go. Eventually Matt followed that through by giving her a passionate kiss on the doorstep and watched her go in looking all starry eyed as she waved him goodbye.

Olivia was coming down the stairs as Jen came into the house and noticed her bright countenance, which indicated that the weekend went well.

"Guess I don't have to ask you if you had a good weekend, since it's written all over your face," Olivia laughed.

"Oh Olivia, it was just perfect. From start to finish. It was our first real opportunity to go on a trip like that, and we had so much fun. From the car journey to meeting both sets of parents, it couldn't have gone any better."

Jen looked like she was literally walking on air as she glided through the hall following Olivia into the lounge area.

"I guess I know what you mean. I remember when Steve and I took our first trip abroad together to the jazz festival in Rotterdam. I learnt so much about him that I either previously took for granted or did not fully appreciate, but that was where his true colours shone and where the surprise proposal came from."

Chapter Twenty-one

Olivia had Jen's attention as she floated back down to earth from her high.

"And did you know in that moment that he was the one?"

Olivia paused for a moment as she contemplated before giving her answer.

"I guess I would say yes. As it ignited in me something that was buried deep within me that I did not allow myself to explore. He was in my life for the longest time and yet I did not know that he was the man God had for me. I can be hard-headed like that at times, you know." Olivia smiled.

"You hard-headed? Never," Jen sarcastically responded with a hint of glee in her tone.

"Well, Olivia, my heart has already started talking to me and I am getting the impression that Matt is the one, and if I am reading the signs correctly, I believe he feels the same."

"That's brilliant, Jen." Olivia ran over and gave her a big hug.

"My advice would be to continue to pray about it and allow the Holy Spirit to lead you both. You'll get a lot of outside influence along the way, but as long as you both communicate with each other and involve God in everything you do, you really can't go wrong. I'm quite excited to see how things pan out for you as you really deserve this, hon. Matt is truly a nice guy and you both look good together and make a great couple too. Now I don't want to be the one to say we told you so, but we told you so."

Jen laughed as she recalled being accosted by her and Carol when they first saw her and Matt interacting with each other at the luncheon and had to agree that they really were spot on.

"Okay, okay. So, you called it first and saw what we didn't see, but we just naturally hit it off that first time so I guess you can call that 'like at first sight,' eh?"

They both laughed as Olivia stayed in the lounge and Jen headed up the stairs to get herself and things sorted.

3 Weeks Later…..

It was the start of the week at Belmont Medical Centre, where the senior staff met first thing to look at and discuss the schedule for the week. The senior consultant started off by commending how efficient the surgery was running following the merger and felt that all the staff, old and new, handled the transition well and the now newly formulated team appeared to be working harmoniously together with no major concerns to report. Several key staff went through the agendas with regards to their specific department, with the last item on the agenda to be discussed coming from the Operations Manager. She took to the floor and addressed the rest of the staff.

"Now we all know that this week is Janet's last week, not only with us, but with the NHS since she is retiring. I know some of us haven't known Janet for that long, but we still want to give her a good send off for all her hard work over the years and her service to the NHS. Michael, since you, Joan and Chris have known her the longest, perhaps you could give me some ideas of what we could do for her? Would she like us to book a restaurant, and we all gather there? Or do you think she'd prefer something low-key at the surgery in the conference room? I can organise everything to look nice and special for her."

Michael was caught off guard as his thoughts weren't altogether at the meeting. He had been stressing over Carol and her unwillingness to slow down and take things seriously. And with him not being at home to monitor what she was doing; it continually sent him in a panic with the endless scenarios that he could encounter on any given day coming home from the surgery.

Michael pulled his thoughts together and came back to the conversation in the room.

"Errm, I'm not too good at these sorts of things, but knowing Janet, being old school, she wouldn't want a fancy restaurant. I think she'd be happy just having something here, as you suggest. What are your thoughts, Joan?"

Michael quickly shifted the responsibility to Joan who he felt would be more suitable to share her thoughts and come up with any suggestions.

Joan was only too delighted to accommodate since she was quite fond of Janet.

"Yes, I concur. Janet would just relish having something at the surgery. It would be personal to her, and I know she would appreciate whatever we plan."

Joan directed her focus to the Operations Manager.

"I don't mind helping you come up with a theme and give you some ideas with regards to planning this. Let's put something in my diary later today and we can get started since we don't have long to go."

"Thank you so much, Joan, as your input would be greatly appreciated. I haven't known Janet long, but for the short time she has been here, her knowledge has been invaluable, and she interacts well with the patients and staff alike."

Janet's surprise party was now in motion, and it fell on everyone to work together to keep it a surprise from her and to ensure that they could keep her away from the conference room at the end of the week where the festivities would take place.

As the senior staff were disbursing to their rooms, Chris caught the attention of Michael and Joan and asked if he could have a quick word with them. They waited until everyone had left the room and went back in.

"You alright, mate? You don't seem yourself,"

Michael asked Chris as he could see that he looked like he had the world on his shoulders. The three of them huddled at one end of the table, since the magnitude of the conference table would have swallowed them up had they spaced themselves out. Joan too expressed concern that Chris didn't seem himself since the merger and wondered if all was well at home.

Chris cleared his throat and explained the reason he wanted to talk with them. He still saw the three of them as the team they were at the old surgery and felt he could trust them with the thoughts that were spiralling around in his mind. He started off by sharing how good it had been for Ben to be reconnected with his grandparents and how he had noticed a difference in his demeanour every time he took him to stay with them. However, he then went onto explain the situation that happened when Tilly took Ben out for the day, and no-one knew where they were. And how worried he felt and had subsequently made the decision to keep Ben away from his grandparents yet knew deep in his heart that it was the wrong decision to make.

Michael and Joan listened sympathetically to Chris and his dilemma and tried to interject support as and when they got the opportunity.

Chris continued.

"The trouble is that before all of this happened, I was thinking of relocating back to Leicestershire so that Ben could be close to his grandparents and had been looking at jobs at various hospitals. I've now heard back from one of them and they are keen to offer me a job, at quite a senior level, but the dilemma I have is, do I take it?"

Chris seemed like he was between a rock and a hard place, in ascertaining what to do best for himself and for Ben.

"Well, Chris, you know my thoughts about family. You only have the one and should make the best out of it. And you know that you can't indefinitely keep Ben away from his grandparents. Yes, it was irresponsible of Tilly to act in the way she did, but you can't blame your in-laws for her actions. Especially as they have been very good to you and Ben over these last few months."

"Yeah, Chris, I'm with Michael on this one. You should see this as a new opportunity to start over and just go with it. Whatever is wrong with you and Tilly's relationship, I daresay it will mend in time, but don't allow this one-off situation to dictate how the rest of your life should pan out. I say give this job offer some serious thought and if it is something you perceive would be good for you and Ben's future, then just take that leap. And don't look back. We'll be alright as you leave us alone here,"

Joan said with a slight smirk in her voice that made Chris smile for the first time since they had started to talk.

"Guys, thank you so much for your advice. I just really needed to hear the perspective of someone else aside from all the mayhem that has been going on inside my head. Oddly enough, Tilly has been trying to communicate with me of late and has left several voice messages stating how sorry she is, which I have just been ignoring. I guess if I'm going to think about moving back anytime soon, I need to sort this situation out first so that Ben isn't caught up in the middle of our issues. Anyway, again, I really appreciate your listening ears and let's keep this just between the three of us until I decide on the job offer." As they got up to leave, Michael confirmed that his lips were sealed, and Joan agreed also.

They all went back to their respective offices, in readiness for the busy day ahead of them with patients, as well as stints at the hospital as part of their specialist fields. Joan and the Operations Manager were able to slot an appointment in the diary for later in the afternoon to discuss arrangements for Janet's leaving do.

Michael's diary was somewhat relaxed as he needed to be flexible to be ready at a drop of a hat to attend to Carol, since she was quite close to her elective surgery date. And Chris glided back to his office somewhat lighter in his demeanour, grateful for the fact he was able to offload some of the burden he had been carrying of late. He had a full schedule for the day seeing patients and got to work as shortly thereafter his first patient was on the way to his office.

Janet's role had changed drastically since the merger and therefore she wasn't as involved in interacting with her previous bosses as in the old surgery. However, whenever she got the opportunity, she'd still pop into their office in between patients to check that everything was fine and that they did not need anything. Old habits were hard to die with Janet, but she was happy with her decision to accept the retirement package that was offered to her. She had no regrets of stepping away from a profession she had given most of her adult life to.

There were various things on her bucket list that she wanted to achieve and was looking forward to a change in pace. Since Janet was a keen gardener, and was meticulous in the way it looked, attending to that was number one on her list to finish off some of the things she always wanted to do and did not always have the time to complete. Since Janet wasn't privy to the plans that were being made on her behalf, she assumed that as most of the staff did not know her that well, that her exit on Friday would be a quiet one. And yet plans were in motion to give her a grand and fitting send off for her faithful years of service.

CHAPTER TWENTY-TWO

Chris felt relieved that his last patient had just left his office and shortly thereafter he would be packing up to go home. He had not taken on any extra hours outside his regular surgery hours, like he did in his previous role. Instead, he wanted to be present in Ben's life and didn't want to continue his form of arriving home just in time to tuck him into bed, thus missing valuable quality time with his son.

As he was updating the computer with the notes of his last patient, his mobile phone rang. The number indicated that Natalia was calling him. It wasn't like Natalia to call him whilst he was still at the surgery, unless it was an emergency, and he answered his phone straightaway.

"Natalia. Is everything okay?" Chris' tone was troubled as he waited for Natalia to speak.

"Hello, Chris, I'm sorry to trouble you, but I just wanted clarity on a matter which has just arisen here at the home."

"Okay, Natalia, what is it?"

"Well, you have a visitor here. She said that she was Ben's aunt and then he came running to the door and they both embraced each other and the next thing, I knew, Ben was showing her into the house."

Natalia appeared frazzled as the situation was out of her control, and she did not have the chance to assess things adequately.

Chris was beside himself with the news Natalia had just disclosed to him.

"Tilly is in my house," he said in a raised voice.

"I'm sorry, Chris, everything happened so fast, and I lost control of the situation."

"My apologies, Natalia. I'm not raising my voice at you nor am I angry with you. I'm just a bit annoyed with Tilly for her insensitivity. What is she doing now?"

"Errm, I can hear laughter from the lounge, but Ben doesn't seem fazed by her presence, which is why I wasn't worried at first, but I felt I should call you, as I really don't know who she is, having never met her."

"No worries, Natalia, you did the right thing. I had started to pack up anyway, so I'll make my way home now. I'll be there in 20 minutes."

Natalia went back into the lounge where she found Ben beside himself in uncontrollable laughter. She really had not seen that side of Ben since she had started working at the home and felt that perhaps his aunt had a positive effect on him. However, she sensed from Chris' tone that he wasn't comfortable with Tilly just turning up and suspected that there was more to the story that she wasn't privy to.

Chris had never discussed his family with Natalia, so she was not familiar that he had a sister-in-law nor what the dynamics of their relationship entailed. All she observed from the short time of Tilly being there is that Ben was a different child around her, and she liked seeing him like that.

After putting down the phone with Chris, Natalia went back into the room to interrupt the joviality that was occurring.

"Hi there. I've just had a word with Mr Harris, and he is on his way home."

Tilly looked up from playing and tickling Ben and acknowledged Natalia.

"Thanks very much and I'm sorry if I had startled you. I was in the area and thought that I'd pop in on the off chance that Chris would be here."

"Oh, it's no problem. Well, let me leave you both whilst I go and finish the dinner as you both appear to be having a lot of fun."

Ben caught his breath. "My aunt Tilly is the best."

Natalia smiled and left the room. She was relieved to learn that she didn't allow some random stranger into the house as that would have been seriously irresponsible.

It took Chris approximately twenty minutes to reach his house, and he immediately recognised Tilly's car as he parked up.

'What is that woman playing at now and why she is here?'

These were all valid questions that were spiralling in Chris' thoughts, which he was about to find out the answers to. Natalia heard the door open and immediately left the kitchen and came to meet Chris, firstly apologising for the situation. Before Chris could shut the door, he was having to console and reassure her that she was not at fault with the way the situation escalated quite speedily out of her control. He told her that he was here now and would sort things out.

Chris went into the lounge where he found Tilly and Ben cosily in a corner reading one of Ben's books. His first observation was to note how clear and confident Ben was reading, with no apparent stumbles. When Ben saw Chris, he shouted out his name and ran towards him for a big bear hug.

"Look Dad, Tilly has come to see me, and I have shown her my room and now we are reading together."

Chris could not deny the excitement Ben was feeling at the thought of his aunt making a trip especially to see him, although he feared it wasn't that innocent and there was more at play here.

"Yes, son, that is great. Why don't you leave me and your aunt Tilly to have a little chat whilst you go upstairs and freshen up for dinner?"

Ben seemed happy enough with the request and speedily charged his way out of the room, running upstairs so that he could be back down to spend more time with Tilly. Now that the room was free of little ears, Chris took the liberty to grill Tilly and ask her what she was doing at his house… again.

"What are you playing at, Tilly? This isn't the first time you have turned up at my house uninvited."

Chris had already coaxed himself in the car on the drive home that he wasn't going to allow Tilly to rile him but instead, for the sake of Ben, was going to be calm and collected and listen to what she had to say. However it was very tempting to just let rip and give her a piece of his mind, which he knew would probably not achieve much.

"Oh, and hello to you too, Chris. That's not a very nice greeting, now, is it?"

Tilly was her usual sarcastic self and enjoyed rubbing Chris up the wrong way, but that wasn't what she came to do. Chris calmly sat on the sofa, ensuring that he wasn't too close to Tilly, and gave her the opportunity to speak.

"Okay, Tilly. To what do we owe the pleasure of your visit?"

Tilly took her time and explained to Chris that she was in the area, albeit quite far from home, carrying out some deliveries and made the snap decision to stop by since he would not answer any of the texts, she had tried sending him to apologise for her previous actions.

Tilly did not feel that Chris took the attempts she was making to try and apologise seriously and did not want her actions to affect her parents not being able to see their grandson.

"Mum and Dad have been besides themselves not being able to talk with or see Ben and I don't want to be responsible for that. If only you would have at least acknowledged one of my messages, then I wouldn't have had to take such drastic measures and turn up on your doorstep, uninvited… again, as you say."

Chris couldn't fault Tilly's rationalisation and knew he should have been more mature in handling her attempt at an apology which was something he needed to work better at. Tilly had always intimidated him in her demeanour and the way she carried herself which is why when he first was introduced to Jill, it was a stark contrast, and he was immediately drawn to her sweet and kind nature.

Chris' tone mellowed somewhat as he responded to Tilly as he could see that she was genuinely sorry. He also took the time to observe how fond she was of Ben and he of her.

"Yes, I did receive your texts but wasn't really in a good place to respond to them. I was still annoyed over the whole situation and now realise that I should have dealt with things in a more mature way."

Chris paused and then shook his head.

"Tilly, isn't it time we called a truce? I don't know about you, but I don't think I have much energy any more to keep this debacle up. It's exhausting."

Tilly laughed.

"I'm not the bad guy you know. I just wanted to have a relationship with my nephew, but you wouldn't let me. Hence the reason why we had to do things the way we did. I don't want anything from you, Chris. I realised long ago that I was second best when it came to you choosing between me and my sister."

"Tilly, please let's not go over that old ground again."

Chris was exhausted for always being blamed by Tilly that he didn't choose her over her sister and yet here it was coming up again.

"You know what, Chris, I will go there. If we are calling a truce, then it is probably the last time we will get to speak about this. I don't even know if you realised how much you had hurt me.

You met me first. We had a little flirt and even a kiss. And I thought we were going somewhere. Little did I know that when I introduced you to my twin sister that you'd swap allegiances. Do you know how embarrassing that was for me? And the worse thing is that I did not even tell Jill about it. So, when you started showing an interest in her, she was none the wiser and did not know at the time how I had felt about you."

Tilly's countenance was softening and for the first time, Chris saw a kinder side to Tilly that he had never seen before. He did not realise that his actions of long ago had affected her in such a deep and profound way and was probably responsible for the way she viewed him.

Chris knew that if Jill had had any clue that the two of them were an item that she would not have entertained him, as that was the loyal type of person she was. It then dawned on him that he had a lot to thank Tilly for as he would never have had the amazing marriage and wonderful son he had, if she had said something.

Chris dropped his head even further in shame as he knew he owed Tilly an apology, which was long overdue.

"Tilly, I am very sorry. I failed to see how my actions back then would have affected you and not getting the proper closure you needed. I've made a few mistakes in my life, and since I renewed my faith, I'm trying to be a better person. You didn't deserve your feelings to be disrespected by me like that, and I apologise for not treating you with the dignity you deserved. Will you forgive me?"

Tilly stared at him with a blank face. Her purpose in turning up at the house was to try and get Chris to accept her apology and now here he was asking for hers. And over a situation that happened a long time ago but affected her in a way that she didn't get the proper closure she needed to move on.

She always wondered what it was that she had done for Chris to reject her and now she realised that it wasn't as huge as she had magnified it in her mind. He simply fell in love with her sister and that was it. Could he have dealt with the situation in a better way? Of course he could have, but sometimes situations don't play out the way individuals envision or hope for.

Tilly realised the fighting with her emotions over the situation was finally over and she had the closure she had craved for and was ready to move forward.

"Yes, Chris, I do accept your apology. I've now got the closure I need, and we don't have to ever discuss or bring this matter up again. We both loved Jill and now we can both love her son, if you will let me," she said sheepishly.

"Absolutely," Chris said loudly.

"I can see how fond you are of each other, and I don't want to get in the way of that."

"Well, I better get going. I have a long drive home."

Just as Tilly was rising and straightening up herself, Ben ran into the room.

"Ahhh. Here's the main man."

Ben ran straight towards her and tried to wrap his little arms around her waist.

"I'm off now Ben, but it was really nice spending time with you."

Ben's faced seemed confused as in his mind, Tilly had only just got there, and they hadn't spent that much time together.

"Aren't you staying for dinner then?" Before Tilly could respond and politely excuse herself, Ben was goading his father.

"Dad, tell Tilly that she has to stay for dinner." Tilly looked at Chris, and he hunched his shoulders as if to surrender.

"You heard the little man, please stay for dinner. You are more than welcome to as Natalia usually makes more than enough. That's if you want to, of course."

Tilly quickly responded,

"Thank you both. I'd love to join you for dinner, but after which I must really leave as I don't want to get home too late as I have an early start."

Ben was overjoyed that Tilly was going to join them for dinner. Chris immediately went to the kitchen to ask Natalia to set an extra place as Tilly would be staying for dinner. Natalia noticed how his countenance had mellowed from the stern temperament that had first walked into the house. She deduced that whatever it was that he and Tilly previously had, they had managed to iron out their differences, and she was grateful for the sake of Ben that they had.

Matt had a follow-up appointment with Steve, which acted as a session to evaluate his progress and finally sign him off with a clean bill of health. The confident individual who met him at the door was certainly not the same person that he had first encountered, who at the time was slightly depressed and slowly losing the will to live.

"Steve, you look great" Matt said as he walked into the house. Steve smiled proudly, recounting the hard work he had achieved.

"Thanks, man, but that was all down to you. If you hadn't pushed me the way you did, I most probably would be here talking to you with a different mentality. You're good at what you do."

"Thank you, Steve. I appreciate your glowing feedback. Now, be sure to let my bosses know so that I get a raise," he said, tongue in cheek.

"Can I get you something to drink?"

"A glass of water would be fine. Thanks."

Steve went to the kitchen to get a glass of water for Matt and himself and came back into the lounge and they both sat at the table facing each other.

"Well, this visit is only a follow-up meeting to assess how you are doing and to finally sign you off, but I can see for myself that you are back to your old form. You've worked extremely hard, Steve, and that's good to see. I wish all my patients had a success story like yours, but it takes sheer willpower and individuals wanting to get better. And from the time I met you, I could see that you were determined not to let your injuries master you and you fought hard, so well done."

Steve appreciated Matt's assessment of the situation. He remembered those early days, following his accident, when he thought, he wasn't going to make it. However, he had a very good nurse in the form of Olivia who stood by his side and encouraged him all the way back to health. Even prior to marriage, she had demonstrated what the vows 'for better or worse; in sickness and in health' signified. Those were qualities that he wanted in a future wife and Olivia possessed them in bucket loads.

"Talking about nursing individuals back to health. Did you ever follow up on that young man I had told you about who I met in the rehabilitation centre?"

"Ahh, you mean Jack?"

"Yep, that's his name, Jack. Seemed such a troubled soul at the time. I had tried to reach out to him after I left, but he didn't answer any of my calls."

"Yes, I did eventually connect with him, and his parents, and I wouldn't worry about him not responding to your calls. He had a lot of emotional turmoil on the inside and found it hard to let others in, for fear that he would lose them again like he lost his friends. But he's a decent lad and is making good progress. I've been helping him navigate walking with prosthetics and he seems to have taken to them quite well. Next time I see him, I will tell him that you were asking after him."

Steve was pleased to hear that Jack was making progress since he often thought about him and wanted to ensure that he stayed upbeat and did not let his injuries define him or affect his future.

"That's great to hear and please do. Let him know that I am still only just a phone call away if he ever wants to talk. Anyway, how are things with you? Still seeing Jen? Well of course you are as Olivia tells me everything," Steve said with a slight hint in his laughter.

"What I really meant is how are things progressing on that front? I hear you even went to see the 'in-laws' recently."

"I can see nothing gets past you as you apparently know more than I do."

Matt thought it humorous that Steve knew quite a lot about his relationship, courtesy of Olivia. But he knew that there was one thing Olivia didn't know and that was what his future intentions were, which he was keeping close to his chest. Matt raised his hands in the air as in a sign of surrender.

"Yep, I must confess, things seem to be going quite well between Jen and myself. She's a great girl and I am lucky to have met her."

Steve quickly jumped in to correct Matt.

"Don't give lady luck the credit as it had nothing to do with luck. This was divinely orchestrated, and you know it. Give God the credit where credit is due. I know you both used to pass each other like passing ships when you were at the hospital. But with you becoming my physiotherapist and then the connection with Olivia and us introducing you to Jen, you both probably never would have met."

Matt smiled.

"Yes, you're right. I probably wouldn't ordinarily have randomly approached Jen, so I guess your accident had some kind of weird purpose, huh."

"Steady on, mate. I didn't nearly die just so that I could put your love life in order."

Steve playfully raised his eyebrows whilst directly looking at Matt and they both sniggered.

Chapter Twenty-two

"Seriously though, do you think she's the one?"

Matt paused before giving his answer as he did not want to give too much away, especially knowing how close he and Olivia was. He did not want the ideas of what he was planning in his heart to seep out before he had the opportunity to execute it.

"I believe so. However, we are still developing our relationship and getting to know each other. I guess time will tell."

Matt did not divulge to Steve that he had already spoken to PT about his deep feelings for Jen as Steve would have probed him further.

"Well, that's good, mate. Sounds like you've got a mature head on those young shoulders of yours, so take your time. But I would stay don't take too long and if you feel strongly that Jen is your future wife, then don't let her slip between your fingers. Don't be like me who stayed in the friend zone way too long that when I eventually tried to shoot my shot, it missed the mark since Olivia only saw me as a friend and nothing more. Again, it took some serious divine intervention to get her to eventually wake up and see me in a different light."

Matt appreciated Steve talking with him so candidly and took in everything he had to share.

"I hear you, Steve, and I intend to ensure that God is at the forefront of all that we do. Anyway, this was only meant to be a brief visit, but if I don't pass on a message, Jen will crucify me."

"Oh yeah, sounds ominous. What's the message?"

"The message is can you occupy Olivia for a few hours on Saturday morning, whilst Jen gets the house ready? She is throwing a small hen-do for Olivia and needs her to be out of the way so she can put up a few decorations and prepare some snacks. I think the style she is looking to do is an intimate afternoon tea party with a few close girlfriends. You know these women; it could escalate into a whole different event by the time they are finished."

Steve had a smirk on his face.

"Tell me about it. I don't think that's going to be a problem. I guess if I tell her, it has something to do with the wedding, she'd more likely be willing to leave. Okay, let me get on with it and try to think up some plausible reason to get her out of the house."

CHAPTER TWENTY-THREE

The Mills were excited and looking forward to the arrival of their twins. Their elective c-section date was in the diary. Therefore, all immediate plans now revolved around that period. Carol was colossal and was experiencing a lot of discomfort, which she had kept to herself for fear of Michael overreacting and committing her to another hospital stint.

Her ankles were often swollen too, and a lot of the time she found it uncomfortable to be on her feet, which meant that she slowed down somewhat from doing the strenuous things that she had been advised by Michael and her obstetrician not to do. Which wasn't a bad thing. Carol also found it uncomfortable to sleep, since her bump usually got in the way of the various positions she'd tried to settle in. Which meant she would get up early, go downstairs and sit on the sofa with her feet up.

Today was like every other morning and Carol had already gotten up before Michael and snuck downstairs to see if she could finish off her sleep. She could hear Michael rumbling around upstairs and couldn't wait for him to come downstairs to make her a cup of tea and a few slices of toast spread with apricot jam.

As Carol sat comfortably with her feet up, her thoughts centred on how far she and Michael had come. This time last year she never would have thought that they would be where they are now, and about to have twins at that. They had really come far, and she was thankful that her mistakes of the past were eventually exposed and in time forgiven. It was a secret she carried for too long and over the years it weighed heavily on her mind. And yet it was something that she couldn't carry indefinitely, especially due to the emotional ramifications of it. Carol couldn't have imagined what life would have looked like, had Michael not been able to get past her previous mistakes and they had gone their separate ways. Carol was grateful to God for being the third wheel in their marriage which was the key to cementing everything together.

As Carol sat there pondering, she felt a slight twinge again. One she had felt a lot recently and which was certainly different from the feel of the babies kicking. As Carol had not been pregnant to this extent before, and had nothing to compare, she could not work out what the twinge meant and put it down to a bout of indigestion and just rubbed her bump with gentle strokes, hoping that would soothe the uneasiness and make her feel better.

Within no time, Michael had come down the stairs to check on Carol and to see if everything was fine. He found Carol perched comfortably on the sofa with her eyes closed, but he knew she was not asleep.

"Ahhh. Here you are Mrs M. So, will it be your usual then? A cup of tea and a few slices of toast?" Michael's voice startled Carol.

"Ssshh. You're so loud. Just whisper. It's only me and you around you know. But yes, I would like my usual and thank you."

Michael quickly went to the kitchen to prepare Carol's breakfast. He wanted to leave promptly at 8 AM, since he had a few things, he wanted to catch up with at the surgery. He came back in with everything Carol had requested, on a floral table-tray and positioned it over Carol so that she would not have to come to the table.

As Carol started to enjoy her breakfast, she could see that Michael looked like he was ready to make a quick dash and with her mouth half-full of toast, attempted to spurt out a few things she wanted to tell Michael before he scurried out the door.

"Oh Michael. Jen called me yesterday to say she was organising a small tea party on Saturday afternoon for Livy's hen-do, so I'll need you to give me a lift please."

Michael raised his eyebrows whilst sorting out his bag.

"Not another event this weekend." Carol seemed surprised at Michael's reaction.

"Why? What do you mean?"

"Well Friday is Janet's leaving do. And now you want me to take you to Olivia's house on Saturday. And don't forget, Sunday is church. When are you going to have a break and take things easy?"

"Michael, you're such an old woman at times. I'm at home all day and every day, where I am getting sufficient rest to last a lifetime. Plus, I don't really have to go to Janet's leaving do, do I? She's your colleague."

Michael sighed and seemed annoyed at Carol picking and choosing what she wanted to go to without putting his thoughts into consideration.

"Well, no you don't have to, but I just thought you'd like to attend with me, and that we could go together as a couple. We haven't been out to many social events together lately and I thought it would be a nice gesture. Plus, I know Janet would appreciate seeing you there."

"Yes, it would be nice to see Janet for the last time, but you are the one who said I should cut down on things, and I really need to be there on Saturday, more than Friday night."

Carol slurped the rest of her tea until it was all gone.

"Anyway, let's not have a debate about this, as I'm running late. Fine. I'll go to the leaving do on Friday on my own and will take you to Olivia's on Saturday. Is that okay with you, madam?" Michael replied awkwardly.

"Perfect." Carol was satisfied that she had got the last word and hoped that Michael wouldn't spend the rest of the day internalising their conversation.

"Okay, let me take these things from you and get out of here. Have a good day."

Michael kissed Carol on the lips, took the tray from her and left it in the kitchen. He grabbed his bag and coat and headed for the surgery.

Now that Michael wasn't exclusively in charge of things, he still liked to get into work early to clear his head and get ready for the day. Being a larger surgery, there were a lot more bodies around in the morning and he greeted the staff that were there in his usual charming manner on the way to his office. He put his bag down and slumped into his comfy brown leather chair. The last conversation he had with Carol was still playing like a broken record around in his mind.

'Why do we always have to do things her way? She can be so selfish sometimes.'

Michael was really annoyed that Carol wasn't going to be there on Friday night and thought it impolite of her that she insisted that he attended on his own. As he carried on rummaging over his thoughts, there was a knock on the door. It was Chris.

"I thought that was a light on I saw in your office. You're early," Chris commented.

"Yeah, I am. I like to come in early just to get things in order and to get ready for the day. I guess old habits are hard to die."

"I know the feeling. I'm here too doing the exact same thing."

They both smiled, unwittingly agreeing that they were just two hopeless workaholics that didn't know how to pull in the reins on things and just relax.

"Actually, do you have a couple of minutes for me to run something by you?"

Chris whispered and seemed secretive as he closed the door behind him and made himself comfortable by sitting in the chair opposite Michael. Michael had a few things he really wanted to concentrate on, but he afforded Chris the time as he clearly looked like he had something he needed to get off his chest.

"Yeah, sure. What is it?"

Chris gathered his thoughts and then just blurted them out all at once like an uncontrollable tsunami.

"Do you remember that decision I was telling you and Joan about that I needed to make?"

Michael nodded his head to indicate that he did as Chris carried on.

"Well, I have decided to take the job offer and move back home. It wasn't something I came to lightly, but I feel it is the right decision for mine and Ben's future."

Chris went on to tell Michael about how he and Tilly had patched things up and that was the clincher in him making up his mind.

Michael eased back in his chair and clenched his hands behind his neck.

"Sounds like you have really thought things through, Chris, and I'm pleased for you. We'll miss you around here but at the end of the day, you need to do what's best for you and your family. How did your au-pair take the news?"

"She understood."

Chris seemed a bit vague when talking about Natalia, almost as if he didn't want to share anything more with regards to her response.

"I think she had already suspected something was on the cards, but she's fine. Anyway, let me allow you to get on with what you were doing. I just wanted to let you know. I'll probably get an opportunity to tell Joan later. I haven't handed in my notice yet, so please keep this under wraps for now," Chris said as he got up and made his way to the door.

"Your secret is safe with me, mate. I'll just act as surprised as everyone else when you eventually announce it."

Michael gave Chris a wink of solidarity, and he understood what it meant.

Chris went back to his office feeling lighter that he had offloaded his intentions onto someone else, which made it even more real.

As he sat down and stared at the computer screen, the conversation with Natalia the night before played on his mind like he was reliving it in real time on his internal big screen. Natalia was in the kitchen clearing up and Chris had called her into the lounge to have a word. He didn't beat around the bush and just came out straight with the revelation that he had been offered a new job, which he had decided to take, and that he and Ben would be moving out of the area.

Whilst Natalia seemed happy for them, she did not know how that would impact her job. Was Chris expecting her to go with them or was this a callous 'goodbye'. He didn't seem to indicate that he was asking her to go with them. And she knew if he was going to be living near his in-laws that her job would be as good as redundant.

Natalia wanted some clarity on the situation and just asked Chris directly if he wanted her to go with them when they left. Her statement startled Chris somewhat as the idea hadn't crossed his mind that Natalia would want to go with them. And then he realised the blunder he had made in not making things crystal clear that her services would not be required any more. He had apologised to her and assured her that he would give her a glowing reference in support of the next family she worked with, which Natalia had no choice but to grudgingly accept. However, Chris did give her a few weeks' notice which would give her an opportunity to get onto the agency to see if they could place her with another family within the said time frame.

'I still need to work on my people's skills, don't I?'

Chris was giving himself a pep talk as he concluded that he could have handled things with Natalia better than he had.

Wednesday morning at the surgery was busy with lots of patients coming and going and staff running around to accommodate the smooth running of things. Joan had called the Office Manager into her office to check on how things were moving along for Friday. The Office Manager confirmed that everything they had planned was developing nicely and that not even Janet had suspected anything, which was unusual for her, as she usually was invested in whatever was going on.

However, ever since she made up her mind that she was retiring, she had adopted a more relaxed attitude and allowed others to take a more upfront role, whilst she settled for taking an easier life, partly due to her not wanting to invest in the lives of the patients if she wasn't going to be working there for much longer.

Joan was pleased with the progress of things and indicated to the Office Manager that if there was anything else she wanted her to be involved in, not to hesitate to ask. After the conversation, Joan went back to what she was doing, whilst the Office Manager made her way back to the front of house and acted like everything was normal so as not to arouse any suspicions with Janet.

As the day progressed, Chris found an appropriate opportunity to speak with the senior consultant with the intention to hand in his notice. After a small discussion between the two of them, Chris' resignation was duly accepted. The senior consultant thanked him for what he had contributed to the surgery in the short time that he was there and told him that he would be missed, and that the door was always open, should he change his mind. He asked Chris how he'd like the news of his resignation to be conveyed to rest of the staff and suggested that perhaps it could be announced at Janet's leaving do. However, Chris declined that option. He wanted Friday evening to be all about Janet, and he did not want the news of his departure to overshadow what was to be a joyous occasion. As Chris left his boss' office, his next patient wasn't due for 15 minutes, so he knocked on Joan's door to see if she had a free moment. He popped his head around the door.

"Hey Joan, have you got a moment?"

Joan looked at her screen and saw that her next patient was due in five minutes. "Not really, Chris. My next patient is due in minutes."

Chris came into her office anyway and closed the door.

"That's fine, as what I have to say will literally take seconds. I've just come from the boss' office and have handed in my notice."

There was an expression on Chris' face that could only be described as sheer joy.

"You did what, Chris? You can't just land that on me in a few seconds and think you can run off. I need details. I need more than that, mister. I'm free in about half an hour. What about you?"

Chris nodded his head indicating that he too could be free at that time.

"Right, that does it. Come back to my office then and we'll talk about this properly," she said with a smirky smile on her face.

Joan's phone rang. It was a call from reception to let her know that her next patient was on the way to her office. As Joan put the phone down, she beckoned with her hand to shoo Chris out of her office. Chris understood what Joan's hand gesture meant and quickly made his way out of her office. As he was going back to his office, he spotted a young girl pushing a pram with a small baby in it and stepped aside so that she could manoeuvre pass him. The young girl smiled and thanked him for his kind gesture and carried on pushing the pram until she got to Joan's office.

After Chris and Joan had both finished with their patients, on cue Chris made his way down the corridor. The smell of filtered ground coffee lured him into Joan's office. He took a seat and made himself comfortable.

"Would you like a cup of coffee?" Joan asked as she poured herself a cup.

"Yes, please, Joan. After the morning I've had, I need something to perk me up."

Joan poured a cup of coffee for Chris and handed it to him.

"Now, mister, you're going to sit there and tell me all about what you attempted to sneakily blurt out earlier. I don't know how you thought you could just drop a bombshell like that and not expect me to be the least bit curious. So how… when did you decide all this then?"

Chris gave Joan a detailed account of things like the version he had given Michael earlier. Joan's eyes widened as Chris was sharing his heart.

"And that's about the sum of it. I feel the time is right and also, I have peace about it too."

They both continued to slurp their coffees as they engaged in conversation.

"I guess there isn't much more to say, especially as you sound so positive and sure that this is the right decision for you and Ben. My advice would be, do what your heart tells you. God only knows that sometimes we get these opportunities and somehow let them pass through our fingers."

Joan had gone off on a tangent, and her thoughts were veering somewhere else.

Chris picked up on that.

"Wait a minute. Are we still talking about me or are you referring to something or someone else?"

Joan quickly realised that she was rambling and caught herself.

Chapter Twenty-three

"Oh, just ignore me. For a minute I was transported down memory lane."

"Is this the locum you are being transported with?" Chris said cheekily.

Joan laughed.

"Stop being naughty Chris, but I must admit, every time I see him, he does make me think, what if? I know we can't change the past, but we had such a good relationship when we were younger, and it's a pity it just fizzled out without us really getting to know what could have been."

Chris understood exactly what Joan meant and was grateful that he had followed his heart all those years ago, when he chose Jill over Tilly. It was the best decision of his life with the only sadness being that she departed this life too early and way before her time.

CHAPTER TWENTY-FOUR

Friday had finally arrived. It seemed a long week of running around trying not to let seep to Janet the slightest hint of what was going on, but everyone did well to keep the secret under wraps. After a busy day, it was time to close the doors to the public. Caterers had already brought in the food and drinks for the surprise party, using the back entrance, which Joan was instrumental in overseeing. Whilst the Office Manager kept Janet occupied at the front of house, external guests, who weren't staff members, were also given a specific time to arrive and had been escorted via the back entrance also. It was convenient that the back entrance had a hallway that led to the conference room, which allowed everything to go according to plan, unbeknownst to Janet. After about half an hour had passed, Joan gave Michael the thumbs up that everything was ready, which was his indication to go and get Janet.

Janet was busy at her desk putting the last bits of her personal items in her bags. In her mind, she really couldn't believe that it was her last day in a profession she had given her life to and momentarily slipped into a glimpse of the past of her first time working with Michael and Joan at Bricket Wood Surgery.

It was at that place where she felt at home. She was respected by the senior doctors and given autonomy to manage the surgery how she felt it should run. Janet also recalled the highs and lows they had there, which was all part and parcel of surgery life. And yet she wouldn't have changed it for anything. Now here she was, about to depart and embark on a new adventure of the unknown. She didn't know how she would handle not working in a surgery surrounded by all the hustle and bustle that goes with it, but she was open to the idea of a new way of life.

Michael's voice interrupted her thoughts.

"Ahh. Here you are, Janet. I thought you had left without saying goodbye to me."

Michael was keeping up the momentum of the element of surprise that was about to be sprung on Janet.

"Of course not, Dr Mills. I could never leave without thanking you and Dr Webb for all that you have done for me. I'm really going to miss you both and the others, but mostly the two of you."

"Well Janet, we're going to miss you too. In fact, there is just one last thing that I'd like to ask you to do before you leave. There are just some things to clear away in the conference room that hasn't been done, and since it's Friday, we didn't want the mess left over the weekend. Would you mind helping us out as I can't seem to find anyone to assist? I just don't know where they all are." Michael raised his hands in the air like he was in a real dilemma of trying to find help, all the while trying to keep his poker face intact so as not to draw suspicions. They were all so close now and he did not want to fall at the last hurdle and spoil the execution of their grand plan from working.

In true Janet fashion, she stopped what she was doing to go and assist Michael.

"Of course, Dr Mills. It would be my pleasure to do this final task for you, since I'm not going to be around anymore for you to ask, now am I?"

Janet said with a smile on her face. She followed Michael down the hallway until they reached the conference room.

Michael opened the door. It was eerily dark and quiet. He looked back at Janet and smiled and on a flicker of the light switch, a crescendo of noise reverberated 'SURPRISE' as there were cheers and claps as Janet entered the room. Janet stepped back in sheer shock and put her hands across her mouth. The first words uttered by a very shaken Janet were

"How? When? Oh, my goodness."

Michael put his hands on her shoulders and manoeuvred her into a packed room of staff, ex-colleagues and some specially invited patients, who knew Janet from the old surgery.

As Janet observed the various faces, it made her feel even more overwhelmed at the magnitude of what was transpiring. Her gaze circled around the room, and she was mesmerised on how a seemingly ordinary conference room had turned into a fest of colour and was decorated with balloons and banners. Her eyes fixated chiefly on the large banner in the middle of the room in red and gold which said, 'Happy Retirement Janet'. And another one that said, 'We're Going To Miss You'. Janet continued to be guided by Michael who directed her to a prominent area where a chair was adorned just for her and where she was to sit for the festivities.

"Oh my," Janet said as she finally sat on the chair.

"I just can't believe that all of this is for me." Michael piped up,

"Well, you better believe it because it certainly is. You didn't think we could have just let you slip away unnoticed without recognising your years of service to the NHS, do you?"

Janet smiled and shyly dropped her head.

"We are all here to honour you. You'll notice that there are some of your ex-colleagues from years gone by. And some of the patients you have so kindly assisted over the years, who demanded to be here."

The crowd started to laugh and jeer.

"There are also your new colleagues who you have only worked with for a few weeks now, but nonetheless, everyone wanted to be here for you. And I can tell you; it has taken some planning and trying not to let you suspect a thing."

Janet responded quickly by saying,

"And you all did a great job as I did not suspect a thing and that's no mean feat."

"And that's what we wanted, so we have achieved our goal. We just hope now that you will enjoy the night and, on that note, Mr DJ, cue the music."

The DJ played the first song of the night, Stevie Wonder's 'Isn't She Lovely' and the evening got off to a great start.

Janet was in her element and spent the evening engaging with her guests and soaking up the atmosphere. The conference room was large enough for individuals to find a space to dance if a particular tune took their fancy. Janet had several of the male guests spinning her around as they danced with her.

Joan and Chris were perched in a corner having what looked like a deep conversation, and Michael playfully reprimanded them from talking shop on what was supposed to be a joyous occasion and Joan put him right.

"Actually, Michael, we aren't talking shop, I'll have you know. I was just asking Chris about his new job and impending move. And he was filling me in on some of the details he failed to tell me as our time was so short in between patients."

"Oh, I see, well, I stand corrected then," Michael said, having been firmly put in his place by Joan.

He went on, "Well, Chris, in a couple of weeks this could be you too; everyone gathered around to see you off."

Chris laughed sarcastically.

"Err, I don't think so. Unlike Janet, I will be slipping away rather quietly. I don't want all the pomp and fuss. I'd rather have a quick drink with the two of you and that's it, so please don't plan anything grand for me as I'll not thank you."

"I guess we've been told," Joan jeered.

"Anyway, don't worry Chris, we'll keep yours low key. We had to do this for Janet as she's special. Not that you're not special, but I'm sure you get my drift," Joan quickly tried to back pedal her way out of her blunder.

"So, Michael, where's Carol tonight? Thought she would have been here," Joan said as she took a swig of her drink.

"I had hoped so too, but she has a commitment tomorrow afternoon. She has been advised by her obstetrician to take things easy, so I guess she didn't want to overexert herself this weekend and chose to give it a miss tonight. I have already given her apology to Janet who seemed to take it quite well. I think she's so mesmerised by all the other people here that it doesn't really matter if one more person isn't."

In Joan's usual style, she wanted to be nosey and press for more info.

"So, where is she off to tomorrow then?" Michael raised his eyebrows.

"Well, they are throwing a small surprise afternoon tea hen-party for Olivia and that's her girl, so you know she would have rather been there than here."

"And I wonder where my invitation has gone then," Joan said, tongue in cheek.

"I'm sure they'll all have a great time as Olivia is a lovely woman, and Steve is a lucky man."

"To be fair, I believe it was a last-minute thing which her and Jen hatched together. I for one can't wait for her and Steve to tie the knot. I can't tell you the years I have had to sit and listen to him pine over that woman. I kept telling him that he should just be brave and go for it. But he kept insisting that they were the best of friends and what if he jeopardised that and got it wrong and now look at them. They're about to become Mr & Mrs Adams in a few weeks."

Chris felt slightly left out of the conversation as he listened to them both talk about a woman he could have been having a relationship with had he not messed things up between them. When he recalled that last time he was at Olivia's house, it now seemed like a lifetime away and he certainly was in a different mindset.

'How could I have been so stupid? What on earth did I think I was playing at? And then trying to sabotage her relationship with Steve. No wonder she hates me.'

From the few times Chris had glanced over at Olivia when they were at church, it was clear that she did not want to have a conversation with him. Especially since she would change direction or pretend to be talking to someone else when she saw him heading in her direction. Chris was clearly repentant for his actions, which perhaps in hindsight were now a bit too little, too late. He had to accept the fact that Olivia might never want to talk to him again, and since he was leaving the area, this was probably a good thing in his mind to make a fresh start.

Not wanting to seem that he was insensitive to their conversation, Chris tried to make his own contributions to the chat.

"Well done to Steve then, for persevering and holding out for his new bride. I'm sure they'll have a happy life together. I wish them well. Err... I'll just go over and say goodbye to Janet, as I really should be going home now to spend some time with Ben. See you both on Monday then."

Chris took the opportunity to exit the conversation which was proving to be too uncomfortable for him to continue.

Whilst he knew he wouldn't have been able to offer Olivia a marriage proposal so soon, it was hard for him to envisage what could have been had he not had his own internal issues that he was dealing with and trying to process. Michael and Joan observed as Chris made a quick dash from them.

"Was it something we said?"

Michael seemed oblivious to what was happening around him and it was Joan that had to put him in the picture.

"Men... honestly. Michael, he was probably just uncomfortable with us talking about Olivia. With what went on between the two of them. I guess he may still be holding some sort of torch for her."

"Ohhh, I see." The penny had finally dropped for Michael.

"I hope he isn't still holding a torch for her as that ship has sailed. To be honest, I don't know if I could have seen that relationship lasting anyway. Chris and Steve are very different in their temperaments and Olivia is more suited to someone like Steve, who brings out the best in her. Anyway, talking about exiting, I too must dash as I have a hormonal wife at home waiting to give me my orders, so I'm going to run and say goodbye to Janet also," Michael said with a glare in his eye.

The evening was a great success and had gradually fizzled to a natural end with guests leaving and filtering out one after the other. Janet was so inundated with flowers and gift bags that the senior consultant offered to arrange a taxi to take her home. As Janet gathered her things and was helped to the taxi by Joan, she couldn't believe what an evening she had had. She felt blessed that so many individuals took the time out of their personal time to ensure that she had a good send off and it was a memory that would forever be etched in her mind.

"Dr Webb. Thank you so much. You don't know what this evening has meant to me." There was a softness to Janet's tone and her eyes were tearing up.

"You are so very welcome, Janet, and please, it's Joan now. No more of this doctor stuff." Janet smiled.

"Yes, of course, Joan. I'll try to remember that when I pop back to see you all from time to time."

"Well, make sure when you visit that it's a social call and not as one of our patients."

They both smiled and Joan closed the taxi door and waved Janet goodbye.

When Michael arrived home, he could hear Carol talking on the phone and assumed it could only be one person. He greeted Carol with a quick shout to indicate that he was home, as he ran up the stairs to take a quick shower before relaxing for the rest of the evening.

"Hey, Liv. Michael's home so I'll have to be going soon as I want to hear all about Janet's surprise do."

Even though Carol did not accompany Michael to the event, that still did not stop her from wanting to quiz him to find out about all the ins and outs of the evening.

"Gosh, don't you hate surprise do's?" Olivia sighed.

"I would know if someone was planning one on my behalf. I just don't know how individuals can't tell."

Carol realised that she had to be careful with her tone so as not to give the game away.

"I think sometimes those who are planning the surprise are quite good at not giving the game away. Anyway, what are your plans for tomorrow?"

Carol decided to stay safe by diverting the conversation to protect herself from slipping up.

"Oh, don't get me started. Steve's mother has something she wants to show the both of us that she thinks would be good for the wedding. I have already told Steve that this is our wedding, and we are doing the planning and making the ultimate decision on things. But you know him. Now that he has made peace with his mother, he wants to maintain it. So, I guess I can go along for a few hours to see what it is she wants to show us. I will stand my ground though and if we don't like something, it's not featuring in the wedding."

Olivia was adamant. She was thankful that her future mother-in-law was not trying to sabotage her relationship or wedding to her son any more. However, she still wanted to retain her sense of individuality and did not want to be bossed around by anyone.

"Anyway, I know you have to go now, but what are you up to also?"

The words that came out of Carol's mouth next, were as cool as a cucumber. Almost as if she had pre-empted the question was on its way and had already rehearsed her answer. "Oh, I'm going to have a well-deserved rest. I think I have been overdoing things a bit over the last few days, and I think the twins have been letting me know that with the kicks and jibes they have been giving me."

Olivia was mesmerised that she and Carol were talking about babies, since it was always her that they both thought would be the first to have one.

"Wowww, Caz, I can't believe that you're nearly on the cusp of giving birth to twins. Do you remember when we lived together, and I had children over for the weekend? I thought you were going to burst a vein, the way you used to be so protective over this and shielding over that? It was if you were glad that children weren't something that was going to feature in your future and now here you are about to have two."

Olivia started to laugh hysterically.

"I tell you, girl; God has got a sense of humour as you just couldn't make this up."

Carol also had to laugh along.

"You're right, Liv, He sure does. Anyway, I better go as I think that might be Michael coming down the stairs."

"Yeah, sure. No probs. I've got a few things I need to do before I go to bed anyway. But please take care of yourself and my godchildren that you are carrying as you know that when they are here, they'll belong to the two of us."

Even though Olivia could not see Carol's expression, she was smiling to herself as she knew that having twins was going to be a huge challenge for her. And any help that was offered to her, she was going to take with both hands.

"Yeah, I will, and you have a great time tomorrow with your future mum-in-law," Carol said sarcastically.

"Oh, stop it, you; you're a real tease, and on that note, I'm saying goodnight."

Michael had showered quickly and came back down the stairs in the lounge where Carol was perched on the settee with her feet up.

"So, you've finished nattering to Olivia, have you?"

Michael walked towards Carol and gave her a kiss on the forehead.

"Who said it was Liv? It could have been anyone."

"Yeah right. With all that laughing that was going on, I think we both know who it was."

Carol smiled as her husband knew her only too well.

"Yes, you're right, Sherlock Holmes, it was my Livy. Anyway, enough about my phone antics, how did it go tonight? Was Janet shocked?"

Carol wanted to know every last detail from start to finish.

Michael was used to the barrage of questions that would ensue and decided to tantalise Carol by pretending he was tired and didn't want to talk about the evening.

"Carol, I'm too tired to go over the whole night again. If you wanted to know how things went, you should have been there."

Carol started to feel stressed out.

"But no, Michael. You know I couldn't be there. You have constantly been on at me to slow down and take things easy for ages. As it is, it's a good job that I didn't go tonight as I felt a bit queasy. The twins have been kicking like crazy."

Carol rubbed her stomach as she was conversing which got Michael's attention.

"Is everything alright, Caz? What did the pains feel like? Did you start timing them?"

"Michael, stop it. As usual, you're being paranoid. These babies aren't due yet. It was probably me eating something I shouldn't have or twisted myself in a certain way. I mean, I've just finished two bowls of ice-cream and I'm sure that's not good for me."

Carol did her best to try and calm down Michael's fears, but he was a born worrier.

"Okay, well, if, you are sure. But at the slight hint of anything that feels unfamiliar or uncomfortable, Caz, you need to let me know straightaway, as it could be the first indications of labour."

"Yes, Dr Mills, I will. Now back to the party."

Michael raised his eyebrows as he knew he'd get no peace if he didn't give Carol a blow-by-blow recollection of the entire evening.

Once he had finished and he could see that Carol was satisfied, he was glad that they could spend a couple more hours together talking about other things before they eventually retired for the night.

CHAPTER TWENTY-FIVE

It was Saturday morning, and the sun was shining brightly. From Michael and Carol's bedroom window, they had a clear view of the trees in their front lawn. The rustle of the trees usually gave them a good indication of how breezy it was outside. Michael had already woken, showered and was downstairs making breakfast. Carol was enjoying an extended lie-in. The truth of the matter is that she was feeling out of sorts and quite achy, which she put down to staying up too late the night before nattering to her hubby.

For the last few Saturdays, Michael had brought her breakfast in bed. However, today Carol wanted to prove to him that she was fit and strong and decided to beat him to it. As Carol made her way downstairs, she could smell the aroma of bacon and knew Michael was treating himself to a good ole fry-up. Carol stuck her head around the kitchen door.

"Hey there, who's that fry-up for then?" she said, smiling, knowing only too well who it was for.

"Hey, you're up. Good morning, darling. Well, it certainly isn't for you that's for sure. I've made you you're usual. Toast and porridge. How are you feeling? You tossed quite a bit last night. At one point, I thought I was coming off the bed."

There was a hint of concern in Michael's tone.

"I'm okay, Michael. I was feeling a bit achy and was trying to get a comfortable position, that's all. Sorry if I kept you up. We didn't mean to."

Carol did not want Michael to stop her from going to Olivia's house later in the day and wasn't going to say anything to arouse his fears.

"Once I've had a shower, I'll be fine. I'm really looking forward to Olivia's surprise hen-do later. I need to be there by 2 PM to help supervise things. Is that going to be okay?"

"Supervise things, huh. You're just too much," he said, smiling.

"Yeah, that's fine. Now go and take a seat whilst I finish off things in here."

Michael brought in his and Carol's breakfast and they enjoyed sitting down and eating it together, a luxury they usually only got to do at the weekend.

"Jen, do you have the iron and ironing board in your room?"

Olivia was frantically running around trying to sort out an outfit to wear for the day. Jen came out of her room with the ironing board under her arm.

"Yes, I do. Sorry. I was doing some last-minute ironing too. Let me get the iron for you."

Jen had been using the iron to flatten out some of the banners the night before that she was going to put up whilst Olivia was gone. Jen didn't want Olivia to catch her doing so, which is why she had been preparing everything in her room.

Both women respected each other's privacy, so they would never barge into each other's rooms without first knocking or being invited in.

"Here you go. So, do you know what you're going to wear?" Jen asked.

"Well, since it looks like a nice day, I was going to wear a summer dress, but they are all crumpled up in my laundry basket as I haven't ironed for a while. The pile just keeps getting higher and I am losing the will to live trying to tackle reducing the pile." Olivia sighed.

"You better get used to it, girl, because when you're married, that pile will be twice as high."

Even though Jen was teasing Olivia, it was nevertheless a reality that she had to come to terms with. The tangible fact being that things would be different going forward. It certainly wouldn't be like living with a girlfriend. She and Steve would be sharing everything together in their house, including the bedroom. Olivia tried to get the image out of her mind. She wanted her thoughts to stay pure, even though at times it was hard to keep them intact concerning that subject. Olivia and Steve did extremely well to ensure that they were not sexually active before marriage. However, on occasions, their raging hormones still tried to rear its ugly head. Which they combated amicably, to avoid temptation, by ensuring that they weren't spending oodles of time late in the evenings on their own.

Olivia snapped back into the present.

"I have a nice cream dress with black dots, so I think I'll wear that."

"Sounds good," Jen reassured her.

Jen was glad Olivia was making the effort with her outfit, as it meant that she would look nice when she got back and was duly flabbergasted by everyone who would be there for her surprise hen-do.

"So, what will you be getting up to whilst I'm gone? You're not working later, are you?"

"No. Thankfully I have the day off. I thought I'd do some cleaning to start off with and then I'll see what takes my fancy."

Technically, Jen convinced herself that she wasn't lying since she did have to clean up and get everything ready for the tea party. Some of the food and beverage items were already stashed in her room. And some of the other ladies who were due to attend were bringing the rest of items with them.

"Ah, thanks, Jen. I'm only sorry I'll not be around to help. I've been roped into going, God knows where, with Steve's mother. Honestly, I should have said no, but Steve was so insistent, and I didn't want to let him down. It better be worth my time, that's all I can say."

"I'm sure it will be fine, Olivia. Also, it gives you the opportunity to spend more time with his mother and get to know her a little bit better."

Jen was trying to be the voice of reason and seeing the positives as opposed to the negatives.

"I guess you're right, Jen. I think I still get nervous around her. Even though I've put behind me what she tried to do to come between me and Steve, I sometimes wonder whether she could flip again. I'm being silly, aren't I? I should just trust God on this and spend some quality time with my future mother-in-law. Thanks, Jen. I needed our little pep talk and feel marginally better."

Olivia felt lighter walking back to her room to get ready for her adventure.

Steve had already been prepped by Jen what time to arrive, how long to keep Olivia away and what time to bring her back to the house. Steve arrived at 10.30 AM and did his usual signature double blowing of the horn to indicate he was outside. Olivia shouted to Jen that she was leaving and swiftly ran outside to meet him. Steve's mother was not with him as the plan was to meet her at the venue. As soon as Jen heard the front door slam, she started to bring stuff out of her room and frantically tried to make use of the few hours she had to transform the lounge into a room fit for a queen's high tea. There were balloons to finish blowing up and the furniture to rearrange. However, Jen was quite strong and used to lifting patients in and out of ambulances, so that part didn't faze her. When she had almost finished putting everything in place, there was a sigh of relief as she stepped back to look at her handy work. The room looked enchanting. It really did look like a banqueting table spread for royalty. And indeed, that is what Olivia was. A special and loyal friend, who everyone that crossed paths with her adored.

On cue, some of Olivia's closest friends had started arriving armed with items they had to add to the ambience of the room. One had a large balloon which said, 'Hen Party' and others had similar items which lent to the theme. The colour scheme was peach and gold.

"Jen, the room looks great. Olivia is going to love this," one of the ladies said.

"Oh yeah, after she has killed us that is," said another.

They giggled away as they completed the finishing touches. In total, there were eight of them, including Jen, and with Carol and Olivia left to arrive, that would make ten altogether. Jen thought that was a good number to have an intimate tea party and one that wouldn't quite overwhelm Olivia, since she had expressed on many occasions that a surprise party wasn't something she could cope with. However, between Jen and Carol, they knew they could not let her get married without doing something for her and it was Jen that came up with the genius plan.

Last to arrive was Carol, who rolled in and made a grand entrance. Quite a few of the ladies had not seen her for a while, since in the latter stages of her pregnancy she had not gone to church. They were surprised to see how large her stomach had got, yet how much she glowed and carried her pregnancy well.

"Wowww, Carol. Look at you," said one of the ladies as she gave Carol a hug.

"You are positively glowing."

Carol smiled as she lapped up the compliment, because at times she felt anything but that, although Michael always reassured her that she looked beautiful which somehow made her feel better about herself.

"Why, thank you very much, Claire. It's been an experience; I can tell you. But by the grace of God, I'm getting through. My apologies, Jen, for being late. I know I said I was going to get here early to help oversee things, however, these two little monkeys had other plans," Carol said, smiling as she gently rested her hand over her stomach.

"No probs at all, Carol. I surprised myself with what I was able to achieve on my own. Also, some of the others arrived early and we were able to accomplish this end result."

"Well, you've all done a great job, and it looks very lovely," Carol said as she feasted her eyes around the room and took in all the intricate details that Jen had managed to capture. "Olivia will be surprised, but eventually she will appreciate it. The setting will be intimate, so I think you got it just right with the numbers, as it won't freak her out too much."

They all chuckled as they knew Olivia only too well. She wasn't one for the limelight or the attention. She was just a humble schoolteacher who loved interacting with her students and seeing them rise to their full potential.

Olivia was getting anxious in the car because she couldn't recognise where Steve was driving to.

"Steve, where are we going and why haven't you given me any details?"

Steve was laughing as he knew Olivia would get curious and want to know every last detail.

"Look, I don't know anything either. All I know is that my mother has given me the address of where to go and asked us to meet her there. I'm in the same boat too, you know." After about an hour's drive, they arrived at the venue. It resembled a big warehouse, and the car park was heaving with cars. Having driven around the car park a few times, and finally finding a suitable space, they spotted Steve's mother at the front entrance waiting for them.

"Come on, you two. We've got lots to see and so little time to do it in."

Mrs Adams led the way, and they found themselves thrust in the busyness of a wedding fayre.

"I thought this might give you some last-minute ideas with the planning of your wedding."

It wasn't quite what the two of them were expecting, since they pretty much had everything in place. However, so as not to spoil the enthusiasm and efforts that Mrs Adams had put in, they went along with the flow and pretended to be engaged by the various stands and high-end wedding items.

Steve kept an eye on his watch as he had already told his mother that they could not stay long. He did not tell her about the surprise party for Olivia, just in case she accidentally let it slip out in the excitement. She was not one for keeping a secret and had often spoilt a special occasion because of her slips. As they walked around, everything looked extremely expensive, a far cry from the simplicity that they wanted for their wedding. However, they were happy with the choices and plans that they had made for their big day and hoped their guests appreciated their vision too.

"Everything is done so well, isn't it?"

Mrs Adams whispered to Olivia as they exited one of several stands that they had visited, which to Olivia all seemed to look the same.

"Yes, lovely. I guess it's what you're looking for at the end of the day."

"Yes, dear, it is. I thought it might give you some last-minute ideas in the run up to the big day."

Olivia appreciated the sentiments and felt guilty that her initial response wasn't as gentle as it could have been. It was obvious that her future mother-in-law had a lot to prove that she was invested in their wedding, considering her previous form. Olivia noticed that Steve kept looking at his watch and wondered if perhaps he was a bit bored. When Mrs Adams was asking a question to one of the vendors, Olivia took the opportunity to quiz Steve on his rudeness.

"Steve. Why do you keep checking your watch? Your mother is going to think we aren't very interested."

Steve realised that he wasn't being very discreet.

"Sorry, I didn't mean to give that impression. I have already told Mother that we can't stay all day, as I've got to go out which means, I need to get you home too."

Olivia seemed puzzled, because previously Steve kept pressing her about going out with his mother for the day and now had something else planned on the same day.

"Where are you going then?"

Steve knew he would be quizzed by Olivia, so he had to have a plan in place.

"I'm going for a fitting for my suit with my best man." Olivia poked Steve in the ribs.

"You never said you and Michael were going out. Sneaky thing. Bet you did that so you wouldn't have to spend the entire day with your mother, eh? You naughty son," Olivia said, laughing.

"Well, if you and Michael are going out, then you can drop me off at Carol's. It would be good to catch up with her since I haven't seen her for a while."

Chapter Twenty-five

Steve's plan was starting to unravel, and he had to think quick on his feet.

"Noooo. I mean Michael is concerned that she needs to get as much rest as she can. With Michael out, this will give her time to relax and chill, and she isn't going to have that if you go around there and then the two of you start nattering for England."

Steve hoped that he had said enough to convince Olivia to change her mind.

"I guess you're right. I'll just go home then. If Jen hasn't finished cleaning the entire house, maybe I can help her."

"That's good, babe, I think it's for the best."

Steve had dodged a bullet, and he knew it. Mrs Adams came back over to them.

"Do you have your wine ordered yet? I was talking to a company across the way, and they are doing a very good deal, but only for today."

Steve realised the time had expired and that they really needed to get going.

"Mother, sorry, but we need to leave now, but why don't you sort that out and we'd be happy with whatever you choose. Won't we, Liv?"

Steve grabbed hold of Olivia's hand and started guiding her towards the exit, whilst communicating with his eyes that they allow his mother to sort things out on that front. He knew it would make her happy, and that way, they would be free to go. Olivia understood what his eye signals meant and complied with his suggestion.

"Yes, Mrs Adams, that would be great. I'm sure you have an excellent palate and will make the right choice."

Mrs Adams' demeanour went up a notch, especially as they were allowing her to contribute to their wedding in some small way.

"Oh, thank you. Now, get going. I can take care of things here." Mrs Adams didn't even have to think twice and went straight back to continue the conversation she had started with the wine connoisseurs, leaving Steve and Olivia to make a quick exit.

Steve drove faster than he normally would, as he realised that he needed to make up time to get back for the specific time Jen told him that she wanted Olivia to be back by. He had texted Jen before he left to give her an indication of his ETA. He got back to Olivia's house after 4 PM, which was half an hour later. As Olivia got out the car, she told Steve to have a good time at his appointment. And in turn, tongue in cheek, Steve told Olivia not to work too hard as she had mentally prepared herself to go home to do a spot of cleaning.

Jen had been monitoring the front window, awaiting Olivia's return. Once she heard the noise of the engine in the drive, she motioned to everyone to come into the lounge area, out of sight. Olivia entered the house, and everything seemed normal. The house would have been quiet as only Jen would have been expected to be there. Just as Olivia was deciding whether to go upstairs first or not, she heard Jen hollering for her from the lounge. Olivia made her way to the lounge and as soon as she opened the door, she was greeted with the loudest roar.

"Surpriseeeeee."

The noise startled Olivia as she came fully into the room to see Jen, Carol and the rest of her friends with the biggest smiles of joy on their faces.

"What on earth? You ladies are terrible. How… when…?"

Olivia just shook her head when she saw Carol, sitting at the table. The penny dropped and she realised that Steve was also in on the surprise.

Carol smiled and said, "We got yah, girl. We got you good and proper."

Olivia had to agree.

"You sure did, but everything looks amazing, ladies."

Olivia observed the intricate details as her eyes circled around at the way the room was transformed. It felt like she had walked into the Dorchester or some other grand hotel.

"How long have you ladies been planning this?"

Olivia had to admit that they really had stunned her as she didn't suspect a thing. If anything, Carol would have been the one to plan something for her.

However, Olivia knew Carol wasn't herself these past few months and, therefore, resolved that nothing would have been planned.

Carol was quick to pipe in.

"You don't think we could let you get married without giving you a good send-off, do you? Anyway, I can't take credit for the idea as it was all your flatmate's. This whole entire event is her vision. I just lent my support from the couch."

"Well, I really appreciate this, even though I'm not one for surprises, but this is intimate and lovely. It's also nice to see the ladies who I feel the closest to."

The hen-do was a great success and everything Olivia would have wanted if she had planned it herself. The ladies made sure that Olivia enjoyed her afternoon, with laughter and fun flowing in abundance. There were also gifts for Olivia to open and her friends did not hold back on ensuring there were sexy lingerie sets that she had to reveal to the group. Her brown nubian skin glowed as she embarrassingly tried to work out what some of the items were. Jen had organised a few games to test the bride-to-be to see how well she knew her fiancé. And being the teacher she was, Olivia passed with flying colours.

Carol was trying to enjoy herself also, but the niggling sensation that she was feeling earlier hadn't really gone away and she excused herself and went to the downstairs toilet. Olivia had noticed that at times Carol looked a bit uncomfortable and thought that it was just down to her being tired. However, she followed Carol and waited for her to come out of the toilet to check if everything was okay. The music was blaring loud, and everyone continued to have a good time. Carol took her time in the toilet and one of the other ladies came outside to use the toilet too, but Olivia directed her upstairs and told her that Carol was still using the downstairs one.

Olivia began to grow anxious as the time was ticking away and started knocking on the door.

"Caz, hon. Are you okay? You've been in there for a while now."

After a few minutes, Olivia could hear crying.

"Caz. What's up? Open the door and let me in."

Carol unlocked the door and was in a complete state.

"Liv. I think I'm losing my babies. I'm bleeding."

Olivia went into the toilet and saw blood on the floor.

"Oh, my goodness, Caz. I don't have a clue what any of this means. Let me go and get Jen. She'll know what to do."

Olivia quickly ran out of the toilet and called for Jen to come out of the lounge. Her tone was calm as she didn't want to alert anyone else as to what was happening. Jen came out laughing as they were now doing karaoke and one of the voices sounded like someone was strangling a cat.

"Oh my gosh, can you hear the racket that Kath is making? She sounds awful."

Jen's laughter soon turned to concern as the expression on Olivia's face looked like she had seen a ghost.

"What's the matter, Olivia? Are you okay?" Olivia pulled Jen aside.

"Ssshh. I don't want to alarm the other ladies, but something is wrong with Carol. She's in the toilet and is bleeding and we don't know what to do."

Jen frantically rushed past Olivia straight to the toilet where she saw Carol sitting down and crying hysterically. Carol looked straight into Jen's face.

"Am I going to lose my babies, Jen? Am I?"

"Calm down, Carol. I need you to bring your breathing right down. Everything is going to be okay. I'm just going to pop upstairs and get my medical bag, but because of the bleeding, we're going to have to get you to the hospital. I'm going to call an ambulance right now. In the meantime, I need you to stay calm. Olivia is here and she'll hold your hand until I get back."

After a few minutes, Jen came back with her bag and got her stethoscope out and started to listen to Carol's chest.

"Well done, your breathing has come down."

Carol continued muttering under her breath contemplating whether she was going to lose her babies or not. She had come a long way from first learning that she was pregnant and getting over the initial shock. For someone who didn't think children would factor in her life, they were now the most important thing to her and the thought of losing them now, wasn't worth thinking about. More importantly, shattering Michael's dreams of him becoming a father was unthinkable and not something she was going to let her mind process.

Olivia continued rubbing Carol's back, reassuring her that everything was going to be okay. By now, the other ladies had got wind of what was happening. What was earlier an atmosphere of joviality had now turned sombre. One of the ladies, Claire, got the others to start praying as that was one thing they could all draw comfort in, knowing that God was in control, and He would ensure that Carol and her babies were safe.

"When the ambulance comes, I'm going to go with them" Jen said.

"The crew will probably be some of my colleagues."

"Well, you're not leaving me behind. I'm coming too. Oh no, what about Michael? We haven't informed him yet. I better call him now."

Olivia went into the kitchen to call Michael.

CHAPTER TWENTY-SIX

The ambulance got to the house quickly after Jen had explained on the 999 call the seriousness of the situation. The paramedics made their way to where Carol was, who had previously fainted and had started to feel weak prior to them arriving. Jen passed on to the paramedics Carol's vitals and what she had observed. After attempting to ask Carol some questions to assess how she was feeling, the paramedics took over and helped Carol onto a wheelchair and into the ambulance. Carol was still muttering faintly under her breath.

"I need Michael to hold my hand. Has anyone got hold of him yet?"

"Don't worry hon. He will meet you at the hospital."

Olivia did not want to alarm Carol that Michael's phone had gone straight to voicemail and that he wasn't picking up. Nor did she want to divulge the fact that neither could she get hold of Steve.

'Where are the two of them and what are they up to?'

Olivia started to feel apprehensive. If Carol was about to give birth, she did not want the father of her children to miss the birth. Michael would be distraught. Jen informed the ladies that understandably they had to wind things up as both her and Olivia would be going to the hospital. The ladies understood and assured them that they would continue praying until they heard any further news. As they travelled to the hospital in the ambulance, Olivia continued trying to get hold of Michael and Steve, but there was still no joy. Once they arrived at the hospital, Carol was rushed into emergency where she was met by her obstetrician who took over her care.

Michael and Steve had finished their appointment at the tailors earlier than expected and decided to go and have a game of squash, since they hadn't been for a while. Michael had been goading Steve for a while now that since he was back on his feet that he was going to crush him the next time they played. Steve wanted to prove to himself that he was back on form, and it was his decision to take up the challenge and head to the sports centre. Once there, they left their personal belongings, including their phones, in the changing room and wasted no time by going at it hammer and nail on the squash court.

They were only supposed to have a quick game, the first one to win three games. However, as Michael won the first two games, Steve was keen for them to change the goalpost halfway through and decided to go to five games instead. They were both exhausted as every smack of the ball against the wall took out any strength they had left. Steve was perspiring heavily. Determined that Michael wasn't going to make mincemeat of him, he won the next two games. This final game was the decider. Michael could see how determined Steve was to win and the kind thing might have been to let him win the game, if only to boost his confidence back to fitness. However, Michael was way too competitive to throwaway a game just like that. That last rally was the most strenuous one. Michael made his last move, and Steve sprinted to get it, but tumbled and fell. Which meant Michael won the point and subsequently the game.

"Ohhh man. I can't believe it,"

Steve said as he picked himself from off the floor.

"Well, you better believe it, mate, cos I won you fair and square. Even though you changed the terms halfway through the game I might add. When are you going to learn, Stevie boy, that when you play with me, you're just outclassed?"

Michael felt pleased with himself and enjoyed gloating.

"Very funny," Steve replied.

"You are just lucky that I'm not as fit as I used to be. But don't worry, I'm getting there. You'll see that when we have our re-match."

Michael laughed as they gathered their towels and headed for the showers.

"I don't know when I'll next get in another game like this. The twins will soon be here, and my time and hands are going to be quite full then."

"That's true, but you might just need to blow off steam now and again. And when you do, I'll be here waiting to wipe that smug look off your face. Anyway, how's Carol doing? We haven't seen her at church for a few weeks now."

"She's doing good. The only trouble is that I can't get her to just stay completely still and do nothing. It worries me that she'll do something that might unnecessarily rouse the babies before their time. We have our planned elective c-section scheduled in the diary. So, if she continues to take things easy, then there shouldn't be any cause for concern. Anyway, lets hit the shower and get out of here, as I need to pick Carol up from your fiancée's house. I'm sure they had a great time and she'll probably be tired by now and want to go home and have a proper rest."

Michael and Steve had a shower, got dressed and started to get ready to leave the changing room. Steve took his phone off vibrate and noticed quickly that he had six missed calls all from Olivia.

"Oh look, my fiancée has been trying to get hold of me. I've got six missed calls from her. I wonder what she wants now?"

Michael laughed whilst also retrieving his phone from his bag.

"A kept man, eh? You better watch that, mate. She'll be keeping tabs on you after you're married too."

Michael's face appeared puzzled as he also looked at his phone.

"That's odd. I've got a few missed calls from Olivia too. I bet things have probably ended early and she's wondering where we are. Carol must be anxious to get home so she's asked Olivia to call you as well to see where I am."

"Perhaps. Anyway, let me call Liv and tell her that we are on our way."

Steve rang Olivia's phone. It didn't have to ring twice as Olivia immediately answered the phone.

"Oh my gosh Steve. Don't you guys ever answer your phone? Where have you been?" Steve sensed Olivia wasn't pleased with them. But neither did he appreciate her screeching at him without even saying hello.

"Babe. Calm down. Michael and I went for a quick game of squash."

Olivia couldn't believe what she was hearing.

"A quick game of squash? Are you serious? I have been trying to get hold of you and Michael for ages. Anyway, there's no time for chit chat right now. You need to get Michael to the hospital straightaway. We had to call the ambulance for Carol. She was bleeding and fainted."

"Oh, my goodness," Steve said in a frantic tone before Olivia could finish her sentence.

"Is she alright? We'll get there straightaway."

Michael could hear bits of the conversation and was hollering at Steve as he was talking.

"What's going on, Steve? Is it Carol? Is she alright?"

Steve relayed verbatim everything Olivia had told him, sending Michael into a frenzy.

"Oh God. It sounds like she might be going into labour. We should have gone straight home after we had our suits fitted. I can't believe it. Here I am playing squash, and my wife is probably lying in a hospital bed in great distress. God knows what is going on and how she is feeling."

Michael clasped his hands behind his head as he tried to process the reality of what was unfolding.

"Come on, Steve, get me to the hospital as quick as you can. I've got to get there in time."

Steve wanted to do all that he could to assist his friend. He could sense the strain and anxiety that he was under.

"Of course, buddy. Don't worry, I'll get you there in time. If it's the last thing I do."

It was convenient that they came in one car and that Steve had drove. They both headed for the car park and immediately noticed a problem. Someone had blocked Steve in and had just left their car stationary.

"You have got to be kidding me."

Michael let out a cry of frustration, questioning how someone could be insensitive and park so badly.

"What are they thinking? You can't park like that."

Steve tried to calm Michael down with the assurance that perhaps the person had only parked there temporarily and would be back soon. However, after having sat in the car waiting for five minutes, Steve realised that they had to rethink their strategy.

"Okay. I'm going to go in and see if reception can despatch a message over the Tannoy and see if we can flush this sucker out."

Steve was gone for what seemed like an eternity, but in fact it was only five minutes. An announcement was made over the Tannoy for the owner of a black convertible Ford Mustang, complete with the registration details, to report to reception urgently. Steve had informed reception the seriousness of the situation and that he and his friend urgently needed to get to the hospital as soon as possible.

Soon after the announcement was made, four young lads casually strolled up to the reception with sports bags on their shoulders. They were goading and teasing each other, pulling off each other's caps, jeering loudly, oblivious to the mayhem they had caused. One of the lads spoke to the person at reception sitting on the other side of the counter.

"Yeah, man. It's my car registration you just broadcasted. What's up?"

Before the staff member could utter a word, Steve jumped in.

"What's up is that you have parked badly and blocked me in. You can't park like that, and I urgently need to get to the hospital. So, if you wouldn't mind, I'd be grateful if you could move your car right now."

Steve was trying not to sound too agitated because he knew that the type of lads he was dealing with, they would probably drag their heels deliberately just to make a point.

"Okay, old man. Keep your hair on. There weren't any available spaces at the time. We do this all the time and have never had an issue before. So, what's your problem?"

They were obviously selfish lads and a law unto themselves. Steve just wanted them to quickly move their car so that he could get Michael to the hospital. In his line of work, he dealt with attitudes like that all the time. Which is what got them into his unit in the first place. Steve walked behind them until he got back to his car. The young lads jumped into their car, opened the sunroof, revved up the engine and sped off in a hurry, tooting their horn and making a raucous trail behind them.

"I see you found them then," Michael said as he rolled his eyes in disgust that individuals could be so insensitive without a care in the world.

"Yes, I did and to them, it's something they do all the time. Can you believe they wanted to know what my problem was? I really had to keep my cool so that the situation wouldn't escalate and turn ugly. Anyway, enough about them. Let's go."

"Don't go down the main High Road as they have roadworks and temporary lights. Go round the back, down Blackwell Street and along by the canal, you'll get to the hospital quicker that way."

Michael was used to driving to the hospital in rush hour and knew all the shortcuts to dodge the traffic.

"Sure will. Thanks for the heads up."

Steve put his foot on the gas but kept his eye on his speed as he didn't want them to be stopped by the police and then be delayed even further. After 20 minutes, they arrived at the hospital. Steve dropped Michael at the entrance so that he could run in whilst he headed for the car park. Michael was familiar with the layout of the hospital and headed straight to the maternity unit. Olivia and Jen were sat waiting, looking anxious and nervous. Michael rushed in. Slightly out of breath from running up the stairs as opposed to waiting for the lift.

"Great, Michael. You're here. Thank God,"

Olivia said feeling a sense of relief that Michael had managed to get to the hospital in time.

"How is she?" Olivia shrugged her shoulders.

"Michael, the last time I saw her, she didn't look great. Just get in there. She needs you," Jen said in a reassuring way that he was not to fear the worse. Michael was scared. He didn't know what he was going to encounter and said a quick prayer under his breath as he made his way to the operating theatre.

Michael needed to be prepped with the standard green surgical gown and mask before they would allow him to go in and see Carol. The obstetrician explained to him that they were going to have to do a c-section now as the first baby wasn't lying in the normal 'head down' position. Also, the baby's heart rate had dropped quite significantly.

To save that particular one, it was decided that both babies should be delivered and put in an incubator machine straightaway. Michael was used to seeing patients in distress several times throughout his career, but when it came to someone close to his heart, that was a completely different story.

Before going into the operating theatre, Michael's mind drifted back to the time when his adopted mother was extremely sick, and he visited her in the hospital. Similar to what he was about to visualise with Carol, he did not know what to expect and it looked like there was a time when he was going to lose her. The emotions he felt at that time, he vowed he never wanted to experience again as it almost rocked his world. Thankfully, his mother pulled through and made a full recovery.

"Michael, you can come in now." One of the nurses interrupted Michael's thoughts and directed him into the operating theatre.

Carol was relieved to see Michael and the enormity of the situation caused her to collapse in a flood of tears.

"I thought you weren't going to get here, but I'm so glad you're here now." Michael held Carol's hand.

"Nothing could have kept me away, babe. I'm here now and I'm not going anywhere."

The obstetrician started to set things up for the procedure. Carol was told she would either have a spinal or epidural anaesthetic once they had assessed her, meaning that she would be awake during the procedure but numb from the waist down. Meanwhile, the medical team got themselves ready to prepare for surgery.

Steve found Olivia and Jen anxious for news in the waiting area, as they hoped for the best.

"Hey. You found us then."

Olivia was relieved that she had someone to hold her hand whilst they all waited not knowing what the outcome would be.

"So, Jen. Do you think Carol will have the babies today then?" Steve said inquisitively.

"Most probably, I would hazard a guess. If the babies were in distress, it would be the safer option to get them out straightaway and put them in an incubator. Carol is brave and she'll get through this. With Michael by her side now, that should be reassuring for her."

"I really hope so, Jen," Olivia remarked.

"I wish I could be on the other side of Michael, in that operating room, holding her other hand. Dear Lord, please be with Carol and deliver those babies safely."

Jen stood up to stretch her legs. Sitting for a lengthy time made them go numb.

"Why don't I go and get us something to drink as I could murder a coffee and do with a walk too."

"Okay then. Could you get me a decaf tea with oat or almond milk? That's if they do that here," Olivia said.

"The café should have alternative milks. I'll ask them anyway. What if they haven't?"

"Then just get me a bottle of freshly squeezed orange juice. In fact, get that instead. Thanks hon."

"What about you Steve? Can I get anything for you?"

"I'll have a bottle of water thanks. Are you going to be okay carrying everything? Should I come with you?"

"Okay, thanks Steve. I could do with an extra pair of hands."

Jen and Steve left to get the beverages, leaving Olivia alone with her thoughts. Olivia sat there trying not to imagine the worse yet continued to worry.

'What if something went terribly wrong and there were complications with the procedure?'

But in her next thought, she remembered that they were people of faith. They were supposed to utter words that were positive as opposed to words that were gloomy.

Olivia recited Philippians 4:13 under her breath.

'I can do all things through Christ that strengthens me.'

However, she personalised the scripture so that it pertained to Carol.

'Carol can do all things through Christ that strengthens her.'

Not long after, Jen and Steve came back with the drinks. They sat there sipping and chatting, waiting until Michael came downstairs to give them an update.

It was a long 45 minutes, but Carol's surgery was successful, and the twins were finally here. Carol was exhausted and yet remarkable all at the same time. On the other hand, Michael had a newfound respect for his wife. The fact that she was able to give him the thing he had always dreamt of being, a father. He watched intently as both babies made their entrance into planet earth, which was a surreal experience. However, after their delivery, the joy of seeing their newborns delivered was soon short-lived as the babies were quickly transported to the NICU. Both babies, a boy and girl, were quite small, but the boy was struggling to breathe. He was immediately connected to a ventilator by an endotracheal tube. Thankfully, the girl just needed some extra oxygen and didn't need to go on a ventilator. The specialist staff placed a nasal cannula over her head to help with her breathing.

Carol still felt light-headed but was concerned about her babies.

"Michael, are the babies okay? Where have they taken them?"

"Don't worry hon. They are getting the best care. Because they are small and were born before the 39 weeks, they just need some help with their breathing. Now you take some time to rest. You were great, Caz. Well done, you did it."

Michael was excited and took a flannel to wipe Carol's brow as she had been perspiring profusely.

"Yes. I did do it, didn't I? But please don't ask me to do that again anytime soon."

Michael was pleased to see that Carol's wit was as sharp as always, and he gently kissed her on her brow.

"I'm just going to go downstairs and let the guys know that you are okay, and the babies are safe and in good hands."

Michael hesitated before he left the room.

"Should I tell them the names of our babies, or do you want us to do that together?"

Carol didn't really care either way. She just wanted to be able to hold her babies in her arms.

"If you want to tell them, that's fine. I don't mind. Just play it by ear. If they ask, then I guess it's okay to let them know. But if they don't ask, then let it be. I just want to see my babies."

"After you have rested, babe, I'll see if the nurses will allow me to take you in a wheelchair so that you can go and see them in the NICU."

Michael went downstairs and found Olivia and Jen still patiently waiting where he left them, with Steve having joined them. Olivia saw him come into the room and quickly rose to her feet for an update.

"Hey Michael. How did everything go? Is Carol okay? How about the babies? Are they well?"

"Calm down, calm down, Olivia. All is well. Carol is recovering nicely, and the babies were successfully delivered and are currently being taken care of in the NICU."

"Oh, thank you, Jesus." Olivia raised her hands in the air appreciative of God answering all their prayers.

Steve got up to shake Michael's hand.

"Congratulations, man. You're now a father. I can't believe it."

Steve was genuinely pleased for Michael. He had finally got the thing he had always yearned for, long before he even had a wife.

Jen too lent her sentiments.

"Yes. Congratulations, Michael. That is such great news. I am so glad we acted when we did and called the ambulance."

"Thank you, Jen. We have so much to thank you for. Had you not responded as quickly as you did, who knows what could have happened."

"You are very welcome. I was just doing the job I am trained to do, but you can thank me by naming one of them after me if you like," Jen teased.

"Oyyye," squealed Olivia.

"Do you mind? They are naming one after me," she giggled.

"Anyway, what did you have?"

"A boy and a girl" Michael proudly said.

There was a unanimous sound of "Ahhh."

Chapter Twenty-six

"And what are their names or is that still a secret?" Michael smiled.

"No, Olivia, it's not a secret. Our son is called Zachary, and our daughter is Zoe."

"Those are such lovely names," Olivia said.

"When can we see them and Carol, of course?"

"Well, you won't be able to see the babies until they are out of the NICU. Perhaps come back tomorrow to visit Carol as she needs her rest now. Having a c-section is a major operation and it takes quite a lot out of an individual. Also, knowing Caz, she'd want to look her best before receiving visitors."

"That'll be right," Olivia chirped, agreeing wholeheartedly with Michael.

"Yeah, Liv. We can always come back tomorrow. Let's leave Michael to go back to his newly extended family," Steve said.

"Okay. But before we come back tomorrow, we have some shopping to do. We need to get flowers for Carol, and cuddly teddy bears for my godchildren."

"Whatever you say, dear," Steve said sarcastically raising his eyebrows.

"I'm working tomorrow, so I'll pop in to see if I can visit Carol," Jen remarked.

"Guys, again, thank you all so much for the part you played, whether that was getting Carol or me to the hospital. We are profoundly grateful to have you all in our lives."

Michael hugged them all and they waved goodbye to him as they left, allowing him to go back to Carol and his new family.

CHAPTER TWENTY-SEVEN

The medical team in the NICU continued to keep a close eye on the twins. Zoe had made significant progress in the few days since she was born with the doctors reasonably happy with her breathing. However, it was still touch and go with Zachary, which was a concern to the doctors, as well as his parents. It broke their hearts to see their little son's body hooked up to machines with various tubes and wires attached to his body, keeping him alive. Carol was now able to nurse Zoe, which she found unfamiliar and strange and didn't feel like she was a natural. However, Michael was on hand to encourage her that she was doing a great job and that she would soon get used to it.

As promised, Olivia had visited Carol the day after the twins were born. Although not able to see the twins in person. Michael had shown her pictures of them that he had taken on his phone, which Olivia had to make do with as a suitable alternative for the time being. Carol was happy to see a friendly face and didn't hold back on all the gory details of the birth, to Olivia's dismay. Jen had also popped in to see her in between her shifts to make sure Carol and the babies were all doing well.

With Zoe cradled in her arms, Michael wheeled Carol to see Zachary, manoeuvring carefully down the corridor and eventually arriving at the designated place. Once they were comfortable, Carol gently rocked Zoe from side to side as she whispered softly in her ear.

"Hey Zoe. This is your big brother. He's not too well at the moment, but we are praying for him that God will heal his body. And we believe that He will do it too because his name means 'God has remembered'. God is going to remember him and then it won't be long when the two of you will be playing with each other. And probably driving your mum and dad crazy at best."

Michael stood behind Carol stroking her shoulders and praying silently under his breath.

'God, I really don't know what is happening to us, but I do know that you are not the author of confusion. I don't believe that you allowed us to get pregnant, only for one of our babies to die. It doesn't make sense. And we aren't going to stop praying until we get our miracle.' In Michael's mind, Zachary would be the one to carry on his legacy, ensuring that the Mills' name lived on.

As he stood there listening to Carol bond with their children, his mind took a glimpse back in time as he remembered the discussion they had had when deciding on names. Carol was superficial, wanting them both to have the same initials. But Michael wanted a bit more depth. He wanted names that had a spiritual meaning.

After much discussion, they eventually settled on Zoe for a girl, meaning '*Life*' the God life. And for a boy, chose Zachary. Meaning 'remembered by God' or 'God has remembered'. Little did they know when deciding on those names, months later, how poignant they would become. And how fervently they would need to rely on God and their faith for a miracle.

Olivia wanted to ensure that Ben's final week at Newmont Primary School was memorable. He had come a long way and had grown in leaps and bounds. She had run it by the Head who had given permission for them to throw him a small class party.

Since their unfortunate incident, Olivia did not have much interaction with Chris and tried to avoid talking to him, if she didn't have to. However, she knew that she would need to get word to him about the party for Ben. Olivia still did not want to give Chris the time of day. She still felt there was something shifty about him, which she didn't trust, and was glad God had other plans for her life that didn't involve him.

Instead, she arranged for the school secretary to make the call. Chris was happy for them to give Ben a good send off and gave his permission. Olivia was in her element getting the plans together and wanted Ben to enjoy his last week with them. Everyone was going to miss him and did not want to see him leave.

When Chris got home that night, he wasn't as late as normal, so he managed to see Ben before he went to bed. Ben couldn't contain his excitement that his class was going to throw a party for him. And Chris had to sit through him painstakingly going over everything that he was hoping it would be.

Natalia had made one of her Polish dishes which Chris speedily guzzled down, leaving the plate clean, followed by getting Ben ready for his bedtime. If ever he got home at a decent time, he would make it a point of attending to Ben since he seldom had the opportunity to do so. Natalia made herself scarce after tidying things up in the kitchen and retired to her room.

Natalia had managed to secure a new position with another family. She was glad that she wasn't going to be out of work for an extended period. The plan was that she finished with the Harris family on a specified Friday and took up her new position the following Monday. The family came as a recommendation from Chris.

One of his patients was enquiring as to how he went about securing an au-pair and he happened to mention that Natalia's position was soon coming to an end. He gave them the company he used and told them to specifically ask for Natalia as she came highly recommended.

He felt guilty for the way things had turned out and felt it was the least he could do to ensure that Natalia was properly compensated for. He had particularly asked his patient not to divulge to Natalia that the recommendation came from him. Therefore, Natalia did not know that her new position was as a result of Chris' input.

Most individuals had already made up their mind about him. And he didn't see the point of trying to change the minds of those who wanted to believe what they chose to believe. He knew in his heart that he had changed and was making inroads to turnover a new leaf. The fresh start was exactly what he and Ben needed.

After Chris had put Ben to bed, he retired to the lounge area, sat on the settee and took out his mobile phone to catch up on his voicemails and missed messages. As he listened to the three messages he had, they were all from his estate agents asking him to call them back urgently.

The time was 7 PM and he wondered if they would still be there. He called the mobile number of the lady who was dealing with him personally. He caught her out of the office, but as he called her on the mobile and it was an urgent matter, she took the call.

"Mr Harris. Thanks for returning my call. I've been trying to get hold of you all day."

Chris hinted a slight concern in her voice that troubled him.

"What is it, Belinda? Is everything alright? Sorry I missed your calls as I had a busy day at the surgery today. And then the battery in my mobile died and I left my charger at home. Oh, never mind, you don't need to be bothered with my mishap."

"Well, Mr Harris, there is no kind way to say this, so I'm just going to rip off the band aid quickly. Unfortunately, the sellers whose house you are supposed to be buying have pulled out. Apparently, they've had some sort of epiphany and don't want to sell any more."

"They can't do that, can they?"

Chris was agitated and numerous scenarios started swirling around in his mind.

"But haven't we exchanged contracts? And I've already paid my deposit. I have a buyer and don't want to pull out now and let them down. I have also given notice on my job and my son's school."

"Mr Harris, I'm sorry for this setback. However, you are within your rights to rescind the contract. I will get back your deposit with interest. And the vendor will have to pay to cancel the registration of the contract, plus any interest at a daily rate. So, I will go ahead and get the ball rolling on this, if that's okay. In the meantime, as you already have a buyer in place, I would encourage you to go ahead with your sale and then rent a house when you get to Leicestershire. You'll be in a much better position to buy something without a chain behind you."

"I guess so, but that's not how things were supposed to pan out."

There was a slight hesitation on the phone and then Belinda spoke again.

"Didn't you say your in-laws were going to be nearby in the area? Could there be a possibility of you staying at their house for a couple of weeks or so, until you secured your own rental?"

Chris sighed heavily.

"That is an option, I guess, but I wouldn't want to be a burden to them. Although they wouldn't think so. They would love to have Ben around the place regularly. Leave it with me and let me speak with them and get back to you. Anyway, thanks for your advice and if you can get the ball rolling on getting the vendors to cough up and settle our legal fees then that would be one less thing to worry about."

"Of course, Mr Harris, I'll start the paperwork tomorrow. For what it's worth, enjoy the rest of your evening. And again, I'm sorry that I was the bearer of bad news."

"Thanks Belinda. It wasn't your fault. I guess it is what it is. You have a good evening too."

The next day Chris woke up with a lot on his mind. From the shattering news Belinda dropped on him the previous night, he did not sleep well, tossing and turning all night trying to establish what would be a suitable solution.

His first thought was that if Jill was here, she would have known what to do.

His second thought was, but then again, if Jill was here, he wouldn't have left the area they established a home in, in the first place.

Everything seemed one big mess. His faith wasn't where it ought to be and, in his desperation, he cried out to God.

'God. I know I have struggled at times with my faith. But I know you're real. And I'm asking you to show yourself clearly in this situation. Make a way some way, somehow.'

Chris had finally come to the end of his tether and did not want to make any further decisions in his life unless he had God's direction.

Having decided to go into the practice later that morning, Chris prepared himself to make the call to his in-laws. Natalia had already left with Ben to take him to school, so that distraction wasn't there to make him feel uncomfortable. Mrs Hunter answered the phone, and Chris took the time to explain what had happened and the predicament they had found themselves in. Before he could even get around to asking if he and Ben could stay there until they got themselves sorted, Mrs Hunter was offering their home as an option. She made the phone call easy for Chris, and it took away any awkwardness he was feeling having to ask.

"Chris, you take as long as you like to find somewhere. You know the house is big enough and we would love to have you both. It's a pity the place where you were buying fell through, but sometimes things happen for a reason."

"Thank you, Felicity. That's very kind of you, but don't you want to discuss it with Frank first and then get back to me?"

Chris didn't want Frank not to have a say in the matter. However, Mrs Hunter wasn't going to let this opportunity slip through her fingers and had to make a quick decision in case Chris had second thoughts and changed his mind.

"Oh, don't worry about Frank. We are one and he'll be fine with my decision. After all, we're family. Don't you forget that."

Chris thanked her profusely and assured her that once he was there, he would make it his mission to secure another home for him and Ben as quickly as possible.

Chris made his way to the surgery and got the opportunity to chat with Joan in-between appointments. He shared his latest news about the move with her. Joan expressed her annoyance at the insensitivity of someone pulling out of a deal, right at the last minute at that.

However, like his mother-in-law, she encouraged him to look at the positives. It could be a blessing in disguise. Perhaps there was something structurally wrong with the house and they might have inherited an inadequate property to live in. Joan confessed to Chris that she wasn't a strong believer like he was, but that perhaps God was shielding him from something more sinister.

In all the thoughts Chris was battling with, he did not even think that it could be something so simple as that. And he was reassured that he shouldn't let this setback unduly worry him.

Thankfully, he had a back-up plan, which meant he could go ahead with the sale of his property and move according to plan. He had already told his colleagues that he didn't want them to make a fuss and that he wanted to exit quietly. And he made Joan promise that they wouldn't go back on that. When they had the surprise party for Janet, he felt that she was deserving of that. He didn't think he was and did not want individuals to say things about him that perhaps they didn't mean. After all, most of the staff didn't really know him that well. Following the merger, he pretty much kept himself to himself, interacting only with Michael, Joan, a few of the other partners and the secretaries. He felt comfortable exiting quietly.

Chris allowed his thoughts to take a glimpse back in time round the period when he left his last surgery. That was the quickest exits of all time. It's almost as if he had to run and run and run. He didn't know where. All he knew was that he couldn't stay there and listen any longer, whilst his name was being dragged through the mud. It was disappointing to him that individuals who had known him for years thought he could do something as unethical as what he was being accused of.

And who was at the centre of it all? Tilly. Even though he had superficially cleared the air with her, he still didn't trust her fully and living with his in-laws would give her access to him and Ben's life. More than he would have wanted to give. His preference would be to keep Tilly at arm's length. And that he happily lived his life, with his son far away from her. And that she lived her life in whatever way she wanted to. Just as long that it didn't entail their paths crossing.

Chris got through the rest of the day and clocked off early for a change. Early enough to be able to pick up Ben from school. He called Natalia to inform her of his plans and Natalia took the opportunity to carry on preparing dinner, since she didn't have to stop halfway through, as her daily schedule would have entailed.

Chris turned up at the school to pick up Ben, unbeknownst to Olivia. He waited patiently outside Ben's classroom and could hear Olivia giving the children their last instructions for the day. She really was a natural and had gone above and beyond to help Ben to become the confident child he had become.

Chapter Twenty-seven

Chris felt that if he wanted to prove to everyone he had changed, he needed to apologise to Olivia, since he had not done so to-date. Well, not to the degree that would have been acceptable to her.

The children started to leave the class in clusters, laughing and giggling with each other as they walked to the cloakroom to get their belongings. Chris saw Ben as he came outside, and Ben was pleasantly surprised and felt immensely proud that his dad was there to pick him up. He gave Chris a big hug.

"Hey buddy, you go and get your coat and wait for me outside the cloakroom. I just need to have a quick word with Miss Dupont."

Chris knocked the door and put his head around the door. He startled Olivia as she thought it was one of her colleagues wanting her attention about something.

"Oh. I wasn't expecting to see you," she said, rummaging through her mind what he could possibly want.

"Did you want to discuss the party we are planning to have for Ben this Friday? I thought our secretary had already given you the details."

Olivia could feel her cheeks hotting up and her throat getting dry, so she quickly took a swig of water from the water bottle that was on her desk. She put down the board wipe that she was using when she heard Chris' voice literally crawl up her back, giving her a chill.

Chris continued to walk into the room and his voice was ever so calm.

"No, I've already got all those details and I'm fine with everything. And thank you for doing this. Ben is excited and can't wait for Friday."

"Well, it's the least we can do for Ben. He's a very special boy and is going to be missed by everyone. His teachers and his peers."

Chris continued,

"If you have a few minutes. I just wanted to have a quick chat with you."

'Honestly, what is it now, Chris? Could this get any more embarrassing?'

"Yes, I have a few minutes. Please take a seat."

Chris walked closer to the front of the room and took a seat on one of the chairs which made him look like a midget.

After wriggling around somewhat in the seat, Chris said

"Actually, perhaps it would be more comfortable if I just stood."

Chris strained his body to get back up into a standing position. Olivia was sniggering inwardly because she knew very well that he wouldn't have been able to hold an intelligent conversation sitting so low and looking up at her. But that was her way of enacting her revenge on him, which no doubt she felt he had deserved.

Once Chris felt he was on an even keel again, he proceeded.

"I just wanted to take this opportunity, firstly to thank you for everything you have done for my son. You have worked your magic on him and he's a totally different boy from the one that first came through the doors of this school."

Chris exhaled and continued. The next part of the conversation was more sensitive but nevertheless had to be said if he wanted to leave with his head held high.

"I also want to apologise for my behaviour towards you. Which was totally out of line and uncalled for. And, for trying to sabotage your relationship with Steve by telling him untruths in an attempt to tarnish your character. I really don't know what came over me that day and I have hated myself for my conduct ever since. I know any offer of an apology I had tried to make before would have been lame, but I did not want to leave without expressing my sincere apologies and to ask if you could find it in your heart to forgive me."

Olivia was truly taken aback as that was the last thing she had expected from Chris. She had thought that what happened between them was always going to be something that was never going to be resolved. And here he was now looking like a shell of his former self, apologising and asking for forgiveness.

Perhaps it was a sign that he was genuinely sorry for his actions and wanted to put things right. Olivia also knew that if she truly wanted to move forward and not have this memory lingering over her, that she had to forgive him. It was what her Christian faith demanded. Whether she wanted to or not. It was clearly in the Lord's Prayer.

'Forgive us our trespasses, as we forgive those who trespass against us.'

As she looked into his deep brown eyes, she forgot how handsome he was and that it was his striking eyes that first attracted her to him. She could also see a softness to him that she had not seen before and felt the warmth of his tone as he spoke.

Olivia cleared her throat.

"I appreciate you saying what you have said, as I can imagine that it couldn't have been easy. Yes, Chris, I accept your apology. So, let's just draw a line under the sand and not speak about this again."

Olivia couldn't quite bring herself to say the words 'I forgive you', but she wanted him to know that she did by what she had said.

"Thank you, Olivia. I really appreciate that. Well, do not let me take another minute of your time. I have a young man to take home, who I am sure is starving and looking to be fed."

That was Chris' feeble attempt at lightening the air. Which worked as he got a half-smile from Olivia which was noticeable from the way the corner of her mouth curved.

"Okay, well thank you. And I most probably won't see you again either, so I wish you all the best. Take care of Ben and I hope he settles well in his new school. He has all the tools to be a confident little boy now, so I don't think he'll have any trouble transitioning."

"No, I guess not. Again, thank you."

Chris turned and walked away from Olivia, mentally walking away from what could have been his future had he not handled things so dreadfully. But in his heart of hearts, he knew that Olivia's heart belonged to Steve. You only had to see the two of them together to see that. And if he was honest with himself, he was happy for her.

Even though he did not vocally wish her well for her future nuptials, he knew she would make the perfect bride with her stunning Nubian features, and that she would be an outstanding wife too.

CHAPTER TWENTY-EIGHT

Chris and Ben arrived home and found the house noticeably quiet. Natalia had already prepared the dinner and was upstairs continuing with her packing. She heard a commotion and stopped what she was doing to go downstairs to serve up dinner.

"Hey you two. Had a nice ride home together?"

Ben smiled and nodded his head and then sped speedily pass Natalia, straddling the stairs two at a time to get upstairs even quicker.

"Take your school clothes off and leave them in the wash basket, as I need to put a wash on tonight. And don't forget to wash your hands," Natalia shouted as he reached the top of the stairs.

"I'll get the dinner ready. Will you be eating with us too?"

It dawned on Chris as he realised how much precious time he had missed with his son. And that he had made the right decision to change their pace of life. He remembered the 'conversation' he had with Jill in the car when she subconsciously crept into his thoughts. She reassured him that home was where the heart was, and the message had sunk home. "Yes, I will. Should I go and wash my hands too?" he said sarcastically.

Natalia giggled. "By the way, thank you."

Chris gave her a puzzled look. "For what?"

"Did you really think I wouldn't work it out?"

Chris continued to look bamboozled, racking his brain as to what Natalia was talking about.

"I know it was your recommendation that resulted in me getting my new job."

Chris sheepishly bowed his head. "Oh. I see. How did you find out then?" Natalia smiled.

"It wasn't hard to work out. I mean, when the agency calls and tells me that a family have specifically asked for me because I come highly recommended, I knew that it was probably down to your input."

"I guess when you put it like that, it's game over."

Chris raised his hands in the air as a sign to say that he had been rumbled.

"I felt quite responsible for you losing your job and I wanted to make sure that you were duly recompensed."

"Well, you didn't have to do that, but I am very grateful and again, thank you."

Natalia left Chris to set the table, whilst she brought the food out, after which Ben had come back downstairs, and he and Chris positioned themselves at the table. Natalia's Polish dishes were always a treat when she cooked her native cuisine, with the strong aroma tantalising their taste buds, giving them an explosion of sensation in their mouths. Natalia sat with them, and they all enjoyed a pleasant time together, with Ben rehearsing to Natalia how happy he was that his dad had collected him from school.

"That's good, Ben, but remember. We don't talk with our mouths filled with food, do we?"

"Oh yes. Sorry."

With Olivia's input at school and Natalia's input in the home, Chris was fortunate to have such strong women supporting him, ensuring Ben's childhood was a positive experience.

After dinner, Chris helped Ben with his bedtime regime and once Natalia had tidied the kitchen and put a wash on, she retired to her room for the evening.

Chris remained downstairs in the lounge and made himself comfortable. He searched for something on the TV to watch as he relaxed. With the remote control in his hand as he was flicking through the channels, his phone rang and interrupted his focus. As he looked at the phone, his demeanour changed slightly. Tilly's name was visible, illuminating like a bright neon light. His first thought was *'why on earth did Tilly feel the need to randomly call him?'*

However, the last time he ignored her calls did not bode well, which resulted in her turning up on his doorstep uninvited. He did not want a repeat of history and reluctantly answered the phone.

"Tilly. What can I do for you?"

"You could sound a bit more welcoming, Chris, and can you turn down your TV?"

Chris rolled his eyes as he muted the TV.

"Is that better?" he said sarcastically.

"Yes, much better. Thank you. Anyway, I just wanted to call as I heard the news."

Chris seemed puzzled. "News. What news?"

Tilly continued.

"Mother told me what happened with the property you were trying to buy. Sorry it fell through."

A conversation with Tilly about his personal woes was certainly not something Chris wanted to entertain.

"Thank you, but you don't need to concern yourself, as we've made temporary plans."

"Yeah, Mother said. And that's what I wanted to talk to you about. I wanted to offer my place also, in case your search for a new property takes a while."

Chris raised his eyebrows at the ludicrous thought of Tilly's pathetic gesture.

"Err. I don't think that will be necessary Tilly. Plus, I don't think staying at your home would be a good idea, given our history. Do you?"

That was a rhetorical question, which Chris wasn't waiting to be answered.

"Anyway, we don't plan to be at your parents' house for too long as I've already started looking for new properties."

"Okay, well, don't say I didn't offer. Anyway, I suppose anything would be better than that old, rundown, red-bricked house that you were planning to buy."

Tilly's words pricked a nerve in Chris' thoughts.

"How do you know what the house looked like?"

Tilly didn't even realise what she had blurted out and quickly tried to come up with a lame excuse. "Ummm. Mother told me when we were discussing it."

"Tilly, your mother could not have told you that, because I didn't even discuss with her the specifics of the property I was buying. So, again. I'm going to ask the question. How do you know what the house looked like?"

Tilly started getting defensive and her voice trembled. And Chris detected that whenever Tilly was lying, her voice trembled. That's how it was when she had accused him of contributing to his wife's demise.

"Oh, Chris you're so dramatic. What does it matter how I knew what the property looked like? You're not buying it now, anyway, are you?"

The penny had finally dropped.

"It was you, wasn't it? You sabotaged our sale, in the hope that we wouldn't have anywhere to live. And then you could be the heroine of the day and rescue us out of our ordeal. Like beggars with nowhere to go. You are unbelievable, Tilly, and very, very selfish too. When are you going to get it into your head that there is nothing that is going to happen between the two of us? Not now. Not never. You know what. I am going to end this conversation now, as I don't want to say something that I am going to regret. But I will say this, Tilly. You seriously need to get some help. See a counsellor or something. You really need to move on, and a counsellor can help you. Or maybe you need God. Yes, that's it. Find God. He will help you. I know He's helped me change to be a better person."

"You can think what you like, Chris, but I had nothing to do with your property sale falling through. A friend of a friend who works at the Estate Agents might have mentioned something."

"Goodnight, Tilly."

Chris put the phone down. Tilly was the same person she had always been, and he felt sad for her. She clearly was still hurting and needed closure. And when Chris reflected on the way he had dealt with the call and what had transpired, he felt proud of himself. It proved that he had changed. Because the old Chris would have exploded and been out of control. However, he remembered that the old Chris had gone, and he had to concentrate on the newer version of himself getting airtime. He didn't have time for Tilly's childless games. She was supposed to be a grown woman and yet she was behaving like she was Ben's age, and he wasn't going to fall into the trap of Tilly's triviality.

The rest of the week was a busy one for Chris. He had left the surgery, and Joan kept her promise, and it was a quiet, inconspicuous departure. However, he did meet up, as a matter of courtesy, with Michael and Joan for a farewell drink. Michael and Joan had been very gracious to him when they found out about him not having an up-to-date licence to practice. It had caused much harm to their surgery at the time, yet Michael and Joan allowed him to return, once he had got his affairs in order.

Michael was still on paternity leave but felt it important to make the time to properly say goodbye to Chris. He told Chris to take care of himself and be happy where he was going to put down roots. Both he and Joan reassured Chris that one day he would learn to love again, because he deserved to be happy. As did Ben deserve to have a new mother. They ended their meet-up on a pleasant note and agreed to stay in contact.

Likewise, Olivia ensured that Ben's last day was equally special. He was made to feel like the king of his class and all his friends and teachers said wonderful things about him. There was a small spread of cupcakes, crisps and drinks. And all the kids filled themselves on sweets and sugar, until their bellies were full, and they were hyper. Ben left school that afternoon on a high, leaving behind friendships and fond memories of his time at Newmont Primary School.

Natalia had also said her goodbyes the day before the move, which turned out to be more emotional than they all thought it would be. Natalia had grown fond of Ben and appreciated how Chris had welcomed her into his house and entrusted her with the welfare of his child and run of the home.

She had accumulated a lot of personal stuff. Mainly clothes, shoes and make-up, to be fair, so her move was quite an ordeal too. Fortunately, some close friends were on hand to help her and eventually everything was wrapped up over a couple of days. Chris completed the sale of his house and exchanged contracts succinctly. He and Ben then successfully made the move back to Melton Mowbray, staying as agreed with his in-laws, until they were able to secure a home of their own.

Two-weeks after the twins' birth, Michael and Carol finally received positive news from the doctors. Zachary had made a dramatic turnaround and was out of the danger zone. The doctors were astounded and described Zachary's progress as what could only be termed as a miracle. They did not specifically want to attribute the credit to God, but Michael and Carol knew better.

The prayers they, their family and friends had painstakingly uttered at a time when there was little hope to grab hold of were gloriously answered. Zachary was given the 'all clear' to leave the hospital later in the week once all the final tests had been completed.

The day had arrived when Michael proudly turned up at the hospital. This time, not to visit Carol and his babies, but to take them all home. To take his mind off things in the weeks prior, he was working hard on the nursery. Carol had given him a few jobs that she wasn't able to do in the latter stages of her pregnancy, and Michael finished them off to the letter. He knew how particular Carol was when it came to her work and that he had to get everything right.

The décor throughout the room had a white theme, with hints of blue and pink accessories. With the help of Steve, he had erected two cots, wardrobes and baby changing units. He tried his best to position the softer things like cushions, rugs and toys how he thought Carol might like them.

"Here you are. Thought you'd never get here."

Carol was excited to see Michael and had got herself and the twins ready in anticipation of his arrival.

"Sorry, love. I got stuck in traffic, but I see you've been busy putting all your things together."

Michael's eyes locked in on the two bags that Carol had piled high with clothing, bottles and various gifts that she had accumulated from her visitors. Michael had with him two baby-seats under each arm.

"Are you okay though?"

Carol had been making steady progress with her health and her doctors were pleased with her improvement too.

"Yeah, I'm doing well. Can't wait to get home though and introduce the twins to their new home. And to show them their room also, which I hope looks nice."

"Well, in my defence, I think Steve and I have done a sterling job. I don't have your expertise eye, of course, and no doubt you'll be moving things around the way you like it when we get home, which wouldn't surprise me," Michael said cheekily.

One of the nurses helped Michael by taking Zoe to the car, whilst he carefully carried Zachary, his heir. Another nurse wheeled Carol to the car. Both nurses wished Carol well, since they had got used to having her around, and waved them all off.

Once home, Carol gave her seal of approval when she observed the room for the first time and appreciated all the effort Michael had put in, with the help of Steve. Did he get everything in the right place or the way Carol would have done it? Perhaps not, in her opinion. But after all they had gone through in the past couple of weeks, it was a trivial thing to get upset over.

Carol and Michael carefully placed the twins in their appropriate cot, which seemed like they were made perfectly for them, with their white bedding and the initial 'Z' hand-stitched on them in the appropriate pink and blue colours. Michael took a moment, almost having to pinch himself as he took in his surroundings. He was now a father and of two at that. His dream had finally come true, and he was now living in the reality, with a loving wife and children of his own.

No one could ever convince him that God wasn't real or indeed answered prayer. The thought of losing one of the precious babies that God had blessed them with was unthinkable, but thankfully Zach pulled through.

"Look how sweet they look in their little cots," Carol said as she gently tucked each twin in.

"Can you believe they are actually ours?" Michael added.

"Err, every time I think of the pain of that delivery… yeah," Carol said sarcastically.

"I guess so."

Michael agreed, forgetting that it was his wife that had done all the hard work, unlike him, who just watched on helpless.

"Anyway, let's leave them to sleep. I need to call Liv to let her know that we are all home now."

Michael engaged the baby monitor and he and Carol tiptoed out of the room, leaving the door slightly ajar.

"Okay, well, you catch up on what you need to do, and I'll go downstairs to see what I can rustle up. Unless you want me to order take-out."

"Take-out will probably take too long to be delivered. How about some pasta? That's quick and easy."

"Pasta it is then. Your wish is my command."

Michael left Carol in the bedroom to go and rustle them up something quick to eat. Whilst Michael was downstairs making the dinner, Carol took the opportunity to have a long bath. Being at the hospital did not afford her such luxuries and it was just a quick shower so that she did not have to stay too long in the bathroom, which she didn't find the most pleasant. It was bog standard in her opinion. Having a long soak was just what Carol needed as she allowed the soap suds to smother her, whilst sinking deep into their oval porcelain bath.

After her bath, Carol slipped into a floral kaftan to feel more comfortable now that she was back in the comfort of her own home. Carol sat on the edge of her bed and called Olivia.

"Hey girl, it's your girl," she said as she glowed whilst talking to Olivia.

"Hey Carol. Are you guys' home now?

Michael told Steve he was going to get you and the twins today."

"Yes, we're home. We got home about an hour ago and I've just had a nice long bath, so I'm feeling very relaxed and clean. And it's a blessing to be home with my two babies and that they are both well."

Olivia was so pleased for her best friend, because it could have gone either way. But thankfully their prayers were answered, and both babies came through their ordeal.

"Anyway, Michael is downstairs making dinner and I just wanted to quickly touch base with you. I have some good news and not so good news, so which one do you want first?"

"Now let me see," Olivia said, pondering in her thoughts as what it was that Carol was about to drop on her.

"Okay, let's go with the positive news first then."

"Oh good, I was hoping you'd say that" Carol said gleefully.

"Well, the good news is that I can now attend your wedding."

With Zach being unwell, Carol thought that she was going to have to miss the wedding and that was something she was praying would not be the case. She had waited long enough for Olivia to eventually meet someone. So, the thought of not being at her wedding would have been devastating.

"Well, that's great news. So, what's the not so good news then?" Olivia braced herself for what was to come.

"That would be the maid of honour duties. We had previously discussed it and were aware that the twins' birth might clash with the date of the wedding. And since they arrived early, and with all that transpired regarding Zach's health, my hands will be too full attending to the twins, and I don't think I can serve or assist you adequately in the manner you deserve. I'm sorry, hon."

Olivia was relieved as she thought Carol was about to drop a serious bombshell on her, like something relating to the health of either one of the twins.

"Caz, you have nothing to be sorry about, as that is totally understandable. I am made up that you will even be able to attend my wedding and that's what is more important to me. As an interim measure, I had pre-empted this might happen and had asked Jen if she wouldn't mind stepping in if it came to that and she was more than happy to do so."

Carol was relieved by this revelation because she did not want Olivia to think she had abandoned her, especially as Olivia was there for her as maid of honour at her wedding.

"Phewww. I'm glad you understand. But praise God, your godchildren will be there, gurgling and cheering you on. Probably puking up all over me too. Plus, I'm breastfeeding so now you see why I wouldn't have been a good maid of honour to you. I'm glad Jen will be there to spoil you. Anyway, let me let you go cos I can hear my hubby calling me. Take care, hon. Speak to you soon."

"Yes, Caz, you take care of yourself and those babies of mine too," Olivia teased as she put the phone down.

CHAPTER TWENTY-NINE

What seemed like an event that would never happen for Olivia was finally here. The day when she would marry the one whom God had approved for her. She had watched so many couples come and go before her and whilst she was happy for them, she always wondered when it would be her turn, when would she be the blushing bride and all the attention be directed towards her.

Olivia's thoughts took a glimpse back to Carol's wedding day. Every detail was in place, and everyone knew what their designated roles were. Like Olivia, Carol had waited a while to find her Boaz, and she was determined that it was going to be a wedding that individuals did not forget in a hurry and would talk about for years to come.

Olivia, on the other hand, couldn't promise the same elaborate affair as right from the start, she and Steve wanted their wedding to be more about their love for each other, rather than all the pomp and glory that sometimes goes along with weddings. Especially where those individuals often got lost in all the fanfare and forgot what the most important part of the day was really about.

Olivia's parents had come down a couple of days prior to the big day and Olivia enjoyed showing her mother the venue where they were going to have the reception and some of the trinkets that they were going to dress the hall with. Olivia knew her dad wouldn't have appreciated all the girlie stuff, and he was happy to hang out with Steve and Michael.

Both sets of parents also got to meet each other for a cosy meal, where Steve's mother was on her best behaviour. She was like a new woman, who didn't want to put a step wrong to be seen jeopardising the wedding. She had learnt her lesson, albeit the hard way. And she knew that if she wanted to be in the lives of any future grandchildren, that she had to put aside whatever prejudices she first had about the marriage.

On the other hand, Mr Adams was not fazed and went along with whatever was happening to keep the peace. He trusted his son's judgement and was confident that Steve knew what he was signing up for. Marriage wasn't for the faint-hearted and Steve had a strong personality which gave Mr Adams confidence and belief that he could handle the ups and downs that came along after the nuptials and signing on the dotted line.

It was a late afternoon wedding, which allowed time for everyone to get themselves ready and to the church on time. The bridesmaids, consisting of two close friends of Olivia who attended her church, and Jen as the maid of honour, were getting ready at her house.

Meanwhile, the men, on the other side of town, all congregated at Steve's place. There was a real buzz in the air at the home where the ladies were congregated. Individuals were frantically running around as they got themselves ready.

The hairdresser had already done the hairstyles of Olivia's entourage, and it was just her hair left to do. She knew exactly the look she wanted, which she felt complimented the style of dress she had chosen, and the hairdresser followed her instructions to the letter. Olivia wanted her curly locks controlled and thus asked the hairdresser to give her a side part and then pin her hair so that it resembled a smooth front with a bun to the side.

The bridesmaids started to get into their dresses, which were dusty blue and crafted from a flowing chiffon material. The dresses featured a halter neckline with delicate pleated details, offering a timeless sophistication. The fitted bodice highlighted their petite waists, whilst the A-line skirt flowed gracefully to the floor for comfort and movement.

Jen's dress was the exact same style, but in cinnamon rose as a contrast to highlight that her role was different to that of the two bridesmaids. They all made their way downstairs to the lounge in anticipation at a first peak of the bride-to-be.

Olivia took her time as she got ready. Every second counted and was important to how she got to this stage. Her mother brought in her dress which was in a white dress carrier, which she struggled with due to the length of the carrier. The hairdresser was just doing the finishing touches to Olivia's hair and her mother started to shed a tear as she hung her dress up.

"Oh Olivia. You look so beautiful. I don't know if I'm going to be able to control myself throughout the service."

She took a handkerchief from her bag and dabbed her eyes.

"Oh Mother, what are you like? And I haven't even put my dress on yet. You're going to be a hot mess, aren't you?"

Olivia said as she giggled.

"I know. I'm going to have to go and apply my make-up again at this rate. Let me help you get into your dress."

It was usually the role of the matron of honour to help the bride get ready, but as her only daughter, Olivia's mother had asked to be given the opportunity on this occasion, breaking protocol.

"By the way, Mum, you look great yourself. I bet you're glad that we stuck to that style, because it really suits you."

Olivia and her mother had chosen the outfit a couple of months prior when Olivia went to visit her parents. Her mother tried on a few styles until she settled on the one she was wearing, a sheath/column scoop illusion knee-length lace chiffon dress with cascading ruffle sequins in its design. She wanted to do her daughter proud and had to make sure her outfit was just right, which complimented the dainty fascinator she had chosen to compliment her dress.

Olivia faced the mirror as she stepped into her wedding dress whilst her mother helped zip her up. Even though Olivia always said she did not want a big poofy dress and wanted it to be fairly simple, there was nothing simple about the way she looked. Her reflection looked back at her and unveiled a radiant bride about to marry the man of her dreams.

"You look absolutely beautiful, Olivia. That dress was made just for you. It hugs you in all the right places in a modest way."

Olivia's mother welled up again as she watched the hairdresser attach the veil to the back of her hair and observed how it sparkled and flowed glowingly behind her.

"Well, Mum. This is it. It's now or never, eh? And I feel so ready for this. I feel at peace."

"You are ready, my sweet girl. You have waited a long time for this, and Steve really is the one. One always knows on their special day when they are marrying the right person.

I knew it when I walked down the aisle to meet your father all those years ago and I can really sense that you know it too."

Olivia's mother gave her a gentle hug, trying not to smudge her make-up or dislodge the veil that her hairdresser had painstakingly pinned in tightly so that it would last the duration of the day.

As Olivia made her way to the top of the staircase, her bridal party and father were at the bottom waiting for the first glimpse of the blushing bride. Aided by her mother behind her holding her train, Olivia carefully glided down the stairs to an eruption of emotion as everyone was taken aback at how stunning she looked and how much she glowed like she was the Queen of Sheba about to address her subjects.

"Wowww Olivia. One word. Stunning,"

Jen said as Olivia reached the bottom of the stairs.

Her father had a glint in his eye as he prepared mentally to proudly give away his little girl. Even though she was now a grown woman, he would always see her as his little girl. The little girl that was the apple of his eye. The other bridesmaids equally gushed over her, and everyone commented on how lovely she looked in her dress, which was an off-white trumpet/mermaid high neck sweep train lace dress that suited her long slim figure perfectly.

Someone had mentioned that the wedding car was already waiting outside, and Olivia's father escorted her to the white Rolls Royce Phantom, with a dark brown leather interior, where the driver tipped his hat to her whilst opening the door to allow her to slide into the back. Her mother, Jen and the two bridesmaids followed behind and got into a Mercedes Machbach with cream leather interior. They too felt quite special as they made themselves comfortable, sinking deep into the soft seats, looking on as Olivia's Rolls led the way to the church.

At the guys' quarter, they had a more relaxed day in the lead up to the wedding. They took everything in their stride. Watched a bit of football. Had a few snacks and enjoyed some drinks. They were all suited and booted in identical navy suits, with Steve wearing a white jacket with a navy cravat. Michael wasn't at the house with the guys. He had agreed to meet Steve at the church.

Even though he now had responsibilities and a family to look after, he still wanted to fulfill his best man duties and not let Steve down. The agreement was that he would stand with him at the front of the church as his best man and do his best man speech, but the rest of the running around would be done by the other guys.

Matt was happy to help out and he became the second in command, responsible for taking up the best man duties where Michael left off from. Steve was perfectly fine with the arrangement as Michael did go out of his way, when his son was at a critical stage, to throw him a small bachelor party, gathering a few guys from church for the occasion.

They ended up frequenting a Lebanese restaurant and stuffed themselves silly with food that kept coming, dish after dish. Even when they tried to tell the staff that they really were quite full, the management told them that as it was a bachelor party, they needed to eat like men. Whatever that was supposed to mean to them. Steve couldn't eat properly for days after that.

"Are you ready, Steve?" Matt cheekily put the question to Steve as he was fixing his cravat in place.

"I was born ready for this, Matt. Especially as I've got the woman of my dreams. The one God made specifically for me. Make sure you don't let Jen out of your reach, especially if you feel she is the one. Is she the one?"

Now it was Steve who was putting Matt on the spot. He smiled and nodded.

"You know, I believe she could very well be the one."

Steve wanted to give Matt some man-to-man advice remembering how he nearly missed his chance had he not been bold enough to take the opportunity when the moment arose.

"I liked Liv for a long time, but I resigned myself to the friend zone, because I was too scared to spoil the friendship we had. And then one day, I thought, if I don't go for it now, it may never happen. I told myself, *'what have I got to lose'*. God's divine ordering gave me the opportunity I needed to shoot my shot and the rest is history. Look, we are here today on our wedding day, about to pledge our lives to each other forever."

Matt was impressed.

"Man. That's a great love story of God's providence in both of your lives. I've got a lot to think about, but I promise you, I won't drag my heels that's for sure. Right, let's get you to the church then."

Matt hollered to the guys in the other room that it was time for them to be making strides to the church. Unlike the ladies, the men weren't chauffeur driven and had to make do with driving themselves to the church. Steve went with Matt and a couple of the other guys, who were ushers, took their cars.

After a short journey, Steve and his entourage arrived at the church, where they were met by PT who was standing at the door and welcomed them in. Guests had already started to fill the church, and the first individual that caught Steve's gaze was his mother beaming from ear to ear, proudly perched on the front row reserved for the immediate family. Her tall elaborate headpiece instantly drew his eyes to where she was sitting and the outfit she complimented it with equally screamed an array of bright dazzling colours.

His father was suited in the same attire as the ushers and sat quietly next to his wife. Next to the Adams' was Charlotte Bramwell with a distinguished gentleman by her side. As her parents could not make the wedding, she was permitted to bring a plus one. He was a gentleman she had been seeing for a while.

As Steve walked down the aisle and acknowledged all the eyes that were fixated on him, he cheekily gave Charlotte a wink. In his mind, he laughed as he thought that the gentleman Charlotte was with was definitely the type of man her parents would approve of, and he was happy for her.

On Olivia's side of the church, Joan was close to the front. She too had a plus one: the locum that she used to date many years ago. They had been spending quite a bit of time together and she felt comfortable to use the wedding as the opportunity to go public and showcase him to her friends.

A few rows behind Joan were Carol, her sister Jenny, and the twins. Carol specifically chose that row in case the twins got unsettled and she had to make a quick exit in order not to interrupt the proceedings with a screaming child belting out at an inappropriate time.

She waved to Joan, who came over to see her and meet the twins for the first time.

"My, My. You've got your hands full, haven't you?" Joan teased.

"Tell me about it. This is their first official outing and I'm hoping that they behave themselves for their auntie Olivia and uncle Steve."

"I'm sure they will. They are so cute."

Carol couldn't miss the opportunity to be inquisitive.

"And the gentleman next to you. Is he with you then?" she said cheekily.

"Oh, Carol, I have missed you and your nosey self," Joan laughed.

"Yes, he is with me. If you're good, I might introduce him to you later."

"Oh good. I shall look forward to meeting him."

"Anyway, let me get back to my seat as I just wanted to quickly say hello and to see the twins."

Steve's stroll to the altar seemed like he'd never get there. He eventually arrived, where a smiling Michael was waiting for him.

"Hey mate. How are you doing?"

Michael embraced Steve with a man hug, quick, to the point and not prolonged.

"I'm good, mate. I'm ready and looking forward to the day."

"Well, just enjoy every moment, because it goes fast enough and then after it just becomes a blur.

Well, that was my experience anyway. I wish I took the time to take it all in, but slower, appreciating certain aspects of the day. But Carol had us on a tight timetable and you know what she's like, especially when she has a plan in her head."

They both smiled at each other knowingly. The musicians played an array of soothing music, whilst the rest of the guests filtered in. Just like Steve and Olivia planned, it was a small number of guests, consisting of close family and friends. They had no intentions of sending an invite to the whole church congregation to attend, because they did not feel it was warranted.

Many couples who had gone before them had felt that they needed to extend an invite to the entire church, which turned into a nightmare when trying to cater for all those guests. However, Steve and Olivia felt it was their special day for them to celebrate with a selected few.

PT came over to Steve and Michael to give them the heads up to take their position as he had received word from the head usher that the bridal party had arrived.

Olivia stood at the doorway of the entrance to the church. The organist played the song 'On the Wings of Love' as the bridesmaids and ushers made their way down the aisle. All eyes watched as they swayed in time to the music.

Then it was time for the main attraction. PT asked everyone to be up on their feet for the arrival of the bride. Again, breaking away from protocol. Olivia wanted her mother and father to walk her down the aisle.

Her mother walked her down the first half of the aisle to Luther Vandross' 'Here & Now' and her father was positioned in a suitable place to walk her down the rest of the aisle to her groom who was waiting with anticipation. As Olivia was nearing the altar, Steve turned around to watch her reach him and was astounded as to the beauty he was beholding as she smiled and stood next to him. They quickly exchanged greetings.

"Hey, you," Olivia said.

Chapter Twenty-nine

"Hey back at you, Liv. You look absolutely stunning."

Steve couldn't hide his feelings.

"You scrub up well yourself," Olivia teased.

PT welcomed everyone to the wedding of Olivia Dupont and Steven Adams and acknowledged the families of both couples. He referred the guests to their programme, and everything ran according to plan. There was a time of worship with upbeat songs selected by Olivia and Steve that they loved to sing and were special to them. Steve had a surprise for Olivia and had a friend of his, who went under the pseudonym of Anniebee, play the saxophone, since he knew how much Olivia loved the cool smooth sound of the sax.

It was a lovely surprise for her. Carol read a scripture and was so chuffed that she was able to do so and that she did not miss Olivia's big day. The couple made their heartfelt vows to each other. Had their first legal kiss, which had the guests gushing because there was a real sense of love in the air, which was evidently clear for all to see. The couple were invited to the vestry by PT to sign the register and whilst they were gone, the guests were treated to more solo singing and an upbeat number from the worship chorale.

After a short while, PT came out and announced to the audience the new Mr & Mrs Adams, which followed an eruption of cheers, claps and jeers as Steve and Olivia made their way back down the aisle as man and wife. The guests followed and filed out joyfully right behind them, where Steve and Olivia posed outside the church for photographs by the official photographer and their guests. The bridal party joined them as well as the family and had a selection of photographs. Michael allowed Matt to take over whilst he went back to be by Carol and his children's side.

In between the photographs, Carol took the opportunity to run over and give Olivia a big hug, expressing how happy she was for her and how radiant and glowing she looked. She also hugged Steve and told him to look after her best friend, or he would have her to deal with, something Steve did not want to be on the receiving end of and readily agreed.

Steve and Olivia were whizzed off by their chauffeur to another location to take more intimate one-to-one pictures with their bridal party. The immediate family also went to the private location whilst the rest of the guests headed for the reception. Carol had felt it would be too much for her and the twins to go also and told Michael to go with the bridal party, whilst she and Jenny headed straight to the reception instead.

CHAPTER THIRTY

The rest of the evening reception was equally as eventful as the ceremony and what transpired earlier. The catering, speeches and dancing was a euphoric occasion with guests enjoying everything that Olivia & Steve had visualised for their nuptials.

For their first dance, as man and wife, Olivia & Steve smooched closely to The Bee Gees' soulful tune, 'How Deep is Your Love'. After, the guests took to the dance floor in their pairs. Michael & Carol, who left the twins sleeping soundly in their travel carry cots under the watchful eye of their aunt Jenny. Joan and the Locum. Charlotte Bramwell and her date. And Matt & Jen.

Matt was especially glad to finally have the opportunity to get up close and personal with Jen. They had literally crossed paths for most of the day, occupied with their respective duties, that they didn't have chance to make time for each other. Amid the surrounding couples, Matt held Jen attentively, with his hands gently around her waist. The aroma of her distinct perfume, Diamonds Emporio Armani, reminded him of how good she smelt whenever she was close to him. A scent he couldn't deny that made him wish Jen was more than his girlfriend.

"I can't believe this is the first opportunity we've had to ourselves," Matt said as he glided Jen along the dance floor.

Jen smiled as she enjoyed being caught up in the moment of imagining herself as a bride one day and what it would really feel like. Mindful that her and Matt were drawing closer towards each other with their conversations taking on a more serious nature, Jen felt like a proposal was imminent. However, she didn't want to jump the gun and get ahead of herself, conscious perhaps of the fact that she was just caught up in the moment of Olivia & Steve's wedding and her vision clouded with romantic notions.

"Yes, it's been one busy day, but a lot of fun, nonetheless. I can't believe we got them through today. Well, I guess now this is all over I'm going to have to pack up my stuff and concentrate on the big move."

Jen was glad for the way things had worked out and in her favour. Steve had agreed to move out of his bachelor pad to live with Olivia, with the objective in due course to sell Olivia's house and for them to buy a property together. And to avoid Steve having to vet several potential candidates to rent his flat, they gave Jen first refusal. Jen was only too glad to take them up on their offer.

"Yes, that is true, but you know I'll be there to give you a hand. I'm not going to let you go through all that by yourself."

Matt was ever the true gentleman, especially when it came to doing things for Jen.

"Oh, my knight in shining armour, how kind of you. That would be great. I have booked a small van to assist with the move as I really don't have that much bulky stuff by way of furniture etc. It's just my clothes and exercise equipment."

"Well, thank goodness for that," Matt said playfully.

They both smiled and made their way off the dance floor as the DJ changed the pace of the music to a more upbeat tempo which demanded more energy.

"Think I need a drink before I can shake a leg to the buoyant tunes coming up," Matt said.

"I totally agree," Jen said, laughing.

"Let's see what we can get at the bar."

It was an open bar with the drinks flowing freely and, of course, the special wine that Mrs Adams had chosen and got a good deal on at the wedding fayre.

As the evening started to reach its peak, Mr & Mrs Adams made a beeline for Olivia & Steve, who spent the evening mingling with their guests, ensuring everyone was having a good time.

"Steve, can we have a word with you both before we leave?"

Mr Adams said in his gentle tone, pulling them both away from Carol & Michael, who themselves were also getting ready to leave. The Adams' wanted to express their gratitude to Olivia & Steve for planning and organising such a splendid day, in fitting with their style, and for allowing them to be a part of it, considering a few months prior how badly it could have ended had they not changed their stance on their son's relationship.

Mrs Adams gave her son a big hug, followed by one for Olivia. She squeezed Olivia's hand tightly after they came out of their embrace, a touch they both understood the meaning of. Mr Adams reached into his inside pocket and pulled out an envelope which he handed to Steve.

"Now, we told you that we wanted to handle the cost of your honeymoon. So here is a little something for you both. Don't look at it now. You can open it when you are both in the comfort of your own home. And please don't say it is excessive, or you can't accept it, because this is our special gift to you both."

Steve rolled his eyes as he went in for another hug with both of his parents.

"Thank you both in advance guys. Liv and I will appreciate it, wherever we are going." He smiled.

Olivia also wanted to add her thanks.

"Yes, Mr & Mrs Adams, thank you very much for your generosity."

"None of this Mr & Mrs Adams any more, Olivia. We're family now. It's Mum and Dad to you."

Olivia appreciated Mr Adams' assertion of the new salutation she was to refer to her in-laws by going forward. She smiled as she watched them walk away.

Olivia's mind drifted back a jiffy to the unpleasant scene of the last time she was handed an envelope and asked to read it 'in the comfort of her own home'. That envelope was given to her by her now mother-in-law and had contained a fake prenup. The expression on her face that ensued after the exchange haunted Olivia for days. But God had supernaturally turned things around and here they were now treating each other with the utmost respect. That was the power of forgiveness. Not allowing situations to fester but dealing with matters swiftly so that they are resolved in an amicable way.

A tap on Olivia's shoulder brought her back to the present. It was Carol who wanted to say goodbye as her and Michael were about to leave.

"Hon. You're a married woman now. I can't believe it. You've entered the wives club. Good luck, sis."

They both started cackling which prompted puzzling looks from Steve and Michael wondering what the two best friends found so funny.

"When are you guys going away for your honeymoon?" Carol asked inquisitively.

"That's a good question. We've just been handed an envelope from Steve's parents, so I guess we'll know soon, eh?"

"Anyway, you know it's going to be somewhere nice, so you don't have to worry in that respect. Remember, they've got money, girl," Carol said cheekily.

"Anyway, we must go now. We've never stayed out this long before with the twins. However, because this has been a remarkable day for two special people, we had to make an exception. Take care of yourself and we'll talk soon. Or when you come up for air that is."

Carol couldn't help herself with that naughty comment, which set them both off again in fits of laughter.

Michael also gave Steve his best friend/best man pep talk.

"Now take care of that bride of yours. And remember, talk about everything. No matter how small or insignificant. It's all important in the grand scheme of things at the end of the day and will save you much heartache in the long run."

Michael tapped Steve gently on his back.

"Yes, I will and thanks for today. I've appreciated your input. We'll touch base soon man."

Olivia also thanked Jenny for coming to the wedding and she, Carol & Michael and their children all made their exit.

The DJ continued to play instrumental tunes as one-by-one the guests filtered out. Olivia's parents also left and made their way to a nearby hotel that they were staying at. It was an emotional farewell for Olivia as she was now a married woman and not the single daughter that she had always been perceived as. Her future conversations with them would now take on a whole new direction and that was something she'd have to get familiar with.

Steve similarly had a good catch up with Charlotte Bramwell. She told him how proud she was of him for sticking to his convictions throughout and for truly knowing what he wanted. Steve appreciated her sentiments and told her that he too wished her only the best. He hinted at her date appearing to be a nice person and that she should take one day at a time and enjoy the journey. She smiled as she took in his advice. In Charlotte's estimation, Steve was now considered an expert in the field of love with a successful relationship to emulate that had led to marriage.

Matt & Jen were two of the last people to leave the venue, having ensured that everything was wrapped up with the catering team and the DJ. All that was left to do was for them to give Steve & Olivia a ride back to their home. And for Jen to pick up her small holdall that was already in her room. And for Matt to give her a lift to her new digs. She was staying there for a couple of days until she got the rest of her things.

Olivia & Steve thanked Matt & Jen profusely for all their help throughout the day and for the lift home. Whilst Matt waited in the car, Jen quickly dived upstairs and wriggled out of her bridesmaid dress, which she flung over a chair in the corner of her room. She changed into a baggy sweatshirt and skinny jeans and tied her hair back in a ponytail. She grabbed her holdall, ran down the stairs and slammed the door. She chose to exit discreetly and not comment or say goodbye to Olivia & Steve as she didn't want it to feel awkward or embarrass anyone.

Matt had turned off the engine, but when he saw Jen come out of the house, he revved it up again as Jen put her holdall on the back seat and got into the car. Matt drove off. In his mind, he did not want the evening to end, especially as it was only just after 10 PM.

"I know this may sound random, but do you want to go somewhere for a quick coffee?"

It was almost as if he had read Jen's mind, as she too did not feel like going back to an empty flat by herself either. She knew that neither of them would feel it appropriate for them to go back to the flat, as that wasn't their style.

"It's almost as if you were reading my mind. Yes, I'd love to."

Matt was made-up on the inside and was glad his time with Jen wasn't going to end just yet. They drove to a local cafe bar that opened late and sold hot drinks and pastries. The venue offered a relaxing ambience, where soft jazz music played in the background, which was just right for conversation levels.

Matt & Jen ordered a hot drink each and indulged themselves with a dessert of their choice. The conversation between them flowed easily. From the first time they had encountered each other, conversation was never a problem. Matt had known for a long time that Jen was 'the one'. He could easily have asked her to marry him then and there, but he knew that no woman would appreciate being proposed to over a latte and cream bun. It was from that point he decided in his heart that he needed to think of a special way that he could propose to the woman of his dreams.

They talked about taking another road-trip to see their respective parents and Matt wondered if that would be an appropriate time to do it, with both parents available to witness the special occasion. He had a lot to think about, but he wanted it to be soon as he did not want to let any further time pass by without telling Jen how he really felt about her.

They spent an hour or so at the venue, after which Matt dropped Jen back to Steve's flat. He told her that he'd be back the next day to pick her up for church. He gave her a gentle kiss as Jen exited the car on a high, like she was walking on air.

EPILOGUE

In the six months that followed, there were significant changes in the lives of the various friends. A couple of weeks after their marriage, Steve & Olivia got the opportunity to go on their honeymoon, courtesy of his parents. They waited until Olivia was on summer break from her teaching role and took a two-week holiday to Egypt, staying at the Reef Oasis Blue Bay Resort & Spa. It was a relaxing break where they got to experience the attractions of Egypt, such as seeing the famous Pyramids, having fun in a hot air balloon, as well as riding camels and quad bikes through the desert. Their final night was taking a boat ride on The Nile over a romantic dinner and watching the sunset as it glazed stunningly over the deep blue water. On returning home, they put into motion their plans to sell both properties and were successful in securing a beautiful four bedroomed town house situated close to Michael & Carol's vicinity.

The Mills' surprised themselves as to how quickly they took to parenthood. Zach & Zoe were the apples of their eyes. The role was busy and hands on, but they were enjoying every moment and couldn't imagine their lives without the twins. They had made major changes to their lifestyle to spend as much time as a family.

Carol had made the decision to take a two-year sabbatical, leaving her business in the capable hands of her assistant. He continued to liaise with her on certain key projects, but most of the work she left him to make the decisions on.

Michael had left the surgery and took on a private consultancy role, which meant he did not have to work as strenuously as he did when he worked at the surgery. It took a bit of time getting used to it when he first made the transition, but he adapted quickly, freeing up his time to be there for Carol and his children.

Michael had continued to stay in contact with Chris and was happy to learn that he was doing well. His job was panning out, having been promoted to a senior level, thereby enjoying a sound work environment. Regarding his house situation, he was only at his in-laws for a month or so, before he was able to secure a property for himself and Ben. With the property being close to his in-laws, he did not need to employ an au-pair as his in-laws were on hand to take Ben to school and pick him up whilst Chris worked.

Neither did Chris have to be concerned about Tilly being around as she had taken a new position abroad. With Chris reiterating to her that there was never going to be a future between them, Tilly wanted to remove herself from having to be around him. She took a role at an NGO in Papua New Guinea, offering her expertise with helping to secure medicine to rundown areas where money for medicine was scarce. Tilly felt that she needed to do something with her life that she could be proud of and giving to others seemed a good start and the right way forward.

Chris also shared with Michael that he found a church where he was able to put down roots and build relationships. He was part of a cell group when he first got there and over time had met a lady, who also was a widower. It was talking about their similar shared experiences that naturally gravitated them towards each other. It was early days, but they were taking things slowly and enjoying each other's company. The lady also had a child, a daughter about two years older than Ben, and by blending the families together through their shared adventures, the children found a friendship in each other, which filled a gap in their lives of growing up as an only child.

Matt & Jen's love story also continued to flourish. Jen had found new lodgings with one of Olivia's bridesmaids, who was also her friend and attended their church. They both were happy with the way their arrangement was working. Their jobs continued to keep them busy with Jen in her role as a paramedic and Matt as a physiotherapist. Matt remained connected to the hospital for certain sessions, and he and Jen would use those opportunities to meet up for lunch. Jen would grow anxious as each time they went out together; she would anticipate that a proposal would transpire, but there was much disappointment.

However, Matt was quietly scheming up a surprise in the background, unbeknownst to Jen and her wildest dreams. It was only when Matt told Jen that he could see that she had been working hard and needed to take a break to go and see her parents and his that he was able to execute his plan.

He had been liaising with both mothers who had been organising an intimate dinner in a private lounge at a restaurant near Jen's parents' house and were aware that he had planned to propose to Jen. Matt had already asked Jen's parents for her hand in marriage, and they were quick to give him their blessing. What Jen thought was going to be a relaxing weekend to see both parents, she was stunned to find out that when she least expected it, the thing she desired most was realised. Matt, with the help of the mothers, did a great job in surprising Jen in the presence of the people most precious to them. It was an emotional and intimate setting and Matt's proposal was well articulated and heartfelt, which was accepted enthusiastically by Jen. In the weeks that followed, they would start their pre-marital classes with PT, as was the normal requirement for engaged couples who were planning on getting married.

The ladies would often meet up from time to time to catch up on each other's lives but had not met up for a few months due to their busy schedules. A luncheon had been scheduled at Italia Bellini, a restaurant that was a favourite of Carol and Olivia's and Jen was being introduced to it.

The day had arrived.

Olivia picked up Carol, arriving at the restaurant 15 minutes early. Jen was en-route. The restaurant had reserved their favourite table for them, and they were showed to their table by a waitress. They quickly settled in and made themselves comfortable.

"It's like we've come full circle, Caz. I'm sure the last time we were here was just before you got married."

"I know. That seems such a long time ago now."

Olivia continued.

"I mean, you're now a mother of two six-month year olds. My lovely godchildren, I might add. And I'm a married woman. Wow! Who would have thought when we were sharing a house all those years ago that our lives would change so drastically, in such a short space of time?"

The friends took a few moments to reflect on how good God had been to them.

Matt had given Jen a lift to the restaurant. Just before she got out of the car, he teased her as to how she was going to share her good news with the others.

"I note you're wearing your diamond rock. The ladies will notice it straightaway, especially Carol. You know that nothing gets pass her." They both smiled.

"No. I have a plan." Jen took off her engagement ring.

"I'm going to put this little beauty in my pocket for now and then execute my little plan at an appropriate time during the meal. They are going to be beside themselves. Gosh I'm so excited. It's only been three weeks, and I haven't told anyone yet. Have you?"

Matt confirmed that he too had kept their engagement close to his chest waiting until they were both in agreement to share the news with their close friends.

"Okay, well, you better go in then and have some fun."

Matt lent over and gave Jen a kiss as she got out the car.

"Enjoy yourself sweetheart."

"I intend to. Thanks, hon. I'll get a lift from the girls so don't worry about coming back to get me."

Jen made her way into the restaurant and immediately was met with the sound of cackling coming from a far side corner of the restaurant. Olivia was waving her hand and beckoned Jen towards them.

"Hey ladies,"

Jen greeted Olivia and Carol with a kiss on each side of the cheek. She took her coat off as she sat down and draped it on the back of her chair.

"Am I late?" Jen asked.

"Oh no, Jen. Caz had put the twins down for a nap and wanted to leave in that window, so I picked her up early and we thought we'd just come straight here instead of hanging around."

Carol weighed in by sharing with Jen that the restaurant was a place where she and Olivia had their best girlie chats. And if the walls could talk, they would reveal a lot of their deepest secrets.

The ladies ordered from the menu and settled into general chit-chat as to what was the latest gossip. Carol updated the ladies on what was told to her confidentially by Michael about Chris being in a good place and being in a new relationship. But in true Carol style, she wasn't fazed at all that she had casually blurted it out in conversation. Olivia wasn't overly interested in what Chris had been up to but was glad that he had finally got his life together.

She was pleased to learn what that might mean for Ben, if things were to progress into marriage for them. Especially since Ben always used to tell her that he wished he had a big sister.

Equally, Jen showed no emotions either and felt relieved that she had a lucky escape, especially considering the man God had brought into her life, who was polar opposites to Chris.

Carol also updated them on life as a busy mother of two and shared how the twins constantly kept her and Michael on their toes. It was demanding and yet rewarding at the same time. Olivia had had a couple of opportunities to babysit for the twins to give Michael & Carol a night out, so she could attest to that.

Whilst the ladies had known where Olivia had gone on her honeymoon, they hadn't been told the intricate details. Olivia shared what a great time they had and showed the ladies a few pictures on her phone of her and Steve riding camels, driving on dirt bikes in the desert and, of course, the iconic pyramids. The other two gushed at the spectacular photos. Olivia continued to share that she and Steve were still in the process of settling into their new town house and were enjoying the process of choosing furniture together and doing all the things that newly married couples did when they were bringing two homes into one. Steve was a lot messier than Olivia, so she had her work cut out in trying to keep him in line, whilst trying not to come across as a nagging wife.

"And what about you, Jen? Any news to share?"

Carol felt like she and Olivia were doing most of the talking and wanted to give Jen an opportunity too. Especially since they both could dominate a conversation, if they weren't interrupted.

"Yeah, Jen. Tell us about that fine man of yours," Olivia teased as she watched Jen's face awkwardly shift and her head drop.

"Jen. What is it? Has something happened?"

Olivia felt concerned. She wondered if something had happened to their relationship, and she was too consumed in her own relationship that she had failed to notice that her friend's was failing.

Olivia and Carol quickly exchanged glances, communicating with their facial expressions how they were going to address whatever revelation Jen was about to disclose.

Inwardly, Jen wanted to laugh. She wasn't sure if she could pull off the theatrics of what was unfolding, especially as the mood had changed and the ladies were showing considerable concern.

Unbeknownst to Olivia & Carol, Jen put her left-hand into her pocket and wriggled under the table whilst she slipped the diamond ring onto her finger. Jen was now ready to give her winning Oscar performance.

Jen pretended to sob and reached for a tissue in her pocket to dab her eyes. As she started to dab her eyes, the cut of her diamond ring sparkled and dazzled that it could not be denied.

"What is that?" Olivia shouted.

"Is that an engagement ring?" Carol screamed.

"Yes. Yes. We got engaged," Jen said with a screech of jubilation, stretching her hand in the middle of the table for the ladies to see.

Olivia & Carol sat there stunned.

"You naughty girl," Olivia said.

"You really had us going there for a moment. I could feel my heart beating fast as I thought you were going to say that you and Matt had broken up."

Carol clapped her hands in approval for Jen pulling the wool over their eyes.

"Girl, you really do deserve an Oscar for that performance. I really didn't see that coming."

Everyone was laughing and crying all at the same time. Olivia carefully got up and ran behind Jen and gave her a big hug.

"I'm so happy for you, Jen. This is such great news."

Carol blew her a kiss.

"This is for you, Jen. Many congratulations as you both deserve it. I think you owe us though, as we called it from the start."

Jen laughed as this time she dabbed real tears from her eyes. She was overwhelmed by the love being showed by two women whom she respected hugely and had emulated to aspire like.

"Thanks, ladies. I really appreciate your love and yes, you both were right. Matt and I were meant to be together, right from the start."

What followed next was a barrage of questions as to how and when the proposal happened. Jen answered all their questions, confirming that she had no idea it was coming. She thought she was going to see her parents for the weekend, but instead, Matt had everything organised with the help of both mothers.

Olivia & Carol gushed over Matt & Jen's love story and commended Matt for his excellent choice in the engagement ring he had bought for her.

The ladies had spent the best part of three hours reminiscing and being grateful that they were all living their dream. Each one of them had seasons when things looked like it was all about to fall apart... but God... He showed up in His Sovereignty and turned their sad stories around.

He turned their ordinary lives, into extraordinary lives. He used their mess to relay a message of hope. And the tests they went through were to become their testimonies that no one could take away from them.

They thought they had exhausted all their conversation and shared their good news with each other and were about to depart, but it was Olivia who dared to have the last word.

"Ladies, we've had such a great evening, and I thank you both for being in my life. You both have unique strengths that help keep me balanced. But as we are about to go, I just have one thing that I'd like to ask of you both."

Carol and Jen were intrigued as they looked intently towards Olivia and waited with anticipation for the question. They had assumed that they had explored everything there was to discuss, so they weren't sure what Olivia was going to say.

However, Carol afforded Olivia the liberty and gave her the floor.

"Of course, Liv. What is it?"

"Well, it's an important question."

It was a drum roll moment, and as Olivia slowly deliberated, the suspense was killing the women as they waited for the words to come out.

"Well, spit it out Liv. You've got us here on tender hooks. What is it?" Carol said hastily.

"Okay. Okay. Be patient Caz…."

Olivia took a deep breath and continued.

"The question is quite simply really. I just wanted to know if you both would consider being godmothers to the baby I am expecting?"

There was a look of shock on the faces of Carol and Jen.

"Wait a minute……What?"

Carol screamed loudly, which made the other people in the restaurant turn around to see what the commotion was. Jen was speechless as she put her hands across her mouth. Olivia winked and smiled, as she had rehearsed in her mind what their responses would be to her and Steve's good news.

She rose to her feet and loosened a thickish embroidered throw that was draped around her, which revealed a small bump she was hiding. It was priceless, and her news was the trump card of their time together, as she truly had the last laugh.

That was Olivia's 'drop the mic' moment, seeing the surprised faces of her friends reacting to her 'good news' and it was magical.

The End...

ABOUT THE AUTHOR

As vivid as Andrea can remember, she has always loved writing and expressing her thoughts on paper. She was a keen reader too and, at a young age, could often be seen with a number of books under her arm coming out of her local library.

Years later, it isn't surprising that she would become an author, with this book being the third to her ensemble, with romance novels being her preferred genre.

Andrea is also a keen traveller and loves to holiday with family and friends to different countries experiencing their culture and enjoying the various sceneries.

Going out to dinner, enjoying plays at the theatre and movies at the cinema, as well as going to concerts are some of the things Andrea finds her happy place in exploring.

Andrea is the author of 'Insightful Tips For The Unique Mature Single' and 'Second Glances' and has contributed to the anthropology, 'Black Christian Single'. She enjoys travelling the Globe, attending Christian Retreats and meeting new people. Her hobbies include writing, going to the cinema and theatre, as well as enjoying gatherings with family and friends.

Book professionally typeset by Ruth – raawpro@gmail.com

Book cover design by www.coversincolor.com